T0130168

Praise for the first Abracadabra Mystery

Magick & Mayhem

"Magic, Merlin, and murder are a great mix for this debut cozy. Up to her ears in problems, both magickal and mortal, Kailyn's a fun and adventuresome heroine I loved watching. Crafting a spell, summoning a familiar, and solving a murder shouldn't be this hard—or this fun."
—**Lynn Cahoon**, *New York Times* and *USA Today* best-selling author

"Sharon Pape's *Magick & Mayhem* is spellbinding, with magical prose, a wizardly plot, and a charming sleuth who, while attempting to protect a cast of sometimes difficult and always surprising characters, has a penchant for accidentally revealing her own powers and secrets to exactly the wrong people."
—**Janet Bolin**, Agatha-nominated author of the national best-selling Threadville Mysteries

"*Magick & Mayhem* is a charming, must-read mystery with enchanting characters. A fun and entertaining page turner that I couldn't put down."
—**Rose Pressey**, *USA Today* best-selling author

Other Books by Sharon Pape

*Magick Run Amok**
*That Olde White Magick**
*Magick & Mayhem**
Sketcher in the Rye
Alibis and Amethysts
Sketch a Falling Star
To Sketch a Thief
Sketch Me if You Can

*Available from Lyrical Press, an imprint of Kensington Publishing Corp.

Magickal Mystery Lore

An Abracadabra Mystery

Sharon Pape

LYRICAL UNDERGROUND
Kensington Publishing Corp.
www.kensingtonbooks.com

LYRICAL UNDERGROUND BOOKS are published by

Kensington Publishing Corp.
119 West 40th Street
New York, NY 10018

All Kensington titles, imprints, and distributed lines are available at special quantity discounts for bulk purchases for sales promotion, premiums, fund-raising, educational, or institutional use.

Special book excerpts or customized printings can also be created to fit specific needs. For details, write or phone the office of the Kensington Sales Manager: Kensington Publishing Corp., 119 West 40th Street, New York, NY 10018. Attn. Sales Department. Phone: 1-800-221-2647.

Lyrical Underground and Lyrical Underground logo Reg. US Pat. & TM Off.

First Electronic Edition: April 2019
eISBN-13: 978-1-5161-0872-5
eISBN-10: 1-5161-0872-8

First Print Edition: April 2019
ISBN-13: 978-1-5161-0873-2
ISBN-10: 1-5161-0873-6

Printed in the United States of America

To Jason and Lauren
Who have taught me so much.

Chapter 1

"That infernal machine is naught but an instrument of torture," Merlin grumbled as he staggered toward us. "What possessed you to allow me on it?" With his long white hair that had come untethered during the ride and his rats' nest of a beard he looked more like a wino than a legendary sorcerer from the kingdom of Camelot. He stumbled over his feet and pitched forward into the frothy layers of my Aunt Tilly's lavender muumuu.

"We tried to stop you," I said. "'You won't like it, Merlin,' we said. 'Don't do it, Merlin,' we said. 'Please believe us, Merlin.' Does any of that sound familiar?"

"Well yes, but you must admit everyone on the ride seemed delighted."

"Some people love rides like that," Tilly said.

"In that case, I can refer them to a beefy chap who works in a dungeon and is quite skilled in all manner of torturous devices."

Tilly held him away from her, hands on his shoulders. "Let's see if you can stand on your own without falling over." Merlin wobbled a bit before finding his equilibrium. "There," she said, letting go of him. "Are you at all queasy?"

"Not in the least."

"Count yourself lucky," I said, not having been as fortunate my one and only time on that ride. "I couldn't look at food for hours."

"You appear to be fine," Tilly said to him.

"I am not fine. The whole ordeal has left me famished," he said, as we walked away from the Tilt-a-Whirl. We were in the thick of the forty-fifth annual New Camel Day Fair, elbow to elbow with a few hundred people. Moving from one attraction to another was largely a matter of joining the stream of people heading in the direction we wanted to go. If we weren't careful, we could wind up back on the line for Merlin's nightmare ride.

"You've already had three hotdogs, curly cheese fries, lemonade and two root beers," I reminded him.

"And yet my stomach demands more."

"Does it have a particular request?" Tilly asked dryly.

"Cotton candy," he said without a moment's hesitation. "And a candy apple. I've never tasted either." There ensued a debate on the wisdom of Merlin eating the apple. A quick inspection of his mouth revealed he was missing a number of teeth and many of the remaining ones were chipped or broken. I explained that he could lose the teeth he had left with one bite into the sticky coating. Tilly suggested kettle corn instead, which proved to be a winner.

Two pounds of sugar later, we headed over to the booths where New Camel's merchants displayed their wares. My family had always participated, stocking our booth with our most popular health and beauty products, and Tilly held a drawing for a free psychic reading and English tea. It was a lot easier when my mother and grandmother were alive and there were four of us to take turns manning the booth. Although Tilly and I had managed all right on our own last year, now that we had to oversee Merlin, we'd decided to forgo the booth this once. It was a difficult decision, because Abracadabra always enjoyed a nice uptick in its customer base when folks bought our products at the fair and decided they couldn't live without them.

I'd already been stopped by a dozen people who were disappointed we didn't have a booth. They'd come to the fair, hoping to stock up on our products at the same time. When I offered to open my shop at three o'clock to accommodate them, they acted like they'd won the lottery. Tilly applauded the move as good business. Merlin contended it was a fool's errand to try to please everyone.

The Soda Jerk was the first of the booths we came to. They weren't making sundaes and shakes on the spot, but two of the owners' great-grandkids were there handing out coupons to buy one sundae and get a second one free at their restaurant. Their line was long, but moved so fast that in no time we each came away with a coupon. We walked on past the stands that held no interest for Merlin. He turned up his nose at the vintage clothing shop, the dollhouse and miniature shop, and the recently reopened candle shop. But he was drawn to the display from the old-fashioned toy shop. He browsed for a few minutes while we chatted with the owner, Nelson Biddle. I'd known the man all my life. He was as much a staple of New Camel as our family was. Had it been up to Tilly and me, we would have stopped to say a quick *hello* to each merchant who wasn't busy with customers. But we'd learned the hard way that a powerful sorcerer with a failing memory could wreak all sorts of havoc if he grew bored. When we reached the Busy Fingers booth, Penelope Rose saw us and waved. It would have been rude not to stop. She had a beautiful display of her handicrafts—knitted baby items, crocheted Afghans, and embroidered throw pillows. She was also offering half price lessons in any of the handicrafts, if booked during the fair. The goal of every merchant there was to entice fairgoers to visit their shops and become long term customers.

While we caught up with Penelope, Merlin stole away to the next booth. Since it was Lolly's, I didn't try to stop him. He'd be waiting his turn in that line for a good fifteen minutes or more. She always had the longest line at the fair, because she was known to be generous with the free samples of her satiny fudge. She believed if you wanted to hook a customer on your products, they needed to associate your shop with abundance and satiation. It was a philosophy that had served her well over the years. After scoring their free sample, most of the people in line would also buy a box or two of her chocolates.

Tilly and I had just bid Penelope goodbye and were crossing over to Lolly's when someone in her line yelled, "Hey old man—no cuts." From what I could tell, Merlin had grown tired of waiting and decided to march straight up to Lolly who was handing him a couple of samples. Lolly got to her feet, her cherubic smile stiffening. "Thank you, sir, but I'll decide on the rules and how to enforce them. There's plenty here for everyone."

Without missing a step, Tilly snagged Merlin's arm and dragged him away before he could turn the man into a slug or a maggot. I mouthed an apology to Lolly. She answered with a wink. Tilly made it less than thirty yards with her charge before he dug in his heels, bringing her to a hard stop that could have given her whiplash. "It's not a good idea with all these people around," she muttered as I caught up to them. I followed Merlin's line of sight. He was glowering at No-Cuts-Guy directly across from us in the line.

"No dark magick," I added.

"Fear not, Mistress," he said without shifting his focus. "I will do nothing untoward." I decided to give him the benefit of the doubt. It wasn't like I had much of a choice anyway. Tilly looked at me and shrugged, having apparently come to the same conclusion. Since the day Merlin crash landed in my shop, we'd tried to keep the legendary sorcerer from drawing attention to himself and the fact that he hailed from another time and place. It had been a losing battle from the start. On New Year's Eve,

Tilly and I had finally caved. We resolved to continue giving him our opinions on spells and other actions he was considering, but we wouldn't penalize him for his choices. Unless they were likely to have a deleterious effect on our lives as well.

Merlin was still staring at No-Cuts-Guy. We waited anxiously for something to happen, something to change. I was half-expecting the guy to turn into a frog right there in line. When the spell started working, I didn't immediately realize it. Two squirrels scampered across the grass, coming to a stop near No-Cuts-Guy's feet. They were quickly followed by half a dozen more. Before we knew it, No-Cuts-Guy had an entourage of a dozen chittering squirrels chasing each other around him. The people nearby gave him and his squirrel circus as wide a berth as possible without forfeiting their place in line.

No-Cuts-Guy tried shooing them away. He looked around for help, but since there were no squirrel containment officers wandering around the fair, he resorted to kicking at them. That was unacceptable to Merlin who instantly recalled his minions. Once released from their thrall, they scampered off in every direction. Except for the one Merlin charged with a second mission. That squirrel shimmied up No-Cuts-Guy's pant leg. The expression on the man's face was priceless. He did a panicked little dance in an effort to dislodge the critter. When that proved unsuccessful, he ran off screaming, presumably to the first-aid station or the restroom.

"Doesn't he know you can't run away from your troubles?" Tilly said with a giggle. Merlin had a grin from ear to ear. Everyone who'd witnessed the squirrel incident, as it was destined to be called, was roaring with laughter, until even I had to join in. But someday Tilly and I might have to pay the consequences for allowing the wizard such latitude in casting spells. Our resolution might need some editing.

Still in high spirits, we wandered into the area where one could win a stuffed animal or a goldfish in a little round bowl. After scouting out the various games, Merlin opted to try his hand at darts. "All I must do is hit one balloon on that board," he said.

"It's not as easy as it looks," I told him

"I'll have you know that I'm the finest player of the sport back home." He played three games with three tries each and failed to hit a balloon on any of his first eight attempts. However his last dart sailed straight into the heart of a sky-blue balloon that burst with a satisfying pop. He picked out a gray stuffed bunny with a white fluff of a tail, after I nixed the goldfish. Too many cats in the family. The poor fish would die of a heart attack if it didn't wind up as someone's lunch. When Tilly asked what he planned to do with the stuffed animal, he proposed giving it to Lolly's new great granddaughter. I felt like the proud parent of a child with a generous nature. From there we followed a crowd of people to what we hoped was the petting zoo. Merlin hummed a song as we walked. Although it had a familiar ring, it took me a minute to identify. And I wasn't happy once I did. He was humming the song "Camelot" from the Broadway musical. He must have seen the movie version of it on TV. Tilly chimed in with the words.

"Don't," I cautioned him. "You're trying to send the subliminal message that New Camelot is the town's proper name."

"Oh dear," Tilly said, abandoning the tune. "If I'd realized that, I would never have aided and abetted."

The wizard looked wounded. "Why do you always think the worst of my intentions?"

"It's based on your record to date."

"Is it not possible that the song simply popped into my head on its own? Have you never had a tune take up residence in your head?"

"Not such a convenient one," I replied. All the people passing around us were now singing the song. Great—sooner or later someone was going to realize that by adding two letters to the peculiar name of New Camel, it became the much lovelier and more romantic New Camelot. From there it was a short leap to the fabled home of King Arthur and Merlin, the famed sorcerer.

We had to wait our turn at the petting zoo, but once we were inside the enclosure, Merlin's eyes lit up and he instantly dropped the aggrieved expression as if it had come to the wrong address. Tilly and I knew how much he missed the animals that populated the forest near his home. But his home was thousands of miles away and hundreds of years in the past. He sat on one of the low benches meant for children, and within seconds the baby goats, piglets, lambs and bunnies formed a semicircle around him, vying for his attention the way my cats did. Children complained to their parents that he was hogging the animals. Before irritation could boil over into heated words and actions, Tilly and I told the old wizard it was time to leave. He did not take it well. The animals seemed to share his disappointment and tried to follow him out. In the end, two animal wranglers and a maintenance man had to hold them back so we could leave without causing a mass exodus.

Poor Merlin was further vexed when he realized we'd come to the end of the fair. Of course no New Camel Fair would be complete without a couple of the town's churlish mascots stationed at the exit. Merlin took strong exception to their presence. "Thus the lie is perpetuated for another year.

It is truly a diabolical plot." One of the camels spat at him. He spat right back. Before the animals' owner could add his two cents to the exchange, Tilly and I grabbed Merlin's arms and whisked him out of the fairgrounds, his feet skimming the ground.

I dropped my aunt and our foster wizard at her house, stopped back home long enough to deposit my car in the driveway and grab Sashkatu, who was clearly miffed at being left for hours with the five other cats. We walked across the street to the rear door of Abracadabra. The moment we were inside, he ascended his custom-built steps to his padded window seat with its fine view of Main Street. He'd been my mother's familiar, and she'd spoiled him shamelessly. Not that I'd done anything to remedy the situation since he'd come into my keeping eighteen months ago.

I was turning the *closed* sign to *open* as my first customer reached the door. "I cannot tell you how grateful I am that you were willing to open for me on your day off," Lenore Spalding boomed. She was a petite woman in her fifties, with the vocal projection of a stage actress. Whoever raised her had failed to teach her the difference between an outside voice and an inside one. "For a little bitty thing, she can sure rattle the timbers," my grandmother Bronwen used to say after each of Lenore's visits.

"I'm happy to oblige," I said. "Let me know if you need any help finding what you want."

"Thanks, but I know this shop like the back of my hand." She slipped one of our wicker shopping baskets over her arm and disappeared down the first aisle still talking. "I never thought about it before, but that's a weird expression." Her words carried back to me loud and clear. There wasn't a lot of *Excuse me?* or *What was that?* when you were dealing with Lenore. I'd seen people turn off their hearing aids when they saw her coming.

She returned to the counter ten minutes later with her basket filled to the brim.

"You have enough here to last you an entire year," I said, ringing up her order.

"Trust me, I'll be back in six months, the latest," she said with a booming laugh that woke Sashkatu, despite the fact that he was growing deaf. He opened his eyes, homed in on the source of the disturbance, and yowled at her. "Sorry, sorry. I forgot how much he hates idle chatter." In all the years she'd been coming to my shop, she'd never figured out that it wasn't the chatter he minded, but the decibel of it.

After Lenore left, a steady stream of customers kept me busy until closing time. I was about to lock up when Lolly flew in the door, breathing hard, her face blanched a scary shade of white. "Kailyn, please," she said, her voice shaking badly, "would you—I mean, I need you—to please come with me."

"Of course. What happened? Are you okay?" Ignoring my questions, she grabbed my hand and pulled me out the door. By the time we crossed the street to her shop, she was bent over, gasping for air. She gave herself twenty seconds before leading me into her shop with its lingering scent of chocolate, and then out again through the backdoor to the small yard of weeds and dirt where she kept her garbage cans. A bag of garbage lay beside the cans. And a woman was sprawled face down in the space that remained, with one of Lolly's fudge knives protruding from the left side of her back.

Chapter 2

I brought Lolly inside, because standing out there staring at Ava wasn't doing either of them any good. Lolly was shaking and swaying back and forth. She needed to sit down before she fell over. She was as white as Ava, her hands probably as cold, though I had no desire to test that theory. In any case, it would have compromised the crime scene. I brought her into the workroom and opened one of the folding chairs she kept there for resting between batches of candy. I offered her water, but she refused it. In times of deep distress, I've never craved water, or any beverage, not even Tilly's calming tea. I don't know who decided it was the thing to give a person in a traumatic situation.

A moment later, she sat up straight and clapped a hand over her mouth. "Oh—good heavens. Kailyn, my brain must be scrambled. I have to call my family!" She started to push herself up with the arm rests. I could see the flimsy chair collapsing under the pressure and dumping her onto the floor. That was the last thing she needed.

"Stay there, please stay there. I'll get you the phone." She had a landline in the candy room. I'd seen it on previous, and much more pleasant, visits. I found it perched beside the sink and brought her the handset. She spent a minute dithering over which of her children to call and decided on Bonnie. I remembered Lolly describing her as the most level-headed of her children. Bonnie's exclamation of surprise and horror was loud enough for me to hear. Some news comes as a shock no matter how level-headed you were. Murder was definitely on that list. The victim's body in your mother's yard made it a top five contender.

"Okay," Lolly said, handing back the phone and breathing a little easier. "She'll get in touch with everyone else. She's my own little take charge, you-can-count-on-me Paul Revere. Always has been."

Paul Curtis made it to Lolly's in less than five minutes, well ahead of Detective Duggan. He'd been the officer on duty at the New Camel substation when I called 911. I led him past the display cases in the front of her shop and into the workroom. Before going out to the yard, Paul stopped and laid a reassuring hand on Lolly's shoulder. It probably didn't fit police protocol to show compassion for a potential suspect, and I was pretty sure he wouldn't have done it in front of Duggan.

When the forensic team arrived, Paul showed them to the crime scene and left them to their work. He asked Lolly if she was doing all right or if she felt the need to call her doctor. Paul had known her all his life, same as me, and it had to be difficult to think of her as a murder suspect.

"No thank you," Lolly murmured. "I'll be okay. It's just the shock of it."

Paul looked at me and shook his head as if to say *poor Lolly*. I nodded in agreement. Since it wouldn't be appropriate to make small talk under the circumstances, we tried not to look at each other. Paul wandered into the front of the shop, peered outside, then circled back to the workroom, clearly at odds over what to do until the detective showed up.

He must have done five laps before coming to a stop and asking Lolly if he could use the second folding chair. She didn't seem to have heard him, so I gave him the go-ahead. He set it up a few feet from her and sat down. "I don't have an exact ETA on detective Duggan," he said looking from me to Lolly and back again, "but I'm going to start the interview." He seemed to be waiting for our reactions. Lolly was off in another world. I shrugged. It sounded like a good idea as long as Duggan didn't start the interview over when he showed up. I had a strong suspicion he might, unless he'd mellowed a lot since the last time we butted heads, back in November.

"Lolly?" No reaction. "Lolly?" Paul raised his voice. She came out of her trance, looking around like someone who's been fast asleep and isn't quite sure where she is. "I'd like you to take me through the hour or so before you discovered Ava Duncan's body in your yard."

"Oh, okay," she said, sitting up straighter in the chair. "I had a booth at the fair like always. I left there—let's see—must have been around four thirty. I packed up the leftover candy and other supplies and drove back here."

Paul was jotting down notes on a little pad as she spoke. "Would you say you got back here five forty-five or so?"

"That sounds right. I put everything away, tied up the garbage from the morning and took it out to the cans in the back. That's when I almost stumbled over Ava's body." Tears sprang up in her eyes. "Such a terrible thing."

"About five o'clock?" he prompted.

She nodded, wiping away the tears with the back of her hand.

"What did you do immediately after you found her?"

"I dropped the bag on the ground and I ran over to Kailyn's shop."

"Why didn't you call nine-one-one?"

"I don't know," she said. "*Get Kailyn* is what popped into my head."

"When she ran into my shop, she was scared out of her mind," I said.

Paul cleared his throat. "I have to ask you not to intervene on her behalf. It taints her answers. By rights I should have asked you to stay in the other room."

"I'm sorry. I'll go wait there." The last thing I wanted was to make things worse for Lolly. I was looking out the front window when Detective Duggan finally arrived. He had to elbow his way through the growing crowd just to reach the front door of Lolly's shop. From what I could see, it was a crowd composed mostly of her extended family. With few exceptions, they all still lived in and around New Camel and were as closely knit as a family could be without being conjoined at the hip. Her four children were there with their spouses and their kids—Lolly's sixteen beloved grandchildren. There was also a contingent of Lolly's siblings, their spouses and kids with more family members joining the throng as the alert went out by phone, text and Facebook messaging.

Although Paul had immediately cordoned off the property with yellow police tape, it hadn't held up to the antics of the younger cousins who treated the unexpected reunion as a dandy place to play their own version of cops and bad guys. The parents, who were usually on top of their offsprings' behavior, were too distraught over Lolly's situation to keep after them, and the kids knew it.

Duggan marched into the shop with a grim expression hardened on his face like cement. He whipped past me and headed into the rear of the shop, muttering, "Figures *you'd* be involved." If the comment was intended to make me scurry away, he still didn't have a clue about me. I followed in his wake and watched him stride out the back door, letting it slam closed behind him. He didn't say a word to Lolly or Paul, who was already on his feet. It was hard to know if Duggan was angry at the world for dumping another murder in his lap, or angry with the circumstances that had prevented him from getting there sooner. It was likely a combination of the two topped off by the bonus of finding me at the scene.

I went to stand beside Lolly. From there I could see Duggan and the two-man forensic team sidling past each other as if they were at a square dance and the caller had yelled *do-si-do.* Ava was sprawled across most of the tiny yard, but she wasn't up to moving out of anyone's way. Duggan studied her, making a circuit of her body as best he could. He conferred briefly with the other men before taking a shortcut to the door by stepping over her. There had to be a superstition about doing that, but it didn't come to mind. Although we Wildes didn't believe in superstitions, we may have been responsible for starting a few of them over the years.

To Duggan's credit, he must have assessed Lolly's condition well enough to realize that hauling her down to the police station could be the tipping point, making an emergency room visit necessary. He told Paul to take me into the front of the shop. I'd been through this enough to know that he wanted to question us separately to see if our stories matched. I didn't know if Paul would admit to letting me stay in the room earlier. If he were smart, he wouldn't.

When Paul showed Duggan his notes from that brief interview, the detective didn't brush them aside. He read them, nodded and said, "Thanks, I'll take it from here." There'd clearly been a shift in their relationship during the months they'd been off my radar. *You go Paul,* I cheered silently. I just wished Duggan would lose the drill sergeant persona and treat Lolly with the deference due to someone who'd reached her golden years as a model citizen, with the exception of one speeding ticket when she was rushing to the hospital to meet her first grandchild.

There wasn't much distance from the front door to the back door of Lolly's shop. Even though the retail space was separated from the workroom by a wall, that wall had an open archway on one end connecting the rooms and making it easier for Lolly to carry the candy trays back and forth. Given these inadequacies, Duggan lowered his voice to a raspy whisper. I was still able to make out some of what he was saying to Lolly, until Paul started talking to me.

"Six good months—I thought maybe all the killing around here had finally stopped, and then your call came in. Hey—sorry—that didn't come out right," he said, stumbling over his words. "I... I didn't mean to suggest it was your fault or anything." He was still awkward talking to me. I felt bad, but I had no idea what I could do about it. Maybe if he had a girlfriend, he'd get over his crush on me. It wasn't as if we'd ever had a relationship—except maybe in his mind.

"No problem—I didn't think that," I said, partly to relieve his mind and partly to make him stop talking so I could hear what was going on in the workroom.

Paul went over to the window and peered outside. "That's quite a crowd out there." He seemed determined to keep up the chatter. I went behind the counter and plucked a milk chocolate turtle and a chewy caramel from the trays. He seemed delighted to accept them. With any luck they would keep his mouth busy for a little while and let me hear what was happening in the other room.

"Was there any trouble between you and Ava?" Duggan was asking. Lolly must have shaken her head, because he went on to another question. "There are two ways into your yard. Through a padlocked gate, which wasn't tampered with, and through your shop, but your security system wasn't tripped. Can you explain how the body wound up back there?"

"No," Lolly replied, her voice as thin and breathless as a little girl's. I should have told her to insist on having an attorney present. A lot of help I was.

"That's good stuff," Paul said, licking chocolate off his finger. "But I ought to pay for it." He reached into his pocket, found five dollars, and set it on the counter. "Would you let Lolly know that's from me?" I promised I would. A few more minutes elapsed before Duggan called me back there. He already had Lolly's answers; it didn't matter if she sat in on my interview. Paul went with me and leaned against the marble island where the candy magic happened.

With Lolly still seated, there was only one empty chair. Duggan told me to sit down. It would have been nice to think that he was being gracious, but I knew better. He wanted the high ground, the position of power. He asked me the same things I'd overheard him ask Lolly. No, I didn't know of any problem between Lolly and the deceased. I didn't know about Ava's death until Lolly told me. I didn't hide evidence or change the location or position of the body. Yes, I called 911 before I called anyone else.

"Why do you think Lorelei ran to you before calling the police?" he asked. For a moment, I had trouble connecting Lolly with her given name. Like most people in town, I'd never known her as anything but Lolly.

"I don't know for sure, but I guess when she found Ava it was such a shock that she kind of blanked. I was just across the street, so she ran to me for help."

"Why didn't she go to Tilly?"

I explained that my aunt was closed for the day, but that I'd opened my shop for a couple of hours. Duggan questioned me for several more minutes about my ties to Lolly, how much I knew about her life apart from her work, which wasn't much beyond her family's activities, and how well I knew Ava. The answer to that one was *barely.* She'd visited my shop a few times. Duggan closed his notepad and tucked it back in his shirt pocket. It was now or never if I wanted to ask him the question that had been nagging at me since he walked in the door. "Should Lolly be retaining a lawyer?"

"It wouldn't be a bad idea," he said flat out, no *probably,* no *maybe,* to soften the blow.

Lolly recoiled in her chair as if his words had a physical impact on her. Although I'd asked the question, I wasn't prepared for such a blunt answer either. What had I expected him to say? *No, of course not. We all know Lolly couldn't possibly have harmed anyone. We'll get it straightened out in no time.* "What happens next?"

"Given her extensive family ties here, her age, and her health, I'm not taking her into custody at this time." He turned to address Lolly directly. "Don't leave town, or I will find you and throw you in jail so fast it will make your head spin."

I went to Lolly and took her hand. "She's not going anywhere, Detective. There's no need for threats. She's not some hoodlum." I knew I'd overstepped my bounds about a second too late. Paul winced in anticipation of the detective's wrath.

Duggan squinted at me with one eye as if he were taking aim with a weapon. "You looking to warm up that cell for her, Ms. Wilde? You're lucky I understand that you're just trying to protect your friend. Oh—one more thing," he added on his way out of the workroom. "I'll be conducting a search of your house, Lorelei. So your house and this shop are off limits until further notice."

Paul raised his hand to us in what looked like a half-hearted wave, but was probably just meant to be discreet and escape Duggan's attention. I helped Lolly out of her chair and walked her to the front of the shop. I gave her the five dollars Paul had left for her, which seemed ridiculously petty when words like *murder* and *prison* were being bandied about, but I'd made a promise.

When we walked outside, a murmur of relief rose from Lolly's family. She grabbed my hand. "Kailyn—I need to talk to you."

"Of course," I said, completely clueless. "First you should try to rest, eat something. Let your family take care of *you* for a change. I'm on the case. We'll talk soon."

"No," she whispered urgently, "you don't understand. I lied to the detective." If she'd told me she was from another planet I wouldn't have been more surprised than I was at that moment.

Unable to wait any longer, one of Lolly's youngest grandchildren broke away from her mother and ran up to her. She wrapped her pudgy little arms around Lolly's knees and hugged her with all her might. I nodded to Lolly and she nodded back with a smile as she bent down to her granddaughter.

Chapter 3

After feeding Sashkatu and his brethren, I called my aunt Tilly. She'd be hurt if she learned about the body in Lolly's yard through the grapevine before she heard it from me. She listened without interruption, accompanying my words with a counterpoint of heartfelt *oh mys* and *oh dears*. "You know what this means," she said. "I was right again."

"Your last premonition was months ago, on Thanksgiving, but nothing came of it." I couldn't let her get hysterical again about being labeled the Angel of Death. "There have to be some parameters. A death that happens within days of your prediction may be a valid concern. One that occurs months later shouldn't be." I spoke with all the authority I could muster.

"You're quite certain of that?" she asked warily.

"As sure as I can be."

"All right then," Tilly said, "I must bake Lolly something appropriate and visit her at the first opportunity. Muffins and scones, I should think—comfort food."

"Now that you mention it," Merlin piped up in the background, "I could do with some carrot muffins."

"He's the only one I know whose hearing has improved with age," Tilly said dryly. She was pulling out her baking trays, muffin tins and mixing bowls. I could barely hear her over the clatter, so I left her to the baking.

As far as I knew, word of Ava's death hadn't yet reached the local media. The one reporter who covered New Camel was always running between high school sports and Four H events. If he spent his time shadowing Duggan, he'd have nothing to show for most of his days. No matter—after Travis arrived, news of the latest murder would be everywhere.

He was at my door, before I could decide whether to order Chinese or Italian. He hadn't bothered to change out of his newscaster suit, but he was no longer wearing the tie or jacket and his dress shirt was open at the neck, the sleeves rolled up. He had a brown shopping bag that smelled like a trattoria. He set it down on the kitchen counter and gave me a *hello* kiss that went on long enough for me to forget I was hungry. "I've missed you," he whispered in my ear, the rich timbre of his voice plucking at all the right nerve endings.

"I can't believe you stopped to pick up dinner on the way. When we talked, you were determined to get here before dark."

"I called the restaurant, and they met me at the curb with it." Travis unpacked the bag, which held two foil-covered heroes and two salads in clear plastic boxes, dressing on the side, and a stack of napkins. I grabbed paper plates, forks, and the iced tea from the fridge, while he unwrapped the sandwiches. "There's meatball for me and chicken Parm for you. If I got it wrong we can switch or split them."

"I'm good with the chicken, but I can't eat more than half of this—it's huge." We took our plates to the table and dug in. "Was it still light enough to get some decent footage of Lolly's place?"

Travis washed down a mouthful of hero with iced tea. "Yeah, but the cops didn't make it easy."

"I'm pretty sure that's not their job."

"Whoever put up the crime-scene tape went overboard. The place looked like it was toilet-papered for Halloween."

The image that came to mind made me chuckle. "That would be Paul giving Duggan what he asked for—in spades."

"There was no way to get near the backyard without moving it."

I put my hand to my heart and feigned shock. "Don't tell me that stopped you!"

He grinned. "I hopped the fence at the ceramic shop next door and got some decent shots of the yard—if you could call it a yard."

"It's utilitarian—a place to stow garbage cans."

"And apparently, a petite murder victim. Did you know the woman?" He took a hefty bite to finish off the first half of his hero.

"She came into my shop a few times over the last couple of years. The first time, she mentioned that she moved here for a job, but she never elaborated. Aside from that, our conversations were confined to what kind of products she needed."

"Was she a customer of Lolly's too? Or did they have more of a relationship than that?"

"A customer. I didn't get the sense there was more to it, and under the circumstances I didn't want to start questioning Lolly. She was not in good shape and she still had to sit through the interview with Duggan." I put down my sandwich for a sip of iced tea, then ate a few more bites before giving up.

Travis was well into his second half. "Not crazy about it?"

"It's delicious, it's just me—I guess I'm filled up on worry. My mother always warned me about that." I intended the words to come out with humor, but they dropped like stones. Travis reached across the table for my hand and held on to it while he polished off his dinner and drained the iced tea. The turmoil inside me slowly quieted. He was better than Tilly's best tea, but I had no intention of sharing his particular formula with anyone else. He was looking at me with his head tilted to one side as if he was trying to assess my state of mind.

I managed a smile that felt lopsided. It was the best I could do. "How would you like a full report from the time Lolly ran into my shop, until I left her with her family?"

He popped the last bit of hero into his mouth. "I wouldn't turn it down." He squeezed my hand before letting it go. We adjourned to the living room, where Sashkatu had already claimed his spot on the top ridge of the couch. When we sat down, he opened one eye to see who dared disturb his snooze. We received a look that said *one needn't rock the entire couch when one sits on it. A little more finesse would be appreciated in future.*

"We beg your majesty's pardon." Travis had developed an affinity for Sashki, and I was convinced it was mutual. A few weeks earlier, I'd caught the two of them snuggled together in bed. The moment Sashki realized he'd been made, he jumped up and yowled bitterly at Travis as if he'd been held there against his will.

Travis put his arm around my shoulder and drew me tightly to his side. We stayed like that while I gave Travis as complete a synopsis of my hours with Lolly as I could recall. No detail was too small to mention. But when I reached the end, I hesitated, not sure it was right to betray Lolly's confidence in one respect. On the other hand, Travis was my partner. We'd be investigating the murder together, so he needed to know everything I knew. Why was I reluctant to repeat what she had whispered to me? Didn't I trust him implicitly? The answer was immediate. He wouldn't be in my bed or anywhere else in my life if I didn't. And yet betraying a confidence was difficult for me. I needed Lolly's permission.

Travis caught the hesitation. "Was there something else you were going to say?" I explained about wanting Lolly's okay before sharing any more information. He nodded. "I would expect no less from you." I could name a couple of ex-boyfriends who would have handled the matter with a lot less understanding.

"She said she'd call me. My guess is she's waiting until she has a few minutes alone. We didn't have much time to talk at the shop. Paul showed up less than five minutes after my call, then forensics arrived, and eventually Duggan. As soon as he let Lolly go, her family closed ranks around her like a Viking shield wall. Any thoughts based on what I've told you?"

"Given the information we have at this point, I'd rule Lolly out as a suspect, if for no other reason than she's too smart to kill someone at her own shop."

"Plus she's Lolly!" I refused to entertain the possibility that she was guilty. "There isn't a single hateful bone in her body." And I couldn't imagine changing my mind, regardless of what she'd lied about. "The killer was definitely trying to frame her, otherwise why steal her knife to use as the murder weapon?"

"Are you certain it wasn't just a generic knife you can buy anywhere?"

"It was definitely Lolly's. Her daughter bought her a set of candy-making utensils engraved with her initials for Christmas a few years ago. They're Lolly's pride and joy. It was the first thing I checked for when I saw the knife. But who would want to frame her? Everyone around here knows she isn't capable of murder."

"That's it then," Travis said as though he'd had a light bulb moment. "All we have to do is find the one person who doesn't know Lolly very well and we'll have our killer." His delivery was so deadpan and the suggestion so absurd that I dissolved into laughter. It felt good to let go, but wrong to be laughing at such an awful time. I shook my head, annoyed with myself.

"Cut yourself some slack—you needed that. Laughter is great at lowering stress levels."

"It feels so disrespectful. I keep thinking about poor Lolly being caught up in this mess. When she woke up today, she had no idea what was in store for her."

"You need to put the worrying and empathy on the back burner for now and focus on how we can find the real killer." He was right of course. "There's one unimpeachable fact," he continued, "Ava was murdered. Now who had a motive to kill her?"

"I know almost nothing about her, but I'll reach out to the other shopkeepers and my friends."

"Okay, we have the beginning of a plan. I'll check with my contacts and search social media for information about Ava." I was about to ask Travis if he had to head back to Watkins Glen, when my phone rang. We both sat up straight like teenagers caught breaking the rules. *Lorelei* popped up on Caller ID. "Lolly," I said, after juggling the phone and nearly dropping it, "how are you doing?"

"Well, as my ten-year-old granddaughter likes to say, 'I'm lower than a pregnant ant.'" She was trying hard to sound upbeat.

"You don't have to pretend with me." If I knew Lolly, she'd spent the last few hours assuring her family that she was coping just fine. She probably wouldn't have agreed to move in with one of them if she'd been able to stay in her own home. I hoped the police would let her back in quickly.

"Thank you for reminding me." She issued a long wobbly sigh. "I've known tired in my life, times when I felt beaten into the ground, but murder adds another dimension that makes it hard to breathe."

"Try not to torment yourself. Travis and I will track down the killer and get answers to all the questions." She thanked me again, and I waited for her to broach the subject of lying to Duggan. When she didn't, I thought she might be waiting for me to ask about it. "Lolly?"

"Oh there you are. I thought maybe I didn't hear you say *goodbye.*"

"No, I'm here. Did you want to tell me something about your interview with Duggan?"

"My good Lord, *that's* why I called. I think I'm losing my marbles."

"Your marbles are a little scattered for the moment, but whose wouldn't be?"

"Is it terribly pushy of me to ask you to come by tomorrow? According to my son the lawyer, one should never talk about sensitive matters over the phone."

"No problem. Where will you be?"

"Officer Curtis called a little while ago to tell me I can go home. I intend to be back there first thing in the morning." I heard Bonnie in the background telling her she shouldn't be alone at a time like this. "I'll be home in the morning," she repeated firmly, as much for her daughter's benefit as for mine.

Chapter 4

I opened my eyes to the soft light of early morning. Merlin was staring at me from the foot of the bed. He didn't seem to care that five of the cats were climbing on him and knocking each other off to bounce on the bed and try again. Sashkatu was perched on my dresser regarding the youngsters of his clowder with the resigned forbearance of an elder statesman. Travis was already up. I heard water running in the kitchen.

"Are you awake, Mistress?" Merlin asked. "Tilly told me that it's not polite to wake someone unless it's an emergency."

"Is there an emergency?" I sat up, one leg over the side of the bed, poised to take off. "Is it my aunt?"

"No no, she's fine, which is why I didn't rouse you sooner." He looked like he was expecting praise for his patience, but he wasn't going to receive any from me. I fell back onto my pillow. "How was I supposed to stay asleep with the cat gymnastics on my bed?"

"Tilly never said I couldn't wait nearby until you awoke. As for the cats, I can't be responsible for their activities."

I groaned. "Okay, Merlin, I'm awake. Why are you here?"

"I want breakfast, and Tilly is still sleeping."

I threw back the covers and reached for my bathrobe on the chair near the closet. It sailed into my hand. Magick was lovely when it worked properly. I pulled it on as I climbed out of bed. "Then why didn't you sit on her bed to wait?"

"Although I love the lady dearly, she can be upset by the strangest of things."

"Imagine that." I shoved my feet into my slippers and led the parade of the furred and bearded down the stairs. Travis was at the sink rinsing out his coffee cup. He was wearing the same pants and shirt he'd had on yesterday. After learning about Ava's murder, he had to choose between going back to his apartment to pack a change of clothes and trying to make it here before sunset. The journalist in him had chosen the latter course. A smile lit his face when he turned and saw me—a neat new power I'd acquired, more special because it owed nothing to magick.

"I told Merlin to help himself to cereal or yogurt," Travis said, "but he was determined to wait for you. I made coffee—there should be enough for a few more cups."

"Thanks. You're heading back to the Glen?"

He set his cup in the sink. "Duty calls, though I'd rather go with you to Lolly's." He caught me around the waist and gave me a goodbye kiss with a side of longing that proved contagious. For a minute, we both forgot we had an audience.

"I thought we came down here for breakfast," the wizard grumbled. The cats backed him up with a chorus of plaintive meows.

Travis laughed. "You'd better feed them before they mutiny. Let me know how it goes with Lolly."

I fed the cats, made Merlin eggs and cheese on an English muffin and took a quick shower. Tilly called to find out if I had our foster-wizard. She'd been up late baking for Lolly and overslept. Since I was going to Lolly's, I offered to take the baked goods along. Tilly insisted she wanted to comfort her in person. I checked with Lolly, who welcomed the idea.

When I was ready to go, Sashkatu was waiting at the door. He'd grown accustomed to spending the day in the shop with my mother, and after she died I'd kept up the tradition. I promised him I'd be back for him soon. He skewered me with a look that said *that remains to be seen* and stalked off, nursing one of his famous snits.

I brought Merlin home, picked up Tilly and we were off to Lolly's house with the basket of muffins and scones. Their irresistible smell reminded me of the last baby shower in Lolly's family, for which Tilly had supplied an enormous basket of goodies. A far happier occasion than this one.

Lolly lived in a cottage that belonged in a fairytale. After her husband passed away and her children left to feather their own nests, she'd downsized. The cottage had all she needed, a kitchen, a family/living room, a bedroom and a bathroom. There was a basement for storage, and an attic that could be dormered if she ever got tired of looking at the same old walls. Large family dinners had been relocated to her children's houses on a rotating basis. When she finished decorating the cottage, it exuded the same warmth and welcome as its occupant.

Lolly opened the door with a brave but shaky smile that dissolved into tears when Tilly embraced her, and started anew when she saw the basket she'd brought. She seemed to have aged overnight. She'd always looked so robust with her apple-round cheeks and dimpled smile that I'd never given much thought to her age. But that morning she looked every bit a grandmother in her seventies. A grandmother in deep distress. There was a bleakness about her, her eyes wallowed in dark shadows, and her shoulders hunched forward as if to protect vital organs.

"There's tea as well," Tilly said, taking charge and leading the way into the kitchen. "I'll put up water, so the two of you can get started." We sat at the drop-leaf table in the dinette with room for three.

"What did you mean about lying to detective Duggan?" I asked. Time was of the essence. There was nothing to be gained by beating around the bush.

"I don't know what possessed me," she said, her voice quaking with emotion. "I've never been a liar. My mother, rest her soul, pounded that out of me at an early age. But, when he asked me if there'd been any problems between Ava and me, the lie spilled out like it had a mind of its own. 'No of course not, Detective. Ava came to my shop to buy candy. What possible problem could come of that?'"

"But it wasn't true?" I prompted her when her mind seemed to drift.

She shook her head. "Ava and I did have a falling out, because she was having an affair with my son-in-law Elliot." Her words hung in the air, while my brain scrambled to remember that Danielle was the daughter married to Elliot. I'd been knocked for a loop. To me Lolly's family was the big, perfect all-American family who never fought at Thanksgiving, never envied or competed with each other, and certainly never cheated on their spouses.

"Lolly, I'm so sorry. How did you find out?"

"My daughter told me. I'd noticed a lot of tension between her and Elliot, so I sat her down when the kids were in school and asked if she needed my help in any way, or if maybe she wanted to use me as a sounding board." Behind us the kettle whistled. Tilly poured the water into three cups and Lolly excused herself to get honey, lemon wedges and milk. Tilly served the tea and insisted we each take a scone or a muffin before she settled into the seat we'd left for her.

Lolly added milk and a bit of honey to her cup. "At first Danielle pretended she didn't know what I was talking about, but then she broke down and told me the whole sordid tale." Lolly paused to take a bite of her apricot scone before continuing. "Dani found out by pure happenstance.

She was meeting a friend for lunch in the Glen and when she walked into the restaurant she saw Elliot and Ava at a table. They were holding hands, drinking wine and leaning over the table as if they couldn't get close enough." I'd never heard such bitterness and anger in Lolly's voice and I realized that perhaps I didn't know her as well as I thought I did.

"When Elliot looked up and saw Dani, he made a big show of being thrilled to see her," Lolly continued. "He got up and brought her over to meet Ava, said she was an old friend from college and wasn't it an amazing coincidence that they bumped into each other on the street. They'd come into the restaurant to spend an hour catching up. Ava played along and between them they almost convinced Danielle. But when she had a chance to think about it, she couldn't get that first tableau of them out of her head. That night she confronted him. He begged her forgiveness, swore it would never happen again. It was all Ava's fault, she came on to him, wouldn't let him be until she wore him down."

"Men," Tilly said, wagging her head. I wasn't sure what she meant by the comment. Although Morgana and Bronwen had been abandoned by their husbands, Tilly had enjoyed a happy marriage. Maybe she was just trying to be supportive.

"That was the end of it?" I asked, breaking off a piece of my carrot muffin and tucking it in my mouth.

"Everything was quiet for a while. Elliot didn't have to 'stay late at the office' anymore. He spent more quality time with her and the kids. I thought, okay, I could breathe easy again. But about a month ago, I was driving past the Winterland hotel. A car was coming out of the parking lot, so I slowed down to let it pull in front of me. There was a woman at the wheel. A mile or so down the road, she moved into the turn lane and I pulled up beside her. That's when I saw Elliot in the passenger seat. I wasn't even surprised; but I was crazy angry, so angry I was shaking. Not only had he betrayed Dani's trust again, but now *I* had to be the one to tell my daughter. *I* had to be the one who would tear her world apart." Lolly choked back a sob. "If I was ever going to kill someone—that would have been the moment."

Tilly scooted her chair closer to her friend and put her arm around her shoulders as best she could. "That wasn't the end of it," Lolly said. She paused to sip her tea, the scone forgotten on her plate. I couldn't imagine what she meant. "Danielle filed for divorce. Elliot pleaded and begged her to take him back, but she'd had enough. With all that going on, Ava walked into my shop one day. You could have knocked me over with a feather."

Tilly and I were slack-jawed. I recovered first. "What on earth did she want?"

"She came to buy chocolate."

"No," Tilly said, stretching out the word in disbelief.

"And she didn't understand why I refused to serve her. She said, 'I'm here to conduct business. Any smart business owner knows better than to let personal issues affect commerce.' She left in a huff, as if she were the injured party."

I could see that Lolly was drained from reliving the emotional story, but I had one last question before we left. I asked if she had any objection to me sharing the information with Travis. She managed a weak smile. "Not at all. In fact, I'm grateful you're doing this for me. You two make an amazing team."

"I understand why you lied to Duggan," I said when she was walking us to the door.

Tilly put her hand to her heart. "Can you imagine if you'd told him the truth? We'd be visiting you in a jail cell. Now don't you worry," she added, giving Lolly a proper, muumuu-enveloping hug. "They'll find the killer before you know it."

On the drive home, Tilly and I were both quiet, lost in our own thoughts. "If I'd been aware of the havoc Ava was wreaking, I might have been tempted to try a little black magick," I admitted, swinging into my aunt's driveway.

"That's not a subject to be taken lightly," Tilly said, as solemn as I'd ever seen her. "There's already enough darkness in our little corner of the world."

Chapter 5

I started visiting my fellow shopkeepers during what I laughingly referred to as my lunch hour, because lunch was rarely consumed. I tried to keep it at the same time every day so that I wouldn't miss customers who counted on finding me open during my standard hours. On tour bus days, I generally worked right through lunch. The folks who came on the buses didn't live locally and wouldn't be back anytime soon. I couldn't afford to lose their business. For that matter, the other shopkeepers would be attending to business as well.

On the plus side, using lunchtime to carry on my investigation meant I didn't have to open Abracadabra late or get home late—a boon for my gang of would-be familiars who wanted their dinner on time. My grandmother, Bronwen, had called the five young cats *Morgana's Folly*, a name my mother did not appreciate. She'd gone on the familiar-summoning spree with the hope that a new familiar would fix the problems we'd been having with our magick. At cat six, she finally gave up. Apparently, the fault didn't lie in her aging Sashkatu. But since one can't simply give away magickal cats on a street corner, or through craigslist, they became part of my inheritance. Through no fault of my own, I was eligible for the title of crazy cat lady before I was out of my twenties.

For my first lunch hour of sleuthing, I stopped in The Wheel, the pottery shop next door to Lolly's place. The owner, Tess Webster, had opened her business about six months earlier. She'd come over to introduce herself to Tilly and me when she was setting up. She looked to be in her thirties, and usually had a toddler and a baby in the shop with her. Since she was new in town, I didn't have high hopes that she knew Ava, but I didn't want to leave any stone unturned.

I'd only been inside The Wheel once before, when Tilly and I had brought Tess welcome-to-New Camel gifts. Tilly's offering was a trio of breads—pumpkin, banana and zucchini. Mine was a basket of my most popular skin care items. The interior of the shop looked very different from the other shops in New Camel. It was more bare bones and functional. There were two potters' wheels, two rectangular wooden tables that reminded me of the ones in my high school art class, a desk with a computer, and a kiln in the back of the shop. A bookshelf ran along one wall, the titles on the books' spines covering every aspect of the history and art of pottery, as well as more practical volumes on how to go about throwing a pot. A Pack 'n Play was near the opposite wall and a quilted cradle rested on one of the tables.

I loved Tess's work, the beautifully decorated pots, each unique in shape and style. They were on display in glass-fronted cabinets that kept them safe from the curious hands of children and the often careless hands of adults. I would have bought one on that first visit if I'd been able to choose just one.

Tess was putting a pot in the kiln to bake when I walked in. Her brown hair was pulled back in a ponytail and a clay-smudged denim apron covered most of her jeans and T-shirt. Throwing pots was not a glamorous business. Tess set the timer and joined me in the front of the shop. She seemed happy to see me. "Aren't you missing someone?" I asked. The baby was asleep in her cradle, but I didn't see the toddler anywhere.

"My husband took the day off to spend with the whirlwind, otherwise known as Conner. He wanted to give me a break."

"Sounds like you found a winner."

"Let me get back to you on that. Today might just cure him of that winning charm." She pulled out two chairs from under the table where the cradle was perched. "Sit, please. I'd love some grownup conversation that's not punctuated by crying or complaining. Wow," she added, "I just heard myself and I sound like the worst mom."

"No way, I don't know how you create such beautiful pieces, teach classes and watch two little ones at the same time. And that doesn't include taking care of a household."

Tess laughed. "Most of the time I don't know how I do it either. I'm like a tightrope walker—if I look down, I'll lose my footing and we'll all wind up in a pile on the floor."

"I guess you know what happened to Ava Duncan," I said, when there was a pause in the conversation.

"Unfortunately, I had a front row seat for it. When I heard the first police car screech to a stop next door, I looked outside. At that point, there was nothing going on in front of Lolly's shop, so I looked out back into her yard. I saw that poor woman lying there with the garbage cans like she'd been discarded, thrown away. It's ironic really—we moved here to raise our family in a peaceful place where we wouldn't have to worry about things like that."

"New Camel *was* that place until last year," I said. "And if it's up to me, it will be again. In fact, that's the reason for my visit." Tess cocked her head. "My boyfriend and I have been investigating the murder cases around here and closing them before the police. But please don't repeat that to anyone, especially detective Duggan. I'm not exactly his favorite person."

"My lips are zipped." Tess pulled an imaginary zipper across her mouth. "I had the dubious pleasure of speaking to him myself."

"Would you mind if I asked you a few questions regarding Ava's death?"

"Sure—anything that can help. You have a much nicer approach than he did."

"Jack the Ripper probably had a nicer approach than Duggan," I said. "Did you know Ava? Ever see her before yesterday?"

"She didn't look at all familiar to me. I'm certain she never came in here." The baby was making little noises in her sleep. Tess leaned over the cradle to check on her.

"Did you happen to see anyone in Lolly's backyard before the police arrived on the scene?"

"No, but I had no reason to be looking before the sirens."

"Did you hear any shouting or arguing coming from next door in the days or weeks before Ava was killed?"

"Not that I can recall. This town is usually so quiet, I would remember if I heard something like that."

"Have you noticed anyone walking around town, checking things out, maybe trying to get a look into the yards behind the shops—that sort of thing?"

She didn't answer right away. I saw her look at her watch and worried she might have reached her limit with interrogation, even if I was a lot nicer than Duggan. I was hitting her with one question after another, because I knew a customer could walk in at any moment. The longer Tess took to reply, the more I expected to be shown the door. She was probably trying to come up with a polite way to go about it.

"No one stands out in my mind," she said finally. "Between working and caring for the kids I don't have much time to be observant. And if someone wanted to scope things out and remain anonymous, they'd just have to wait for a bus tour to come through and they could blend in and never raise any suspicions." She had a good point. "I'm sorry I'm not being much help."

"No, actually you have a valid point. I'm the one who should be apologizing. I didn't mean to pummel you with questions. I just want to clear Lolly's name and get Ava's killer off the streets as soon as possible." The timer rang on the kiln, punctuating my words.

"I totally understand," Tess said, rising. "And I'm rooting for you. It scares the hell out of me that the killer could still be around here. What kind of person sneaks up behind you and plunges a knife in your back?" A frisson shook her body as she headed to the kiln. "And poor Lolly. From the day we moved in, she's been so kind to us. Of all people, she doesn't deserve to be caught up in this mess."

"Have any of your customers commented on Ava's death?" I asked once Tess returned to her seat.

"It happened so recently, I've only seen a few of the people who take lessons from me. Their reactions were basically, 'Did you see it happen?' and 'Why would anyone want to frame Lolly?'"

"If anyone does voice an opinion about who killed Ava or why, would you let me know?"

"Absolutely." The baby was fussing again, all her tiny limbs going at the same time. It didn't take long before she worked herself up to a strident wail. Tess lifted her out of the cradle and patted her back. In moments she quieted, but every time Tess tried to put her down, the crying began anew. "I think Emmy needs a diaper change. I have her things in the bathroom. I won't be long."

"That's okay, I should be getting back to my shop anyway. I'll be in touch." I was reaching for the door when it flew open, and three-year-old Conner ran in, followed by a man who I assumed was Tess's husband. He was nice looking in an outdoorsy way, with a neatly trimmed beard that put Merlin's mangy one to shame. I could picture him living in the wilderness, splitting wood for the fire, staring down a Grizzly or a moose.

Conner stopped in his tracks and looked up at me with a frown. "Who are you?" he asked in an accusing tone.

"Conner, buddy, that's not polite." His dad squatted down to his level. "Here's what you do." He stood and extended his hand to me. "Hi, I'm Ben Webster, Tess's husband, and this is our son Conner."

I shook his hand. "Nice to meet you, Ben. Nice to meet you too, Conner. My name is Kailyn Wilde." I held out my hand and after a wary moment, he put his small hand in mine.

Ben grinned. "Good job, Conner." He gave his son a high five. "Nice to meet you too, Kailyn, and thanks for being part of the impromptu etiquette lesson."

Tess poked her head out of the bathroom. "Kailyn owns the shop across the street." Ben said it looked intriguing and he'd been meaning to check it out. Conner had clearly lost interest. He made a beeline for his mother who was coming out of the bathroom holding Emmy. He was so intent on reaching them that he wasn't looking where he was going. His foot caught the edge of the Pack 'n Play. It would have been better if he'd fallen there, but he managed to stay upright, stumbling forward out of control and headed straight for the side of the kiln. Tess and Ben shouted for him to watch out. He couldn't. It was all happening too fast. In the split second before Conner went headlong into the kiln, I focused my energy on it and nudged it out of his way. He fell, spread-eagle on the floor.

For a minute, no one said anything. Conner sat up and looked at the bruise on his knee with a quivering lower lip. Ben and Tess reached him at the same time. Ben checked his knee and deemed it okay. "This calls for an emergency ice cream cone," he proclaimed like a doctor issuing a prescription. Conner sniffled, caught between tears and a smile.

"With sprinkles?"

"A double dip of them!"

"And a cherry, like on a sundae?" Conner was getting into the spirit of it.

"No matter what the cost!" Ben set him on his feet.

"Mama, mama," Conner tugged on the bottom of Tess's apron. "Can Emmy have one?"

Tess bent down, the baby still in her arms. "Thank you, Conner, that's very generous. You're a wonderful big brother, but we'll have to wait until she's older." Tess gave him a big kiss.

"No mushies," he protested, rubbing at his cheek.

"That was awful close," Ben murmured to his wife. "There must be a guardian angel watching over him."

"A guardian angel for sure," Tess repeated, looking directly at me. Ben and Conner took off for The Soda Jerk, and she laid Emmy back in her cradle. "That kiln moved out of the way," she said in an accusing tone. "Ben couldn't see it from where he was, but I did."

"I've read that under severe stress, the brain can alter how we see things. It can make time seem to stretch out or stand still, even change how we perceive distances."

"I've heard things like that too," she said with a big old serving of doubt in her voice. I needed her to focus on the important part of what happened. "I'm just really glad Conner wasn't badly injured. In the end that's all that matters, right?"

"Well yes..." There seemed to be a *but* on the tip of her tongue. I had to get out of there. The longer I stayed, the more she would question what happened, along with my part in it. I checked my watch as casually as possible. "I didn't realize how late it was—I've got to run before I miss any customers. I'll be in touch. Take care." I tried to sound natural and light-hearted, but I missed it by a mile.

Chapter 6

"I fear you may have opened an ugly can of worms," my grandmother Bronwen said.

She and Morgana had dropped by for one of their visits from beyond the veil, their energy clouds, serene and white. I had expected a rebuke when I told them how I saved Tess's son, but I refused to let them undermine the peace in my heart.

"At best it was an impossible decision," Morgana chimed in. "Had I been in Kailyn's predicament, I may well have done the same thing." *Was my mother taking my side?!*

Gray peaks rose in Bronwen's cloud. A storm loomed. "I'm not saying I wouldn't have myself. I was simply pointing out that she will need to be careful should gossip spread."

"Maybe the gossip that spreads will be about how she saved the little boy," Morgana responded. I kept waiting for her cloud to flare red, but it remained a snowy white.

"Ever since your mother started that course in happiness, she's become a wimp," Bronwen muttered. "All the fight's gone out of her—she's insufferable." So I was right, they did enjoy the sparring. But since it's impossible to argue without an opponent, Bronwen was clearly determined to scuttle my mother's plans for peace.

"You could benefit from the course too," she replied evenly.

Bronwen's cloud crackled and flashed with lightning. "I have no wish to undergo a lobotomy of the spirit."

"It's not a lobotomy of any kind." Morgana sounded calm, but telltale fissures of red were making her cloud look like a drunk's eyes the morning after. She was losing the battle with herself.

"Ladies," I said. "I have a question." They turned their attention to me with a tilt in their axes that reminded me of the way dogs tilt their heads when they're trying to understand. "Have you ever considered how you might be feeling, if only one of you had died in that accident?" My question was met by total silence, which itself was impressive. My mother and grandmother were seldom at a loss for words and never at the same time. I watched the stormy gray ebb from Bronwen's cloud and the red drain from Morgana's. Without another word, their clouds blinked out together. Why hadn't I thought to pose that question until now? It had certainly been on my mind for some time. I had no idea if it would soften their interactions, but at least I'd given them food for thought. I doubted a permanent détente was possible, or even desirable in the long run. As Bronwen had told me on numerous occasions before her death, they didn't argue, they debated. "Exercising the brain is critical if one wants to keep it fit." I didn't know if that was true in their present states. For that matter, I had no idea how one *thought* without an actual brain, but since the dead were not allowed to enlighten mortals about the great unknown, I'd have to wait until I found out for myself.

Sashkatu found me in the kitchen drinking the last of my coffee. He frowned at me with eyebrows cats technically don't have. The muscles of his face had always been more expressive than any cat I'd ever known. When I didn't instantly react, he began trilling at me. If he'd said, *Get on with it, human!* he wouldn't have been any clearer. I checked my watch. It was nearly nine-thirty. I grabbed my purse and we were out the door.

We crossed the street to the back door of Abracadabra. I turned off the alarm and Sashkatu headed straight for the window ledge with its memory foam pillow to ease his aging joints. I turned the *closed* sign to *open* and unlocked the front door. It was rare for me to find a customer waiting. But of course, that morning there were two.

I apologized for being late. Beverly Ruppert marched in first, greeting me with a cool *hello*. "I wouldn't have waited, but I'm completely out of the under eye smoother." I knew she was angling to be compensated for her time. She pumped all the merchants in New Camel for discounts and freebies for one reason or another. Of course, when the situation was reversed and she kept you waiting at her salon, she was quick to point out that stylists ran late at every salon—it was to be expected, the same as in a doctor's office. Arguing with her was pointless, so most of us ignored her broad hints and hoped she'd stop patronizing our businesses.

I didn't recognize the second customer. She had about five years on me. Although she was pretty, she wasn't drop-dead gorgeous, but there was something about her—the word that popped into my mind was *polished.* Her blonde hair was short, cut to the line of her jaw. Her makeup was subtle, highlighting her blue eyes and high cheekbones. Her beige suit had simple lines, but fit her as if it had been custom-made. She wore graceful heels, but not stilettos. Small gold crescents hugged her earlobes and a flat, gold chain rested just above her clavicle. There was a gold band on the third finger of her right hand. She was either married or wanted to give that impression. The only off note was the Apple watch. It looked too big and clumsy on her wrist. I wondered if she'd had trouble deciding whether to wear it with her otherwise perfect outfit. Maybe she believed that allowances should be made for the convenience of technology. All of this went through my mind in the few seconds after Beverly moved off and the newcomer approached me.

"Sorry to keep you waiting," I said.

"No problem. It's a beautiful spring morning and I spend entirely too much time indoors." Her voice was smooth, no rough edges. I wanted to ask what she did for a living, but I wouldn't. No one likes a nosey merchant.

"Is there something in particular you're looking for or would you prefer to browse?" I asked.

"I've had a number of people tell me that I could not leave this town without visiting your shop. If only twenty percent of what they claimed is true, I'll be a customer for life."

"Oh good, no pressure."

She laughed. "I have a meeting to make at ten, so would you put together a few of your best sellers for me?"

"I'd like to oblige, but it's really not possible without knowing more about you, what you like and don't like, what will work best for you at this point in your life."

"I've given you license to sell me the most expensive items you have, and you won't accommodate me?" She seemed both taken aback and curious.

"I have a reputation to protect. This shop has been in my family for many years. Maybe you could come back when you have a little more time?"

"I'll tell you what, I'll cancel my lunch meeting and come here instead. Will that work?"

"I didn't mean for you to inconvenience yourself."

"I'm afraid you can't have it both ways," she said amiably. "Either I take your advice and come back later, or you put a few things together on the fly for me now."

"I'll be happy to help you during your lunch hour," I said, forced into choosing on the spot. I was willing to bet she never hesitated to make decisions.

"Terrific. I'll be here at one o'clock."

After she left, Beverly came up to the counter with her basket. "Some people! Who does she think she is, giving you an ultimatum like that?" Her hoarse whisper was loud enough for Tilly to hear next door. "I would have thrown her out of my salon if she tried that with me." I didn't say anything. "Any chance of a discount for wasting my time this morning?" she asked sweetly.

"I'm sorry. No discounts on Thursdays after the first Wednesday of a month without an *R* in it." I smiled and handed her the tote with her purchases. Judging by her expression, she left the shop still trying to make sense of what I'd said.

The rest of the morning was slow. Spring could be that way. Folks were busy airing out their houses, cleaning winter's debris from their gardens and planting fresh annuals and vegetables. Buses brought the occasional group of tourists on the weekends. Day trippers seemed to be waiting for the warmer temperatures when they didn't have to bother with jackets and walking from one shop to the next was a pleasant saunter instead of a race to get out of the nippy wind. Winter wasn't quick to let go of Schuyler County. It hung around in the early morning and crept back in after sundown.

Polished Lady, who turned out to be Whitney Reynolds, returned at one o'clock sharp. During the hour we were together, she told me she was an interior designer in town to oversee work on the new Waverly Hotel. She was easy to be around, with a quick wit. For all her attention to style, she didn't take herself too seriously. By the time she was finished shopping, she'd spent over three hundred dollars. The sum was even more impressive when you took into account that I keep my prices low. We Wildes believe that everyone should have access to the best health and beauty aids magick can supply.

A number of locals came in during the afternoon for refills of products or simple spells. On days when I wasn't busy, it was nice to chat with people I'd known most of my life. After so many years, many were like extended family. I especially loved to hear stories involving my mother and grandmother.

In the time that remained before closing, I made up more of our allergy elixirs. Most of them contained Quercetin, which reduces inflammation and is a natural antihistamine. Combined with vitamin C, Sabalia and other botanicals, it worked fairly well. With the addition of a magick spell, it brought raves.

At four fifty-five, Sashkatu roused himself and came down from the window ledge via the custom steps Morgana had designed for him when age and arthritis first started taking their toll. He'd always seemed to have an inner clock that told him when it was time to eat. As a child, I believed he must have eaten a clock, like the crocodile did in Peter Pan. I would put my ear to his belly to listen for the ticking. Even though I never heard it, neither my mother nor grandmother were able to disabuse me of that belief. I gave it up on my own at the age of seven, when I realized the kind of clock I had in mind couldn't possibly fit down his throat.

Sashki stretched his velvety black body until he seemed to double in length, then gathered himself to sit and wait for me to do the many pointless things humans do. I was about to set the security system, when the shop phone rang. I stopped to answer it. Sashkatu wasn't pleased. If he'd been able to roll his eyes, I'm sure he would have.

Travis answered my *hello* with, "I have the dates for Ava's wake and funeral." He had a habit of ignoring the social niceties when he had news to impart. And I had a habit of teasing him about it.

"I'm fine, thanks. How are you?"

He refused to be detoured. "The wake is tonight and tomorrow. The funeral is Saturday morning."

We knew Ava grew up in Williamsville, a suburb twenty minutes outside Buffalo, and that her parents still lived there, so it wasn't a surprise that she'd be waked and buried there, but a girl can hope. "Buffalo is two and a half hours away," I said, trying not to groan and nearly succeeding.

"Exactly—road trip!"

Chapter 7

Travis was happy about the trip to Williamsville. For him it was a change in routine and a chance to learn more about the latest murder victim. For me the trip came with complications. It meant having to burden my aunt with six more cats. She'd have to go to my house twice a day to feed them and clean their litter boxes. She lived close by and never complained about the added responsibility, but she was getting older, and I worried about all she already had on her plate. She was the only living family I had left.

"Of course," she said without hesitation when I called to ask her. "Who knows what you might discover that could lead you to Ava's killer."

"Are you sure it's not too much for you?"

"For goodness' sake, dear girl, it's just for one night. We all have to do what we can to keep Lolly out of prison."

"Fear not, I am here to help your aunt," Merlin piped up in the background—that alone had the power to make me stay home.

"Ignore him," Tilly said firmly. "Everything will be just fine here. You'll feed the cats breakfast before you leave, and I'll see to their dinner and breakfast the next morning. I'm glad that's settled. Good night." She clicked off. I sat there looking at the phone in my hand, feeling like *I'd* been bamboozled. I had to laugh. With my mother and grandmother largely out of the picture, Silly Tilly had come into her own.

I packed my overnight bag, but left my demure, little black dress on its hanger so it wouldn't wrinkle—a distinct perk of driving over flying. We'd be attending the wake, but not the funeral. At wakes one could talk to other attendees and eavesdrop on conversations that might yield useful information. Funerals were a lot more structured and formal. Plus I barely knew Ava and I didn't feel right invading her family's privacy during such a solemn and difficult ritual.

Sashkatu watched me from the bed, his green eyes narrowing. He understood the signs of an impending upheaval in his life. When I tried to stroke his back, he hissed and slinked away to nurse his pique. I knew it was an act just to make me feel bad, but it worked anyway. I had to remind myself that my aunt would coddle him and give him far too many goodies, because she was accustomed to the portions she gave her big Maine Coon. Sashki didn't come to bed until after one in the morning and when he did, he made a point of smacking my face with his tail a few times to wake me.

Travis had to work in the morning, so he picked me up at noon and we headed northwest.

We had a reservation for the night at a hotel chain in Williamsville. The wake was scheduled from two o'clock to four o'clock in the afternoon and seven to nine in the evening. Since it was a workday, we would wait until evening, when the most people were likely to be there.

We ate an early dinner near the hotel and arrived at the funeral home at seven-thirty. If we arrived too early we would stand out as strangers. Our best bet was to blend into a crowd of people. The parking lot of the funeral home was almost full when we drove in. Travis snagged one of the last two spots. As we walked to the entrance, it seemed like everyone around us was stopping to greet friends and family. The greetings were subdued and sober, the hugs maybe a little tighter and longer than on days when death hadn't come into their lives.

Travis took my hand and drew me closer to his side. He was probably thinking about his brother, as I was thinking about Morgana and Bronwen. I squeezed his hand and he came up with a lopsided smile for me. Ushers from the funeral home opened the doors for us. In the lobby, we checked the sign with the chapel number for the Duncan wake. It was the only one listed, which meant that everyone there had come to pay their respects to Ava and her family. When someone died young, it seemed to pierce the heart of even the most jaded souls.

The line to enter the chapel made a double loop around the central hallway. "Let's wait until there's no line," I whispered. "We can make better use of our time if we circulate and keep our ears open."

Travis nodded. "You take this front section and I'll hit the back half. I watched him weave slowly around the knots of people who weren't in line, looking for a likely conversation to listen in on. I was about to begin my own gossip odyssey when a woman on my right said the magic word—*Ava*.

I stayed where I was, facing the entrance and checked my watch as if I was waiting for someone.

The woman who'd caught my attention reminded me of a younger, more petite version of Beverly, from the way she looked, right down to her lack of discretion. Her voice rose above the many muted conversations as if what she had to say was too important to be hushed.

"Well that's what I heard," she snapped as if someone in the group had challenged her words. I was sorry I'd missed them.

The older woman next to her clucked her tongue. "Same old, same old." I couldn't tell if her comment was a rebuke to mini-Beverly, a remark about Ava or a general comment about the state of things in the twenty-first century.

"I still don't think she deserved to be killed," the one man in the group said in a low sandpapery voice.

"Ha," mini-Beverly said, more like a bark than a laugh. "I'm not surprised to hear that from a man." The other women looked uncomfortable. The ones in my peripheral vision studied their shoes or manicures, but no one responded to the remark. The man walked off shaking his head, perhaps too wise to start an argument given the venue. Someone quickly changed the subject to *poor Val and Teddy,* Ava's parents.

What I'd heard from mini-Beverly and friends would be easy to interpret as a condemnation of Ava's errant ways with men, but it could easily have applied to other aspects of her life. It would be foolish to jump to conclusions when I didn't hear the beginning of the conversation and I didn't know anything about the people speaking or what they had to win or lose. I moved on, trolling for other remarks that were likely to be about Ava. The few snippets I picked up were decidedly kinder than what I'd heard from the first group. *So young, so much potential... never said a harsh word about anyone.... my kids loved to have her babysit back in the day...*

By the time the line to pay our respects had dissipated, the crowd in the hallway was also thinning out. I caught up with Travis at the entrance to the chapel. "Any luck?" I murmured.

"Not much. You?"

"A little. We'd better go in or they'll be getting ready to leave." There were only two people ahead of us in the chapel. Val and Teddy Duncan were standing off to the side of the coffin. The young man who was on Val's other side had to be their son, Liam. He was taller than his parents and bore a striking resemblance to Ava. There was a woman sitting in the first pew. What drew my attention was her long red hair. Even in the subdued lighting of the chapel, the color was dazzling. Travis and I waited at the top of the aisle to let the other couple have their private moment with the family. After they moved away, we approached the Duncans. They looked dazed, shell-shocked like soldiers in war. Val frowned, trying to place us. Teddy stared into the distance as if he was past caring who anyone was. I introduced myself and Travis. We expressed our condolences.

"May I ask how you knew my daughter?" Val asked.

"Ava was a customer of mine in Watkins Glen." I didn't mention that Travis was a reporter. We didn't want them to think he was there to make a circus of their loss. They'd probably had to deal with enough intrusions by the media, with more on the way. Murder sells.

Val reached for my hand. "Thank you for coming all this way." She turned to her husband, still holding on to me. "Teddy, this woman came here from Watkins Glen, because our Ava shopped in her store. Can you imagine?"

Teddy nodded, and made an effort to focus on us. "Thank you." His voice was flat, without inflection, like robots in old sci-fi movies.

Val put her hand on Liam's shoulder and introduced him.

"Nice to meet you," he said, shaking both our hands. "It's a comfort to see how many people have gone out of their way to honor my sister." His voice broke on the last words. More people were coming down the aisle to convey their sympathies, so Travis and I reiterated ours and stepped away. We were walking back up to the door when I noticed Lolly's son-in-law Elliot. He was sitting in one of the last rows, staring in the direction of Ava's casket. At least he didn't break Dani's heart over a meaningless fling. Not that she would find comfort in knowing it.

We drove the short distance back to the hotel in silence, lost in our own thoughts. Regardless of how I felt about Ava, her family's grief had affected me. It was hard to turn off those feelings and dive right into analyzing the remarks I'd heard. Travis must have felt the same way. It wasn't until we were back at the hotel that he finally spoke. "I've been to my share of wakes, but that was rough." He dropped his car keys, phone, and wallet onto the dresser.

"I feel like we snuck in there to go through their dirty laundry. I keep telling myself they'd want to know who was responsible for their daughter's death, they'd want to see that justice is done."

Travis pulled off his suit jacket and tossed it over the desk chair, adding his tie a moment later. "I think you're right on both counts. But to do that, we're going to have to talk to them for background on Ava at the very least." He was right of course, but it always felt wrong to question people in mourning. Travis understood my reservations. As a reporter, he'd learned to make peace with his conscience in order to do his job. I still struggled with mine. "If we don't talk to them," he said, "it will be like investigating this case with our hands tied behind our backs. I can assure you that Duggan doesn't have any reservations about talking to them. In fact, I'm sure he already has."

I sank into the armchair facing the blank screen of the TV and kicked off my heels. "Maybe we should contact Liam first. That way he can broach the idea of working with us to his parents."

"I like that. And depending on how close he was to his sister, he might even know things about her that the parents never got wind of."

"There's one problem," I said. "The funeral is tomorrow and we're leaving."

"We'll call Liam Monday. If he and his parents are amenable, we'll come back up here another day. It'll be worth the trip for what we stand to learn." We spent some time discussing the remarks we'd overheard at the funeral home, and concluded that even if the attendees knew Ava played fast and loose with morality, they chose not to denigrate her at her wake, with the exception of mini-Beverly.

Chapter 8

Travis dropped me off at home in the early afternoon and headed back to the Glen to anchor the evening news. All the cats but Sashkatu came to greet me. He was lying on the top ridge of the living room couch, regarding me with an expression that said, *Well look who's here.*

I walked up to him. "Would your Highness like to accompany me to the shop?" He seemed to be deliberating. I gave him a minute before adding, "The offer expires in fifteen seconds. If you want to go with me, you'd better hustle your bustle." He got to his feet, stretched, yawned, and took his sweet time descending the couch to his personal steps that he took to the floor. He could out-diva the best of them.

When we reached the shop, I went through the connecting door to Tea and Empathy to thank my aunt for helping out with the cats. Her shop was locked and dark. She rarely took off on the weekend. I called and found her at home. Her *hello* was rattled.

"What's wrong?"

"We're fine," she said sounding anything but fine. "Of course I'd be a lot finer if our wizard friend would lay off the spells." I heard Merlin protesting in the background that he didn't know it was a spell.

"It sounds like you could use some help—I'll be right over."

"That won't be necessary," Tilly said. "I've got everything under control." A loud crash punctuated her words. "On a related matter, I may have to kill Merlin."

"I'm coming."

"Hold it," she said firmly, "You need to open your shop for at least part of the day. I've made up my mind. This can wait until you close." But what if *I* couldn't wait until I closed? What new trouble had Merlin wrought?

Should I ignore my aunt's wishes and run over there? Lately she got her back up if she thought I was trying to baby her. Pride was a big deal in my family. I decided I'd do my best to wait.

As it happened, I didn't have long to dwell on those matters. Customers kept me hopping for the next three hours. It was a good thing I'd left a sign on the shop's door and a message on the phone that I was away until Saturday afternoon. Most of the people who came in were locals, but there was a smattering of day trippers who were out for a ride and needed a destination.

Every last person who entered my shop wanted to know why Lolly's place was shuttered and strung with police tape. And they wanted to know when she would reopen. Many a sweet tooth left disappointed.

I closed my shop at four thirty, a compromise between Tilly's edict and my need to know what was going on at her house. I carried the sleepy Sashkatu home and fed the gang, before calling to let her know I was on my way.

She opened her door for me, her curly red hair limp and her face shiny with perspiration. "Brace yourself," she warned me as I stepped into the foyer. *Brace myself?* Was I about to see something that horrific? A moment later her meaning became clear. I was thrown back against the wall by an invisible force that hit my chest with such momentum that it knocked the air out of my lungs. My face was slathered in sticky, foaming moisture. My hands flew out to fend off my attacker and my fingers sank into...*fur?*

Merlin ran into the foyer yelling, "Off beast—off I say." It took Merlin and Tilly pulling and me pushing to finally remove my assailant.

"What is that?" I was bent over, trying to catch my breath.

"A common mongrel," Merlin said. "A cur, a mutt—take your pick."

"A very large one," Tilly added. "It's best if we sit down. That way we won't have as far to fall if he launches himself at us." She and I took the couch in the family room and Merlin settled into an armchair across from us. They both seemed to be coping better than I was, but then they'd had more time to adjust to the situation. I kept scanning the room for the invisible dog, which made no sense and yet I couldn't help myself.

Tilly understood what I was doing. "If he's running at you, you can feel the air he displaces a few seconds before he's on you. It helps to remember that he's not vicious, just big and exuberant." I had no problem with big exuberant dogs. I loved dogs of all sizes, shaggy and short-haired, enthusiastic and reserved. In fact, before Sashkatu and I bonded, I'd been summoning a dog to be my familiar. It was that very spell that had plucked

Merlin from his time and dropped him into my storeroom, highlighting the difficulty we Wildes were having with our magick.

I looked from Tilly to Merlin. "I need some answers, like why is he here? And why is he *invisible?*"

"Merlin was deep into reading the family scrolls again," Tilly said. "He's determined to figure out what's wreaking havoc with our magick. It seemed like a safe enough activity for him to pursue, but I was wrong. Really wrong. He was reading a paragraph aloud, trying to make sense of its meaning, when this mountain of a dog appeared."

"What Tilly dear is trying to say is that I didn't realize I was reading a spell. And that spell inadvertently summoned a dog. A huge dog. An enormous dog. A—"

"Yes," I interrupted, "that much I'm clear on. But why is he invisible?"

"I was trying to send the beast back from whence he came, but instead I somehow rendered him invisible."

"Have you tried the spell to reverse spells?" I asked.

Tilly sighed. "It seems you can't reverse spells when they're layered as in this case,"

"So we have to make him visible before we can reverse the spell that brought him here?"

"Yes," they said in unison. I felt a sudden rush of air, as if a high-powered fan was blowing in my direction. I scooted back against the couch pillows to brace for the attack. A second later he was on me. Slobbery tongue, nails that needed clipping, fur up my nose and in my mouth. By the time he moved on to Tilly, I felt like I'd been tarred and feathered. I told myself things could be worse. He could have been ferocious, hungry for human flesh.

Isenbale, my aunt's Maine Coon, yowled. I'd forgotten about him in the confusion. I followed the sound and spotted him on the top shelf of the built-ins that framed the fireplace. Tilly had set a bowl of water up there for him, and he appeared none the worse for his unhappy circumstances.

"My poor baby," Tilly lamented.

"What of me?" Merlin said, disgruntled. "Am I not to be afforded sympathy? I had to carry him to the litter box—twice."

"You're the only one tall enough to keep him out of the dog's reach," she said.

"Do either of you remember the spell that made him invisible?" I asked.

"I do," Merlin said. "Send—" Tilly and I yelled for him to stop.

"Please write it down for me," I said more calmly. "Do *not* say it aloud."

"Ah yes, I see your point." He reached for the pad and pen on the table next to his chair, scribbled the few lines, and handed it to me. I read it silently.

Send this dog back where he's from.
Spare no time; do not delay.
Keep him safe, let no harm come.
Take him from our sight today.

That was it—the last line of the spell was the culprit. Or rather Merlin was for not properly vetting the words before casting it. My mother and grandmother had drummed into me how important it was not to use words that could mean more than one thing. When I told Tilly that I'd discovered the problem, she was thrilled. She wanted to go bake something for a celebration. I pointed out it would be easier to accomplish if she waited until the dog was no longer there to trample her. Merlin was understandably less thrilled. He didn't like being told that he created the problem.

Now I just had to devise a spell to make the dog visible again. After that we should be able to send him back with the reversal spell. It took me more time than I expected and it wasn't the most elegant of spells. In my defense, it was hard to be creative when I had to keep defending myself from the invisible beast. I repeated the words three times.

There's a dog within this house
That nobody can see.
Make him visible again,
And safe we all will be.

I didn't realize I was holding my breath, until it exploded from my lungs the moment the dog appeared before me. Tilly and Merlin had not been exaggerating. He was one of the largest dogs I'd ever seen. He had long white fur that would have benefitted from a bath. His black eyes, in all that whiteness, reminded me of a snowman. I told him it was great to see him, while fending off another, slobbery attack.

I was about to reverse the spell that had brought him there, when Tilly jumped up and insisted on saying a proper *goodbye* by planting a kiss on his long snout. Merlin said a more formal farewell and apologized for having dognapped him in the first place with the ancient incantation.

I recited the reversal spell ten times, and as the last word cleared my mouth, he disappeared. None of us dared move until we were positive he'd left and wasn't merely invisible again. Then Merlin rescued Isenbale from the shelf. Tilly went off to the kitchen to bake away her stress, and Merlin followed her, throwing out suggestions. I went home to collapse on the couch with a pint of Rum Raisin ice cream.

Chapter 9

Travis and I had to interview Lolly's daughter, Danielle. There were questions she alone could answer. For starters, did she have an alibi for the time of Ava's death? I didn't intend to ask for Lolly's permission to speak to her, but I did want to give my friend a heads up. Travis advised against it. We weren't with the police and we had no official standing as private investigators. If Lolly talked her daughter into not cooperating with us, we'd be at a great disadvantage in trying to solve the case. Although telling Lolly felt like the right thing to do, I wasn't exactly looking forward to the phone call. She'd told me about her son-in-law's affair with Ava in confidence, which made me feel a bit like a traitor. If I hadn't known about it, Danielle wouldn't even be on our list of suspects. On the other hand, although Duggan might not know about the affair yet, it was only a matter of time before he stumbled over it in his investigation. He wouldn't have any qualms about questioning Dani. A week ago, if anyone had asked if I would ever dread talking to Lolly, I would have laughed at them. In the end, I decided to speak to her in person.

I considered a low-key place like The Jerk, but there would be too many potential eavesdroppers, too many inquiring minds. I decided to invite Lolly over for lunch instead. When I ran it by my aunt, she suggested we use her shop on a day when she didn't have any readings scheduled. That way Lolly and I could have lunch at one of her lovely tea tables in the solitude of Tea and Empathy. Our own private restaurant. Tilly insisted on making us a proper tea. She'd even stay and serve it. Merlin would be left at home.

Lolly seemed happy enough to accept my invitation, but I detected a slight wariness in her tone that I'd never heard before. When life turns you inside out and upside down, I guess it shakes all the certainties out of you like so much loose change. Accepting anything at face value becomes a luxury you can no longer afford. My heart sank. I was about to prove her misgivings right.

The next day at one o'clock I closed my shop for lunch and went next door to wait for Lolly. She came bearing a slab of rocky road fudge she'd made with one of her granddaughters. Tilly came out of the kitchen, launching a hug fest. I'd known Lolly's hugs all my life. These were different, stiffer, as if she were holding back. As if her wariness formed an invisible barrier between us that never existed before. Tilly and I shared a brief look that told me she'd felt it too.

Lolly was extravagant in her praise of the beautiful table my aunt had set for us. She'd used the fine china handed down from our ancestors, who'd crossed the ocean in the seventeenth century to start a new life in the colonies. Tilly brought out her most prized three-tiered serving dish for the tea and set it in the middle of the table. The large bottom tier held the dainty quartered sandwiches, the second held the scones with raspberry jam and clotted cream, my personal favorite. On the third tier were the mini pastries I was usually too stuffed to eat.

Lolly and Tilly took their seats while I fetched the teapot and filled our cups with the special peppermint blend my aunt had chosen for its calming and mood elevating properties. The two friends were already chatting about Lolly's grandkids when I joined them. She told us about their latest antics while we ate sandwiches of cucumber with Swiss cheese, egg salad, and cream cheese on moist date nut bread. We laughed at the story of Faye, the precocious two-year-old who begged her mother for glasses so she'd be able to read.

By the time we reached the scones, the conversation was flagging. There was no way to keep it upbeat when there was a big old elephant in the room waiting to be addressed. I asked her how things were going.

"Not great," she said. "Elliot moved out, the kids are crushed, and Dani has the best motive around for killing Ava. She doesn't know that I have the next best motive. I never told her about the fight I had with that bit—horrible woman."

"Actually, I want to talk to you about the case," I said, forcing myself to maintain eye contact when my impulse was to look anywhere else.

She put down the scone she'd taken. "Okay... should I be worried?" She looked from me to my aunt.

"No, of course not," Tilly said a bit too freely "We're on your side. What could you possibly have to worry about?" I knew she meant well, but she might as well have said, *we'll make sure someone else is the killer. What's the point of practicing magick if you can't help out a friend?*

"I'm sure you realize that if Travis and I are going to investigate the case properly, we'd be remiss if we didn't interview Danielle. I just wanted to give you a heads up about it. We intend to speak to Ava's parents and to her brother in the next few days as well."

"I understand," Lolly said stiffly. "I guess I was hoping you knew my Dani well enough to know she couldn't have killed Ava."

"Lolly," I said, "I honestly don't believe she killed Ava." It wasn't exactly a lie. I didn't think any child of Lolly's could commit murder. Yet how many times had people said the same thing about a relative or a next-door neighbor, only to discover that in a moment of extreme anger or pain the least likely people can do the most unthinkable things? "The main reason we want to speak to Dani is to find out if she knows something or heard something that can point the investigation in the right direction." Great, I'd blundered into the same trap as my aunt—the need to make Lolly feel better.

* * * *

Travis called me after the evening newscast. I was still on the couch, having watched him anchor the show with the gravitas and authority of an elder statesman. Sometimes I had trouble connecting that man with the charming, witty guy who made my heart dance by walking in the door.

"Don't beat yourself up over it," he said, after I told him about my conversation with Lolly. "You're a good, kind person who doesn't like to inflict pain on your friends. That's an asset in my book. Besides, you've proven more than once that you're not a softy when it comes to the bad guys. So, no harm, no foul."

"But I shouldn't give up my day job, huh?"

He laughed. "The magick? Not that it would be easy to do, since it's part of your DNA and all. Not to mention that it saved our collective butts on a number of occasions."

"Thanks for the pep talk. I'll call Dani tomorrow. I have no idea what kind of reception I'll get. She's been going through hell." One of the would-be familiars, a sweet American Shorthair my mother had named Filormeu, climbed into my lap. Sashkatu wasn't on his throne atop the couch, so she was seizing the chance to cuddle. She curled into a ball, purring in deep contentment as I stroked her back.

"We'll have to coordinate the appointments we make," Travis said. "I spoke to Ava's brother Liam today."

"How was he?"

"About how you might expect—he can't believe she's gone. He feels guilty because he wasn't able to protect her like he did when they were kids. Logic doesn't hold any sway. It's the kind of useless guilt we all carry around in one form or another." I knew he was talking about himself and his brother as much as he was Liam and Ava. "He remembered us from the wake. When I explained that we were investigating his sister's death, he seemed reluctant to meet with us. I should point out that he'd spent the morning with the inimitable detective Duggan, and as we know, that can sour anyone on investigators for life. He asked what more we could bring to the table. I told him we had a much better record of closing cases. That piqued his interest."

"Then he's willing to meet with us?"

"Willing to give us a chance is probably more accurate."

"What about his parents? If we're driving back up there, we need to speak to them too. It's not exactly around the corner."

"Yes ma'am!" Travis said in a clipped, military tone. "Working on it, ma'am!"

I laughed. "Sorry, I didn't mean that to sound like a command."

"Did you ever consider a career in the army? You know—'be all that you can be.'"

"I'm pretty sure I'm maxed out. If I take on anything else, I won't have any time for you."

He gasped. "That's it then—the army can't have you!"

Chapter 10

Beverly was my first customer the next morning. She never came in this frequently. I tried not to take it as a bad omen. She marched in like a woman on a mission. Her nostrils were red and swollen, her eyelids puffy. She dabbed at her nose with a crumpled tissue, looking altogether miserable.

"According to my doctor, I've developed allergies," she said, sounding a lot like Elmer Fudd. "Can you believe it? Who suddenly develops allergies at my age?"

I made the mistake of telling her what she didn't want to hear. "Actually, you can develop allergies at any stage of life."

"My question was rhetorical, Kailyn. Let's leave the diagnosing to the MDs. I'm here because I need something to take care of these horrid symptoms. Hair dressers have to be up close to their customers. Mine are not going to want me anywhere near them like this." As usual, if Beverly was unhappy, she had a knack for spreading it around. Between her moody personality and her penchant for gossiping, she was lucky she was a talented stylist or her shop would have closed a long time ago.

She collapsed into the customer chair, sniffling and snorting and told me to bring her the best products I had to fix her problem. I was tempted to say, *It's a good thing you clarified that or I might have brought you the second-rate ones.* But Beverly's sense of humor was deficient at the best of times.

I returned with a few different options, including Nettle Leaf and local honey. They all worked fairly well on their own, but with the addition of the Wilde family secret ingredient, they worked like magick. "Try each of these individually so you can decide which you prefer," I said as I rang up her purchase.

"Did you know that Ava was having an affair with Elliot Marsh?" she said without preamble. She liked to shock people, hit them with the latest news from the grape vine and feast on their reactions.

"Is that so?" I said evenly, robbing her of the pleasure.

"You know that Marsh is Lolly's son-in-law, right?" Beverly was clearly frustrated with my lackluster response.

"Yes, I do"

"And that's all you have to say on the subject?"

"It's none of my business. Or yours, for that matter." Beverly narrowed her puffy eyes at me, probably considering a scathing comeback. Instead she chose to impart more bad news.

"Everyone believes either Lolly or Danielle killed Ava. They had motive and opportunity." She paused to wipe her nose and judge if I was properly shocked. I maintained my neutral expression and added a little smile.

Denied again, she went for broke. "They could have killed her in the shop, rolled her out into the yard and claimed they found her there and were being framed by the real killer. Anyone else would have had a much harder time planting the body. Lolly keeps the chain-link fence around the backyard locked. Another killer would have had to throw the body over the fence. Not an easy thing to accomplish without being seen—especially during the day." Which was probably why the killer had chosen the day of the New Camel Fair to take her life. With everyone at the fair, all the shops were closed.

Beverly had barely made it through her closing argument before a coughing fit seized her. I had to go over to Tilly's to get her a glass of water. "I'm sure Detective Duggan has thought of all that as well," I said, as her respiratory system calmed. When she was ready to leave, I handed her the mini tote with her purchases.

She managed a stiff *thank you* as she stepped away from the counter. But then she turned back to me. "If I were a gambler, I'd bet good money that Lolly had a hand in Ava's death."

"And I'd take that bet," I said. Sashkatu, who'd apparently had enough of her, jumped down from his ledge onto the counter, hissing and crouching as if he was about to leap onto her. I winced for the pain it must have caused his poor joints. Beverly shrieked and ran for the door. "I should call the police on you for endangering the public with such a dangerous animal—" She slammed the door shut behind her, cutting off her own words.

Sashki padded back along the counter to me with a definite swagger and fixed me with a look that said, *that's how to handle such a distasteful creature. I'll expect some remuneration in my dinner bowl.*

* * * *

During my lunch hour, I called Danielle. She didn't seem at all surprised to hear from me. I had to assume that Lolly had prepared her and probably stressed the fact that she had nothing to fear from me. The sooner I found the killer, the sooner the cloud of suspicion hanging over the town would evaporate. I refused to think about the possibility that the killer was Dani. It wouldn't be, I assured myself, because it couldn't be.

She said she was available the next day at ten o'clock. Her two older kids were in school full time, but the youngest was done with preschool before lunch. It meant opening my shop late, but the sooner I was satisfied about Dani's innocence, the better I would sleep at night. Although I hated to admit it, Beverly may have gotten to me after all.

I'd barely hung up the phone when it rang in my hand. "Hi stranger," Elise said. "Can I interest you in some beef stew?"

I had a peanut butter and jelly sandwich waiting for me behind the counter for lunch and no idea what dinner would be. Beef stew sounded fantastic. "When did you have time to cook it? Or did Zach take up cooking?"

She laughed. "Zach? You mean the kid who would live on pizza if I let him? Nope. All the credit goes to the slow cooker I've owned for ages and never used. I dragged it out of the closet in desperation. The boys and I need to eat smarter. Less takeout, more home-cooking. I threw the meat, potatoes and veggies in this morning before I left for work and it cooked while I did my best to mold young minds."

"So you don't actually know how well your experiment turned out."

"If it's terrible we can order pizza. Say *yes,* please say *yes.* It's been weeks since I've seen you and I'm in desperate need of adult company."

"Not to worry—you had me at beef stew. I'll be over after I feed my kitties."

* * * *

Noah opened the door and gave me a quick kiss on my cheek. He wanted to know what was in the foil covered plate in my hand. "Dessert, no peeking," I said, sweeping the cake up out of his reach. He was growing so fast, I wouldn't be able to get away with that maneuver for much longer. He ran off to the family room where it sounded like a superhero war was being fought on TV.

I found Elise in the kitchen, setting the table in the nook. She grabbed me into a hug that almost knocked my surprise dessert onto the floor. I shrieked and juggled the cake, narrowly avoiding disaster. "You didn't have to bring anything," she said when she realized what had almost happened. "But since you did, what is it?" She reached for the edge of the tin foil—like mother like son, but I didn't try to stop her. Her eyes widened. "Is that one of Tilly's amazing coffee cakes?"

"I try to keep one in the freezer for just such an occasion."

"If *I* did that it wouldn't be in there for very long. And I'd be buying bigger pants." She called the boys to dinner and started ladling the stew onto the plates. It smelled amazing. Noah put his cell phone in the docking station on the counter and slid into his seat. Zach thundered down the stairs and into the kitchen. His face lit up when he saw me—the perfect antidote for Beverly.

"I didn't know you were coming, Aunt K." He gave me a peck on the cheek, before sliding in next to his brother.

"I knew," Noah taunted. "You would have known too if you weren't upstairs talking to your girlfriend all afternoon." I heard the pain in his retort. They'd reached the great divide. Zach was in love, and Noah didn't understand what had suddenly changed and stolen his brother away.

Elise looked at Zach with one eyebrow arched. "Forget something?" He did a great rendition of the teenagers' long suffering sigh, got up and docked his phone too. We served the boys first, then took our plates to the table. Zach dug into the stew like he hadn't eaten in a week. Noah picked at it, ate a little, and pushed the rest around his plate.

"So guys, what's new?" I asked, hoping to brighten the mood. "Noah, has baseball started yet?" He nodded "Still playing shortstop?" He nodded again. I felt like a comedian who couldn't connect with his audience. It was a tough room tonight.

"When can I come watch you in a game?"

He perked up a bit. "Mom has the schedule."

"Aunt Kailyn and I will work it out," Elise said.

"Ten, fifteen years from now when you're playing for the Yankees, I want to be able to say, 'I watched you play when you were just starting out.'" That finally got a smile from him.

"Except I may want to play for the Mets," he said, clearly getting into it and testing my loyalty.

"I think I could live with that."

"I couldn't," Zach protested. "In this family, it's always been the Yanks or no one."

"Well that's too bad," Noah said. "I get to make up my own mind, right Mom?"

"Yes, but you won't have to make that decision for a good long time."

"It's not up to you, it depends on which team offers to sign you," Zach muttered under his breath.

"Ma," Noah whined.

"Zach—please let it go." The rest of dinner continued in much the same fashion. I understood why Elise had begged for some adult time.

After dinner and dessert, the boys went their separate ways. Noah went back to his movie, Zach grabbed his phone and bounded up the stairs. "Guys," Elise shouted after them, "you'd better have finished your homework." She made us tea and we went to sit in the living room.

"The constant bickering is exhausting," Elise said when we were settled together on the couch. "They've always done it to some degree, but now there's resentment and malice in it. I'm glad you got to see it for yourself or you might have thought I was exaggerating."

"As an only child I have nothing to compare it with," I said, "but I feel for you."

"I'm afraid I'm becoming part of the problem. By the time I get home from teaching, I'm tired from dealing with more than a hundred other teenage personalities."

I sipped my tea and set it down on the low table in front of us. "I thought you were enjoying teaching again."

"I do enjoy *teaching*. It's the rest of it I'm struggling with." She sighed. "Part of the problem is a new kid in one of my classes, Logan Sheffield. He transferred here from a private school and he's having a hard time connecting with the other kids. From day one, he came in with a chip on his shoulder—everything here is crappy compared to his last school. Maybe that's true and maybe it's just a defense mechanism, but no one wants to buddy up to an attitude like that."

"What do his other teachers think of him?" I asked.

"We actually had a meeting about him. They're finding the same problems I am."

"Has anyone talked to his parents?"

"I talked to his mom. Dad was at work. She was very nice and she sounded sincerely concerned about Logan. But she's having problems with him at home too. It seems they've had some financial difficulties recently. She didn't go into the details. That's why they had to pull him out of the private school. In fact she was going to look for a part time job, but she and her husband agreed that she needs to be around for Logan at this point."

"Is there a school psychologist?"

Elise nodded. "Failing like the rest of us."

"I would never consider using a spell on him or any child, but maybe I can help you deal better with all the stress you're under at school and at home."

"You can do that? I mean, I know you can do just about anything, but could there be any downside to it?"

"No, but if you should decide you don't want it, I can reverse it." I let Elise consider my offer without elaborating on the benefits. I didn't want to influence her decision. I picked up my mug. The tea had cooled enough for me to drink it.

"I'm in," she said brightly. "The alternative would be asking my doctor for pills and I don't want to go that route. So, what do I have to do?"

"You'll need to write the spell down with pencil and paper. Whenever you feel your stress level rising, just repeat the words three times." Elise went to the kitchen and returned with the requisite pencil and paper.

"Ready."

"This is an old spell handed down from my grandmother to my mother and on down to me. I believe it goes all the way back to my great, great, great grandmother—I've lost track of how many greats are involved."

She smiled. "In other words, it has stood the test of time. Thanks for telling me that."

I recited the spell slowly enough for her to write it down, and then I asked her to say it with me:

I can cope, this much I know,
Though the winds of stress may blow.
I can cope, this much I know;
I will calm and I will grow.

"That's easy enough," she said.

"Remember, spells get their power from your belief in them. You can't just pay them lip service. You have to take them into your core, since you don't come by the gift naturally. It may take you some time to get the hang of it. Don't give up. I know you've got what it takes." Elise was bobbing her head, hanging on every word. "And now I'm going to shut up, before I become part of your stress."

We spent the next forty minutes talking and laughing about more mundane things past and present. By the time I left, she was in a noticeably better frame of mind.

Chapter 11

From the top of her naturally blonde head to the tip of her petite toes, Dani Marsh looked nothing like her mother. And their differences didn't stop there. Whereas Lolly had never met a ruffle she didn't like, Dani was a pared down conservative. Ruffles, bows and sequins were anathema to her. When she was a child, Lolly would buy her frilly dresses, and Dani would promptly chop off the hated bows and ruffles, rendering the garments unwearable in the process. In the end, Lolly gave up and made peace with her daughter's right to be her own person. It was better for their relationship and easier on her wallet.

I arrived at Dani's house at the appointed hour with two coffees and two brownies from the Breakfast Bar. She lived between New Camel and Watkins Glen in the big colonial where Elliot, her almost-ex, had lived since birth. His parents, who had moved to Florida, gave the house to their only son as a wedding gift. It was by any measure an impressive gift. But Dani didn't like colonials. She thought they looked pretentious, especially if they had Doric columns, as this one did. Since she couldn't change the exterior of the house, she insisted on redecorating the interior in her spare, utilitarian style. As it turned out, the five bedrooms came in handy. She and Elliot filled three of them with kids, and still had one left for an office/guest room.

My hands full, I was trying to press the bell with my elbow. Dani must have seen me walking up to the house, because she opened the door at that moment. I was caught off balance and stumbled over the threshold. I thrust the cardboard coffee tray and bag of brownies at her in case I went down. She grabbed them and backed away from my bumbling entry. I surprised both of us, by managing to stay upright.

Once I was no longer auditioning for a role in a Three Stooges reboot, I was able to take a good look at Dani. The toll her husband's dalliance had taken on her would have been evident to even a casual acquaintance. It had been made worse, no doubt, by the murder of his paramour and the suspicion cast on Dani. She looked tired, but not the kind of tired that a good night's sleep could fix. It was the emotionally-drained tired of the soul that's only cured by the passage of time. She was pale and drawn, her usually sparkling hazel eyes, dull. We touched cheeks and air-kissed *hello*.

She led the way into the kitchen and set the coffees and brownies on the hexagonal table near the bay window. "I don't know how you take your coffee, so I left it black," I explained, taking a seat.

"Perfect, I like it with just a drop of sweetener—easy enough to add." She took the lid off the coffee and added a packet of faux sweetener to it.

I took the brownies out of the bag. "I imagine Detective Duggan has already called on you. With walnuts or without?"

"Without, thank you," she said, making me glad I'd bought both. "Duggan was waiting outside in his car when we got home that day, you know, the day my mom found... her. The kids were overstimulated, and I was so worried about my mom and so jumbled inside—it was the worst time to be questioned."

"That's exactly why he did it. The worst time for you equals the best time for him. He was hoping you'd slip and divulge something incriminating about yourself or your mom."

Dani broke off a small piece of the brownie and put it in her mouth. "There was nothing to divulge."

I drank my coffee, finding it harder than I'd expected to question her about so personal and painful a subject as her husband's infidelity, especially since she was still going through the divorce and all it entailed. "I'm sorry to have to ask you about Elliot and Ava," I said. "If there was any way around it, I would take it in a heartbeat."

Dani nodded. "My mom and I are just grateful for your help. Pretend I'm a stranger."

"Thank you," I said, knowing it wasn't possible. "As you're aware, the fact that Ava was having an affair with your husband, gives you and your mom a motive to kill her. The fact that she frequented your mom's shop and was found dead behind it means you both had opportunity unless you have a verifiable alibi for that day and time. Do you have a key to the shop?" I was praying she'd say *no*.

"Yes." Another strike against her. "Duggan pointed out that if my mom or I were to confess, he'd do what he could to cut us a deal with the DA."

"What did you say?"

"I told him we couldn't do that, because neither of us is guilty." She broke off another piece of the brownie, then put it back down on her napkin and pushed the whole thing away. "I'm sorry. It's delicious, but my appetite is AWOL."

"Stress destroys my appetite too. It makes some people, like my aunt, want to eat everything in sight." Dani made a half-hearted attempt to smile. There was no point in stretching out her misery. *Jump in and get it over with.*

"How did you find out about Elliot and Ava?" I hated testing her, but I had to see if Lolly's story matched hers. I wouldn't be much of a sleuth if I let it slide because I was close to them. Maybe PIs should be prohibited from working on those near and dear the way surgeons are. No one can be objective when it comes to family and friends. Travis should have been doing this interview. But he wasn't here, I was.

"It was pure coincidence," she said, repeating what Lolly had told me. Of course, they'd had enough time to coordinate their stories. Since I couldn't hook her up to a lie detector, I'd have to take her words with the proverbial grain of salt. There was a spell that prevented a person from lying, but given the imperfect state of my magick, it was useless.

Dani looked up at me. "It was like I was *meant* to find out. At least that's the way it felt." Elliot probably saw it as the day his luck ran out.

"Once the ME establishes the time of Ava's death," I said, "Duggan is going to ask you where you were and what you were doing during that time. You need to have a verifiable alibi. Can you give me a general idea of your activities that day?" Motive and opportunity would go out the window if she could prove beyond a doubt that she was elsewhere.

Dani was biting on her lower lip. "I had a ten o'clock appointment with my divorce attorney and then I ran some errands. I didn't pay strict attention to the timing of them. Who does, unless they're planning to commit murder and need to establish an alibi?" She had a point, but it wasn't likely to do her much good.

"You should try to come up with a basic timeline for those activities before Duggan puts you on the spot. If you saw someone you know at each stop, they could help account for your time. When do your kids get home from school? They're too young to be left home alone, so that would be another part of your alibi. Unless you use sitters."

"If I need someone to watch the kids, it's always a family member."

"Did you use one of them that day?

"No, I make a point of being here when school lets out, and I take them with me if I need to go out again. I don't ask for help, unless it's absolutely necessary. We all have busy lives."

"After you found out about the affair, did you ever threaten Elliot's life or Ava's, maybe in the heat of an argument?" Dani shook her head. "Did you ever confront Ava on the phone or in person?"

"Never. I didn't want anything to do with her. What she did to my family was beyond despicable. I'll never understand women who don't give a damn if they hurt other women. But in the end, I lay the blame on my husband." I was relieved to hear that she hadn't confronted Ava. It would only have made matters worse. I was all out of questions, at least until the ME released his report.

Switching hats from investigator to friend, I asked Dani how the kids were doing in school and what activities they were involved in. She shared some funny anecdotes, and by the time I left, she seemed to be in a better frame of mind.

"You're sure she never spoke to Ava—I mean *never?*" Travis asked when I called to update him.

"I've known Dani all my life and if she said she didn't, I believe her."

"You know my theory. Everyone is capable of killing under the right circumstances. No one gets a pass in a murder investigation."

I sighed. "The next time I go to see her I'll be sure to bring the thumb screws." I expected a laugh, or a chuckle, but Travis was in solemn newscaster mode. "Even if I could believe Dani killed Ava, there's no way she'd frame her mother for it." When I dig in my heels, Travis has learned to back off. Or change the subject.

"Listen," he said, "I know it's short notice, but if you can make the trip up to Buffalo tomorrow, I'll call Liam and see if we can meet with him and then with his parents in Williamsville."

"I'm glad to hear we won't be interviewing all of them together. Three is definitely a crowd in a murder investigation."

"From what Liam said, we may have to talk to his folks together. They're pretty much holding each other up at this point."

"I bet they don't even know their daughter left a broken family in her wake."

"And if they did, do you think they would love her less or miss her less?" Travis asked. I thought about my family and how they might react to news that I'd destroyed a marriage. They'd probably have a hard time believing it. And if they discovered it was true? They'd be disappointed in me, but they would never stop loving me. Travis was right.

Chapter 12

Tilly said she'd be delighted to cover for me the next day. She didn't have any readings scheduled in her shop. I felt guilty about asking for her help again. Her willingness and my guilt were becoming a pattern for us.

"Believe me," Tilly said, taking my two hands in hers. "If I didn't want to do it, I would say so."

I had my doubts about that. Tilly always had a problem saying *no* to me. I remember my mother warning me not to take advantage of her. "She loves you to distraction. You must never abuse that kind of love." But since my mother and grandmother had been taken from us, Tilly was the only family I could go to for help. Even if our new circumstances should have eased that restriction, it sure didn't make a dent in my rasher of guilt.

"You're absolutely certain it's not too much for you?" I repeated for the third or fourth time. "I mean you take days off to rest from your own work and running my shop can be tiring." We were standing in her kitchen where she'd just finished cleaning up after a whirlwind of baking for a friend's surprise party.

"First of all, the reason I need time off has nothing to do with being tired. If I were to spend every day in other people's minds, I'd lose my own in short order. Working in Abracadabra is therapeutic for me. I grew up in that shop alongside your mom just as Bronwen did before us. It's the link we have with our ancestors who came to this land over four hundred years ago. So just say *thank you, Aunt Tilly,* and let it go."

"Thank you, Aunt Tilly. I love you." I reached out for a hug and found myself pulled into the generous folds of her new emerald green muumuu. When I surfaced, it occurred to me that I hadn't seen hide nor hair of Merlin since I'd arrived there. What made it all the more curious was that he hadn't been sitting in the kitchen during the baking process. "Our wizardly friend is awfully quiet," I said.

"I know. Isn't it grand? He's gotten so involved in reading and translating the old scrolls that he actually forgot to eat lunch yesterday." That was hard to believe. "Has he found anything interesting?" Since childhood I'd been fascinated by the arcane appearance and meaning of the words in the scrolls. It was like a secret code guarding other secrets that none of us had the key to unlock—until now.

"He's been closemouthed on the subject, but there's a definite twinkle in his eyes when he speaks about it—or rather, refuses to speak about it. I've decided to enjoy the calm before the next storm." Although that plan might prove foolish down the road, I could understand its appeal.

I texted Travis that we were on for the next day. Half an hour later, he texted back that the interviews were set and that he'd pick me up at nine. With that settled, I had to decide on the more immediate questions of which shopkeeper would have the pleasure of my company at lunchtime. I was still hoping one of them knew more about Ava Duncan than I did. I settled on Stratford and Son's Variety Shop. I didn't expect to learn much from the older Stratford, but the son, Leo, was about the same age as Ava when the killer stopped her clock.

I made sure Sashkatu had enough water and put the sign in the window that I'd be back at two. The day had grown warmer than the meteorologist predicted. By the time I'd walked the three blocks to the Variety shop, I was thinking of ditching the investigation and spending my whole lunch hour outside. My overly strict conscience wouldn't have it. *Some Nancy Drew you're turning out to be. The first nice day and you're ready to forget the trouble your friends are in.* I assured myself I'd done nothing of the sort and to prove it, I went straight into the store.

In the past decade, the Variety Shop had become the largest store in New Camel by consuming the shops on either side of it. The merchandise ran the gamut of tourist items made everywhere but here. T-shirts emblazoned with the name New Camel and pictures of a cartoonish camel were probably the biggest sellers, followed by sweatshirts for those days that were colder than expected. There were camel salt and pepper shakers, camel coasters, camel napkin holders, camel key chains and every other possible knickknack one could imagine in the shape of, or with the image of a camel.

The first and only time Merlin went into the store, he became so incensed by the merchandise that he worked himself into an alarming shade of crimson. Worried that he'd suffer a stroke, my aunt dragged him out of there as he launched a blustery diatribe at the elder Stratford.

"I was merely trying to set the fool straight," he'd said indignantly once they were outside.

I don't think I'd been in the shop more than a couple of times myself. I suppose if I had company visiting from out of town, I might take them there to pick up souvenirs. But for better or worse, we never had guests—with the notable exception of Merlin. And when I figured out how to send him back to King Arthur's court, I certainly wasn't going to let him take items from the twenty-first century back with him. He'd already muddied up history enough by vanishing from his own time. Not that it was his fault. I'd been summoning a familiar and apparently lassoed the legendary sorcerer instead, setting him on a crash course for my storeroom.

Stratford senior was helping a couple at the front of the store. Leo was restocking merchandise near the rear. The resemblance between father and son was remarkable. Both were tall and thin, Leo slightly more so. Both had dark hair and blue eyes, though Lester's hair was thinning, the blue of his eyes fading as if used up by thirty extra years of living. The men's features were mirror images. Leo's mother was nowhere to be seen in her son, until you got a glimpse of his personality. If Leo was entirely his father on the outside, he was entirely his mother on the inside. He was a people person, friendly, always ready with a joke, making friends of every customer. Word around town was that Leo had turned the barely solvent business around and made it flourish. By contrast, his father was dour and stingy with a smile. I'd heard that when he tried to smile more at his son's urging, the result was more horrifying than friendly. His face wasn't made to work that way.

"The bewitching lady from the magick shop," Leo said with a grin when he looked up and saw me approaching. "What can I do for you? Did you suddenly find yourself in need of some American kitsch?"

"To be honest, I came by for information." I'd decided to be straight forward with him. "Do you have a minute?"

"More than one for a fellow shopkeeper." He set the box of camel magnets on the counter and leaned back against it.

"Did you know Ava Duncan?" Her name had an immediate effect on him. He was pretty good at masking it, but I caught the subtle wariness in his eyes.

"Yes, I did. Terrible what happened to her."

"Was it?"

"A young woman was murdered—you don't think that's awful?" I'd clearly knocked him off balance with my comment—as intended.

"I guess that would depend on your perspective. She did tear a family apart."

"So did Elliot. He chose to cheat on his wife."

"As the old saying goes, *it takes two to tango.*"

Leo shrugged. "Hey, I don't know enough about their affair to assign blame. For that matter, I barely knew Ava."

"How did you meet her?"

Leo took a moment before responding. He must have been weighing his options. Should he be honest and link himself to a murder victim or lie and put an end to the subject? "I met her at a bar right after she moved to the Glen," he said finally. "She looked lonely, so I bought her a drink and we talked for a while." *Play it low-key,* my inner Nancy Drew cautioned me. *He has information. Don't scare him off.*

"If you don't mind me asking, was that the beginning of a relationship between the two of you?"

"A short-lived one, as it turned out. After one dinner and a movie, she stopped returning my calls. Maybe she'd met Elliot. In any case, I'm a quick study, so I moved on with a little dent in my pride." Leo was hard to label, by turns self-confident and self-effacing. "I take it you're investigating her death?"

I laughed. "Pretty obvious, huh?"

"You might say your reputation precedes you."

"One last question?"

"I didn't kill her," Leo said, jumping the gun.

I grinned. "That wasn't my question, but I'll be sure to make note of it. I was hoping you'd tell me a little about Ava. I never met her."

"She was down to earth, not pretentious, what you saw is what you got. I thought she was pretty, but not everyone did."

I thanked him and asked him to call me if he thought of anything else about her that might be important—like why someone would want to kill her. "Has Detective Duggan been in to talk to you?"

"You already had your last question," Leo said with a mischievous twinkle in his eyes. "But I'm in a generous mood. The detective has not yet made an appearance, and I would prefer to keep it that way."

"He won't hear anything about you from me. The less I see of that man, the better I like it too." On the walk back to my shop, I tried to make sense of the two different women Ava seemed to be, the nice down-to-earth woman Leo knew, and the arrogant home wrecker Lolly described. Maybe the problem lay in my prejudice against Ava. I wanted to believe that any woman capable of stealing Elliot away from Lolly's daughter had to be a temptress, a Mata Hari that no man could resist. If she was just an ordinary woman, then much of the blame for the affair rested squarely on Elliot's shoulders. If Ava wasn't irresistible, why hadn't he resisted her for the sake of his family, the sake of his marriage? It was possible that Dani and Elliot were already having problems when Ava came along. Timing—so much of life seemed to come down to timing. One thing was clear to me. I couldn't continue to let my personal feelings about Lolly and Dani cloud my thinking.

Chapter 13

Travis and I left for Buffalo the next morning. We had an appointment to meet with Liam at noon. His lunch hour was the only time he had available for us. He'd started a new job at an accounting firm and often had to work late. "Low man on the totem pole" was how he'd characterized it to Travis. The problem was finding a private place in which to hold our meeting. Restaurants were crowded at that hour and Liam's apartment was too far from his office. He suggested a pizza joint where the business was mostly delivery to local offices. It would have to do.

The drive was pleasant. The day was spring at its best, with pale blue skies and all the cherry trees in bloom. After I gave Travis a brief summary of my meeting with Leo Stratford, neither of us seemed inclined to talk about Ava's death. We'd be doing that soon enough. Instead we kept the conversation light. He talked about the new season of baseball, and I talked about planting more annuals. When Morgana and Bronwen were alive, Morgana had loved gardening and I'd inherited her love of flowers. She'd buy flats of impatiens, petunias, salvia and other flowers whose names now eluded me. Travis offered to spend a day helping me with the project, which I appreciated beyond measure. But I knew the odds were not in my favor. There was bound to be a news emergency that would keep him in Watkins Glen, if not farther away.

"My mom loves planting flowers too," he said. "You have that in common. Every year she drags my dad to the nurseries to help her. I'm not sure if she knows just how much he hates trailing behind her, especially in the hot houses. I once asked him why he doesn't tell her and just refuse to go. His answer was, 'eh, it's just once a year. I'll survive.'"

"Sounds like they have a good marriage," I said. He took his hand off the wheel and closed it around mine with a little squeeze. Was that his way of saying he hoped we could have a marriage like that someday? I pushed the question out of my mind. I wasn't ready to think about forever.

"Since we're on the subject of our parents," he said, "mine would like to meet you." He gave me a quick glance to judge my reaction. I made a point of keeping my expression neutral.

"I'd love to meet them too. The only problem is I can't ask Tilly to help out again so soon after this." I wasn't sure if I was looking for obstacles to delay the inevitable, but I had to admit it was a distinct possibility. "And now with the investigation, we shouldn't be away that much." The trip to Manhattan made Buffalo seem like a walk around the block.

"They're willing to come to New Camel." His smile told me that he thought he'd solved the problem.

"Have you considered the ramifications of them coming here?" He clearly hadn't, or he wouldn't be looking so pleased with himself.

"I'm not sure what you mean. Sooner or later they'll have to learn about your special...talents."

"Yes, but maybe little by little would be better than a sudden total immersion. It would be like throwing them into the water with alligators, before telling them *these* alligators are vegetarian and friendly. How strong are their hearts?"

He laughed. "Strong enough."

"My shop alone will be a surprise. Even though your mom sent you to Abracadabra to buy some products for her, it doesn't look anything like a beauty counter at the mall."

His smile drooped. "Right—I forgot about that."

"Then there's the often unpredictable Tilly, and let's not forget the inimitable Merlin, who could accidentally turn your parents into any number of creatures both real and mythical. I think that would flap your unflappable mother."

Travis didn't have an immediate response, but trying to find his way around Buffalo might have had something to do with it. The navigation system was telling him to go straight, but the street we were on was a dead end. He turned off the insistent voice and tried the app on his phone. Fortunately, it recognized the problem and rerouted us. We had a limited time with Liam. We didn't want to spend it lost on the streets of Buffalo.

We found the pizzeria with two minutes to spare, but there was the issue of where to leave the car. Travis saw someone pulling out of a spot on the next block. He gunned the engine, made it through the intersection on a yellow light, and claimed the prize.

"I hope they have decent pizza," he said, maneuvering into the tight spot. "I'm starving." I was too, but I had a less critical palate, having only once tasted the 'real stuff,' as Travis referred to New York City pizza.

We made it to the pizzeria before Liam. The shop was old but clean. There was a counter where you could view the different pies and place your order, a refrigerated unit from which to select your beverage, and four tables for anyone who wanted to eat there. No one was at the counter or occupying the tables when we arrived. Liam ran in as we were ordering. Travis asked him what he'd like and added it to our slices along with three bottles of overpriced water.

We sat at the table in the alcove near the door for its semblance of privacy. The phone kept ringing with orders, and delivery guys were in and out. It was clear no one was interested in us or our conversation. We made it through the pleasantries with a minimum of words and took a few bites of the pizza before getting down to the business of our meeting. "What can you tell us about Ava that might give us a clue about why someone would want to kill her?" Travis asked.

Liam took a minute to finish chewing. "She was a good person and she thought everyone else was good and kind and honest."

I washed the pizza down with water. "You mean she was naive?"

"Sort of, but she had street smarts and business smarts. Trusting the wrong people was her one blind spot." He sighed, shook his head and bit off another piece from his slice.

"Do you know of anyone in particular who betrayed her trust?" Travis asked. "A boyfriend maybe?"

"Yeah, there was a boyfriend Brock... damn, what was his last name?" Liam took a swig of water and swirled it around in his mouth as he tried to remember. "Davenport—that's it—Brock Davenport. My dad asked Ava how she could trust a guy with a movie star name. She got pretty mad at him. You have to know my dad. He's a kidder. Ava knew that, but his teasing got under her skin anyway."

I put down my pizza. It was difficult to eat and interview someone at the same time. For the present, having my questions answered took priority. "When did Ava and Brock break up?"

"About a year ago, before she started the new job in Watkins Glen."

"Do you know what caused the break up?"

"She said he was too controlling and temperamental. Personally, I didn't like him from the get-go."

"Why is that?" I asked.

"I could never put my finger on it. Maybe it was his swagger. He had a way of making you feel—small. I don't know if that's the right word for it." Travis dropped the last third of his pizza onto the paper plate and threw his napkin on top of it. "Do you happen to have his address?" Liam shook his head. "Just his cell phone. Do you want it?" Travis and I said *yes* in unison. In less than a minute, Liam found it on his phone and texted it to us.

I picked up my pizza and took a nibble, but it had cooled too much. I dropped it back on the plate and pushed it away. "How did Brock take it?"

"How would I know? It's not like the guy confides in me."

Travis knew where I was going and hopped aboard. "Did he keep calling, beg her to take him back?"

"Yeah, he wouldn't let her be. He made all kinds of promises to change."

"Change?" Travis pounced on his answer. "In what ways?" I knew what he was thinking. If the behavior Brock promised to change rose to the level of physical abuse, it could be a little hop, skip and jump to murder.

Liam chased down his last bite with water and shrugged. "To be a better boyfriend, I guess. I don't know much about what irritates women, or maybe I'd have a woman in *my* life."

"We need to know exactly what he promised to change." Travis wasn't letting up now that he had the scent of information. "Liam, think! This is important!" His voice remained low, but his tone made it seem like he was yelling. He was forgetting his manners and he couldn't afford to do that. Manners were important when you didn't have the clout of a detective's badge.

Liam sat back in his chair, as if he were trying to distance himself from Travis. We could lose him. I tried to catch Travis's eye to warn him, but his focus was so tight on Liam that he might as well have been wearing blinders. When he got no response, he tried a different tack, like a sailor trying to catch the wind. "Did Ava tell you what final straw made her break it off with Brock?"

"I don't know man," the accountant replied with some attitude of his own. "Why don't you ask my mom when you see her. I'm sure she knows more about Ava's personal life than I did."

I had to dial things back if I wanted to keep the dialogue alive. I hadn't made the trip up there to let Travis blow it. "Liam," I said in a conversational tone, "do you know if Davenport was ever abusive to your sister?"

Liam shifted his gaze to me. "I never saw any signs of physical abuse, but I suppose it could have been covered by her clothing."

"After the breakup, do you think it's possible Brock was stalking your sister?"

Liam seemed to relax talking to me. He was no longer plastered to the back of his chair. "Ava never used that word, but maybe she didn't want to scare us. I know for sure she was really happy to be moving." There was a long pause before he said, "You think Davenport is the one who killed her." He said it as if he'd finally put two and two together. It made me wonder how good he was at accounting.

Travis realized he'd gone off course. When he opened his mouth again, he was more cordial. "It's far too early in our investigation to say for sure. You'd be surprised how often things change as more information becomes available. Every suspect seems the most likely until you learn more about the next one."

Liam glanced at his watch, but I didn't want him to leave yet. We needed to know more about Ava. "Did your sister get along with everyone or did she sometimes rub people the wrong way?" I asked to draw his attention away from the time.

"I think most people liked her, but she could be opinionated and stubborn."

"Do you know if she considered anyone an enemy?"

Liam got to his feet. "Not offhand. Sorry—I've got to get back to work." Short of tying him to the chair, I had no way to keep him there. We thanked him for his time and his help.

What I needed was a hot slice of pizza. Back in college, I was the only one in the dorm who didn't like eating cold pizza from the mini fridge. But it was far from the only thing that set me apart. Travis ordered a slice for me and a second one for himself. We sat at the table eating and rehashing the interview. He apologized for going off the rails. "I thought Liam was holding back and that a push might help. I was wrong—about pushing—but I still think he knows more than he's saying."

"When we talk to his parents later, they might give us a clearer picture of Ava and Brock." I was sitting opposite him now and I locked my eyes on his. "You seriously cannot go at them the same way you did with Liam. They're still in a state of shock and they're grieving."

Travis put his right hand over his heart. "I promise to be the quintessential gentleman. You may have to poke me to be sure I'm breathing."

Chapter 14

We had a four o'clock meeting with Valerie and Teddy Duncan in their home. Liam had worked out the details for us. According to him, they hadn't required any coaxing. As lost as they were, they were determined to seek justice for their daughter.

We found our way out of Buffalo and over to Williamsville with no trouble. After checking into the same hotel where we'd stayed for Ava's wake, we killed some time walking through the park across the street. I was too nervous about the meeting to enjoy the weather. I was worried the interview might exacerbate their pain and equally worried that Travis might forget his pledge in the heat of the moment. I gave myself a pep talk. I'd never acted inappropriately in the past, unless you counted my first time at a funeral at the tender age of six, when I told the family that their deceased grandmother looked nicer dead than she had alive. At the time, I thought I was paying them a compliment. As for Travis, I'd never heard him question anyone as aggressively as he had Liam, but he'd seemed properly chastened afterward. I had every reason to believe it wouldn't happen again.

Based on the tightening knot in my stomach as the afternoon progressed, the pep talk wasn't working. I'd noticed that men could shake off uncomfortable feelings more easily than women. For men what was done, was done. Time to move on—*Sorry, my bad. What's for dinner?* For women, misgivings lingered like a never-ending cough after a bout of pneumonia.

Four o'clock found us at the Duncans' door. Valerie invited us inside. Her eyes were no longer red and swollen. The grief had burrowed under the surface. She'd applied some mascara and eyeliner that only succeeded in making her look severe rather than sad. Since we'd last seen her, she'd had her hair done at a salon and fixed in place with so much hairspray it reminded me of a shirt that was stiff from too much starch. I imagined it would slice into my finger if I touched it. We followed her into the kitchen, which was clean, but showing its age. Teddy was installed at the round table in the dinette, which was covered in a green vinyl tablecloth and set with cups, dessert plates, utensils and napkins. He rose to shake our hands and thank us for our efforts to find Ava's killer. He tried to summon up a smile, but it wouldn't stick. Valerie asked us to sit and offered us coffee. I'd smelled it brewing when I walked in and I could see the full carafe sitting in the old Mr. Coffee machine on the Formica counter. Since she'd gone to the trouble of making it, I didn't feel right declining. I should have told Liam to make sure his mom didn't fuss for us. But Tilly would have reminded me that sometimes social conventions helped get you through the day when nothing else could.

Valerie poured the coffee into our cups, then disappeared into the small pantry and returned with a variety box of donuts that she opened and put on the table near Travis and me. "Please help yourselves. They're store-bought, but very good."

They looked good. Teddy reached across the table to pluck a donut covered with powdered sugar. That broke the ice. Travis took a chocolate one, and I caved, going for a sugary one. Valerie was the only holdout.

Travis took out his pad and pen. In deference to the tragic circumstances, we'd decided not to record the conversation. We would do our best to respect their privacy. Not an easy feat given the circumstances.

"Please let us know if you need to take a break," I said before I asked my first question. They both bobbed their heads. "To the best of your knowledge, did Ava have any enemies?"

"I can't imagine that she did," Valerie replied. The question seemed to have taken her by surprise. She glanced at her husband for corroboration.

"No—no way," Teddy sputtered with a little spray of powdered sugar. "Everyone loved her."

Travis had some chocolate on his chin. I didn't want to reach over and wipe it like a mother would. Instead I offered him my napkin and motioned to my chin. Hardly subtle when we were sitting in such close proximity to the Duncans. He got the message and wiped it away without missing a beat. "What about her ex—Brock Davenport?"

"Oh yeah," Teddy said, "the guy with the Hollywood name. He acts in local theater. He's absolutely sure he'll get discovered any day now. Meanwhile he waits tables. I can't understand what a girl like Ava saw in him."

I sipped my coffee and wiped my mouth, in case I had a ring of sugar around it. "Did he harass her after they split?"

"I was worried about that," Valerie said, "but when I asked her, she claimed he took it in stride. 'Just a blip in his day,' is how she put it." So Ava had confided in her brother more than in her parents—at least when it came to Brock. Either she didn't want to worry them or she didn't want to hear *I told you so* from her dad.

"Can you give us the name of the company where she was working?" Travis asked. It had been on our list of questions for Liam, but he'd bolted before we could get to it.

"Monroe Enterprises," Teddy said. "According to Ava, they do research and development involving large magnets."

"We don't really know what they're working on," Valerie said. "Ava wasn't part of the science staff. She worked in the business office where she was head of accounting—directly under the business supervisor. Numbers were always her thing." I could hear the uptick of pride in Valerie's voice for a moment before it dropped like a stone under the weight of her new reality.

"I've read that most murder victims are killed by someone they know," Teddy said in the silence that followed. "Does that mean the cops and you guys talk to everyone Ava knew before you go looking at strangers?"

"We do, as a general rule," I said, "but I can't speak for the police." I'd always thought it had to be worse to know your assailant, but maybe it was worse to die just because you were at the wrong place at the wrong time—nothing more than a big old cosmic mistake.

Valerie drew her arms across her chest and shuddered. "Murder, no matter who commits it or why, is horrible…it's horrible."

"Was Ava happy at her new job?" Travis asked. I was glad he was sticking with the less emotional topic of her employment.

"She seemed to be." As Valerie spoke, her arms relaxed, and her hands came to rest in her lap. "She'd made new friends. One of her coworkers, a girl named Angie, lived in the same building she did. They car pooled to work most days." A smile tweaked at her lips. "She told us about this adorable little town of New Camel. She wanted us to come visit for a weekend so she could show us around her new world." Valerie's smile vanished and tears welled up in her eyes. So much for safer topics. I suspected there wouldn't be any for a long time.

"You probably misunderstood her," Teddy said. "The town must be New *Carmel.* Who would name a town after a camel?"

"It was New Camel," Valerie insisted. "My hearing is just fine, thank you."

"It actually is New Camel." Travis piped up, before it became a full-blown argument.

"I stand corrected." Teddy sounded miffed. Travis and I looked at each other. Time to get out of Dodge, before we created more tension for the couple. I wished I could ring a bell and tell them to go to their corners and cool off, but the best thing we could do was leave and let them find their equilibrium in their own way. We thanked them for their time and hospitality and asked them to call us if they thought of anyone who had a reason to kill their daughter.

"I doubt Duggan would have left," Travis said on the drive back to the hotel.

"He probably would have stayed and used their anger to find out if either one was hiding anything. Are you second guessing our leaving?"

"No, but being unwilling to press people who are in distress has kind of been my Achilles' heel as a journalist too. I sometimes wonder if it's the reason I haven't gotten further in my career." So that was the reason he'd been uncharacteristically hard on Liam. He was trying to push the envelope. For better or worse, Liam's reaction had brought that experiment to a close for now.

"But could you have lived with yourself after intentionally causing someone more misery?"

Travis stared straight ahead, his eyes fixed on the road as if he was afraid to look at me. "To be honest, I don't know."

"That's okay," I said, "because I do."

Chapter 15

"Am I glad to see you," Tilly said when I walked into my shop. She'd never greeted me like that after I returned from a trip. In fact, she was the least likely person I knew to throw guilt around that way. I immediately checked the tufted window ledge and was relieved to find Sashkatu ensconced there, regarding me with sleepy eyes that said, *You're home. Very nice. Just keep it down.*

I wheeled my overnight bag against the counter so it wouldn't trip anyone who came into the shop. "What's wrong, Aunt Tilly?" I met her as she came from behind the counter, looking lovely in her new flowered spring muumuu. I had to wade through a lot of frothy layers to hug her properly. "Are you all right? Is Merlin?"

"Merlin is Merlin," she said, shaking her head. Three words had never been truer, but they posed more questions than they answered.

"Please tell me he didn't turn himself into some creature again."

"He didn't, but he's been making my life a trial nonetheless."

"What has he done?"

She threw her hands in the air. "I don't know yet. He has some grand news that he's refused to tell me until you returned."

"I was only gone overnight. What grand news could possibly have happened over the past twenty-four hours?"

"As we've both learned, it doesn't take much for Merlin to go overboard. If he's to be believed, he's been nearly crawling out of his skin with the need to impart his news, but he insists we must both be present."

"Where is he now?"

"In my shop, burying his frustration under a pound of brownies." At that moment, the wizard strode into Abracadabra by way of the door that connected to Tea and Empathy.

"Aha!" he said marching over to us. "I thought I heard Kailyn's sweet voice." He was all smiles as if he hadn't driven my poor aunt batty waiting for me.

"I hear you have some good news to tell us." There was little point in reprimanding him. He wouldn't absorb a word of it until he'd regaled us with his news.

"Good news—humph," he said, taking umbrage at my remark. "It's *grand* news. Make no mistake about it." Tilly rolled her eyes.

"I'll thank you to be more respectful, Matillda. Now ladies, please accompany me next door where you can both be seated." Tilly and I shrugged at each other as we followed Merlin.

Sashkatu joined the parade, trotting past us to catch up with the wizard.

Once we were all installed at a tea table and Sashki had crawled into Merlin's lap, he cleared his throat and began. "As you know, I've been studying and translating your family's ancient scrolls, in particular the sections that dated back so far that the words were incomprehensible to you. Not long after you left on your jaunt, Kailyn, I came upon a section that is quite remarkable. It is not the type of information to be shared in helter-skelter fashion. It is to be revealed to a family as a whole, if at all possible. Since you two are the only remnants of the once thriving Wilde clan, I waited for both of you to be present." He paused as if waiting for applause or a cry of *Huzzah*, neither of which was forthcoming. He managed to swallow his disappointment and continue.

"According to the scrolls, you, Matillda Wilde, and you, Kailyn Wilde, are my progeny, my great, great, great and so forth, grandchildren."

It took a minute for his words to sink in and for my brain to sort out their full meaning. I glanced at Tilly, but she was still busy digesting the news. Merlin was braiding and unbraiding sections of his beard while he waited for our reactions. "It is grand news, momentous news," I said, choosing my words with care. "But are you absolutely sure? It's the sort of news you don't want to have to take back. That kind of disappointment would be devastating." I was overstating the issue, but Merlin thrived on drama and pumped up accolades.

He looked as if he was caught between delight at my initial words and indignity over my doubting his translation skills. "I would never have told you if I had the slightest misgiving about its veracity."

"Great Grandpa!" Tilly said, grasping his hands in hers.

He pulled them away. "Don't call me that. It makes me sound old and feeble." Tilly apologized, with a wink to me.

"But you are our grandfather, although many generations removed. Exactly how many, I wonder…" She started counting on her fingers, which quickly proved insufficient.

"Stop it!" Merlin thundered. "Stop it this instant! I will not be mocked by ungrateful children." Tilly had pushed him too far.

She bristled. "I am not ungrateful, humor simply helps me cope with sudden changes. And you, my wizardly, greatest grandfather, are far too thin-skinned."

"If that was an apology, it was sorely lacking."

"I never said it was an apology. It was an explanation and a statement of fact." I recognized the signs—their sparring could go on for hours, especially since Merlin was well-fueled with sugar and caffeine. But I had a store to run despite my new illustrious parentage. I also had questions dancing on my tongue.

"Excuse me," I said, raising my voice to be heard over theirs. "Merlin, I read somewhere that you never had children. The stories—"

"Are wrong," he said, turning to me. "I sired a number of male children during my life, but they were either stillborn or perished shortly after their births. I always assumed my magick was too strong a burden for the wee ones to bear. It was the deepest regret of my life—having no heir to carry the magick on to future generations."

His face brightened. "But now through your family's records I am reborn. They write of a baby girl I fathered. Her given name was Cerelia. She was strong enough to survive, although her mother had tearfully assured me that she too had perished. Mayhap the woman was afraid I'd take the child to live with me. And she was right. I would have wanted to help her magick grow to its full potential. In any case, Cerelia grew up and had three daughters of her own and so on down through the centuries—to both of you."

"It sounds like females are the only ones strong enough to carry the magick," I said, "and yet you were the first and a male."

"Do you know how I came by the magick?" Tilly and I shook our heads. "When I was old enough to understand, my mother told me about the night she was visited by a supernatural being who lay with her. In the morning, she told herself what she remembered of that night was only a strange dream. But when she gave birth to me exactly nine months later, she could no longer fool herself. As for my ability to survive with the magickal DNA, perhaps I was simply stronger by dint of being the first."

I'd always taken the magick in my family for granted, but now that I knew it came from Merlin, I wondered what it might mean for any male children I might have. Part of me wished Merlin had kept his grand news to himself. I didn't like the unsettled feelings it left in the pit of my stomach and the unanswerable questions it planted in my brain.

Chapter 16

I didn't tell Travis about Merlin's news when I spoke to him that night. I didn't think of it as being secretive. I considered it a kindness not to burden him until I had a chance to absorb it myself. My clowder of cats must have sensed the whirligig of emotions on tour inside me and they came to give me comfort. I appreciated their motives, if not the way they went about it. They vied for turns in my lap and on my shoulders like they were playing a game of musical chairs to upbeat music only they could hear. Sashkatu watched them for a while from the rug near the fireplace, before taking matters into his own paws. He climbed onto the couch with the help of his custom stairs. With a minimum of hissing and growling, he sent the bunch of them slinking off to other quarters. He settled into the vacancy in my lap like a king who'd beaten back pretenders to his throne. I stroked his soft coat to the peaceful tempo of his purring, which restored some much needed quiet to my soul.

The next morning, he and I were at Abracadabra bright and early, he on his window seat and I at my desk, when there was a sharp rapping on the front door. It was still locked, because I didn't open for another half hour and I'd planned on using the time to pay bills. No matter what else might be rampaging through my life, bills were as reliable as the dust on my merchandise.

I swiveled in my chair to see who couldn't wait until the hour plainly posted on the door. Ben Webster? I'd actually expected to find Tess on my doorstep one day, not her husband.

He knocked again with the same urgency. I couldn't in good conscience ignore him. The bills would have to wait.

"Coming," I called, as I made my way around the counter to unlock the door.

He stepped inside, wearing a well-made suit that didn't jibe with my initial impression of him as an outdoorsman. "Sorry to barge in so early, but I'm on my way to work and I had to talk to you without Tess around."

"That sounds mysterious. Would you like to sit down?" I pointed to the chair I kept near the counter for weary shoppers and bored husbands.

"No thanks, I don't have much time."

"Then how can I help you?"

"My wife won't stop talking about how the kiln moved out of Conner's way. She's certain you had something to do with it. From where I was standing, I couldn't see what happened, but she's been obsessing about it, talking about witchcraft and maybe even moving again. I hope you'll forgive me if I'm off base, but I'd like to hear what happened from you." His tone was pleasant enough, but his eyes were boring into mine as if determined to detect any lies. I made an executive decision and hoped it wasn't reckless.

"I've been learning how to move objects with my mind. I'm sure you've heard of people who can do that."

"Yeah, but I figured it was just a magician's trick, like you'd see in Vegas or on TV. But you couldn't have set up a trick like that with Tess there the whole time. And you didn't get up to push the kiln out of the way, because you couldn't have reached it in time." His expression dared me to offer up an explanation.

"Telekinetic ability is rare, but it does exist. People have been pushing the envelope in every field of endeavor. Stretching the power of the mind is no different. That's what Tess saw. I'm just glad I was able to prevent Conner from getting hurt." Was I ever going to hear about this from my mother and grandmother!

"I need to see this for myself, if I'm going to help my wife get past her fears."

"I can't always do it," I said. At least not since our magick had become erratic. "My adrenaline must have kicked in that day and helped."

"Please show me," he said, despite my disclaimer. "I'm just six months at my new job. I cannot pack up and move again." He sounded desperate.

"All right, I'll try." If I pretended I couldn't do it, he'd think I'd been lying. I had to give him a little example of telekinesis if I wanted him and Tess to accept it and let it go. "Put a coin on the counter." Ben found a quarter in the pocket of his pants and set it down as I'd requested. On a good day, I could have made the quarter spin on its edge or do a little tap dance, but I settled for sliding it across to the counter to me and back to him again. He looked at me with open-mouthed amazement.

"It's taken thousands of hours of practice, and Zen-like mind control." He thanked me for the demonstration, adding that he had another question, if I didn't mind. "Okay," I said, wary of what was coming.

"What are all these products you sell in here? Tess is concerned they may be illegal or dangerous." She'd been in our shop on one occasion and she'd seemed delighted with the basket of products I'd given her as a welcome to our town. Why didn't she see the irony in fearing me, precisely because I'd saved her son from harm? I knew what my mother's answer would be: "Fear trumps everything." I didn't want to believe that, but Tess was making a good case for it.

"I sell only natural, plant-based health and beauty products. Feel free to browse through the aisles." I had nothing to hide, at least not on my shelves. Ben did a quick circuit of my shop, thanked me and was out the door and off to work three minutes later. Bronwen appeared as the door closed behind him. Her cloud was dark blue with yellow swirls, a combination I'd never seen before. It couldn't be good.

"Kailyn, why on earth did you tell that man about your telekinetic ability?"

"Nice to see you too, Grandma." I couldn't resist—the day had gotten off to a rocky start and I needed to lighten it up.

"It's always lovely to see you, but putting me on the defensive doesn't change the question." Although it did soften her tone. "Why did you admit to having telekinetic power?"

"Because lying can raise more suspicions than being honest. Tess saw what she saw. I hope my explanation puts her concerns to rest."

"Your intentions are fine, dear girl, but you're mistaken if you think that tiny bit of truth will put an end to her probing. And don't tell me I'm being old-fashioned. Those who ignore the past will make the same mistakes—or something like that." My grandmother had never been very good at remembering quotations. Apparently, death hadn't helped.

"I promise to keep that in mind," I said, trying my best to sound contrite. *Tess, please don't make me regret my honesty.*

"We'll keep this conversation between us," Bronwen said. "No need to involve your mother." I thanked her—one less lecture felt like a gift. "There is another matter I wish to discuss with you. I've noticed that you haven't pressed on with your teleportation skills."

I had no rebuttal; I was guilty as charged.

"I keep meaning to, but then I run out of time."

"And yet one must never rest on one's laundry."

"I think you mean *laurels,*" I said.

Bronwen looked surprised. "Well that makes a whole lot more sense than laundry. In any case, you have to practice teleporting with an object, a breakable object, increasing the size and weight over time before you can consider trying it with a living creature." I promised to get on it at the first possible opportunity. "That's my girl. Now is as good a time as any. I'll leave you to it."

I didn't want to argue with her, but teleporting in and out of my shop when a customer could walk in at any moment wasn't the best idea.

The rest of the morning was quiet. I had time to pay the bills between customers and do a bit of dusting—two of my least favorite chores. When lunchtime rolled around I decided to stop in and chat with a couple more shopkeepers, part of my continuing efforts to find out if any of them knew something that might be useful to our investigation. Since my stomach was grumbling about being empty, I promised it a tall vanilla ice cream soda at The Jerk. It was a weakness I blamed on Morgana. She'd instilled in me the belief that ice cream was a perfectly acceptable lunch from time to time.

My first stop was the new candle shop and its proprietor, Lucy Gale. Although she'd never met Ava, she thought her death was sad and tragic and about ten other adjectives. She was a human thesaurus—wonderful to have around if you had a thesis to write, but hard to break away from when there was an ice cream soda in the offing.

Next was the train shop, a favorite of kids and dads alike. I'd never cared much for the trains. I was all about the miniature villages the trains passed through and the tiny people inhabiting them. Ollie Ollifson, who was proof that some parents shouldn't be allowed to name their children, was a big barrel of a man who'd never outgrown his love of trains. He didn't know Ava by name and didn't recognize her photo, but he stared at it for some time as if trying to summon up a memory that wasn't there. He was sorry he couldn't help me, but would I like to play with the trains before I left? When I declined, his face fell in utter disbelief. Most people who walked into his shop probably did so because they shared his love of trains. I was the odd one out.

Chapter 17

"Your buddy just walked in," Margie said as she set the soda down in front of me. I followed her line of sight to the front door and saw Elise Harkens waiting to be seated. "Back here," Margie called, waving her over. When Elise saw me in the booth, she burst into laughter.

"I want exactly what she has. No, on second thought make mine strawberry."

"You got it."

"You should have told me you needed a lunch date," I said. "I always have time for you."

"You've been working the investigation during your lunch hour and I didn't want to put additional pressure on you."

"It's funny that today is the first day in a while that I decided to treat myself instead of eating my brown bag PB and J."

"And today was a half day for parent/teacher conferences or I wouldn't be here either."

"So… tell me what's going on in your corner of the world—kids okay?" I'd been their babysitter until they were old enough to be home alone without killing each other.

"They're good. I have some news about me though," she said coyly.

I narrowed my eyes at her. "You've been holding out on me." We kept in touch by phone even when we couldn't meet in person, but she hadn't told me anything in weeks that would have made her eyes twinkle like they were twinkling now.

"I wanted to see your reaction in person."

"Well here I am."

She took a deep breath and let it out slowly. "I'm sort of seeing someone."

My eyebrows took flight. "Sort of?" I couldn't contain the grin that was spreading across my face. "Isn't that like being a little pregnant?"

"Sort of—meaning I've had dinner with him a couple times now. I really need some input before I commit to more. I talked to my sister, but she sees everything in black and white, yes or no, take it or leave it. I need you and the way you see things with the whole color spectrum."

The busboy brought Elise her ice cream soda. She took a sip that went on and on. "I didn't realize how thirsty I was or how good an ice cream soda can taste."

I snatched the soda away from her. "Who. Is. He? I'm not giving this back until you tell me more."

"His name is Jerry, short for Jerome, Simmons. He's tall and nice looking, of course not in the same league as Travis, but not too many men are."

"What does he do?"

"He's a dentist who recently joined the group I use for the boys. Their regular dentist was away when Noah chipped a tooth a couple of weeks ago—I told you about that."

"I remember, but you didn't say a word about Dr. Jerry."

"You could say we bonded as he bonded Noah's tooth. Before we left, he asked me out and I shocked myself by saying *yes*. I'm not usually that impulsive, but I immediately liked him. He must have felt that way too."

"Divorced, widowed?" I asked. By the time people were approaching forty, *never married* was rarely their status.

"Divorced for five years, a boy and a girl a little younger than my kids. His ex moved to Watkins Glen for a job and he wanted to stay in their lives."

"It's not easy to start over in his profession without taking a big financial hit. Sounds like a good father. And after five years, you're not just a rebound for him."

"But what about me? Do you think I'm just lonely?"

"There's nothing wrong with wanting company. People are basically herd animals. We need other people. Besides, it's not like you're going to elope with the guy tomorrow. You want to know what I think?" She bobbed her head. "When you talk about him, you light up and twinkle. For now, that's all you need to know. Stop second-guessing yourself. You're allowed to have some fun." I polished off my soda.

"You're right. My sister told me I was getting ahead of myself. I don't even know what that means. I love her to pieces, but we're polar opposites. She's never been able to give me sensible advice."

"When do I get to meet Dr. Jerry?" I asked.

"How about a double date whenever Travis gets back in town?"

"I may come down with a toothache before then," I said with a sly smile. "Did I forget to mention that the practice is limited to children? Now can I have my soda back or are you planning to finish it too?"

* * * *

The medical examiner was scheduled to release his report on Ava Duncan's death that night as a lead-in to the local evening news. Anyone who had seen her body in Lolly's yard already knew she'd died from a fudge knife in her back. The ME had probably been waiting for toxicology results before going public. Although I didn't expect to hear much that I didn't already know, I felt obliged to watch just in case. Since I was investigating the case on Lolly's behalf, I couldn't afford to overlook any scrap of information.

The young reporter, who was in charge of the while-we-wait chatter, summarized what was already known about her death, made more poignant by the sobering video of a black body bag leaving Lolly's shop and being loaded into the coroner's van. The room quieted as the chief of police stepped onto the podium, strode to the microphone, and introduced the ME. When the younger man joined him there, the chief stepped back to give him room.

The ME was all business. He read his report in a monotone that started to lull me to sleep. In the end, the only thing I learned was that there were no drugs in Ava's body at the time of her death. He glossed over her time of death with a broad reference to the afternoon she was discovered. Duggan had probably asked him not to be more specific with the public. That made it harder for Dani, and any other suspects. She'd have to account for her time over many hours. I'd already discussed that with her. The only thing I could do now to help her would be to find the killer and disprove their alibi. The police chief came back to the lectern and the two men fielded questions from the assembled reporters. The only problem with the reporter filling in for Travis was that he wasn't Travis.

Travis was in New York City, filling in for one of the national news anchors away on vacation. Over the past six months, he'd heard murmurings that he was going to be offered a permanent position there, but somehow the opportunity never materialized. Until it did, he was at the ready every time they needed him to fill in. It didn't matter that the trip to the city took five hours or more. Who measured dreams in hours and minutes? His parents and I were an enthusiastic if uncoordinated cheerleading troop.

I ate salmon and salad in the living room, watching Travis nail the news. He had the perfect voice for it, deep and resonant, reassuring regardless of the current state of the world. He called after the show. It was becoming our tradition, wherever he was. "You were great," I told him.

He chuckled. "It's the objectivity I appreciate the most. Listen, before I drove down here, I spent hours trying to find a listing for this Monroe Enterprises where Ava supposedly worked. I checked with the secretary of state for the state of New York. Then I scoured the internet. I even tried NAIC and still came up empty. As a last resort, I spoke to commercial realtors for this region—nothing.

"NAIC?"

"They provide multiple ways of looking up a company when you only have limited information to go by—got me nowhere."

"Maybe her parents had the name wrong. I'll give Liam a call tomorrow to double check."

"Great. Now I'm off to meet my folks for dinner. Fair warning, they may hold me hostage until I set a date for them to meet you."

"I've been giving it more thought and I decided it's wrong to keep putting them off. It's just nerves on my part. You have carte blanche to arrange a meeting. We'll make it work."

"Okay, thanks. But for the record—no matter how it goes, nothing will change between us."

"Wow—somehow that makes me feel both reassured and twice as nervous. Is it going to be awful? Will they think I've cast some horrible spell over you?" I had an image of them hiring one of those organizations that snatches people out of cults and reverses their brain washing.

Travis laughed, but it sounded forced. "Don't do this to yourself. It's going to be fine. Worst case scenario, it may take them a little while to adjust to this new paradigm, like it did with me."

"You're right." I tried to sound more relaxed, but it sounded as forced as his laughter. We'd get through it. In the end, we'd be one happy family. Now I was getting ahead of myself.

Chapter 18

I'd almost forgotten there was a bus tour scheduled for the next morning. It would soon be the height of the tourist season and I, along with all the other shopkeepers in town, was busy spring cleaning. It was important that everything sparkled and shined. The window washers had been through the week before and now the last of winter was being swept out of each shop. The cherry trees that lined the streets were decked out in their showiest pink blossoms, and the New Camel Chamber of Commerce had crews hanging baskets of scarlet, pink and white impatiens from the old-fashioned light poles. Everyone seemed energized and optimistic. But the best sight of all that late May morning was Lolly back in her candy shop.

Although she was still a person of interest in Ava's death, Duggan had removed the yellow police tape and allowed her to go back to work in time for the tourists. Mayor Tompkins must have had something to do with it. I would have loved to eavesdrop on the conversation between those two men. I know what I would have told the detective: "The yellow crime tape in the middle of our quaint little town will be a scary reminder of our rising murder rate. Word of mouth about it will spread fast and far. And don't forget about Lolly's candy shop. In every survey done by our tourism board, otherwise known as Edgar Abernathy, her shop was the number one attraction by a seven to one margin. We need Lolly and her shop if we want a vibrant tourist season." But apparently the mayor was successful without my help.

I walked over to welcome Lolly back and found the shop to be a veritable whirlwind of activity. Her daughters were busy cleaning while she concentrated on making her delectable wares. No small order. All the shelves in the display cases had to be filled. Under normal circumstances, she'd only need to refill a tray or two at a time as they ran out. This was like the day many years ago when she'd first opened her shop. She'd been a lot younger back then, she was quick to point out. "There's no way I could do it today without my kids' help." Dani pulled her head out of the display case she was cleaning. "Don't let my mother fool you, she's been here since dawn working harder than any of us." I didn't doubt it for a second. The whole town smelled like the inside of a rich chocolate truffle. I wanted to ask Dani how she and her mother were holding up, but I decided this was not the time for it. I returned to my own shop, where Sashkatu was on his window ledge warming his old bones in the morning sunlight, and I got back to cleaning every nook, jar, and cranny. He watched me work with the contented sigh of the elderly who have earned the right to rest.

Once I was satisfied with how the shop looked, I went down the hall and through the connecting door to Tea and Empathy. Tilly was baking and setting the tea tables with fine china and shining silver flat wear. Merlin was planted on his high stool at the entrance to the kitchen, watching the oven timer tick down. When he turned to me, I stopped dead in my tracks. The wizard had undergone a metamorphosis. Somehow my aunt had sweet-talked or badgered him into letting her trim his beard and hair. He could have graced the cover of *Sorcerer's Quarterly*, had such a magazine existed. He was wearing a white shirt and beige pants that were exact replicas of the much coarser shirt and burlap pants in which he'd traveled across the centuries. But the new garments were clean and made from finer fabrics. There was only one person in New Camel who could have created such well-tailored clothes—Evelyn, muumuu maker extraordinaire.

"You look so handsome," I said, "I almost didn't recognize you."

Merlin rubbed his palm across his manicured beard. "I don't know what all the fuss is about. I was perfectly fine before Matillda dressed me up like some dandy. I've never cared much about appearances—just ask Arthur or Lancelot."

The timer rang before I could point out the impossibility of his suggestion. Tilly came around the wall that divided the rest of the shop from the kitchen. She stopped when she saw me. "Kailyn—I thought I heard voices back here." I kissed her slightly damp cheek and whispered in her ear that she'd done wonders with the wizard.

"I finally had a meltdown about untangling his beard and mending his rags. Don't even ask how much Evelyn took me for, the old miser. I should have learned to sew when my grandma Gwyneth wanted to teach me.

When you're young, you ignore opportunities, because you think they'll always be available."

"Tilly, my dear," Merlin said sweetly, "shouldn't you be removing the scones from the oven before they burn?"

"I'm going, I'm going," she muttered. "He's like a timer with a nagging function." Through my aunt's windows, I saw people walking on the sidewalks in small groups. The tour bus must have arrived early. I said *goodbye* and hurried back to my shop. The general consensus among the shopkeepers was that when day-trippers came early, we opened early. It was just good business sense to cater to the tourists in every way we could. I wanted to call Liam and Brock, but it would have to wait until after the bus left.

The passengers on the tour were older women, from fifty all the way up to one woman who was approaching the hundred-year mark, and she made sure everyone knew it. She had her routine down pat. "I'm Teresa and I'll be one hundred years young come August the twelfth," she announced as soon as she cleared the threshold. "My family is making me a big party to celebrate. It's going to be spectacular." Her mind was still sharp for her age, but her body required the help of a wheelchair. "This is Debra," she added, introducing me to the stocky middle-aged woman who was ferrying her around. "She was afraid to come in here. She's a marvelous companion, but scared of her shadow."

"Now I've told you, Teresa," Debra said, "I'm not scared, I'm just cautious. Better safe than sorry, you know."

Teresa laughed. "If someone says *boo*, she'll be out the door lickety-split." Debra shook her head and smiled. "She can be a trial, this one."

"Enough talking, let's go for a spin around this place. Maybe we'll find some eye of newt to make you brave."

"Or bat wings to mellow your sharp tongue," Debra replied, steering her down the first aisle. There were two people waiting at the counter to pay, so I hurried over to ring them up. Most of the women had never been to New Camel, but they'd clearly heard about my shop, because they came with lists of specific products in hand.

When the bus pulled out of town at two o'clock, I was tired and hungry. I peeked in at Tilly's and scored a leftover scone with clotted cream and raspberry jam. With only a few hours left of the business day, the only shoppers likely to come in were locals who knew what they wanted and needed little help from me. I decided to try a call to Brock, but as it was ringing, Valerie Duncan beeped in on call-waiting. "I hope I'm not getting you at a bad time," she said, her voice thin and fragile.

"Not at all. What can I do for you?"

"You asked us to call if we thought of anything that might help you with the investigation into..." Her voice trailed off, the words still too difficult to say.

"Yes," I said quickly, so she didn't have to finish the sentence. "Sometimes the smallest clue can break a case wide open. I'm glad you called. You'll always find a ready ear with us."

"Thank you," she said, sounding a little more confident. "A few months after Ava started her new job, I remember her telling me she was worried about its longevity."

"Did she say why?"

"She thought the company was flirting with insolvency. When she broached her concerns to the head of accounting, he told her not to worry about it. They expected a large infusion of capital in a matter of days. She should just ask the creditors to be patient with them for a bit longer. She could blame the holdup on the government if she had to."

"Did Ava ever tell you if the problem was resolved?"

"No, but she never said she was worried about her job after that, so I assumed it had worked out." I thanked Valerie and assured her she could call anytime. I clicked off the call, but I couldn't get Monroe Enterprises off my mind. First there was Travis's difficulty in finding a listing for the company, and now this new financial wrinkle, and the fact that the government was involved.

Chapter 19

Calling Brock Davenport, Ava's erstwhile boyfriend, was on my to-do list for that evening, but the cats came first. After they ate, we played a lively game of chase the laser dot. As I'd come to expect, Sashkatu abstained. Lying along the top of the couch, he regarded the other cats with regal contempt and an expression that said, *You're making utter fools of yourselves chasing that ridiculous red dot around.* They didn't seem to take Sashki's disdain to heart. They played on enthusiastically for another twenty minutes, at which point they went off in search of their favorite places to snooze.

I joined Sashki on the couch and dialed Brock's number. By the fourth ring, I was thinking of the message to leave on his voice mail. But he picked up at the last moment, making me switch gears and stumble over my words. "Mr. Br... Mr. Davenport," I said, "I'm... my name is Kailyn Wilde. I'm a private investigator looking into Ava Duncan's death."

"Yeah, you and the rest of the known world." Brock was not a happy camper. I wondered who, aside from Duggan, had contacted him. "I'll give you the same big scoop I gave them—I didn't do it. Now leave me the hell alone!" He hung up with the thud of an old-fashioned receiver being slammed down. Apparently, there was an app for that.

I had one more call to make. Liam answered the phone with a cheery uptick to his voice. "Kailyn—are you calling to let me know you've found the killer?" There were times when Caller ID was a benefit and times when I wished it had never been invented. It gave the person on the other end a chance, albeit a brief one, to ready themselves for the coming conversation.

"Unfortunately not yet. I just need to check on some information. What's the name of the company Ava worked for?"

"Monroe Enterprises," he said without hesitation.

"Do you know if that's the full name?"

"Far as I know. That's how Ava always referred to it. You can check with my folks."

"They're the ones who gave me the name. Did your sister ever show you where she worked?" It was a long shot, but worth asking.

"No, I never got around to visiting her in Watkins Glen," he said with a sigh. "I kept meaning to make the trip. You know how it is—work or something always got in the way. I had no way of knowing—" He cut himself off. "It's a regret I'll carry for the rest of my life."

"We're all haunted by regrets like that." It was all I could think to say. I was about to thank him and say *goodbye,* when he threw out a question that caught me off guard. "Are you seeing that guy Travis or do you just work together?"

"Both." I wondered where he was headed.

"You could do better, you know, professionally as well as personally."

I started to laugh, but I caught myself in time to mask it as a hiccup. "Thanks for the advice." I tried to keep the sarcasm in my mind from seeping into my tone. It must have worked, because Liam continued without the slightest hesitation.

"One day you'll realize I'm right. When that happens, I'll be here. *I* know how to treat a woman." He said the last phrase in a deep register that was clearly not natural, because his voice broke halfway through it. The result was not sexy or masterful as he'd no doubt intended. Rather, it made him sound like an adolescent going through the changes from boy to man. I told him I'd keep his offer in mind and wished him a good night, before I could say something that made me *persona non grata.* At our meeting at the pizza place, he'd joked that he didn't know what irritated a woman or he might have one in his life. It was clear he still had no clue.

Although the call hadn't helped clarify the name of Ava's firm or why it was so difficult to locate, Liam had given me an idea about how to wangle an interview with Brock Davenport. It wasn't foolproof, but it might get me in his door. The only problem was Travis. If I ran the plan past him, he might veto it because it required that I pay Ava's ex a visit by myself. If I didn't tell him about it, he'd be angry I'd gone behind his back. I got it—that's how I'd feel under the same circumstances. I spent a good chunk of the night weighing my two lousy options. A third option, forgetting about Brock altogether, was a non-starter. At this point in the investigation, he was a lead suspect. Giving up on him because he didn't invite me over for tea and cookies was ridiculous. If anything, his refusal to be interviewed was a reason to go after him at any cost. In the end, I decided to tell Travis about my plan, leaving out provocative words like *at any cost.*

* * * *

When the doorbell rang at nine-twenty that night, the five younger cats ran for their hidey holes. Only my stalwart Sashki remained with me to face whatever awaited us on the other side of the door. Although I'd recently recast the wards that protected the house and grounds, I wasn't as certain of their strength as I had once been. Six months earlier, I'd learned the hard way that where there was a murderous will, there was a devious way around the wards. I peered through the peep hole and was met by another eye peering back.

"Who is it?" I demanded, not to be messed with. No easy prey in this house.

"Don't you recognize my eye?" came the injured retort. I unlocked the door and threw it open. Travis caught me in his arms and held me in a hug I could have lived in for the rest of my life.

"Hold my place," he said, extricating himself from my embrace and heading for the powder room down the hall. I ducked into the kitchen to put the kettle up to boil. He found me there, watching the kettle in spite of the old saying. "What happened to holding my place?" he asked, coming up behind me at the stove and putting his arms around my waist.

I turned in the circle of his arms so that I faced him. "I hold your place whenever we're apart."

I finished brewing Tilly's comfort tea and filled two cups that we carried to the table. She'd infused the tea with an extra spell meant to mollify the drinker. She was trying to help me stack the deck in my favor when I told Travis my plan. Although I hadn't expected him for another day or two, she'd insisted on giving me the tea leaves before we closed our shops for the night. I should have realized then that she might have had a premonition he'd be dropping by ahead of schedule. I don't always put two and two together in time to do me any good. Tilly would never have told me outright—she was a big fan of happy surprises.

Travis hadn't eaten since breakfast, so I made him two sandwiches of peanut butter and apricot jam on multigrain bread.

"It's hard to go wrong with the old PB&J." he said, wolfing them down.

While he ate, I told him about my phone calls to Liam and Brock Davenport as a lead-in to my strategy for getting an interview with the would-be actor. He listened without interrupting, but the furrow between his brows was deepening as I spoke.

"I don't like it," he said, after washing his last bite down with the tea. "You're going to talk him up, flatter him, tell him you can't imagine why Ava broke up with him—basically convince the guy that any sane woman, including you, would invite his attentions. If the FBI used such a ploy, the civil liberties folks would be yelling *entrapment*. It's a dangerous road to travel."

I hadn't expected such flat-out disapproval. He wasn't usually that rigid. "I understand your concerns," I said. It was hard to keep my tone calm when my hackles were rising. If he tried to use a similar tactic to get an interview with a suspect, he'd be astonished if *I* objected. The old double standard was alive and well.

"Does that mean you're going ahead with it regardless of my input?" *Drink the tea, Travis! Please drink the tea!*

I picked up my cup, hoping to coax him into doing the same. "You're over-thinking the risks." It worked, but only for a few seconds.

He set his cup down hard enough for some of the tea to slosh onto the table. "No, I don't think you understand the risks. Davenport may have killed Ava."

"If he wasn't a potential killer, I wouldn't have any reason to question him," I pointed out. "But it wouldn't be a bad idea to check out his past, see if he has a record. Can you ask one of your police contacts?"

Travis didn't immediately respond. He shifted his position in the chair and finished his tea, before finally looking up at me with a sheepish smile.

"I already checked his background, right after we talked to the Duncans." I wanted to know why he didn't tell me at the time, but that subject would have to wait its turn.

"And the answer is...?"

"He has no criminal record, but he does have two orders of protection against him, filed by former girlfriends."

"Was he ever charged with breaking those orders?"

"No, but that could change in a hot-tempered heartbeat. Order of protection or not, Ava might have been his final straw."

"Why am I just hearing about this now?" I didn't like being managed or treated like a second-class investigator, because he worried about me. Some women might find it sweet and protective. I wasn't one of them. Travis and I had banged heads about this more than once, and he wasn't a slow learner.

"You're not going to believe that it slipped my mind, huh?" I shook my head. "Then the truth it is, when I found out about the orders of protection, I knew you'd rush right over to question Brock. And I still have this need to protect you. There was an article I read that claimed protecting loved ones is built into the male psyche—primitive genetics we still haul around."

"I don't doubt it. But I'm pretty sure your big, brawny, evolved brain can override those ape-man instincts if you try hard enough."

"Why not think of men as the weaker sex? I need reassurance that you won't take chances that can get you killed."

"I'll be careful not to paint Brock into a corner." I said.

"Not good enough."

"Then what will ease your mind?"

Travis drummed his fingers on the table. "Wear a wire," he said as if he'd just thought of it. "Wear a wire so I can monitor the situation from my car."

I laughed, more from surprise than amusement. "You can't be serious. In every cop show I've ever seen, the person wearing the wire is found out and killed."

"That's TV. Besides, if you're going to pose as a freelance writer to get an interview with Brock, he'd have no reason to be suspicious of you."

"Do you realize you're kind of arguing my side for me?"

"Yeah, I just heard myself. My college debate team would taunt me mercilessly if they were listening." He looked like a sad puppy.

I sighed. "Okay, I'll wear the wire if it will make you feel better. But don't forget my magick is always with me and it's much more effective. If anything goes wrong, I can teleport back home before you can jump out of your car and race to my rescue."

"As long as there are no hiccups in your magick that day." He had a point.

"Touché—magick and a wire it is."

Chapter 20

Two days later, the phone rang at four in the morning, waking me from a deep sleep. I bolted up. Whenever the phone rings in the wee dark hours, my worst fears rush to the front of my mind. Tilly's semi-hysterical voice allowed my heart to subside from my throat. At least she was alive and well enough to be worked up over something. I tried to clear the cobwebs from my brain. "Aunt Tilly, please calm down. I can't understand a word you're saying."

"It's Merlin," she said, panting as if she'd just run a mile. "He's gone. Merlin is gone. He's run away or he's been kidnapped. What shall we do?! What shall we do?! The old fool will get himself killed or wind up in a mental insti…" By the end of the sentence, her voice had risen to a range only heard by dogs.

"I'm going to call 911," I told her, making an effort to keep my own voice steady and reasonable, although my thoughts were in a whirlwind. "Then I'm coming over there. Meanwhile you should get dressed."

"Yes of course, I'll get dressed. That's what one does in such a situation."

Paul answered my call at the local police substation. He sounded a little groggy. I heard the low drone of the TV in the background. It couldn't be easy staying awake through the night shift in a town where the phone rarely rang. Although the murder rate had gone nuts over the past year, other criminal activity had virtually flatlined.

"Kailyn—what's wrong?" My name must have popped up on his computer screen.

"My cousin Merlin is missing. Tilly's afraid he's run away." I left out her concern about kidnapping, because it seemed far-fetched given our financial situation and the fact that Merlin's true identity was a well-kept secret. "I know it has to be forty-eight hours before you act on a missing adult, but Merlin suffers from dementia." I hated to say that about him, but it was somewhat true and it would allow the police to act immediately. "I'll put out an APB on him. I'll need a recent photo or a good description. I'll run by to grab those from you. Or should I go to Tilly's?" I heard his chair scrape against the floor as he pushed back from the desk. I told him I'd meet him at Tilly's.

Unfortunately, we didn't have any pictures of Merlin. If and when we managed to return him to his own time, we didn't want to leave any unnecessary evidence of his journey to the twenty-first century. A description would have to do.

I threw on the clothes I'd taken off a few short hours ago, tried not to wake the cats, who might decide they were hungry, and quietly let myself out. I reached Tilly's house as Paul's cruiser pulled up to the curb. Tilly had left the front door unlocked for us. We found her in the kitchen whipping up a batch of brownies. Some people take drugs to relieve anxiety, my aunt baked. She was dressed in a lavender muumuu and gray sneakers with turquoise accents, but she hadn't combed her hair. Her red curls stuck out from her head as if she'd taken the blender to it. When she turned to me, I could see in her eyes just how distraught she was. I put my arm around her shoulders. "It's going to be okay." I don't like making promises that aren't mine to keep, but we *had* to find Merlin. Failure was simply not an option.

I described Merlin for Paul as best I could: elderly, long white hair and beard, blue eyes, medium height. "Don't forget about his dessert belly," Tilly interjected.

Paul stopped writing and looked up at us. "You mean a beer belly?"

"No, a dessert belly from eating too much candy, cake and ice cream," she explained.

"My aunt can be a bit of an enabler," I added.

Paul was caught between smiling and trying to remain serious—an expression that might have drawn the attention of Leonardo da Vinci, had he been here. "Does Merlin have any friends or favorite places he might have run off to?" Paul asked once he got his lips under control.

"He doesn't have any friends here. And his favorite places aren't open at this hour," I said, thinking of The Soda Jerk, the Caboose, and every pizza shop in the county.

"Was he upset about anything? Did he have an argument with anyone?"

"Not that I'm aware of…" I looked at my aunt, who was stirring the brownie batter for all she was worth. I knew the sign. "Aunt Tilly—what happened?"

She put down her mixing spoon and turned to us with a soulful sigh. "We had a little spat last evening about the TV. He wanted to watch that infernal western channel again and I told him it wasn't going to happen. He took himself off to bed in a huff. You know how unreasonable he can be, Kailyn." I nodded, but I knew that she could be as stubborn as he was unreasonable. The combination didn't make for easy compromises.

"One last thing," Paul said, looking over the description we'd given him, "do you know what he was wearing?"

"I can tell you in second," Tilly said taking off for Merlin's room. Paul and I followed. She did a quick check of the closet. "He's still in his nightshirt," she said, "and barefoot."

"Nightshirt?" Paul repeated. "You mean like from the eighteen hundreds?"

More like from the Middle Ages, but who was counting? "Yes, he has some peculiar habits."

"Okay, I'm heading out," he said. "If Merlin is barefoot he won't have gotten too far. Try not to worry. I'm sure we'll have him home in no time."

"Unless he gets it into his thick head to use magick to elude the police," my aunt mumbled after we heard the front door close.

"Will you be okay alone here if I drive around and look for Merlin?" If the choice was between sitting at home and waiting or joining the search, I'd join the search every time.

"Yes, of course. No one is likely to kidnap me with my arthritis and bunions. And I feel more hopeful now that the police are out looking for Merlin."

It occurred to me that I should put a sign on the door of my shop to let folks know I'd be closed until a family emergency was resolved. I asked my aunt if she had readings and teas scheduled, but she didn't. One less thing to worry about.

I spent an hour driving in circles looking for the wizard. By the time I got back home, the cats were milling around the kitchen. Sashkatu was waiting for me in the foyer, cleaning his paws. He glanced at his siblings and back at me with an expression that said, *the riff raff are getting testy.*

I fed the whole crew and gave Sashki his breakfast in the solitude of the powder room as he preferred. I wrote out the sign for my shop, but when Sashki followed me to the front door, I tried to explain that I wasn't actually going to work and after a minute or so, he seemed to get the gist of it.

"You can come with me to Tilly's" I offered, "but I know you and Isenbale don't get along." The big Maine Coon was a bit of a bully and set in his ways. He'd never had to share his home with another animal.

Sashki didn't waste any time deciding if he wanted to go to Tilly's. He climbed up to the top of the couch and settled in for a nap. The message was as clear as if he'd spoken the words—*spare me.*

After taping the note to the door of my shop, I drove back to Tilly's. We were sitting at the kitchen table with cups of comfort tea and brownies— the breakfast of champions. Considering the tiny size of New Camel, I'd expected the police to have corralled the old wizard by now. Doubts were beginning to crowd out my certainty that he couldn't possibly have been wizard-napped. I kept my dire thoughts to myself. Nothing would be helped by another round of Tilly hysteria. When my cell phone rang, both of us flew off our chairs as if they'd had heavy duty springs installed.

"Turn on the TV," Travis said without preamble. "My network." Tilly and I hurried into the family room, I turned on the TV and we dropped onto the couch as the set flashed on. The words *Breaking News* covered the screen, but quickly dissolved to a newscaster behind a desk. "The town of New Camel, New York seems to have a pied piper to rival the legendary one from Hamelin. Hugh McNamarra is on the scene—Hugh."

"Thanks, Phil," the reporter said. "We're here to find out about this rather strange procession marching through our town. Take a look." The camera shifted away from the reporter to a shot of the street, and there was Merlin front and center in a nightshirt that stopped short of his knobby knees. He was walking barefoot along a residential street with an entourage of cats at his heels. There must have been three dozen of them, with more joining by the second. They were fanned out behind him like a bizarre bridal train.

"For those of you who don't recognize this location, we are just one block away from the entrance to the Interstate. It's imperative that this elderly man and the cats following him be stopped as soon as possible. We just got a report that the police are setting up a blockade at the entrance ramp. One patrolman is here monitoring the scene. The camera moved away from the reporter to show the police car parked across the street a block behind the procession. My cell beeped with a text. It was Paul Curtis, telling me he'd found Merlin. He appeared to be fine, but I should come down to help deal with the situation ASAP.

Tilly scooted to the edge of her seat, squinting at the picture. "Kailyn— his eyes are closed."

I shifted my focus from the phone to Merlin. "He must be sleepwalking. Has he ever done that before?"

"Not that I'm aware of." I knew what that meant. When Tilly slept, she *slept!* Merlin could have sleepwalked every night since he'd moved in with her and she wouldn't necessarily have known it.

The reporter was giving a play by play of the event. Since there wasn't much happening, he was quickly reduced to hyping the potential dangers that lay ahead and describing the cats in the procession. "The Ragdoll toward the end looks like Mrs. Freely's Reggie, and if I'm not mistaken, the two Siamese belong to the Banks family. Now here's the odd thing—I know for certain that many of the cats you see here are indoor cats. Their owners must be scratching their heads, wondering how their pets got out and why they're following the old man at the head of this odd parade."

I had to get down there quickly, which meant teleporting. Tilly was all for it and promised the brownies would be waiting when I returned. I had one thing to do before beginning the process. Since I didn't dare appear out of thin air in front of all the people there and the even larger viewing audience, I had to pick a place out of sight to *land*. I studied the area around Merlin's location. He was moving so slowly, he shouldn't be too much farther along when I arrived. I chose the backyard of a Cape Cod, half brick, half slate gray clapboard with white shutters, for my destination. There was always the possibility that someone might be looking out a window and see me materialize, but it was much more likely that all the residents were on their front lawns watching Merlin and the cats.

I quieted my mind and slipped into a meditative state. Drawing energy from the mitochondria in each cell of my body, I recited the spell:

From here and now to there and then
Attract not change, nor harm allow.
Safe passage guarantee to souls
As well as lesser, mindless things.

Quick as the proverbial wink, I found myself in the backyard of the Cape. I looked left and right—I was alone. I made my way around to the front without attracting any attention. As I'd anticipated, everyone was glued to the Merlin spectacle. The reporter I'd seen on TV was across the street with his cameraman. Paul Curtis was a block away, conferring with a man I didn't recognize. Other news vans were arriving and deploying their personnel. Merlin's little stroll was turning into a full-scale media circus.

I walked up to the wizard and called his name. No reaction. His eyes remained closed. *How on earth had he managed not to walk into a car, a building, or even a telephone pole with his eyes closed?* I grabbed his arm and shook it. No reaction. When I let it go, it fell to his side. The reporter was saying that waking a sleepwalker can cause them to be disoriented and have confused, even violent reactions. Terrific, but first I had to figure out how to wake him.

Paul trotted up to me and without pausing, motioned for me to follow him. I didn't have any tricks up my sleeve, at least none that I could use in public, so I kept pace with him. He stopped about fifty yards ahead of Merlin and planted himself in the street directly in the sorcerer's path. I positioned myself next to him. As the wizard approached us, Paul held up his hands and yelled for him to stop. I did likewise. No reaction. He was apparently sleepwalking *and* deaf. *Had he drunk an expired potion? Eaten a toxic berry? There was so much abloom in spring and his knowledge of North American plant species was limited.*

He was nearly upon us, but I held my ground beside Paul, wondering what he planned to do next. He pulled a Taser out of its holder on his belt. "It's low voltage," he assured me. But before I could voice my concern, he shot it at Merlin. The wizard and his entire procession quivered like a single organism, but didn't falter in their stride.

Paul stowed the weapon, seconds before we collided with Merlin and company. I could tell by the hard line of Paul's jaw that he intended to stand his ground, even if that meant being trampled by one old man and a horde of cats. He widened his stance; I did the same. The wizard would have to go through the two of us if he didn't stop. I'd begun to think that maybe he *could* see where he was going through some third eye magick. At least that would explain why he wasn't bumping into things.

Sirens wailed, heralding the arrival of an ambulance. If anyone needed medical attention at this point, it was probably the reporter who'd been keeping pace with us. He was in danger of hyperventilating with excitement about the coming slow-mo collision.

Merlin's leading foot came down on my instep, knocking us both off balance. I recovered, but he fell forward, stumbling over Paul's feet, banging knees with him, and teetering back and forth before going down. I winced when he hit the pavement butt first, but the impact finally woke him. The cats, no longer in his thrall, appeared disoriented as if they'd just awakened from a long nap. Their owners rushed onto the street to scoop them up and take them home.

The ambulance rolled up to us and two paramedics hopped out to offer assistance. I had a whole new problem on my plate. If they talked to Merlin for more than a minute, they'd come to the conclusion that he was deranged. From what I could tell, he wasn't badly injured. He didn't hit his head and since he was already on his feet, he probably didn't have any broken bones. Tilly's cooking had padded them well. He didn't need to go the emergency room. As for the few bumps and bruises, we could heal them better than the doctors could.

The paramedics were insistent about taking the wizard's blood pressure, in spite of my repeated efforts to intervene. One of them was trying to hold him still while the other wrapped the pressure cuff around his arm. Merlin was flailing at both of them. They looked like they were performing a Marx Brothers routine with hands flying everywhere. And things were about to go from bad to worse. I saw the look in Merlin's eyes—he'd had enough and was about to resort to magick. I couldn't let him turn the EMTs into toads. For one thing, they were only trying to help him. And for another, there were way too many people watching, including a worldwide audience.

"Stop," I shouted over their voices. That got their attention. "This man is my cousin. He suffers from dementia. I handle things for him and I'm taking him home right now."

"Do you have his proxy or a power of attorney?" asked the EMT holding the pressure cuff.

"Well no, not with me." Or at all for that matter. But this scenario had to end with Merlin, Tilly, and me eating brownies in her kitchen. I turned to Paul, who was clearly deep in his own dilemma. He should be supporting the paramedics, but I hoped his heart was siding with me.

"Officer Curtis," I said. "Would you please vouch for me? For us?" Paul was a quick study and clearly still had the hots for me. If he could have ridden to my rescue on a white horse, he would have. I felt terrible about using him this way, but I was out of options.

"Listen John, Eddie," he said in a good-ol'-boy undertone. "I know this family. I've seen the paperwork—it's on the up and up. If they want to refuse treatment, I've got their back. Really appreciate the help." He'd told a flat-out lie for me. I couldn't let it ever come back to bite him.

The taller of the two men shrugged. "You say so, Curtis." He turned to me, "Miss, if you change your mind later—"

I cut him short as graciously as I could. "I know, thank you both." Merlin hadn't stopped glaring at them. If I didn't get him out of there in the next few seconds, he was going to give them a parting gift they would never forget. With the help of the viewing audience and the reach of social media it was guaranteed to go viral. There'd be no place on Earth we could hide.

Chapter 21

I was helping a local customer when Shannon Bell walked into my shop. She had very white skin and very red hair. Her eyes were the same golden brown as the spray of freckles across her nose. I was sure I'd seen her somewhere before, but I couldn't immediately place her. I said I'd be with her shortly. She seemed happy enough to explore on her own. After my other customer left, I found her in one of the aisles looking at a jar of fade cream. I asked if I could help her with anything.

"I was just browsing until this caught my eye," she said. "Does it really work? The ones I've tried, promised a lot, but didn't deliver."

"I can tell you all of my customers come back for more. I know it's none of my business, so please forgive me, but I hope you're not trying to fade those wonderful freckles." A flush rose in her cheeks.

She laughed. "As you can see, I also need something to keep me from blushing so easily." I walked toward the end of the aisle and plucked a bottle off the top shelf.

"This is a blend of passionflower, valerian and other botanicals that should do the trick." *Along with a bit of magick.* "I'll be happy to refund your money on both products if you're not happy with the results."

She grinned like a kid who's just discovered ice cream. "How can I go wrong?"

"May I ask what brought you to my shop?" I liked to know if new customers came because of a recommendation or because they were driving through New Camel and were intrigued by Abracadabra's façade straight out of the Middle Ages.

"I actually came to talk to you," she said as I went behind the counter to ring up the sale.

"Well you've got my attention. What about?"

"Ava Duncan. She and I are—*were* best friends since the first day of kindergarten." The scene at the wake flashed into my mind. She was the redhead in the first pew. I nearly pinched myself to make sure I wasn't dreaming.

"How did you hear about me?"

"Since Ava died, I've been calling the Duncans to check on how they're doing. Valerie was like a second mother to me. During our last conversation, I asked how the investigation was going. She said the detective on the case treats them like an annoyance and it's hard to get any information from him. She's really grateful that you and your friend are on the case too, because you're a whole lot more compassionate than the detective. Valerie gave me your number in case I thought of something that might help. I didn't call you, because I wanted to meet you in person before I shared any part of my dear Ava's life." Her eyes glistened with tears, but she squared her shoulders and blinked them away. "Can we schedule a time I can come back to talk to you?"

"Do you still live in the Buffalo area?"

"Yes, but it's no problem for me to drive down here again whenever it's convenient for you. I'd do anything to help find Ava's killer." I glanced at my watch. It was eleven. Not that it mattered. I'd already made my decision.

"Why don't we talk now if that works for you?"

"But what about your business?"

"I'll take an early lunch hour. One of the perks of being your own boss." I put the clock in the window indicating I'd reopen at twelve thirty. Since Tilly was out having her hair cut and colored, followed by lunch with friends, Tea and Empathy seemed like a better venue for our conversation than my shop.

I ushered Shannon into the tearoom and settled her at one of the little tables while I put up water for tea—my aunt's calming blend.

"This smells wonderful," Shannon said as I filled our cups.

I set the pot on the table and offered her lemon, cream and a variety of sweeteners. We both chose lemon.

After a few sips, Shannon seemed to relax. The tightness in her voice faded. Her words flowed more easily. "Do you have questions you want to ask me?"

"I wouldn't know where to begin," I said. "You must have certain things in mind that prompted you to drive down here."

She nodded. "I'm finding this harder than I expected." Her lips tipped up in a wobbly smile that flickered for a moment and then died. "I think you need to have all the information possible, but I can't help feeling a little like I'm betraying Ava and her family." The tears she'd banished earlier spilled over her lower lashes.

I grabbed the box of tissues Tilly kept on her counter for times when her readings aroused strong emotions. Shannon took one and dabbed at her wet cheeks. "Liam has had challenges in his life," she said, "which means every member of his family has had to deal with them too."

I wanted to let her tell the story at her own pace and without interruption, but a question found its way past my best intentions. "What kind of challenges?"

"Addictive behavior. It started in junior high with drinking. The Duncans put him in therapy. He'd do well for a time and then relapse. I felt awful for Val and Teddy—such good people. It wore them down. As a last resort, they'd sent him away to one of those military schools. Whatever they did with him there seemed to work, or maybe he just learned how to hide the problem as he got older. He graduated and even managed to make it through college with a few detours from time to time. Ava was always his champion. Whenever things went south for him, she was there. And he adored her for it."

"He's been in recovery since then?"

She shook her head and paused to drink her tea. "He traded alcoholism for gambling, thanks to some of his college buddies. At least that was how his parents looked at it. They kept bailing him out of debt. They're not wealthy people, but they inherited a substantial sum of money when Valerie's aunt passed on about five years ago. They put the bulk of the money away as a legacy for Ava and Liam. When the gambling got out of hand, they threatened to write Liam out of their will, unless he joined a program. The fear of losing out on the money finally motivated him to find help."

I put down my empty cup. "I imagine that didn't last." Addiction was a slippery devil.

"He was okay for a little while. We all held our breath, hoping it would last. Three months ago, he showed up on Ava's doorstep, desperate for the money to pay off another gambling debt. But she simply didn't have the cash. She called me after he left that night. She was afraid for his safety. He'd gotten involved with some bad people—people who would just as soon shoot you as talk to you."

"Did Liam find the money he needed?" I blurted out.

"Yes. Somehow he always managed to get what he needed—no doubt another low-life to pay off the first one."

"Did he go back for help?"

Shannon sighed. "What do you think?"

"Do you know if Ava ever told their parents he was still gambling?"

"The last time we spoke she was struggling with the decision. She knew that telling her parents would break their hearts."

"Do you think it's possible that Liam killed her to keep her from telling them?"

She shook her head. "Their relationship was the one good thing in his life. I just thought you should have a complete picture of Ava's family. The Duncans are reluctant to speak about Liam's problems. They think they're somehow responsible for his failures." She finished the last of her tea. "Is it okay if I help myself to a refill? This tea is awesome."

"Enjoy. I can always brew more." Shannon refilled her cup, adding a spoonful of honey this time. "There's something else I want to ask you, but if I'm getting too nosey, don't be afraid to tell me so."

Shannon laughed softly. "I imagine private investigators have to be nosey to do their jobs. Besides, now I'm curious about this question of yours."

"Were you aware Ava was having an affair with a married man?"

Shannon nodded. "Ava was terribly conflicted about it. She was a good person who would never choose to hurt another soul. When she started seeing Elliot, he swore to her that he was divorced. She fell hard for him and she was devastated to learn he was married. She was determined to break it off, but he just wouldn't leave her alone." I had trouble feeling any sympathy for Ava. Shannon must have seen it in my eyes. "You know his wife, don't you?" she said.

"Yes, I know Dani, and their children, and her mother." It was hard to keep the bitterness out of my tone. Neither of us spoke. I'd put her in a difficult position. Her loyalty was with her best friend who wasn't around to defend herself. I would probably have felt the same way if I were in her shoes. I had to remind myself that Shannon wasn't responsible for Ava's behavior. As Morgana liked to say, *don't shoot the messenger.* I liked Shannon and I was grateful for her help and candor. Before the silence became unbreakable, I had to set things right between us. "Let's close the door on that aspect of Ava's life," I said. "We're not responsible for anyone's behavior but our own."

She looked relieved. "Done and done."

"I have one last question. Do you know Brock Davenport?"

"Sure, he was Ava's boyfriend before Elliot wooed and won her."

"Do you think Brock loved her?"

"So he said, over and over again. And maybe he did. The thing with Brock is the drama—everything is overblown. I suppose that's the actor in him. Sorry if I sound cynical. I was glad when she broke it off with him. Until she told me he was stalking her. He claimed he just wanted to protect her, because he knew how dangerous men can be." Her words set off chills in my spine. "I was scared for her, so I did some homework and found out that there were two orders of protection against him from two other women he'd dated."

"Did he ever hurt them?"

"I don't think so. He was never arrested or charged with disobeying the orders."

I brewed more tea and we talked for a while longer about more mundane subjects. I thanked her for coming to tell me about Liam. She thanked me for trying to find justice for her best friend.

When she left, I called Travis to give him a play by play of her visit.

"It's crazy what you find when you scratch the surface of an ordinary family," he said. "Liam clearly had a motive to kill his sister."

"I know, but Shannon said he and Ava were very close."

"I've found you can't put too much stock in the opinions of friends or even family members. The closer they are to the situation, the more their perspective is tainted by emotion. But I have a contact up in Buffalo who might be able to help us out."

"Why am I not surprised?"

"I met the guy when I was doing a piece on biometric hand scanners. His company makes them and services them. They're in most of the big firms now. If Liam's place has one, my guy could find out if he was at work the day his sister died."

Chapter 22

On Tilly's first free day, I asked her to fill in for me at Abracadabra so that Travis and I could put our plan in motion. She was tickled to be part of it, if only vicariously. I'd called Brock Davenport a second time, using a phony name, and a phonier southern accent. He'd sounded suspicious at first, possibly because another recent call requesting an interview was still fresh in his mind. But once I explained that I was a freelance writer doing a piece on local theater and the actors who keep it alive, his qualms seemed to fall away. Publicity was a powerful lure, especially to a man who believed he was meant for stardom, but hadn't yet found the means by which to climb that slippery ladder.

The interview meant another trip up to Buffalo for Travis and me. We were glad Ava was murdered in May and not February, although I don't think she would have been happy with either choice. We hoped to make the roundtrip in one day. Travis's schedule was hectic and I didn't want to impose on my aunt more than necessary. It was certainly a doable, if not tiring, drive. And if it led to catching a killer, the hours in the car were a small price to pay.

Travis was at my house eight sharp in the morning to wire me up. We couldn't do it in Buffalo, since there were not likely to be any coed restrooms. A friend with the Watkins Glen police force had shown Travis how to use the equipment, but there seemed to be a bit of a learning curve to it, exacerbated by his determination to leave no room for error. If it malfunctioned, my life would be in jeopardy. He refused to add my magick to the equation, because it wasn't a hundred percent reliable.

He attached the microphone, then went outside to see if he could hear me. He thought there was too much static, so he tried a different transmitter. When he couldn't get the volume high enough, he switched out the microphone, but the new one wouldn't stay put. I zipped my lips, but my patience was wearing thin by the time he was satisfied.

I'm a squirmer on long car trips, a trait Travis became aware of early on in our eleven-month relationship. I'm constantly changing position, crossing and uncrossing my legs, sitting with my legs tucked under me, but when I wriggled and stretched to grab my purse from behind his seat, he begged me to sit still or I'd dislodge the microphone. The trip felt twice as long in statue mode. At least I wouldn't be wired up on the way home.

I was wearing what Elise and I agreed was professional freelance writer chic—a skirt and blouse with heels, suit jacket optional. Elise insisted I borrow her slim-line, leather briefcase that could double as a purse.

My appointment with Brock was at noon. Travis found the apartment building and drove past it without stopping. He pulled over a block away to let me out of the car. After I walked back and went in, the plan was for him to circle around and park at the curb in front of the building. If there was no place to park, he'd double park as if he was waiting for someone to come down. If a cop came along and told him to move, he'd explain that he was there to take his hundred-year-old grandmother to her surprise birthday party. If that didn't touch the cop's heart, he didn't have one, and Travis would be out of options. I, however, still had magick.

I pressed the bell for Brock's apartment and he buzzed me in without asking who I was. I took the elevator up to the seventh floor. He opened his door when I was walking down the hall.

"Joyce," he said giving me the once over with a grin that would have done Little Red's wolf proud. "Come on in." He definitely had a movie star vibe about him—tall, dark and handsome. But something was missing. His features were so regular that he looked photo-shopped. I wasn't surprised that he'd never been discovered. His likeness had been discovered a thousand times over.

I smiled back as he ushered me inside. "I really appreciate the opportunity to speak to you," I said in my best Southern accent. "Y'all are just perfect for my article."

"And I look forward to telling you about the acting life in the boondocks." He led me into the living room. The apartment bore the mark of a talented designer. It radiated masculinity, but with strategic accents of the romantic. Brock must have gone into a hole to pay for it. He probably subscribed to the theory that if you lived like you were successful, the universe would respond in kind. There were plenty of self-help gurus and books to support the claim.

He motioned to a grouping of tan leather armchairs separated by a cherry wood end table. "Will this do or would you prefer to sit in the kitchen or dining room?"

"This is perfect," I said, taking the chair on the right.

"Can I get you coffee, tea, maybe a cold drink?" The host with the most.

"I'm good, thanks." I opened the briefcase and took out a legal pad for notes and Travis's tape recorder. "Is it okay if I tape the interview? I don't want to forget anything." Of course, the wire I was wearing was also taping it, but for different reasons.

"Yeah, for sure." We spent the first twenty minutes, beating around the acting bush. He listed the various productions in which he'd appeared, starting with the role of Oliver in the first grade and culminating in his recent audition for a small, but important, role in a Broadway show. He didn't get it, but the director told him it was only a matter of time before his name was on a marquee. Brock wasn't a glass half-full kind of guy. He was a glass spilling over with champagne. I bet there was a bottle of bubbly chilling in his fridge for that first big break.

"Does your troupe have a dedicated location for all its performances?" I asked, the question designed to set up a good segue for me to venture off topic. If done well, he shouldn't realize what was happening.

"We do now. But back when I first joined, we took what we could get. We performed in storefronts, in schools, even above a pharmacy."

"I bet you have stage door groupies," I said with a flirty little smile. "I can imagine the young women crushin' on you." Travis had tried to talk me out of using those lines, saying Brock might get the wrong idea about how I felt. But that was precisely why I'd insisted on keeping them in my plan. I knew that a man like him would eat it up and let down his guard. I watched his reaction. He didn't disappoint. He sat up straighter in the chair, ran his hand over his hair, and gave me that wolfish smile. No humble shoe-scuffing for Brock.

"I've had my share."

"Do any of them stand out in your memory?" I knew instantly that I'd hit a nerve. He struggled to prop up his smile, but after a few tortured moments he let it go.

"One," he said. His whole demeanor changed. His shoulders slumped, his lips compressed into a tight line, and the playful twinkle was gone from his eyes. "She was murdered."

My hand flew to my mouth. "Oh, Brock, I'm so sorry. She must be the girl I read about—Ava Duncan?"

"Ava, yeah—my Ava." He didn't sound like he was acting, but when you're dealing with an actor, can you ever be sure?

"Horrible, just horrible. Do the police have anyone in custody?"

"Not that I know of, but they won't tell me anything." *Could that be because you're considered a person of interest?*

"Do you suspect anyone?" I asked.

"I never liked her brother."

"As in you think he murdered her?"

"Maybe, who knows?" He threw his hands in the air and popped up from the chair as if he couldn't bear to be still for another second. He paced back and forth, back and forth in front of me, staring at the floor. "I keep going over in my head everything I know about Ava—all her friends, coworkers, family. Did she have a secret, darker life I didn't know about? I've been driving myself nuts. I try to push her out of my mind and focus on my career. The acting helps. You have to give it a hundred percent or you're shortchanging the audience and making things harder for the other members of the troupe."

He stopped in front of me. "The son of a—who killed Ava had better hope I never meet up with him, because I'll make sure justice is done—the old-fashioned kind—a life for a life." He spit out the last words and there was a steely glint in his eyes.

"It can't be easy to put that behind you," I sympathized, "especially with the case still open." I realized my mistake as soon as the words left my mouth. Brock's face hardened. His eyes narrowed.

"What happened to that accent of yours? What are you trying to pull here?" He was standing over me, glowering. I tensed, expecting him to grab me and drag me out of the chair. I had a spell of protection around me, but sometimes that only softened the impact, minimized the injury.

I stood up, eye to eye with him, or more correctly, eye to chest with him. "You can't blame a girl for trying," I said sweetly, trying to defuse the situation. I was worried about Travis's reaction to what he was hearing. He might already be pounding his way up the stairs to rescue me and that could turn into something a lot uglier. "I was desperate for an interview with you." I wriggled past him, snatched up the recorder, and headed for the door.

I heard Brock's footsteps behind me. I didn't turn around—that always slows you down. I was only a few feet from the door when his hand clamped down on my arm and he yanked me around to face him.

"I should make you pay for deceiving me. Otherwise how will you learn not to do that again?" His words were strangely calm and measured.

"That wouldn't be smart when you're already a suspect in Ava's death," I pointed out, in case his anger had blotted out everything else.

He laughed. "You're lucky I'm not the kind of guy who likes to hurt girls." He gave my arm another twist before letting go. There was more I wanted to say, but my mother taught me not to outstay my welcome. He reached over me and opened the lock. "Get out of here."

He didn't have to tell me twice. Elevator or stairs? If I had to wait for the elevator, Brock could still come after me—the stairs won. "I'm okay," I said for Travis's benefit. "Coming down the stairs." I sprinted across the first landing and directly into Travis. He held onto me, his heart beating against my ear.

"Do you want to report this to the police?" he asked as we walked down to the lobby.

"What would I say—that he grabbed my arm and held me against my will for twenty seconds before letting me go? Besides, I don't want this incident to color the case when we're not sure he's the killer. For all we know he's all bark and no bite. I had the feeling that if I screamed he would have let me go even faster."

On the long drive back to New Camel, I fleshed out the meeting for Travis by describing his body language, the look in his eyes. "Bottom line," Travis said, "do you think he killed Ava?"

"You mean the old *if I can't have her, no one can* motive? I honestly don't know. On one hand, Brock is too invested in his future to risk spending it in prison. On the other, he's arrogant enough to believe he could get away with murder."

When we were close to New Camel, I called Tilly to let her know she was off cat duty. I'd be back in time to feed my brood. I was in the middle of filling their dishes, when Morgana and Bronwen popped in. The cats always seemed to take their visits from beyond the veil in stride. At that moment, dinner was their priority anyway.

Although I was tired from the trip, I was happy to see my mom and grandmother. They didn't visit as often as they once had. I guess absence does make the heart grow fonder. Their clouds were both frothy white. They bounced gently as if they were surfing on air waves beyond my ken.

"You look good," I said. Over the past eighteen months, I'd become so accustomed to seeing them as energy clouds that it no longer seemed strange to judge their well-being by the color of those clouds.

"We are learning to be mellow and go with the flow," Morgana said in a lilting tone. "That's probably why we look well."

"Of course there isn't the kind of friction here that there is on Earth," Bronwen added. "It's hard to say how well these lessons would translate over there."

"You seem to be adjusting better too."

"Yes," said my mother, "but I miss the simple pleasures of having a body, despite all its ills and never-ending upkeep. I miss food most of all, turkey with homemade cranberry sauce, crisp, salty French fries, ice cream in every form—shakes and floats, cones and sundaes—and plain vanilla with apple pie." She sighed. "The great irony is that without a corporeal body we don't have to worry about putting on the pounds, but without a body, we aren't capable of eating anything." Her voice had become peevish.

"Mellow, Morgana, mellow," my grandmother cooed.

"Telling me to mellow only irritates me, mother." The edges of Morgana's cloud had turned red, the color seeping slowly into the rest of the cloud. I didn't want their visit to end in an argument.

"Mom," I said, "maybe when you're willing to move on from your current level, the cravings will fade away." Their deaths had been so sudden and unexpected, they'd had trouble severing their ties to me and Tilly and all things earthly. It was like they'd moved to a new home, but were stuck in the foyer. Although I didn't want to lose touch with them, moving on might finally bring them peace.

"I didn't come to discuss that," Morgana said briskly and her cloud winked out.

"It's a work in progress, but we'll get there," Bronwen assured me, before she too vanished.

Hearing my mother list her favorite foods made me want them. Since the only one presently in my house was ice cream, I was reaching for the freezer door when my mother reappeared. I shifted my hand to the refrigerator door instead and took out the water. "Forget something?" I asked, casually pouring myself a glassful. It would have been mean to rub her nose in the ice cream she missed.

"As a matter of fact, yes. We forgot to tell you the reason for our visit. We bumped into Ava Duncan. She was very pleased that you're investigating her death." Questions flooded my mind, but not in any sensible order.

"What do you mean you bumped into her?" popped out first. "Were you bopping down the street and your clouds banged shoulders as you passed each other? How did you recognize her if you'd never met her? Did she tell you who killed her?" Finally the important one.

"Whoa, Kailyn," Morgana said with a laugh. "Things over here don't work the way they do on Earth. I used the word *bumped* to give you a sense of what happened in terms you would understand. Although we never knew Ava on Earth, it was clear to us who she was."

"I'm having trouble understanding this." I wanted answers, not metaphors. "Forget my other questions and answer just this one. Did she tell you who killed her?"

"Yes, but no one is permitted to pass such information on to the living. It involves matters that are still playing out and they must unfold without interference."

I didn't like her response, but at least I understood it. "If you can't tell me who the killer is, why even mention it to me?" I heard the testiness in my tone, but I didn't care. It seemed she'd come back for the sole purpose of teasing me.

"I mentioned it, because Ava wants you to know she's delighted you're investigating her death and very grateful for your kindness to her parents."

In less than a minute, she'd roused my anger, and then made me feel bad about it—the mother/daughter tango that seemed to survive even death. "Thank you," I said. "Please let her know we're doing everything in our power to find justice for her." After Morgana left, I was no longer in the mood for ice cream. I made myself a cup of tea and sat on the couch to brood over our relationship. Old and wise, Sashkatu climbed up on the couch to provide solace. He rubbed his velvety head along my jaw and under my chin, before curling up in my lap. He'd served my mother and me as pet and familiar; maybe she and I weren't as different as I'd always believed.

Chapter 23

A four-star restaurant by the name of Seasons opened in early May at the Winterland ski resort outside New Camel. Some folks said the timing was strange, since the ski season had ended two months earlier. Other folks claimed that the new restaurant was meant to distract the public from the Waverly Hotel's grand opening in July. Winterland had always made money during the off season by hosting family reunions and catering parties large and small, including weddings. They didn't want to lose that revenue to the newcomer.

Travis and I had to wait three weeks for a dinner reservation on a Wednesday night. Weekends were booked through the fourth of July. But everyone agreed that the real test of the ski resort's strategy would come when the Waverly opened its brand-new doors.

Having to wait so long to dine at Seasons made it seem like an event worth dressing up for. I wore a red, off-the-shoulder dress for the occasion, and what Tilly called *ridiculously* high heels. She and Merlin had stopped by with a sample of her new butterscotch brownies with dark chocolate chips. With the temperature in the low fifties, she didn't have to convince me to take along a shawl. She added a lovely little spell to make it heat to seventy degrees as soon as I put it on.

Travis arrived at my door in chinos, a lightweight sweater and a sports jacket, clearly dazzling my aunt. She made him do a slow three-sixty so she could appreciate the full effect of his sartorial splendor. "You two are dressed to kill," she said, making us both laugh. It took her a second before she realized what she'd said and cracked up too.

"What's so funny—or have you all lost your minds?!" Merlin groused from his perch on the second step of the stairway, where he was surrounded by five adoring cats. Sashkatu, who was watching the whole to-do from the top step, yawned widely like a grandfather who wishes the young ones would leave so he can go to bed.

Tilly explained the double entendre to the wizard, but he shrugged it off. "It's obvious none of you has ever been properly entertained by a good court jester. Come Matillda, I could do with a little nap before dinner." They sounded like any old married couple, but if the truth ever got out, it would emblazon headlines around the globe.

We walked into the restaurant on time and were asked to give them a few minutes while our table was readied. That gave us a chance to peek into the four rooms, each one decorated for a different season. Although winter was far from my favorite season, the Winter Room dazzled with icicles hanging from the ceiling and pine trees in every corner, their boughs layered with glittering snow. It was like looking inside a snow globe. I could only imagine how it would look decorated for Christmas.

The three other rooms were every bit as lovely, though not quite as stunning as winter. Since requesting a particular room often led to a longer wait for a reservation, Travis and I hadn't expressed a preference. When our table was ready, we were escorted to seats in the Summer Room. A large atrium was at its center, filled with trees and flowers. If we listened, we could hear soft waves lapping on a beach. The owner of the ski resort had outdone himself.

Although there was a single menu for all the rooms, it changed with the actual seasons. If the food was as wonderful as I'd heard, customers were likely to return again and again to partake of all four.

I'd noticed that the tables in all the rooms were far enough apart to allow for quiet conversation. Our table, tucked into a corner of summer, could almost be called secluded. If this was the newest restaurant trend, I was an instant fan.

Everything on the menu sounded delicious and since neither of us had been there before, we asked the waitress for suggestions. She said it was all *awesome,* but diners were raving about the cold berry soup, served with a dollop of sour cream; and both the pork osso bucco and the rainbow trout with mango salsa. We each ordered the soup; Travis went for the pork, while I chose the trout.

We were enjoying the soup, which was like having dessert before dinner, when we heard a woman's voice raised above the soft murmur of the other conversations. "I don't believe it!" The sound was so loud and unexpected that it gave me a start and made other diners turn to see who was so inconsiderate. I also looked up to find the source, but I didn't have to search far. The owner of the voice was headed straight for our table. It took me a moment to place her—the impeccably attired Whitney Reynolds, interior designer for the Waverly Hotel. She'd visited my shop once and bought three hundred dollars' worth of products. Sales like that are memorable. I remembered liking her too. But that one encounter could hardly be the reason for her cry of joyful surprise at seeing me again. Travis solved the mystery by bumping the table in his rush to stand up. He took two steps toward her and opened his arms. After the hug, they exchanged cheek kisses.

"How long has it been?" he said at a volume that was more in keeping with the other voices in the room.

Whitney lowered her voice. "Ten, twelve years at least." She stepped back and gave him an appraising look. "You haven't changed at all—no fair."

"Not true, but talk about time standing still—I'd recognize you anywhere." I was beginning to feel invisible—no spell required.

"Hello, Whitney," I said instead of waiting for Travis to remember I was there.

She turned her smile on me. "Kailyn, right?" I saw her glance down at my hands—looking for a ring perhaps?

"You two know each other?" Travis said, sounding more incredulous than he should have, given that I owned a popular shop in town. Maybe he was still in a state of shock from Whitney's appearance.

"I went into Abracadabra the last time I was up here." She took a few steps closer to me. "I have to tell you—the things I bought at your shop are remarkable. They're much better than the finest products on the market, and I've tried them all. What's your secret?"

"It must be the magick," I said with a laugh. I'd learned that if I joked about magick, no one took it seriously, yet I was being completely honest.

"You're not going to tell me. Well I can't say that I blame you. Did you ever consider marketing your products nationally—hell, globally? You'd rake in millions, become a business tycoon." The very last thing we Wildes ever aspired to be. I'd be hunted and hounded for my powers by governments and criminals alike.

Travis shook his head. "Whitney never did think small." Our waitress appeared to inquire if we'd like another chair brought to our table. It wouldn't be any trouble because it was a four-top. Whitney started to decline, but Travis insisted she join us if she was dining alone. "Right, Kailyn?" he asked, assuming I'd be all for it.

I liked Whitney a lot, but I didn't wait three weeks and buy the red dress so I could share the evening with a third wheel who seemed to share a strong history with my guy. "Of course," I said. Many women would have caught the slight demur in my words, but Whitney didn't seem to be one of them. Or she wanted more time with Travis despite how I felt about it. *Watch your step, Miss Reynolds, magick also has a dark side.* And there were times it was awfully tempting to cross that line.

With our guest settled in her chair and another soup on its way, Travis asked what brought her upstate. After a ten-minute answer, she asked him the same thing. I could have given them a more succinct version of both stories, having heard them before, but I just ate my soup.

At the first pause in their conversation, I asked the question that had been on my tongue since Whitney arrived. "So—how do you know each other?" I was rooting for them to say they were cousins, but I knew in my bones it was a different kind of closeness they'd shared.

"We went to high school together," Travis said, spooning up the last bit of his soup.

"Yeah, that's all it was," she chided him. "The way I remember it, Kailyn, we dated exclusively for the last two years of high school. Everyone thought we'd get married. There was even a pool to pick the date he'd propose." Travis looked like he wanted to crawl under the table.

"What happened?"

Travis jumped on the question. "We went off to different colleges, met new people, did some growing up and by Christmas break of our sophomore year, things were different between us."

"You bet they were." The playfulness was gone from Whitney's tone. "One of those new people you met was sharing your bed. That's what changed between us." *Still happy you insisted she join us, Travis?*

"C'mon," he said. "We were kids. Feelings change." He was trying to put a better spin on it, but I could tell from Whitney's face that there wasn't enough spin in the world to fix how he'd treated her.

"Your feelings may have changed, but mine didn't." Her words were charged with emotion. For a moment, I thought her voice was going to crack. But she remained dry-eyed and in control.

"I didn't know," Travis murmured.

"Let's be honest—you didn't want to know." She sighed, and her mouth turned up in a weak smile. "But that was all a long time ago and skeletons are best kept in their closets. Just kick me if I say another word about the past." She turned to me. "Kailyn, tell me how you two met." I rattled off a quick capsule about Travis's first time in my shop, omitting our contentious dialogue about magick. It was pretty sketchy, but she didn't seem to notice. For the remainder of the meal, we all worked to keep the conversation light, but the undercurrent of emotions buzzed in my head, making it difficult to enjoy the food. Whitney picked at her chicken. Only Travis cleaned his plate. Keeping his mouth full was a good way to keep from stuffing his big foot in it again.

Whitney left before dessert, claiming she had work to finish. We went through the social ritual of *goodbye*—the embrace, the air kiss, along with the declaration that we should get together again, insincere on my part if not on theirs.

"I'm sorry about all that," Travis said once we were alone. He reached across the table for my hand. I placed mine in it. "I hope you realize I'm no longer the clueless kid she was describing."

"You did sound pretty clueless, even heartless." I couldn't resist a little teasing payback for his having ruined the evening. The waitress appeared to ask if we'd like to see the dessert tray. Before I could decline, Travis said, "Absolutely." He squeezed my hand when she went off to fetch it. "We are going to salvage part of this dinner."

I can skip desserts I read about on a menu, but I have a harder time turning down a tray of delectables right there before my eyes. Spring being prime time for strawberries, many of the desserts made use of them. Travis chose the strawberry short cake and I fell hard for a plate of chocolate-covered strawberries and almond biscotti. He regaled me with funny behind-the-scenes stories from the newsroom and between the laughter and the sugar rush, I was able to put Whitney out of my mind.

Chapter 24

"Men compartmentalize much better than women do," Tilly said when I told her the whole sordid tale the next morning. She'd just pulled a tray of blueberry scones out of the oven in her shop and insisted we sit down to taste them. I pointed out that we had only five minutes before opening our doors to customers, so she told me to eat fast or save the rest for later. I sat down next to Merlin, who'd already installed himself at a table as soon as he heard the word *taste*. Pavlov would have loved him.

Tilly handed out scones and napkins and took her seat. "I guarantee you, as soon as Travis dropped you off last night, he shoved any uncomfortable thoughts and feelings about the incident into a closet and slammed the door shut. You, on the other hand, have probably been reliving every moment of that dinner in a never-ending loop."

Wise Tilly was at the top of her game. I plucked a warm blueberry out of my scone and popped it into my mouth with a sigh. "So what do you suggest I do about it?"

"Let it go," Merlin said, spraying bits of scone as he tried to talk around a mouthful of the pastry. "Let it go, let it go, let it go."

"Frozen?" I asked.

"He watched it three times this week," Tilly replied. "But it's not bad advice. Travis is a good man who's crazy about you. Of course I don't know Whitney. You might want to keep an eye on her." I had no idea how to simultaneously "let it go" and yet keep an eye on her, but our five minutes were up. Tilly's first client was knocking on the door.

I wrapped my uneaten scone in a napkin and headed back to Abracadabra. Unfortunately no one was at my door to distract me. Sashki was deep into his first nap of the day. I busied myself by doing inventory in my storeroom and making a list of supplies I needed to reorder. Not my favorite chore. I was more than ready for a break when Travis called. He'd heard back from his contact in Buffalo. According to the biometric hand scanner in Liam's office, he was at work in Buffalo the day his sister was killed, hours away in Watkins Glen.

When lunchtime crawled around, I decided to get outside for some fresh air and pop in on a few more of the shopkeepers to see if they could add anything useful to my knowledge about Ava. The mild spring air was soft against my face. It lifted my spirits with every breath. I passed the shops I'd already visited and went into Fido & Friends, the specialty pet store, Blooming Bags, where every purse was handmade by the Finnegan twins, and the Gatwick Gallery, which focused on artists from the surrounding areas. The first two stops didn't net me any new information. None of the shopkeepers had heard of Ava until after she was murdered. I stayed long enough to be sociable, asking after their families and catching up on small town gossip that was more kind than malicious in spite of Beverly's influence.

I entered the art gallery with half my lunch hour spent. The gallery owner, Tina Gatwick, came out of her backroom when she heard the door open. She was holding half a sandwich, tuna by the smell of it. Like most of New Camel's merchants, she was informal with her clientele. It was no big deal for her to welcome visitors with her lunch in hand. She was a forty-something graphic artist who'd left Boston and the rat race behind to live a gentler life in rural New York. She supplemented her income by illustrating children's books. Computers had made it possible for her to live the life she envisioned.

"It's been a long time since you've brightened my doorstep," Tina said, hugging me with her empty hand. "What can I do for you today?"

"You may have heard that I'm investigating Ava Duncan's death." I'd stopped carrying her newspaper photo with me. Her image had appeared on TV, online and in the papers so often that most people could recognize her faster than an uncle they only saw at weddings and funerals. "I've been canvassing the shops, hoping to find out as much as I can about her."

Tina shook her head and sighed. "I hung out with her from time to time, because I was friends with Angie—I was the old lady of the group," she chuckled. "The three of us would have dinner together or see a movie. And now they're both gone."

"Both? What happened to Angie?" I might have hit the shopkeeper information jackpot.

"That's the weird part—no one seems to know. Come in the back and sit." I followed her into an all-purpose room with a desk and laptop, a small fridge, a microwave and a table and chairs that had seen better days. "Can I offer you water or coffee?" Tina asked as we sat across from each other. She was still holding onto her half a sandwich. The bread was sagging from gravity.

"Thanks, I'm good. Please go ahead and finish your lunch."

Tina looked at the sandwich in her hand as if she'd forgotten she was holding it. She took a bite and washed it down with the bottle of water on the table. "Although I knew Angie longer than I knew Ava, most of what I know about her disappearance came from Ava. They both worked at Monroe Enterprises and lived in the same apartment house in the Glen, plus they were close in age. It was easy for them to become tight quickly."

It struck me that she was reassuring herself about why Angie became closer to Ava, as much as she was explaining their relationship to me, but I didn't hear ill will or jealousy in her tone.

"What did she have to say about Angie's disappearance?"

"One day Angie didn't show up for work. She didn't answer her landline or her cell. Ava went upstairs and rang her bell, but there was no answer. She spoke to Jorge, the building's super. He didn't have much to add. He said he was used to seeing her and the kids every day, so after a few days went by, he rang their bell too. Then he checked in the basement for their suitcases. All the tenants have a space there for storage. When he saw they were gone, he figured the family went on vacation. Only it was the first time Angie hadn't mentioned it to him beforehand.

"Ava convinced him to use his key to check the apartment—just in case. She could be very persuasive." Tina took another bite. It took a lot of self-control for me to wait quietly until she was ready to continue. "The place looked exactly the way it did when they were living there. Neat as a pin. All that was missing was their clothing and personal items."

"Something might have happened while they were on vacation," I said, not believing it myself. Any abduction or tragic accident involving a family would have made the news.

Tina finished the last of her sandwich. "I'm sure she would have mentioned a vacation to me or Ava. It just doesn't track. And it's even harder to believe that she uprooted her kids, left the job she was married to and disappeared. That job paid her enough to take good care of her kids, including medical benefits. What mother in her right mind would walk away from that?"

"Maybe she wasn't in her right mind. People sometimes snap from all the responsibility on their shoulders."

"Not Angie. I've never met a more centered woman. And where her kids were concerned, she was a regular wolverine."

Cue the Twilight Zone music, I thought dismally. Instead of getting information on Ava, I'd stumbled onto another mystery. And I had the feeling that Angie's disappearance was somehow linked to Ava's death. I asked Tina if she knew where Angie's family lived.

"I'm not sure. She grew up in New Jersey, but I don't think her folks still live there."

"What is Angie's last name?"

"She took her maiden name back after her divorce—Neumann."

I stayed and chatted a while longer, until I checked my watch and realized it was time to get back to my shop. I headed back at a jog and found Lolly trying to open my door.

When we were inside, I gave her cheek a kiss and we held onto each other for a few extra heartbeats. She smelled like she'd taken a bath in chocolate. "Best perfume ever," I said, releasing her. "Is this a quickie visit, or can you stay for a while?"

"Dani's watching the store. Everyone in the family is keeping an annoyingly close eye on me. They're driving me daft."

I escorted her to the customer chair and hopped up on the counter. "Tell me how you're doing."

"I suppose things could be worse. Business has been better than usual for this time of year, although that probably says less about my candy and more about my notoriety."

"Trust me—it's about the candy. How's the arthritis?"

"What can I say—it's very devoted. The medicine you gave me is a blessing though. I don't think I could manage without it."

I made a mental note to whip up a new batch for her with a double dose of magick. "Unfortunately, stress is bad for arthritis."

Lolly smiled her dimpled smile that pushed up her cheeks and instantly erased twenty years. "Hold on—you mean stress is good for some things?" That sounded more like the Lolly I knew and loved. She rummaged in the pockets of her denim skirt and came away with a little white bag which she held out to me. "Fruits of my labor." I peeked inside—dark chocolate butter crunch, one of my favorites. I thanked her, but she held up her hand to stop me. "Wait, I come bearing information too."

I arched an eyebrow at her. "What have you been up to, lady?"

"With all the foot traffic in my shop lately, I figured I should at least be trying to ferret out something useful for my case. And I did! You've been trying to find the address of that company where Ava worked, right? Well, I not only have that for you, but I also found out that Monroe Enterprises recently changed its name to Eagle Enterprises!"

"You're unbelievable!" I said, hopping down from my perch to hug her again. She pulled a piece of note paper from her apron pocket and handed it to me. "Eagle Enterprises, One Comstock Lane." I wondered if my navigation app would have it. If not, Travis and I were back to square one.

"What's wrong?" Lolly asked.

"I still have no idea where this is."

"Nelson mentioned it was a couple of miles south of town if that helps."

"Knowing the general area is a big help. Is that Nelson Biddle?" I asked, as if there were any number of Nelsons in our tiny town.

"Yes. I hadn't seen him in a dog's age. He ambled into my shop the other day and said he came to visit—to shore up old acquaintances. Said he got the idea from the girl in the magick shop." I guess I hadn't asked him the right questions when I stopped in there. But it was nice to know that my lunchtime visits were paying off in investigative gold and encouraging more camaraderie among the shopkeepers.

"His visit was lucrative for me too," Lolly said. "Nelson had forgotten how much he loved my fudge. His eyes were as wide as a child's when he saw all the flavors. He bought a quarter pound of each one. Candy makes kids of us all. Kids with money to spend. And on that note, I should be getting back to work." Lolly hauled herself out of the chair. At the same time, my phone rang and the door chimes jingled, announcing the arrival of a middle-aged couple I'd never seen before. Lolly and I mimed our goodbyes with blown kisses and waves.

I welcomed the newcomers and invited them to browse—I'd catch up with them in a minute. Travis was on the phone, sounding fine and as if our dinner *interruptus* was the last thing on his mind. Although I needed to update him on everything I'd learned, it would keep. Customers came first. I said I'd call back when I wasn't busy. If it came out a little brusque, he could just tuck that in the same compartment of his mind as our dinner.

Chapter 25

"Sorry about that," I said when I found them in the aisle with liniments and creams.

"No need to apologize," the woman said. "I'm convinced that my phone only rings when the doorbell rings. It's nice to know that it's not just me."

"Well now that you have my undivided attention, how can I help you?"

"We need something for the aches and pains of living."

"All of these topical preparations are basically the same," I said. "Some people prefer the liquid, some the cream. In addition, herbs like ginseng, valerian root and St. john's wort can be taken as teas to work systemically—throughout the body. I have a variety box of them if you don't know which one you prefer."

"Just choose one, for Pete's sake," the man said. He was standing behind her, so he didn't see his wife roll her eyes for my benefit.

"Have you been in the candy shop across the street?" I asked him. "You won't find better chocolate or fudge anywhere."

His eyes brightened immediately. "I'll have to take a look." He was out of the aisle and headed to the door in five seconds flat. "Melinda," he called over his shoulder, "if they have your favorites, I'll get some for you."

Once he was gone, she told me she'd take the liniment and the variety box of teas. "He's a good man, my Robert," she said on our way to the front of the shop. "He's always thinking of me—even when he's annoyed with me." I set her products down, "Listen," she whispered, as if her husband might still hear her, "Seeing as how he's not here now, I want to ask you about magick spells. My friend raves about the one you gave her."

"What type of spell did you have in mind?"

Since I wasn't whispering, she must have realized there was no point in it. "This may sound silly, but it's getting harder and harder to cook anything that appeals to Robert. All he wants is fried food, red meat, or cheese, and butter on everything. The doctors tell him he's courting a heart attack or a stroke, and I nag him about it until I can't even stand the sound of my own voice. But he refuses to change. The man is as stubborn as a jackass, pardon my French."

"Generally, a spell works best when the person it's intended for is onboard with it and knowingly participates. But in your case, that doesn't seem likely."

"It's worth a shot," Melinda said. "I've got to do something to help him. He can be a huge pain in the rear, but I don't want to lose him." Tears welled in her eyes.

"That's why you're going to try this spell," I said, wishing I could be more reassuring. Magick didn't come with any guarantees. We Wildes knew that better than anyone. I set her products on the counter, handed her a pad and pencil from my desk, and asked her to have a seat.

"You're going to write down the spell. It's part of the process that helps you connect with it," I explained when her brows knit together. "You'll need to rewrite the spell with a pencil before you try to cast it as well."

"Every time?"

"Yes, for it to work the most effectively." Unless she had some magickal DNA she hadn't mentioned.

"You should know that the spell won't make him hate the foods he loves—that wouldn't be ethical. It will simply make healthier foods more appealing." Melinda looked disappointed, but she said she understood. I went through the spell slowly, so she could write it without error:

Healthy foods are drawing you,
Veggies, fruit and fish.
Presented with alternatives,
It's for them you'll wish.

"Say it before dinner, before he looks at a restaurant menu, before he goes into a grocery store and before anything else involving food. If the spell is not working, you can repeat it up to five times in a row, but if it still doesn't work, it's pointless to continue."

"Thank you so much," Melinda said, getting up. "I'd like to pay for everything before Robert comes back and asks too many questions." After I rang her up, she paid in cash and I handed her a receipt that she dropped into her purse. At her request, it didn't include the spell. "I hope you don't think I'm awful for trying this on him."

"Not at all," I assured her. "It speaks of love and caring." At that moment, Robert returned with a shopping bag of his own.

"You will not believe the amazing candy in that store." He sounded the way he must have sounded when he was a kid. "I bought too much, but I couldn't help myself."

"That's okay, dear," Melinda said, patting his arm. "We'll make it last a long time, because it's too far to come right back for more. On the way home," she said as they walked to the door, "we should stop at the fish store for some wild salmon and then the farmers' market for fresh vegetables."

"You have *got* to taste the dark chocolate caramels," Robert said, lost in a sugary high. Melinda was going to have her work cut out for her.

I was about to call Travis back when Elise came in with a jaunty step and a smile. "Playing hooky?" I asked.

"It's after three and school's out for the day. Has it been so busy in here that you've lost track of time?"

"I guess so." I came from behind the counter to hug her. She was smiling the way she did when she had some good news to impart. It was a smile that made her look like the teenage girl who'd been my babysitter over twenty years ago. "Okay, I know that look. What's got you bubbling over inside?"

"Well—I'm here for us to plan a double date." It took my brain an extra second to make sense of what she was saying.

"With you and Jerry the dentist?"

"Yes, but when you meet him, it would be so much better if you just called him *Jerry*." She struggled to keep a straight face, but the dam burst when I cracked up.

"I promise to have it all together when I meet plain ol' Jerry." We spent a few minutes checking our calendars and came up with a list of dates we were both available, but we still had to square the dates with Travis and Jerry.

Elise apologized for not having the time to really catch up. She had to take Noah to the orthodontist. She promised a phone session before the end of the week. It made me happy to see her so lighthearted. It was time—close to a year since the huge upheaval in her life.

After she left, I picked up the phone again and finally reached Travis. I told him about Angie and the Monroe Enterprise name and address. It was hard to believe it wasn't even twenty-four hours since we'd been together. He was psyched about the information. "We have to check out the company, her coworkers, managers," he said. "I'll try to find a phone number, otherwise we'll have to show up unannounced and hope they like surprises. Oh—speaking of surprises." I heard the change in his tone from determined reporter to wary boyfriend, which put me on alert. Had I been a dog, my ears would have pricked forward and my muscles would have bunched, spring-loaded for action.

"What's up?" I asked, hoping the surprise would be a pleasant one.

"My mother called to tell me she and my dad are coming up to the Glen this weekend." He was clearly trying to sound like it was the best news he'd heard in years. I liked Elise's news a lot better. "They'll be here two nights. Can I arrange a meal together so they can meet you?"

I was speechless, even though Travis had told me more than once that they wanted to meet me. I should have known his mother wouldn't wait forever. From the way he'd described her, she steamrolled through any and all obstacles to get what she wanted. In this case meeting me was her goal—I hoped I didn't get flattened in the process.

"Sure," I said, hesitation tugging at the word.

"How about Sunday brunch at the Grotto? That way they have a nice meal with us, and then we send them on their way. No chance for another get-together on this trip."

"I see you've given this considerable thought."

"Ad libbing where my mother is concerned doesn't usually end well. But you need to remember that she's sweet and kind and loving too."

"We should be able to make it through one brunch without any disasters," I said doing my best to sound upbeat. I was already trying to remember if there were any spells that could help. If not, I could create one. Of course a spell itself might lead to disaster. Sometimes the best plan was to do nothing, but I wasn't good at doing nothing. Like most people, in spite of every indication to the contrary, I believed I could manipulate fate.

"Let's try to get through this without magick," he said as if he'd been reading my mind. "If we keep it simple, there will be less to go wrong. I think my mother will be amenable to meeting the rest of your family another time—especially the deceased members."

"Not to worry—Bronwen and Morgana can only manifest in the house and shop." For which I was enormously grateful. I had a hard enough time keeping Merlin under control. Two energy clouds following me around would be my undoing. I knew Travis wanted me to promise I wouldn't use magick, but I didn't feel I could make that promise in good faith. "I'll make every effort not to use magick, except as a last resort."

"And I get a veto." He was playing hard ball, but he knew his mother better than I did.

"One veto and we both pray it never comes to that."

"Deal," he said. I clicked off the call feeling like I'd just agreed to have my hands tied behind me during a gun fight.

Chapter 26

Two days later, Travis picked me up for our trip to Eagle Enterprises. With the correct name to go by, he'd had no trouble finding their phone number. That was the easy part. He'd called me in the evening to detail his battle with the company's automated system. After spending half an hour following prompts and pressing numbers in an effort to reach a human being, he opted to leave a message. The voice mail picked up, stated it was full, said *goodbye* and hung up. As a result, we were not expected at Eagle Enterprises.

Based on the vague directions Lolly had passed on to me, our plan was to leave no driveway unexplored in a three mile stretch south of New Camel. In a populated suburban area like Long Island or Westchester that would have been a monumental task, but in the rural environs of our town, it was a manageable number, especially going south from town.

I was in charge of spotting driveways. Many of them were overgrown; a few no more than broken macadam or cement where grass and weeds flourished side by side. We followed them to their end anyway. Given the thick vegetation, pot holes and ruts, we were lucky to be in an SUV. By the end of the first mile, we'd found three abandoned houses in various stages of disrepair, as if Mother Nature was nibbling away at them in an effort to reclaim her land. Saplings were attacking the houses from all sides, along with snakelike vines and weeds that stood six feet tall. I wondered what had become of the people who once lived in these houses.

"Depressing," Travis mumbled as we bumped along the remnants of the last driveway.

"Mile two will be better," I said, hoping to be prophetic. For once it worked. The only driveway we came to was mostly intact, and the house it served still in excellent shape compared to its neighbors. But it was just a house and we were looking for a larger structure. One big enough to house research and development under a federal contract and a business office with a number of different departments. No way all of that could fit into someone's basement.

We didn't come across another driveway until the end of the second mile. At first it appeared to be nothing more than a wide hiking trail. Travis took an informal poll as to whether or not we should explore it—two for and no one against. We turned onto the dirt path, encouraged by how well the foliage had been cut back from it.

Our first surprise came when we rounded a bend out of sight of the road and found ourselves on a paved drive. The dirt path was clearly to thwart unwanted visitors. Eagle Enterprises didn't want to be bothered. Or maybe it was the federal government that had mandated the security measures for the company.

We hadn't gone far on the road when we came to a guard house overseeing a vehicle barrier. Travis stopped alongside the security booth that was large enough for two people. That day it was manned by one guard sporting the uniform of a security company. "I would have thought they'd have military personnel in charge of security," I murmured.

Travis shushed me. "I'll take care of this." I understood. If one person did the talking, we wouldn't risk contradicting each other—still, I didn't like being *shushed.*

The guard stepped out of the booth. He was no retired cop gone to seed. He was under forty, tall and muscular with a neck that looked too wide for his head. I could picture him as a linebacker on a football field. He was top notch security with a gun on his hip and maybe a license to kill. *Really, Kailyn?* Okay, no license to kill, but I was certain if you made one wrong move, you'd be on the ground with his knee in your back and your hands in cuffs. Travis rolled down his window. The guard leaned in.

"How can I help you?" he asked.

"Gee," Travis said with an awkward chuckle meant to show we posed no threat. "I didn't know my late cousin worked in an armed camp."

The guard was stone-faced. "What can I do for you?"

"Can we get a pass to visit the business office?"

He peered past Travis to me. I cranked up a sweet, innocent smile. "Who is it you want to see?" he asked. Oops, now we had a problem.

Travis went with a version of the truth. "You may have heard about Ava Duncan being murdered?" he said with a well-timed catch in his throat.

"Terrible thing, sir, but Detective Duggan has already been here. What exactly is the nature of your visit?" I'd bet Stone Face didn't even cry when Bambi's mother died.

"I'm hoping maybe Ava's coworkers can give us a lead that may have slipped their minds when they were talking to Duggan. He can be formidable." This conversation was getting us nowhere. Another exchange or two and we'd be asked to backup, turn around and leave. I had a spell in reserve for just such an eventuality. It was a little ditty my grandmother taught me when I was three and my friend's dog was standoffish with me. Given the situation, I couldn't say it aloud, so I ran through it three times in my head:

Trust us you can,
Trust us you must
You have no choice,
But to trust us.

"That's not—" Stone Face frowned and shook his head. "You're lucky I happen to be in a charitable state of mind. I'll call the supervisor of the business office and ask him to give you and Miss Wide Eyes there fifteen minutes to talk to some of your late cousin's coworkers. You pull any nonsense, I'm the one you'll have to deal with."

"That's very generous of you," Travis said, trying to mask his bewilderment. The moment the guard stepped back into the security booth, he turned to me.

"Yes, I did," I said before he could ask the question.

"Is it okay if I thank you when we're on the way home with all of our body parts intact?"

"I wouldn't have it any other way."

Stone Face gave us a little map of the building and pointed to the spot where he'd circled the business office. It could be accessed by a separate door from the main entrance. "If you go snooping around anywhere else, you'll find yourselves in a ton of trouble."

"We understand," Travis said solemnly. "Thank you." Stone Face hit the switch that lifted the barrier arm and we drove through, half expecting him to change his mind and come running after us with his gun drawn. But nothing happened.

When the building came into view, I was surprised by its size. It was hard to believe something that large could be completely hidden from the road. The door indicated on the map was the first one we came to. Travis pulled into the small parking lot adjacent to that end of the building. When we reached the door, it was locked. There was a red button next to it and a security camera above it. The guard had said the supervisor would know we were coming, so I hit the button. There was a responding buzz, and when I tried the door again, it swung open. We entered a small vestibule, from which it was immediately clear that Eagle Enterprises had spent the bare minimum on its business office. Although it was essential to its continuing operation, the big bucks went elsewhere.

We let ourselves through an unlocked glass door and wound up at the receptionist's desk where the name plate read: Hannah Overmeyer. The bearer of the name was young and would have been pretty, except for the black kohl eye makeup against her pale skin that gave her a ghoulish appearance.

"I was told to expect you," she said with a smile. "I'll be happy to introduce you to the women who worked with Ava." She pushed back from the desk and came around to where we stood. "I'm so sorry for your loss," she added, lowering the wattage of her smile. "We miss her here." Travis and I murmured our thanks. I felt like a fraud. We weren't Ava's cousins. For that matter, we'd never met the woman. I told myself it was a little lie, a fib that didn't hurt anyone and could possibly lead to finding her killer.

We followed Hannah into a large area that had been divided into cubicles with walls that went only two thirds of the way to the ceiling and no doors. She kept looking back at us over her shoulder as if she was afraid we'd get lost along the way. Or because her supervisor had emphasized the need to keep an eye on us.

"That was Ava's office," Hannah told us as we walked past one of several offices with walls that went all the way to the ceiling and doors. "Her replacement is in there now, but she didn't know your cousin, so we won't disturb her." She stopped beside a bank of cubicles to the left of the office. "These are the people who work in accounting." She took us into each of the six cubicles and briefly introduced us. Everyone was polite and sorry for our loss.

"I've been told that you were given fifteen minutes here." She checked her watch. "There's ten minutes left. Please keep that in mind. I'll be at the front desk if you need me."

"No problem," Travis said. Once she was out of earshot, he whispered, "you take the first three and I'll take the others." Given our time constraints it was the best way to go about it. I did my best to make the minutes count, but my mini interviews with Joan and Krista netted me little. There was a general consensus that Ava was a nice person and a good colleague to work with. They were in agreement that Angie had been Ava's closest friend there, at least until things got tense between them a month or so before Angie split. They claimed to have no idea about what caused the friction between them.

Travis and I were back at Hannah's desk at the appointed time. "Any chance we could chat with Ava's supervisor for a minute before we go?" he asked.

"Let me see," she said, dialing his extension. Judging by her side of the short conversation, he wasn't thrilled about the prospect. She hung up and flashed us a smile. "He's really bogged down with work, but he said of course he'd take a few minutes to talk to Ava's cousins." She pointed to a short hallway to my right with a door at the end of it. "That's Mr. Nash's office."

Nash was wearing a brown suit, cream shirt and blue and brown striped tie. He had a neatly trimmed moustache and goatee that were probably meant to offset his balding pate. "Come on in, have a seat," he said, standing behind his desk. "I was so sorry to hear about Ava. What a loss." Once we sat down, he took his seat again. "I can tell you that she was a hard worker, got along with everyone, a great member of our work family here at Eagle Enterprises. His tone was as bland as his clothing, his words lacking emotional substance. "It's incomprehensible to me that someone just walked up to her and stabbed her in the back. What's become of this world?" He shook his head. "Was there something in particular you wanted to ask me?"

"We'd heard that she and Angie had a falling out. Would you happen to know what it was about?"

"I'm as much in the dark as anyone," Nash said. "I don't think it was work related or I would have heard about it through the office grapevine. You might want to check out Ava's social circle outside of work. If you'll excuse me, I'm snowed under here."

"One last thing," Travis said. "Do you happen to know why Angie left her job here so suddenly, packed up her kids, and disappeared a month before Ava was killed?"

"All I can tell you is that she has parents who live out of state. Perhaps one of them took ill and needed her help."

It was too generic an answer for me. "If that were the case, why didn't she just ask for time off? Or at least tell you she was leaving?"

Nash turned his hands palm up and allowed himself a little chuckle. "I'm afraid I have no answer for you. It wasn't as if Angie confided in me. We were as surprised as anyone when she didn't show up that day. Caught with our pants down, so to speak. We tried to reach her for a week, then we had no choice but to move on and hire a replacement. If one cog goes missing, the whole engine comes to a grinding halt. No sooner were we back up and running at full steam than Ava was murdered. I can tell you—finding someone with her experience was considerably harder. It's as if someone is targeting our business office," he added ominously.

I wanted to say, *Wouldn't it be more productive for an enemy or competitor to target your scientists rather than your bookkeepers?* What I did say was, "You've got to be so careful these day—espionage is everywhere." In spite of my good intentions, a bit of sarcasm dripped into my voice.

Nash's brow lowered over his eyes, reminding me of drawings I'd seen of Neanderthals. "You are more right than you know," he said. "Now if you'll excuse me, we are still playing catch-up around here. If you return to reception, Hannah will show you out."

On the short drive back to town, Travis and I compared notes on the six women who worked in the accounting department.

"There was something they weren't telling me," he said. "I've conducted enough interviews over the years to know when people are holding back information."

"I had the same feeling. It was like they were worried about saying the wrong thing—or being overheard saying the wrong thing. Whatever Eagle is working on must be very hush—hush."

Travis pulled to the curb in front of Abracadabra. "I'm curious as hell about that government project."

I opened the car door. "I'll try to come up with a plan." I didn't say what I had in mind or he'd have me wearing a wire again along with a flak vest. I could teleport into the facility after-hours, snoop around and teleport out. I'd have to go it alone, though. I wasn't strong enough yet to take someone with me.

"Don't even think about it," Travis warned me. "I know what's going through your head and it would be a great way to get yourself killed or thrown in federal prison for attempted sabotage and treason."

Chapter 27

The next day Tilly asked me over for dinner. She wanted to try a new recipe for chicken pot pie that she'd seen in a magazine while waiting to see her ophthalmologist. She'd made a similar dish in the past, but it never turned out quite right. The crust was too heavy and sagged into the mixture of chicken, veggies and sauce. She'd taken it hard. After all, the crust was the pastry part of the recipe—the part she should have excelled at.

Merlin encouraged the new attempt. Not only did he love the dish from his other life in Camelot, but he thought it would be the perfect opportunity to update us on his latest discovery in the ancient scrolls. I was thrilled about not having to figure out dinner for myself, which often meant eggs, grilled cheese, or takeout.

I fed my clutter of cats. With six of them, it actually seemed like the most appropriate term to use. Bellies full, they settled in for some serious preening, to be followed by their evening nap. I decided to forego the car and get some much-needed exercise by hoofing it to Tilly's house. Okay, a block can hardly be called exercise, but it was better than nothing. Perspective mattered. If I owned one of those techy exercise bracelets, it would probably be nagging at me all the time to get some exercise. In my defense, it was hard to run a business, care for a household of felines, solve murder cases and still have time to workout at a gym. My mother had tried to come up with a spell that would work the muscles of couch potatoes while they stayed firmly planted on the couch. None of us expected it to work, so we were just mildly disappointed when it didn't.

"I've never known a spell to work if it promoted laziness or other poor behavior," Morgana summed up at the time. My own experience with creating spells had proven her right. I imagined censors beyond the veil, passing judgment on each spell as it was created. In my vision, they wielded celestial black markers to strike down attempts to shortcut one's way through life's trials.

Merlin opened the door when he saw me coming up the walk. He looked like a crazy professor. His hair stuck out around his head as if he'd been struck by a brainstorm, complete with electricity. His eyes were bright, twinkling with excitement over the pot pie or his newest discovery in translating the scrolls—probably both. There was more than a bit of the showman in the wizard, and even an audience of two was enough to energize him.

Tilly announced that we had to eat first, because the pot pies were ready, and reheating them might destroy their perfect, golden crusts. Merlin didn't argue. To his way of thinking, nothing trumped food. These pies turned out as amazing as everything else that came out of my aunt's oven, proving that the failed pot pie should be attributed to a problem with that recipe. Tilly lapped up our praise. Merlin went so far as to pronounce them better than the pies served in King Arthur's dining room. The three of us were so stuffed that the idea of dessert was met by groans. Merlin suggested it be put off until after his revelations. Tilly and I remained seated at the table. The wizard stood at his place. "My progeny, who gave rise to your ancestors, emigrated from England to this vast land well before it was a country. Have you ever wondered why they chose this specific spot to set up shop?"

"I have," Tilly and I said in unison.

"Ley lines, my dear ladies. It's all about the ley lines."

"Wait—I know this," Tilly said, holding up her hand to stop Merlin from providing the answer.

The wizard waited, imitating a clock tick-tocking its way to the end of her allotted time. "Not helping," she muttered.

"All the game shows have some form of music when the contestant is thinking," he said in his defense.

"I've got it," she called out. "Ley lines are lines of energy beneath the Earth's surface."

"We have a winner! Give the little lady a prize! Sorry, I don't actually have any prizes," he added in a whisper, as if there were a larger, viewing audience from whom he was keeping the truth. "But it does add a little zip to the presentation and I do love saying it."

"I remember reading something about electromagnetic energy with regard to Stonehenge," I said. "Is that related to ley lines?"

"Another winner!" he proclaimed. "According to the scrolls, ley lines carry electromagnetic energy. Stonehenge was built over a nexus of ley lines. Some believe that makes it an energy portal. But that doesn't concern us at the present time." He took a dramatic pause before continuing. "It is my theory that something has disrupted the ley lines here and that is why we are all experiencing problems with our magick!"

Tilly and I gave him a sitting ovation—it had been a long day. Merlin accepted with a gracious, if wobbly, bow. "And now, Matillda," he said. "Bring on dessert!"

* * * *

I spent a ridiculous half hour trying to decide what to wear to brunch with Travis's parents. Everything I owned seemed either too buttoned up, too girl on the prowl, or too retro flower child. I called Travis for an opinion. "You'd be fine in jeans or chinos and a blouse," he said. "Don't over think it." I finally settled on dark-wash jeans, a white tailored shirt, and a blue tweed blazer with gold buttons. I stuck small gold hoops in my ears and slipped my feet into my most comfortable flats, because it's hard to be charming with grouchy feet.

I arrived at the Grotto ten minutes late, not because I was trying to make an *entrance,* but because a large family of Canadian Geese couldn't decide which side of the street they preferred. It was very cute for the first minute or so. At minute five, I took matters into my own hands, before an irritated motorist decided he had a hankering for roast goose.

I left my car where it was and went to stand on the closer side of the road. I'd fashioned a spell for the very same problem several years earlier. I repeated it silently three times. For the benefit of the onlookers, I included a lot of gesturing for the geese to come to me. It would be better for them to think of me as the crazy goose whisperer, than as a worrisome, spell-casting witch.

In less than a minute, the geese were off the roadway and I received a round of applause, punctuated by the horns of the cars now stuck behind mine. I hopped back in and threw the car into drive. You really can't make some people happy.

The Grotto was busier for Sunday brunch than I would have thought. A good half of the patrons were dressed in their church finery. I fit in with the other half. Travis saw me come in and waved to catch my attention. As I threaded my way through the maze of tables, my first impression of his parents was of a handsome couple approaching sixty in conservative style.

Travis's father was tall and lean with well-cut silver hair and intense blue eyes. His mother was more petite than I'd pictured her. Based on Travis's accounts, she'd been magnified in my mind's eye so that I'd expected her to tower over her husband. She was quite the opposite, one of those women with delicate features who can pull off short hair and minimal makeup and still turn heads. I immediately felt big-boned and awkward around her.

Travis introduced me to them as Kitty and Gary. Gary was old school. He got up when I reached the table and pulled my chair out for me. I sat between him and Travis. I wondered if Travis had purposely left the empty seat where I'd be somewhat insulated from his mother or if it was just the way it had worked out. I apologized for being late and told them it was the fault of geese. I left out the part about the spell.

"We have the same problem on Long Island," Gary said. "They don't have any natural predators there, so their population is out of control."

"We liked it better back in the day when they wintered in Chesapeake Bay," Kitty added with a dimpled smile. The waiter arrived before I had a chance to look at the menu, but I didn't want to hold things up. I listened to what everyone else was having and decided to order the French toast with bananas and caramel sauce like Kitty. I wasn't trying to insinuate myself into her good graces. I'm just a sucker for anything sweet. If I ordered eggs Florentine like Travis or eggs Benedict like Gary, I'd be craving the French toast for the entire meal and the rest of the day.

We chatted about our families, our histories, favorite things and pets. Travis steered the conversation away from anything too deep or dark, determined to make this first meeting with his parents a pleasant experience for all of us—except for him. I'd never seen him on edge like that. I did my part to keep things light as well. We almost made it through the meal without incident. The French toast was amazing. I was sipping my coffee, finally relaxing, when Kitty mentioned my magic shop. "The shampoo and conditioner Travis bought for me at your shop last year are truly miraculous. I've never found anything that comes close. If you don't already have a patent for them, you should. Look at my hair—it wasn't this thick in my twenties."

The busboy came by to refill our cups, and Kitty waited until he was gone, before continuing. "The next time my son is in your shop, please remind him to buy me two bottles of each. And if you have a cream or gel to diminish the dark circles under my eyes, I'd be indebted to you. Some mornings I look like I just went five rounds with Rocky."

"I promise," I said. "And I'll throw in some samples of my other products."

"Sign of a good salesperson," Gary said with a laugh. "Get the customer hooked on things she doesn't even know she needs yet."

"No, no. I've just found that my customers like trying different things without spending a lot of money on them upfront."

Travis grinned. "My dad's just messing with you."

Kitty gave her husband a slap on the forearm. "It's best to assume that Gary is always joking. But getting back to your shop—I wish we'd had the time to stop there. It will be a priority the next time we're up here. I'm fascinated by how you created all the products you sell. It must take a great deal of research."

"I have a degree in botany, but I can't take credit for most of my inventory. I guess you could say it's been the family business for a long time."

Kitty shook her head. "Travis told me about your mom and grandma. Such a tragedy."

Three tables away, I noticed the hostess seating Tess and Ben Webster with their son Conner. I hadn't bumped into them since the day I saved Conner from smashing his head on the kiln in his mom's ceramic shop. Conner must have recognized me too. While his parents were fiddling with the kiddy seat, he took off—headed straight for me. I had no idea if Tess was still afraid of me or what she might say in public. But I couldn't think of a worse time for such an encounter. I considered escaping to the ladies' room, but it was at the other end of the restaurant. Short of crawling under the table, there was nothing I could do to prevent what was about to happen. I felt like the girl tied to the train tracks with the train bearing down and no hero in sight.

"Look Mommy—lady from your shop." Tess looked up and followed his pointed finger to me.

"No Conner, no!" she called out as she squeezed past tables to reach him. "Conner, stop!" Conner wasn't listening. He was grinning, pleased with himself for finding me. By then the entire restaurant was watching the race. Would Conner reach me before his mother reached him? I wasn't giving any odds.

"Lady, why you not come back to see us?" he asked, tripping over his own feet and lurching forward head first into my lap.

"Don't you dare touch him," Tess said, scooping him up in her arms. Conner immediately started wailing. "Don't you ever come near my boy again," she added. Ben had reached our table and was trying to calm his son, hush his wife and apologize to me at the same time. Tess didn't want to be quieted. "I don't care, Ben. I don't care if it is white magic." She turned back to me. "Stay away from us, stay away from our son or I'll... I'll get a court order to make you stay away!" She turned abruptly on her heel and stormed back to their table. Conner was sniffling. He didn't understand what he'd done wrong or why his mother was yelling at the nice lady.

"Please forgive us," Ben said. "My wife is a little distraught." I was too dumbstruck to say anything. Gary and Kitty were completely in the dark. It was left to Travis to grab the reins of the situation. He motioned for the waitress to bring our check and told the rest of us he'd catch up outside.

I couldn't get out of the Grotto fast enough. Everyone in there had been treated to a dandy show. It was bound to be the talk of the town in Watkins Glen and by tomorrow in New Camel. I led the way out of the restaurant, trying not to look at the expressions on the faces we passed.

"That woman is clearly disturbed," Kitty said. We were standing together near their car after brunch. "I felt so bad for her husband. And for *you.* What on earth did she think you would do to her child?"

I explained about the day I'd stopped in the ceramic shop to chat. When I reached the part where Conner was on a collision course with the heavy kiln, I switched out magick for quick reflexes. "Fortunately, I was close enough to grab him out of harm's way. Somehow the situation got turned around in her head and suddenly I've become the boogey man."

Gary gave me a fatherly pat on the shoulder. "Don't give it another thought. Proof of your innocence was evident to everyone in the restaurant—that little boy was delighted to see you again."

"She may have been off her meds," Kitty added as Travis trotted up to us.

"Hey, I'm just glad we were able to finish our meal in peace before they walked in." He reminded his folks they should get started on their trip home. There was always a lot of traffic on a Sunday afternoon. Kitty gave us fair warning that they'd be returning in the not too distant future to see New Camel, particularly my shop, and to meet the rest of my tiny family. I said I looked forward to it.

They hugged us both goodbye. "Don't you let what happened in there trouble you," Gary said as he slid behind the wheel. I smiled and nodded. The odds were he and Kitty would have put it out of their heads before they were halfway home, but for me it would remain ever present. Too many people had witnessed it and heard what Tess said. People who knew Tess and knew there was nothing wrong with her mind. Over the next days and weeks, they would make it their nosey business to ask her what the brouhaha was all about. And they'd pass her answer on to friends and family.

Chapter 28

My mother popped into the bathroom as I was getting ready for bed. Her energy cloud was a queasy combination of chartreuse and puce that I'd never seen before. "I was afraid of just this sort of thing," she started with, instead of *hello.*

I spit out the toothpaste in my mouth. "Me too." I meant both the incident at brunch and her inevitable rant about it, but I didn't say that out loud.

"The question for now is how to handle it," Morgana continued.

"Handle it?" Bronwen appeared in the mirror giving me a start. One moment I was looking at my own reflection and the next I was looking at her cloud infused with a lilac hue of calm. "There is no way to *handle* it. Anything she did now would only etch it more permanently into everyone's brains."

Morgana looked appalled "Your advice is to do nothing?" To let rumors fly uncontested until they eventually impact her business? Lead to threats on her life?"

"The rumors will fizzle out as long as Kailyn holds her head high and refuses to get down in the mud with Tess Webster and the gossipmongers. Even if a few people stay away initially, it won't be long before they realize they can't buy remedies half as potent as the ones they get at Abracadabra. You'll see how quickly they decide that a little magick isn't such a bad thing."

I patted our hydrating cream on my face and neck. "Do I get a say in this?"

"No," my mother said, "there are some things your elders should decide."

"Yes, of course you do," my grandmother countered, popping out of the mirror for emphasis or perhaps to stare her daughter down. "Morgana, you need to accept the fact that we're dead. We won't always be able to advise her. She's the one who's living. She must make the decisions that will impact her life."

I couldn't ignore them any longer and I didn't want to squeeze past them to reach the hall. "Do you want to know what I think?" They both turned to me, at least I think they did. It can be hard to tell with clouds. "I don't intend to say a word about the incident unless someone brings it up. If they do, I'll answer them as honestly as I can without mentioning magick." I didn't wait for their reactions. I'd already spent far too much time worrying about the brunch, which was ridiculous because no amount of worrying could change anything. I had a business to run and I needed sleep. I drew in my breath to make myself as narrow as possible and slid between them to make my escape. They could follow me of course, but I was banking on the fact that they much preferred sparring with each other.

* * * *

I had no idea what time they took their leave, but when I went into the bathroom the next morning I was the only one there. Except for one of my cats who loved curling up in the sink, providing it was dry. I showered, applied eyeliner and mascara, and ran a brush through my hair.

I fed the cats, made a cup of strong coffee that I poured into a thermos, and ran upstairs to pull on jeans and a light sweater. It was the time of year when it was hard to know how to dress. I rounded up Sashkatu, who'd fallen asleep on the powder room floor after breakfast. We were crossing the street to my shop when a car came barreling toward us. I grabbed Sashki and jumped out of the way. The car screeched to a stop and reversed to where I was standing with Sashkatu in my arms. My knees were trembling, making no promise to keep us upright. The driver rolled down the heavily tinted window. I thought he wanted to make sure we were all right and maybe apologize. I stepped closer to the car. That's when the back door flew open. A guy as big as a linebacker was on me before I could react. When I opened my mouth to scream, he slapped a hand the size of a ham across my mouth. The driver handed him some packing tape to shut me up. I tried to fight him, but with Sashki in my arms it was impossible.

The linebacker demanded I drop the cat, but Sashki leaped at his face, raking his claws from the guy's eye to his chin and jumping to the ground before he could retaliate. The linebacker screamed, but the driver told him to shut up before the neighbors heard him and called 911. He settled for muttering a string of epithets under his breath while he pulled my hands behind my back and bound my wrists with plastic cuffs—the kind police use. He threw me into the backseat, clambering in after me. Blood was dripping onto his clothes. "Damn cat ruined my shirt," he grumbled. "He's lucky he got away. I would've liked to wring his neck."

"Shut your trap, Boscoe," the driver snapped. "We got what we came for." He hung a U-ie and sped out of New Camel. "Get the blindfold on her."

The linebacker named Boscoe pulled a frayed and dirty-looking bandana out of his jeans' pocket. He pulled it across my eyes and tied it at the back of my head. It was too tight, pressing into my eyes, but I couldn't say anything with the tape across my mouth. All that came out were unintelligible sounds. The driver told me to shut the hell up or he'd have his colleague knock me out.

For a while I tried to keep track of where they were taking me. But after twenty minutes and too many left and right turns, I gave up. Instead I listened for sounds that might help orient me along the way. If my mouth wasn't bound with the tape, I would have laughed at myself. It wasn't going to matter where they were taking me if their goal was to kill me. Yet if that was their intention, why wait to do it? A dead body is much easier to transport than a living one with a mind of its own. Maybe whoever had paid for their services wanted to kill me themselves. My time in the car could be put to better use by creating a spell to supplement my protection wards that had been MIA so far today. I would only use the spell as a last resort. Using my abilities to save a child from harm had come back to bite me. I didn't want to find out what the blowback would be from using a spell to cause harm.

We drove for what seemed like an eternity, but was probably no more than an hour. Time drags when you're not having fun. I didn't know what was hurting more—the tape, the blindfold or the plastic cuffs abrading my wrists. I decided they all played second fiddle to the fear twisting in my gut. I might have finally gotten myself into more trouble than I could survive. With me out of the way, Whitney could swoop right in and guilt her way back into Travis's heart. That thought reawakened my survival instincts more than any other. I wasn't ready to join Morgana and Bronwen in the great beyond.

The car made one final turn and we bumped along a badly rutted road for five minutes, before the car came to a stop and the driver turned off the engine. Boscoe opened the door and pulled me out of the car. I smelled fresh vegetation and moldering layers of dead leaves. It was shaded, little light making it through the blindfold. And it was deeply quiet.

"Don't take off the blindfold and tape until we get her inside," the driver said. We went a couple dozen steps. I was jerked along by the arm, tripping over the uneven ground and my own feet. I didn't bother to complain. Not only wouldn't they understand me, but my comfort was clearly the last thing on their minds.

A door creaked open. The driver told me to watch my step. *Very funny*, I thought as I tripped over the threshold and went down hard on my knees. The linebacker pulled me up, almost wrenching my arm out of the socket. If I got out of this alive, I was going to need the best remedies my aunt and Merlin could whip up.

One of my captors closed the door behind us. Whatever this place was, it smelled old and stale with a note of mildew. A light went on. At least there was electricity. Boscoe pulled off the blindfold. For a minute, all I could see were spots and flashes of light. It took a little while, but once I could see properly again, there wasn't much to take in. We were in a small, one room cabin without much in the way of amenities. An old cot with a stained mattress was pushed against one wall. Across from it was an ancient sink, a dorm-sized fridge and a small shiny microwave that looked anachronistic among the other things.

"This I'm gonna enjoy," the linebacker sneered as he ripped the packing tape off my mouth. I wanted to scream, but I wouldn't give them the satisfaction. It did me good to see the long, red welt on his face compliments of Sashkatu. I'd been worried about him from the moment he scratched Boscoe and jumped down. But he hadn't appeared to be limping. I told myself over and over that he was a wily and resourceful cat. If Tilly or Merlin didn't hear him yowl through the back of the building that housed our shops, he would go around to the front door where they would be sure to see him. Tilly would be worried about me when she saw him there alone. She'd run for the connecting door, only to find it still locked. She'd call my house and cell phone and when I didn't answer, she'd dial 911 and get in touch with Travis. The police might refuse to start the search until forty-eight hours had passed, but I knew Curtis would help in whatever capacity he could. And Travis was probably out looking for me even now.

Chapter 29

Boscoe and the driver were looking around the accommodations as if they had never been there before. Now that I saw the driver standing, he and Boscoe reminded me of Abbott and Costello in the old sitcoms Tilly used to watch. The driver was short and stout like Costello.

"Why did you kidnap me?" I asked. "What does your employer want from me?"

The driver smirked. "You'll find out."

Boscoe edged closer to him and whispered in his ear loudly enough for me to hear. "Hey, you told me you didn't know."

"Never mind what I know or I don't know," the driver snapped, pushing Boscoe away and rubbing at his ear the way a child rubs a kiss away from his cheek.

"Any chance you could uncuff me?" I asked. "I need to use the bathroom." There was one door set into the wall opposite the front door. Three possibilities came to mind. It could be a backdoor out of the cabin, a bathroom or a closet. I was wishing hard for a bathroom.

"If I take off the cuffs, you better not try anything stupid," the driver warned me.

"You're kidding, right? Like I'd have a chance against the two of you."

Boscoe laughed. "She ain't no Wonder Woman."

"Okay, fine," the driver said. He went over to the sink and opened the lopsided cabinet beneath it. "If I can't find a knife or a scissor, you're out of luck." Great—these two rocket scientists brought cuffs, but no means of removing them. I swallowed my frustration and tried to think calmly. I could use a spell to make them fall off, but then I'd be showing them my hand, so to speak. If they got scared enough they might decide not to wait for their boss to put a bullet in me. I was debating what to do when the linebacker pulled a Swiss army knife out of his pocket.

"You know I think this thing has a scissor." The driver came up to him and grabbed it out of his hand.

"Yeah, you think?!" He opened the knife, found the scissor and snipped off the cuffs. We were about to learn what was behind door number two. The driver tossed the knife back to the linebacker and went to find out. The wood was warped and took some tugging to open, but it was a bathroom. He told me not to lock the door or he'd break it down. I figured he meant his large *colleague* would knock it down. I was so happy to see the bathroom that I would have promised him my first born. Luckily it didn't come to that.

The bathroom was tiny and old. There was a rust stained toilet and sink. No window. I stepped inside and closed the door without engaging the lock. While I was taking care of business, I looked for something I could use to my advantage. I had no doubt that MacGyver would have come up with half a dozen ideas. Then it hit me. And one idea was all I needed.

"What's takin' so long?" the driver asked. "Do I have to come in there?"

I opened the door. "A girl needs time to primp," I said with a hefty dose of sarcasm. "Do you happen to know how long we're going to be here?"

"Why? You got a hot date?" Boscoe snorted.

"What if I do? What if it's with a cop? What if the cop is already on your trail?" I knew I shouldn't be baiting them, but I couldn't help myself. Boscoe looked worried.

"You think she's telling the truth?" he said to the driver. "Maybe we should get out of here. I don't like this." He was getting himself worked up. "Didn't like it from the start. I don't know why I let you talk me into stuff. *Easy money*, you said. I haven't seen a penny yet. Why should we take the rap for—" The driver hauled off and punched Boscoe on the chin, which was as high as he could reach. He had a pretty solid right hook.

"Shut up. Try usin' your brain for a change. Even if her boyfriend is a cop, how would he know what happened to her? He probably won't even know she's missing till he goes to pick her up tonight. And how on earth would he find this place anyways?"

If I could get the two of them fighting, I might have a chance to escape. "He may already know where I am. My aunt is a psychic," I said. "Surely you've heard of Matillda Wilde—she's famous. Celebrities come from all over the world for her readings. She's probably homed in on my brain waves and is directing the police here as we speak." I'd pushed too far. I saw it in the driver's eyes as he came at me. He smacked me so hard, my lip split and I fell back onto the cot.

"Shut your mouth or I'll knock your teeth out next time!"

"Do. Not. Ever. Touch me again!" I said, fury whipping through me like a cyclone.

"Or what?!" he snarled.

It was time for the spell I'd created in the car—consequences be damned. I recited it three times to myself:

I am razors; I am knives,
I am needles in your eyes.
I will burn you like hot coal;
I will freeze you like North's pole.

"Or what?!" he repeated, grabbing my arm. He cried out and dropped it instantly as if he were holding a hot branding iron. "What the—!" he bellowed, the arrogant sneer gone from his face.

"What happened?" Boscoe asked.

"She burned me. See?" The driver held out his palm. There wasn't a mark on him.

Boscoe laughed. "Use your brain, sucker—does it look like you're burned?"

"Yeah, well you go touch her and see what happens, bird brain." Boscoe approached me warily. He reached out to touch my arm with his fingertips, but the moment they came in contact with my skin, he pulled away from me with a high-pitched shriek.

"She sliced my fingers," he said, cradling his hand.

"Lemme see." Boscoe slowly uncurled the fingers of his right hand. They both stared in disbelief at his fine, uninjured fingers. "She's gotta be a witch or somethin'" the driver said.

"What are we gonna do?"

The driver seemed to have regained some of his wits. From a safe distance, he ordered me into the bathroom. I did as I was told, looking down, walking like a penitent. "If you try to come out of there, I'll shoot you," he said. I nodded meekly. It was exactly what I wanted to hear.

Chapter 30

It might be my only chance to escape. As much as I wanted to see who had hired these two buffoons to abduct me, I knew it would be foolhardy to pass up an opportunity to save myself. Neither Tilly nor Travis would ever forgive me if I wound up dead. And even if I found out who the killer was, what good would it do if I wasn't alive to tell anyone?

It took me longer than usual to center my mind. Teleportation required more than the casting of an average spell. It was essential to gather the energy of my body and marry it to a sharply focused mind for it to work properly. Being held captive and fearing for my life were not the best circumstances under which to attempt teleportation. Especially if I didn't want to wind up inside a wall, at the bottom of the sea, or underground. I chose my shop for my destination, and waited until I had it together, mind, body and soul, before reciting the spell.

From here and now to there and then
Attract not change, nor harm allow.
Safe passage guarantee to souls
As well as lesser, mindless things.

When I opened my eyes, I was standing near the counter in Abracadabra. I looked for Sashkatu on the tufted window ledge, but it was empty. I didn't really expect to find him there, it was a reflex born of habit. He was probably with Tilly and Merlin. I spent a moment retracting the fire and ice spell in case it was still active. Then I ran next door, pausing at the connecting door to make sure I wouldn't be interrupting my aunt in the middle of a reading or tea. What was I thinking? Once she realized I was missing, she would have cancelled any appointments she had.

I walked in and found Tilly in the middle of a baking marathon. Trays of cookies covered every flat surface, including the tea tables and the palms of Merlin's hands. The combined aromas of peanut butter, oatmeal raisin, and chocolate chocolate chip filled the air with a heady perfume. Sashkatu was sound asleep at Merlin's feet. All present and accounted for. Relief made my knees rubbery. I leaned against the kitchen doorway.

When Tilly saw me, she was so excited she forgot she was holding a tray she had just taken out of the oven. As the tray started to slip from her oven mitts, she valiantly tried to save it, juggling it for a good ten seconds before it flipped into the air and executed a neat spiral dive to the floor, throwing hot pecan sandies everywhere. Merlin leaped into action with the reflexes of a much younger man, catching some of them midair with the tray he was holding. The commotion woke Sashki, who darted into the kitchen to nibble at the cooler edges of the ones that hit the floor.

My aunt threw off the oven mitts and grabbed me to her bosom. "Thank goodness you're all right!" she cried. "I had no place left to put more cookies and my feet are screaming at me." I helped her over to a chair. She wasn't actually complaining. When she was upset or worried, baking was the only thing that kept her sane. The quantity of baked goods she turned out at any given time was a reliable measure of the depth of her love and the width of her concern. They also made for a yummy welcome home celebration.

"You'd best call Travis," she said, trying to catch her breath. "He's nearly as distraught as I was. He threatened to break the story of your kidnapping on the evening news and lambast the police for not doing enough to find you. Duggan threatened to throw him in jail for interfering in police business. So Travis threatened to tell the public your kidnapping was tied to the death of Ava Duncan. And Duggan threatened to end his career. It was like a high stakes poker game. To be honest, I'm not sure if Travis is in jail or not."

I picked up Sashki, who'd had far too much sugar, and carried him back to Abracadabra with me. He was on his ledge fast asleep in no time. I called Travis and waited anxiously for him to pick up. He must have seen my name on caller ID, because when he answered the phone, questions poured out of him.

"Are you okay? Where are you? What happened? Are you all right?"

"I'm fine, but if you want answers you have to give me time to talk."

"Right. I'll be there in forty minutes and you can answer me in person." He hung up without saying goodbye, but called back from the road to ask whether he'd find me at home or in the shop. I said I'd be home. I didn't have the energy to open up, even if there were four hours left of the afternoon.

"Have you checked in with the police yet?"

"No." I sighed, knowing what he was about to say.

"I'm sure you're tired, but it isn't optional. Go down to the substation in New Camel. Hopefully that will spare you an interview with Duggan, at least until tomorrow. I'll meet you there." I went home, got my car and drove down to the New Camel police station. It was absolutely the last thing I wanted to do.

Hobart was on duty. When I walked in, he jumped up and came around the desk to help me into a chair as if I was made of Baccarat crystal and might shatter at any moment. Maybe I was his first kidnapping victim. He took a minute to notify the rest of the Watkins Glen police force that I was no longer missing. He offered me water, which I accepted. I didn't realize how thirsty I was. I took a sip and couldn't stop until I'd drained the glass. He asked if I needed medical attention, which I declined.

"I'll try to make this as quick as I can," he said, resuming his seat. "Your loved ones believed you were kidnapped. Is that what happened?"

"Yes."

"So glad you're okay," he said in the tone of a friend. But then it was back to official police-speak. "I'll need you to give me a detailed account of exactly what happened from the moment you were abducted until your escape."

"I don't suppose this could wait until tomorrow?" I tried to sound desperate, which wasn't hard at that point.

"I understand how exhausted you must be, but we have to go after these guys before they can try this again with you or someone else."

I did my civic duty and recounted everything I could remember, except for two things. I left out the spell I'd used to keep them away from me and I lied about how I escaped. In the version I gave Hobart, I ran off while my captors were fighting with each other and hitchhiked home.

"You know hitchhiking is dangerous," Hobart pointed out. He must have realized how ridiculous he sounded given the circumstances, because he quickly added, "Normally speaking, that is."

"Yes, well I didn't have my phone to call an Uber, so let's just say it was the lesser of two evils at the time." We were wrapping up when Travis arrived.

"Tomorrow you'll have to go through some mug shots and maybe sit down with a sketch artist," Hobart said. "For now, go home and get some rest. I'm glad you're safe."

Travis waited until we were in the parking lot before gathering me into his arms and holding onto me for so long that he might have broken Tilly's record. "I'm not by nature a pessimist," he murmured against my cheek, "but I was really afraid I'd never see you again."

"No worries—if that ever happens, I promise to come back and haunt you."

He laughed, loosening his arms around me, without letting go. "Not as an energy cloud please. They're kind of freaky."

I stopped at my shop to pick up Sashkatu who was still sleeping off his sugar coma. He didn't wake when I put him in the car, which was a good thing. I really wasn't up to a knockdown, drag out fight about it. Travis was waiting at my house. The other cats came out of their hidey holes to see what had brought me home in the middle of the day. They must have held a meeting and determined that Travis could finally be treated like family, because they rubbed against his legs with uncharacteristic abandon. Sashkatu woke up when I set him down on the couch. He looked around, saw where he was and promptly closed his eyes again.

I headed for the kitchen. "On the way here, it hit me how hungry I am."

"You sit down and I'll fix you the best grilled cheese you've ever eaten."

I collapsed onto a chair. "That's quite a statement from a man who's been fortunate enough to have grilled cheese at The Soda Jerk."

"I'll let you be the judge." He rummaged in the fridge and came away with cheddar, Swiss and shredded Romano. What can I say? I love cheese. My stomach gurgled with anticipation. The finished product was as good as I'd ever eaten. He watched me devour the sandwich without saying a word, then led me to the couch in the living room. "I'm sorry to make you go through your ordeal again, but I need to hear everything you told Hobart as well as the parts you left out." Sitting there cuddled against him with his arm around me, I didn't mind the retelling. What had been a chore at the police station, was now cathartic. I didn't have to watch what I was saying.

Although I was finally relaxing, Travis seemed to be absorbing my tension. I felt his body tighten as he listened to my story. "Other than the driver hitting you that one time, how did they treat you?"

"They weren't great in the hospitality department, but they didn't do anything else to harm me. I would have loved to see their reactions when they opened the bathroom door and I was gone."

"How about when they have to admit to their employer that they bungled the job? My motto is never go cheap if you want something done properly."

"They were seriously under qualified for the job. Their talents were better suited to a vaudeville act. They missed their calling by a century or so." He kissed my forehead, then tipped my chin up and kissed me on the mouth. Every nerve and synapse in my body snapped to attention—Travis's own brand of magic.

"I don't know anyone else who would have bounced right back with your spirit and sense of humor after what you went through today," he said.

"I appreciate the accolades, but I have the advantage of magick. It's easier to be brave knowing you can probably teleport out of a situation if you need to." I've always been uncomfortable with praise if I don't think I've earned it. Travis didn't try to argue with me. He seemed to be brooding about something.

"I wish we knew their ultimate purpose in abducting you," he said. "Were they told to keep you in that abandoned house until the boss arrived to *take care of* you? Or was the whole thing designed just to scare you into dropping your investigation into Ava's death?"

"The latter, I think. They could have saved their money, because I have no intention of tucking my tail and hiding under the bed. I keep wondering who would ever hire such bumbling fools."

"Someone without the resources to pay for proven talent or someone who's never been involved in criminal activity."

"Well these guys were bargain basement," I said. "Unfortunately, that doesn't help narrow down our list of suspects—none of them is exactly rolling in money."

Chapter 31

The time I spent looking at mug shots the next day paid off. Boscoe and the driver had several previous arrests and incarcerations for lesser crimes. They'd stepped things up substantially by kidnapping me. Travis tagged along for moral support. As it happened, Paul Curtis's shift in New Camel started that morning. I wondered if Travis called ahead to find out who would be on duty. If the answer had been *Hobart,* would he have already been on the road back to Watkins Glen?

He dropped me at home so I could fetch Sashkatu before opening my shop. I didn't have the strange emptiness in the pit of my stomach that I sometimes felt when Travis drove away and I knew why. Our date with Elise and Jerry was scheduled for the following night.

It was a beautiful day with pretensions of summer. I left the shop door open, with the help of Morgana's dragon statue. The temperature coaxed people from the greater Glen area to come to New Camel for lunch or ice cream and a stroll around our quaint town. The flashy dragon beckoned them to check out Abracadabra. I wasn't overrun with customers like on tour bus days, but I had to eat my PB&J in spurts between helping newbies and chatting with regulars, both of which I always enjoyed.

When the school day ended, mothers left to ferry their children to other activities, and I finally had a chance to sit down since opening. Tilly toddled in from her shop, bearing a hefty wedge of her new chocolate crumb cake for me to try. Once I'd proclaimed it "decadent and homey at the same time," she left with a satisfied smile. Apparently, Merlin had quibbled about it being too sweet. After a year of ingesting every sugary confection he could squeeze into his stomach, he now considered himself something of a critic. If he wasn't careful, Tilly might decide to cut him off.

I was eating my last bite of the not-too-sweet-at-all crumb cake when a group of five middle school girls walked in. They moved as one, like a multi-limbed organism conjoined by some vital organ. Three of them were giggling nervously, the other two looked like they wanted to bolt. I asked if I could help them.

They whispered to each other, before the tallest girl spoke up. "Are you a real witch?"

I flipped the question back to her. "What do you mean?"

"You know—do you have powers?"

"Can you fly like on a broom?" another girl piped up.

"Can you change people into frogs?" a third girl asked timidly.

"Where did you hear this stuff?" I laughed. I've learned to evade questions I don't want to answer by asking questions of my own. It does a masterful job of detouring a conversation.

"It's going around the school," said the tall girl.

"My little brother heard it too, and he's only in the third grade," said one of the others.

"But you're a good witch, right?" asked the timid girl. "I know you saved that little boy's life." I'd already had a good idea where the rumors started, but now I was sure—Tess Webster. I doubted her intentions were to sing my praises. Although I'd saved her son's life, she was afraid of me. Maybe she had some twisted, Rumpelstiltskinian notion that one day I'd come to claim him as my own. When he ran over to me in the Grotto, it must have convinced her that I already had him in my thrall. I had so hoped that Bronwen and Morgana were wrong to be worried about the fallout from my good deed.

"The little boy's family is moving," said the girl who'd been quiet up to that point. "I think they're making a big mistake." She spoke deliberately, as though she'd put a lot of thought into her words. "If anyone had saved a child of mine, I'd consider them my hero and I'd want to stay as close as possible." The other girls murmured their agreement. While we talked, their tight little group had loosened. Now the tall girl wandered over to the table with the crystal display. The timid girl asked if she could look around, and the others followed. Soon they were scattered around the store, asking about all the merchandise, giggling and calling to each other to *come see* this or that. It seemed like a tiny turning point—a baby step or two in the right direction. Even so I knew my mother and grandmother would advocate caution.

* * * *

The long awaited double date was upon us. This Little Piggy, the new barbecue place halfway between New Camel and the Glen, was the winner of our where-to-eat debate. We all wanted a laidback atmosphere and nothing was more casual than eating barbecue. It was impossible to put on airs or be judgmental with barbecue sauce dripping from your chin and fingers.

Elise and I arrived first and were shown to a table in the corner, which the hostess assured us was the quietest spot in the restaurant. The guys came separately, but arrived at the same time. They introduced themselves when they realized they were walking to the same table. Elise did the honors for me. Jerry Fletcher DDS was tall, graying at the temples with an engaging smile. We all hit it off immediately and were so busy chatting that we forgot to look at the menu. We apologized to the waitress when she came by for the second time and promised to be ready if she gave us two more minutes. We all went for the ribs with corn bread, beans and cole slaw—half racks for Elise and me, full racks for the men. This Little Piggy got four sauce-covered thumbs up.

Dessert was coffee and individual blueberry cobblers with vanilla ice cream. Jerry cajoled the waitress into making the scoops extra-large. He and Travis started talking sports, leaving Elise and me with some girl time. She looked at me with a quizzical eyebrow that clearly asked for my verdict on her new guy. I answered with an enthusiastic nod and a grin, glad that he was exactly as advertised. It would have been awful if I'd found him wanting, because I'd never seen her happier.

"So, what's happening with the case?" she asked. "I feel like I'm out of the loop on this one, and Lolly is weighing on my mind."

"Well you've been kind of busy with work and the boys—and Jerry," I added *sotto voce*.

I told her about Brock keeping tabs on Ava, and about Liam's issues. "Nothing new on Dani. But she just can't be the killer—it would destroy Lolly."

"Did you ever find out what went sour between Ava and Angie?"

I took a sip of coffee and set the cup down. "No, but I found out that about a month before Ava was killed, Angie and her kids left town with no forwarding address."

Elise wiped a drop of blueberry pie from the corner of her mouth. "What about her parents? They might know where she went and why."

"I have no idea where they live or how to reach them."

"Maybe Eagle Enterprises still has her in their files. If they do, there should be an emergency contact number, and since she's divorced it's probably her parents or a close friend."

"You are brilliant!" I must have spoken louder than I intended, because the guys stopped their conversation to see what had me so excited. "Jerry," I said, "I hope you know how lucky you are to have this woman in your life."

He chuckled. "So everyone keeps telling me!"

* * * *

The phone roused me from a deep sleep. By the clock on the night table it was close to two a.m. My heart was already pounding when I heard Tilly's fretful voice. "Merlin is missing again."

I flew out of bed, throwing my feline bedmates into a tizzy of their own. Only Sashkatu remained on his pillow. He'd lived through enough human craziness that he was able to take a little more in stride. "How long ago?" I asked, pulling on jeans and a sweatshirt against the colder night air.

"I don't know, I can't be sure. I was on my way to the bathroom for the second time and I peeked in his room like I usually do, but he wasn't there. I searched the house. What if he was kidnapped like you were?"

"I think it's much more likely that he's sleepwalking again. Go make your healing tea and a little something to go with it. When we find him, I'm sure he'll be hungry."

If we were an ordinary family, Tilly would have installed a super-duper lock after Merlin's first sleepwalking episode. But we weren't ordinary. Unlocking spells were easy to cast. Merlin could do it in his sleep.

I grabbed my purse, locked the house and jumped into my car. I was backing out of the driveway when it occurred to me that I had no idea where to go. When I couldn't come up with a reasonable plan of action, I started driving anyway. Doing something was better than doing nothing. I drove for miles, making bigger and bigger circles and becoming more distraught with the passing of each minute. I didn't know where else to look. I pulled into Tilly's driveway behind her red mustang. I was walking to the front door, when a horn honked loud and long. It was so unexpected in the stillness of the night that I jumped and my heart slammed into my rib cage, leaving me breathless.

"Get out of the way or I'll run you down," a disembodied voice shouted. I would have known that voice anywhere. "Are you deaf?" Merlin screeched from the driver's seat of the Mustang. Tilly appeared in her doorway.

"Was that you honking?" she called to me.

"No, Aunt Tilly, it was a crazy old wizard, who may not get to be much older."

Chapter 32

"He spends entirely too much time deciphering those scrolls," Tilly said. She'd shuffled into my shop in her worn-out slippers to discuss Merlin's sleepwalking problem. I was busy dusting in the fifteen minutes before I opened. Searching for Merlin half the night had left me so exhausted, I was certain if I sat down I'd fall asleep. "They're overstimulating his mind," Tilly continued. "I never thought I'd say this, but I wish he'd go back to watching westerns and ordering stuff online."

I finished cleaning the shelf with the cellulite eraser, one of my biggest sellers, and started on the shelf above it. "Look at it this way. If he learns how to fix the problems with our magick, he'll stop sleepwalking and we'll be back to our old selves again—a win-win."

"I suppose," she said grudgingly.

"If you want to stop him from sleepwalking you can always give him one of Bronwen's sleeping pills."

"No no no—they're riddled with side effects. I trashed them as soon as Bronwen passed on. When she concocted them, I think she was getting a little dotty."

"I wouldn't say things like that out loud if I were you. You never know who might drop in and hear you."

"Oops." Tilly clamped her hands over her mouth.

A thought struck me. "Since Merlin sleepwalked into your car last night, maybe his subconscious is pushing him to go find what's been affecting the ley lines."

"Interesting thought. If we spend the day trying to find the cause, maybe his subconscious will let him sleep at night. It's worth a try." She perked up and straightened her shoulders with newfound purpose. "If you need me, I'll be chauffeuring his majesty around."

It was a slow business day, the dusting was done, and when I sat down in my padded desk chair, I was sound asleep in seconds. I awoke three hours later with a stiff neck, feeling a bit disoriented. There were only two customers in the afternoon, so I decided to close an hour early. Even if I missed a sale or two, it would be worth it if I visited Eagle Enterprises and found an emergency contact for Angie.

Despite my long nap, my one concern was that I might not be recharged enough to conduct a round trip. It wasn't that long ago I'd teleported to escape my kidnappers. Unfortunately, the only way to find out was to try it. Honoring my promise to Bronwen, I first sent a glass jar from my storeroom into Tilly's shop. When I went to see how it had fared, I found it sitting on a tea table unscathed—a good sign for a simple inorganic item on a one way ticket, but teleporting a human being was much more complicated, plus I needed a round trip.

My cautious side said I should probably wait a few days to be sure my energy level had rebounded adequately. My more impulsive side argued that I should quit procrastinating and get on with it. That's what I did. I reached the necessary power threshold in short order as if the universe had just been waiting for me to commit. I envisioned the cubicle in which I'd spoken to Krista. If anyone had lingered past the end of the workday, I'd be less likely to be spotted in there than in the open areas. I recited the spell three times and with the speed of a thought I was there.

Experience had shown me that teleporting into a building doesn't trip the security system. No doors or windows had been breached. Motion detectors and video cameras were a different story. The last time I'd found myself in such a situation, I'd created a spell that took care of the problem. I recited it three times.

The building was silent, hunkered down for the night. I didn't bother with Krista's computer. Personnel information would be on the computers in Human Resources. The building had enough night lighting for me to move about without crashing into furniture or tripping over smaller objects, but I could have used a floor plan. It took me ten minutes to find Human Resources in the maze of cubicles and offices. The door was locked. Another spell in my stockpile took care of that. I'd amassed quite an arsenal of spells since entering the world of murder investigations.

The computer on the director's desk was in hibernation mode. I hit random keys and the log on screen popped up asking for a password. Now what? I could try to create a spell to bypass the computer's security, but even with the best intentions, I'd be dabbling in some murky magick. I was on the verge of giving up when I noticed two filing cabinets tucked into a dimly lit back corner of the room. They'd been relegated to the shadows, an embarrassing reminder that the shiny toys of technology couldn't always be counted on to perform. And when that happened, it was good to have old-fashioned paper copies waiting in the wings.

I opened the top drawer of the first cabinet. The folders inside bore peoples' last names starting with the letter *A*. It didn't take me long to find the *N*s and Angie Neumann's folder. Within it were the forms she'd filled out when she was hired, including the emergency contact information for her parents. I whooped a silent cheer and jotted the information in a little notepad in my purse. Mission accomplished.

Although I could teleport back from anywhere in the building, with my energy levels a concern, the safest option was to use the same pathway by which I'd come. I rounded the last corner on my way back to Krista's cubicle and ploughed full tilt into a large cart being propelled by a woman in the uniform of a cleaning service. I could tell by the woman's face that she was startled and afraid she'd injured me.

I leaned back against the wall to assess the damage. I had a nasty gash on the knee that hit the cart and my abdomen felt bruised. Nothing serious. The woman came rushing over to me, babbling in a language I couldn't identify. "Shh," I said, afraid that anyone in the building would hear her. I put my finger to my lips in what I hoped was a universal sign of quiet. In a whisper, I tried to convince her I was all right, but she was practically in tears, gesticulating wildly, no doubt worried about losing her job. I wound up consoling her, patting her shoulder and smiling to convey the fact that all was well, while blood dripped down my leg. We must have stood there a good ten minutes, before she calmed down enough to go back to work.

I slipped into Krista's cubicle with a sigh of relief. By then the bleeding had almost stopped. I'd take care of it properly once I was back in my shop. I closed my eyes and tried to regulate my breathing. It took longer than usual, but I finally felt the tension melting away.

"What the hell do you think you're doing?!" It was a male voice, a very angry male voice. My eyes flew open. The supervisor I'd met on my last visit was standing two feet away, his hands on his hips, glowering at me.

"Mr. Nash—hi," I said cheerfully, not at all like someone who had just been caught trespassing in a company with armed guards and ties to the government. "You must be wondering why I'm here."

"You have one minute to convince me *not* to call security."

"Oh dear, I don't work well under pressure. Perhaps you could give me five minutes? And a quick trip to the bathroom? Bladder issues," I added with an embarrassed little shrug. *Acting like my aunt on a silly day—that's what my brain came up with to save my hide?*

"You have half a minute left and your bladder will just have to cope. You should have thought about that before you decided to break in here."

"Break in? Oh no—I didn't break in. No, no, no—I would never do that. I walked in when the last workers were leaving." *That was better.*

"Regardless of how you got in, you don't belong here! What is it you want?" My brain was groping around for a reason that didn't sound crazy or criminal.

"Silly me," I giggled, "I'd better put plugs in my ears or one day my brain will spill right out. I wanted to personally thank you for the lovely flower arrangement and sympathy card."

"What are you talking about? I didn't send you anything."

"Then who sent it?" I asked with wide-eyed innocence.

"How should I know?!" he thundered, clearly out of whatever patience he'd had before I arrived.

"Oh I get it," I said with a wink, "you're not comfortable with gratitude. You don't want anyone to think of you as a softy. Well your secret kindness is safe with me." I could practically smell the rage ballooning inside him.

"I'm going to let you go this time, but if I *ever* find you anywhere near this building again, I will hand you over to security and file a complaint against you with the police. Do you understand?"

I nodded without another word. *Once you get what you want, shut up before I change my mind.* I'd heard Tilly's husband use those words on more than one occasion. This seemed like an appropriate time to apply the advice.

Nash escorted me out of the building and pointed me in the direction of the guards at the gate. I waved goodbye and started skipping away. I heard him mutter, "Idiot," before the door slammed shut behind him.

Since I wasn't in view of the guards, I scooted off the paved road and into a thicket of trees, vines and brambles. When I was sufficiently screened from anyone passing by, I set about teleporting home.

Chapter 33

My phone rang when Sashkatu and I were walking home from the shop. I wasn't up to a chatty social call or solving any new problems. Teleporting back and forth to Eagle Enterprises had taken a lot out of me and I needed to take care of the cut in my knee before feeding the hungry horde awaiting dinner. But when Lolly's number appeared, I couldn't let the call go to voice mail.

"I just missed you at the shop," she said breathing hard, "but I really have to talk to you as soon as possible." She sounded distraught and didn't pick up on my weary tone, which was not at all like her. I couldn't put her off. She was goodness and sweetness and caring—the whole grandmotherly package. And she always smelled like chocolate. All my efforts to solve the murder of Ava Duncan were spurred on by the fact that Lolly was a suspect along with her daughter, Dani. Concern for their wellbeing swept my fatigue away like a magick broom.

"I'm just getting home. Could you possibly come—"

"I'll be there in five—thank you, dear."

I left the front door unlocked and went into the powder room to work on my knee. There was a good chance that climbing the stairs would reopen the wound. My mother had always kept emergency supplies in each of the bathrooms for just such an occurrence and I'd carried on the tradition. Even if the stairs hadn't been a concern for my knee, it surely was for Lolly with her arthritis.

When the doorbell rang, I called for her to come in. It took her several minutes to make her way down the short hall to the powder room, because six cats insisted on providing a proper welcome even if their owner couldn't. They rarely appeared for anyone other than family. It was a testament to

Lolly that they'd accepted her as one of their own from her very first visit. They were great judges of character and, to the best of my knowledge, had never made a wrong call.

Lolly found me sitting on the toilet lid bandaging my knee. She was so pale she looked like she'd just come from a Medieval bloodletting. "Talk to me," I said, putting the botanical lotions and potions back in the kit and stowing it under the sink. "On second thought, wait until we get you into a chair in the kitchen," I added, afraid she might keel over at any moment. I put my arm around her waist.

She allowed me to lead her to the kitchen table, where I eased her into a chair. "I'm going to brew you some of Tilly's restorative tea." She didn't say anything. Her reticence scared me even more than her pallor. Lolly was always bubbling over with life.

The tea seemed to be taking forever. I helped it along with a quick spell. When it was ready, I poured each of us a cup and sat down. "Can I get you something to eat?" I asked, thinking maybe she'd forgotten lunch and her blood sugar had tanked. She shook her head. Rather than pump her for the cause of her distress, I waited until she had time to sip the tea and let her begin when she was ready.

"Dani made a huge mistake," she said. I could tell she was trying to speak calmly, "and I have no idea how to help her." Tears welled up in her eyes. I put my hand over hers where it rested on the table.

"Tell me what she did. I'm sure it's not as bad as it seems." I shouldn't have said that without knowing anything, but I wanted to give her hope. Whenever I empathized too much with someone's misery, Bronwen would chastise me, saying "false hope just postpones the inevitable. You can't make the sun shine for someone, no matter how much they seem to need it." Her words were etched into my brain, yet they couldn't always stop me.

Lolly took a moment to ready herself the way you would before walking into the doctor's office for the results of a biopsy. "She admitted to me that she did confront Ava." An *oh no* popped into my mouth, but I managed to swallow it. "She found out her address and went to her apartment in the Glen. Thank goodness she doesn't own a weapon."

"How did it go?"

"Not well. They argued. According to my daughter, Ava was as cold as ice, not the least bit sympathetic or willing to break it off with Elliot— not even for the sake of the children. She told Dani that he'd relentlessly pursued her. 'He'll never walk away from me,' Ava said. 'Why on earth would you want a man who no longer loves you?'"

"Did Dani make any threats?" I hated to ask the question, but it was necessary. The police wouldn't have any qualms about asking that and more.

"She threatened to sue her for alienation of affection. When Ava laughed at her, she threatened to... she threatened to kill her." Lolly closed her eyes and shuddered.

I drained the cooling tea in my cup to give me time to think. "Has she admitted this to the police?"

"No and I have no idea how to counsel her."

"When did this take place?"

"At the worst possible time—the night before Ava was found dead." Lolly's voice broke with a sob. The tea could rebalance her body's systems, but it couldn't numb her emotions. Only black magick could accomplish that. And the price for it was too high.

"When Duggan first questioned her, she skipped over the confrontation?" Lolly nodded.

"When did she tell you about this?"

"Two days ago. Keeping it to herself was making her sick. Do you think she should tell Duggan now? Won't it make her look horribly guilty? Look, Ava was the only person who knew about that conversation and she's dead. Maybe Dani should keep her mouth shut?"

"There's a really good chance that Ava told Elliot and she might have also told her best friends. I think Dani has to admit it to the police before they find out from someone else, but I'm no expert on legal matters. If she hasn't retained a lawyer yet, now would be a good time to do it." Lolly clamped her teeth down on her lower lip.

"Listen," I said, "things aren't as dire as you think. From everything I've read, and everything Travis has uncovered, the police don't have any physical evidence linking Dani to the body."

"You're right!" Lolly said. "That means there *is* hope." She stood up and kissed me on the top of my head. "I'm going over to see Dani this minute and tell her in person what you said! It's a good thing I brought my car."

Oh no—did I do it again? Did I give her false hope?

* * * *

"I have information I'm sure you'll find invaluable," Beverly said when she swept into Abracadabra the next morning. I was arranging a new shipment of crystals on one of my display tables. I knew she expected me to drop what I was doing, which is why I didn't even pause to look up.

"I'll be done here in a few minutes," I said. She issued a small *humph* and walked over to the register to wait, drumming her fingernails on the counter to let me know she was annoyed. When I was satisfied with the display, I joined her there. "I'm all ears," I said, forcing a smile that felt more like a grimace.

Beverly produced an equally artificial smile. Neither of us would make great actors. "I thought we could barter for the information."

"I'll have to hear what you have or I can't possibly assign it a value."

"But once I tell you, it will no longer have any value," she pointed out. "You could say you already knew it."

"Look, if you don't trust me to be honest with you, there's no reason to continue this conversation." I went around the counter to sit at the computer. Beverly appeared to be stymied. Her phony smile disintegrated as she tried to decide on a new strategy.

"Okay," she bristled, "I'll take the high road here and trust you, but be forewarned that if you don't play fair with me, I won't come to you with information in the future." She had no idea how tempting that alternative was. On the other hand, she was a sought-after hair stylist and owner of a thriving salon, the nexus of small town grapevines. I'd be a fool to cut off such a rich vein of future information. Besides, treating people unfairly simply didn't square with my nature or the white magick ingrained in my DNA.

"You're going to trust me? How very noble of you," I managed to say without laughing. "What is this information you have?"

"Well, I was in Watkins Glen yesterday to pick up products at the beauty supply store. I'd gotten a late start, because I had to wait for the plumber to unclog a drain in the salon. You can't run a hair salon with a clogged drain." *Imagine that,* I thought to myself. "In any case, by the time I left the supply store it was almost two o'clock and I was starving. I stopped in that little deli-café near the courthouse to have a sandwich—turkey and Swiss on rye with honey mustard." *Thanks, I was wondering about that.* "I took my tray and went to sit down. It was pretty empty. Most people have eaten by two o'clock. That's when I noticed them." *Them?* "They were sitting at the table in the back corner."

"Who was?" Impatience had gotten the better of me.

"Travis and Whitney Reynolds," she said with a smug smile. "I've heard they were high school sweethearts. You hear stories about long lost loves finding each other later in life, but I've never known anyone it happened to." Although I quickly slapped a neutral expression on my face, my reaction was visceral and no doubt obvious. Judging by Beverly's face, she'd thoroughly enjoyed it.

"They were probably just catching up," I said, trying to appear unconcerned. Beverly's grin stretched from ear to ear.

"I don't know why I ever doubted your honesty. Your reactions are plain enough for anyone to read. You had no idea about their date." She knew how to keep digging in the knife. If Merlin had been there, I would have begged him to transmute her into a snake permanently, and no jury of our peers would have convicted us. Not that we had any peers except for Tilly. "How much would you say the information is worth?" Beverly asked sweetly.

"Nothing. And more to the point, I don't remember asking you to keep tabs on Travis. Was that your big news flash? They were having lunch in a deli—oh no, not that. But to prove I'm not just trying to get out of paying you, I'll give you twenty-five dollars store credit. It's a one-time courtesy—don't ever expect me to be this generous again when it comes to gossip about Travis." I watched Beverly lose her smile and any sense of triumph she'd been feeling. If she'd had an ounce of self-respect, she would have apologized and turned down the credit. Instead she marched off to the aisle with the moisturizers. Beverly was never a surprise.

After she left, I tried to shrug off the image of Travis and Whitney that she'd planted in my head. It wasn't easy to do, mainly because it brought up other images: the way Whitney had looked at him that night in Seasons and the way he'd ruined our big night out by inviting her to join us. Little qualms rippled through my heart. I wondered if he would mention their lunch the next time we spoke.

Chapter 34

The rest of the day I saw a steady stream of customers, but only one or two at a time so that I was never alone in the shop. It seemed like they'd all had a meeting and planned it that way. Although I'm always glad to have business, I wouldn't have minded a brief lull, say ten minutes or so, during which I could have called the Neumanns and Travis. They weren't the kind of calls I could make with anyone else in the shop—unless I wanted to add grist to the town's lively gossip mill. I closed up promptly at the stroke of five. I woke Sashkatu and waited for him to go through his ritual of stretching, before we headed home.

After I fed everyone, I played chase the red light and catch the fake mouse with the younger cats. Sashki sat atop the couch, eyelids at half-mast. Once the house settled down for the evening, I sat at the kitchen table with a cup of Tilly's tummy tamer brew, but no appetite for anything else. My stomach was churning like the ocean in a Nor'easter. Now that I finally had the time to make those calls, who to dial first? The Neumanns won, not solely because the case was a high priority, but also because I was dreading the conversation with Travis, afraid to hear the truth about his feelings for Whitney.

After the fourth ring, I expected to be shunted to voice mail. Instead a woman answered with a wary *hello*, catching me off guard. "Mrs. Neumann—Susan, if I may be less formal, my name is Kailyn Wilde. I know your daughter from Eagle Enterprises. She left so abruptly, I was concerned about her well-being." I'd decided to focus on Angie's disappearance and not mention Ava's death, if possible.

"Oh," Susan said, as if she was trying to figure out how to deal with me. "It's nice of you to take an interest."

"I was hoping you'd know where Angie is living now or how I can get in touch with her."

"No… we have no idea. It's been a nightmare for us. She's our only child." She didn't sound as agitated or tearful as parents I'd seen on the news whose adult children had gone missing. But it was unfair to rate her distress by an arbitrary standard. Everyone dealt with trauma and tragedy in their own way. "It's awful to live in such a state of limbo," she continued. "I don't wish it on my worst enemy." There was a catch in her throat and she seemed about to breakdown, but she couldn't quite reach the threshold.

"I can't even imagine what you and your husband are going through," I said. "I'd like to come talk to you. My partner and I have had a lot of success in solving cases." I was vague on purpose, hoping she would take my words to mean *missing persons cases,* when I meant murder cases.

"I don't think that's such a good idea." She hung onto each word, dragging it out as if she were stalling for time, until the cavalry arrived to save the day.

"There's no charge, not even if we find them. You have nothing to lose." I heard a man's voice in the background and Susan saying, "No, it's fine, Chris." A muted exchange followed and then the click of the call disconnecting. Angie's parents knew something. If I could speak to Susan in person, I might be able to find out what it was. But I clearly couldn't do it with her husband around.

I sat there looking at the phone, knowing I had to call Travis. There was a lot to catch him up on, but I couldn't get my mind off his lunch with Whitney. What would it mean if he didn't volunteer the information about their *tête a tête*? It could mean he was simply catching up with an old friend and didn't mention it, because he was afraid I might take it the wrong way. Or it could mean he'd felt the spark between them reignite and felt too guilty to tell me. Had sophisticated Whitney played the guilt card about the way he'd dumped her to press for the lunch date? Even the smartest men couldn't tell when a woman was manipulating them.

* * * *

"Angie and her kids disappeared and her mother isn't interested in the free help you offered." Travis repeated after I detailed my talk with Susan Neumann. "It doesn't make any sense, unless they *know* she *isn't* missing. And why would a woman with young children and a good job choose to give up that security and pretend to disappear? Is she in hiding because she borrowed money from some Mafia character who's now looking to break her kneecaps for not repaying it? I don't think so." He paused for a moment. "Where did Lolly say they lived?"

"Hassettville."

"That's around the corner compared to Buffalo. We ought to take a run up there on a weekday and see if we can catch Susan when her husband's not around to silence her."

"There's something else," I said and related the story about Dani's showdown with Ava. He groaned. "Talk about shooting yourself in the foot."

"I want to canvas Ava's building and see if anyone heard them arguing. I believe what Lolly told me, but Dani may not have been completely forthcoming with her."

"Sounds good. I'll meet you there tomorrow morning at ten."

"It's not necessary. I can take care of it." I heard the grudging tone in my voice and knew Travis would too.

"You don't want me to go?" he teased, feigning insult.

"Come on," I said more lightly, "you know I didn't mean it that way. I was giving you an out if you already have too much work on your plate." If we were going to have a conversation about Whitney, it was going to be in person and at the time and place of my choosing. I just had to be more vigilant about not letting my pique show. We agreed to meet at ten o'clock.

* * * *

I was sitting on the couch, watching *Dirty Dancing* for the twentieth time and stroking Sashkatu's silky back when my aunt Tilly came to visit. She preferred to let herself in rather than ring the bell, because, as she put it, this was the family home where she'd grown up and she was still family even if she now lived a block away. Morgana used to complain that her sister would show up at odd hours and give her a fright. I'd never minded, but there were times when it seemed Tilly would be better served by ringing the bell. That evening was a case in point. I listened to her fumbling with the lock for a good three minutes before she finally managed to let herself in.

When she came into view, the reason for her difficulty was evident. She was holding a cake plate with what smelled like a spice cake slathered in dark chocolate icing.

I jumped up to take it from her. "No Merlin?" I asked, leading the way into the kitchen.

"No—I had to bake this cake to lower my blood pressure because of his Lordship. Plus, I needed a respite from him, so I told him he had to stay home tonight. However, he did exact my promise to bring him back a large piece of cake."

I got busy gathering plates and utensils. I hadn't eaten dinner, but I was fine with cake in its stead. It wouldn't be the first time. Neither of us wanted tea. Instead I suggested vanilla ice cream, which made Tilly wiggle in her chair like a little kid too excited to sit still. I cut two substantial pieces of cake and slid them onto plates. "What on earth did Merlin do to you today?" I asked.

Tilly served herself a large scoop of ice cream and let it fall on top of the warm cake, where it instantly started to melt. "He made me drive him all over the bloody place."

"Oh. I take it he didn't find what he was looking for?" I felt a little guilty for suggesting he try to find the problem with the ley lines.

She handed me the scooper and took the first bite of her dessert. "Oh dear—this is beyond sinful, but it does even out one's disposition."

I helped myself to the ice cream. "You did what you could today and that has to count for something," I said. "Maybe if he continues reading the scrolls, he'll find more information to help narrow the search parameters."

Tilly was dreamy-eyed, beyond caring, on a chocolate and ice cream high. "That would be nice."

"You know how he can be, Aunt Tilly, you might have to put your foot down." However at that moment I wouldn't have bet she could even stand up straight.

"Don't you worry," she said, slurring her words as she reached for the scooper. Before she could lift it, she fell asleep face down in the remnants of her dessert. Since she wasn't going to get messier than she already was, I let her nap there for five minutes, while I wrapped up the rest of the cake. If I kept it in my house, I would whittle away at it all week until none of my clothes fit. When I woke her, I wiped her face with a wet cloth, before putting her and the cake into her car. I deposited them into Merlin's care and strolled back home.

Chapter 35

I parked in the municipal lot and walked over to the building where both Angie and Ava had lived. It was once a two-story middle school, but when the student population dwindled, the classrooms were reconfigured into one and two-bedroom apartments. On the outside, it still looked like a school, red brick and a tall flagpole. On the inside, what had been the school's offices was now a spacious lobby with elevators. I found Travis waiting for me in one of the armchairs. He popped up as soon as he saw me and gave me a quick kiss. It felt dismissive, but I was probably more sensitive since Beverly's visit. I warned myself that if I started over-analyzing everything he said and did, I'd cause a real rift between us and send him running into Whitney's welcoming arms.

"I found the super upstairs painting one of the apartments," Travis said. "His name is Jorge. I explained why we wanted to speak to him and he seemed willing—make that eager—to answer our questions."

"I'll bet he recognized you from the news," I said with a smile that felt too wide.

"That's what he said. I think he has visions of being interviewed on TV. I'm just worried he might pad the truth to make the story more sensational."

"You'll have to start wearing disguises. I think bushy eyebrows and a big nose could be a good look for you. Your star is definitely on the rise, as Tilly would say." I knew I was talking too fast, my nerves amped, courtesy of Beverly. "Have you ever thought about letting Tilly do a reading? You'd be amazed at how good she is. But she's absolutely ethical too. She'd never tell me anything."

Travis was looking at me as if I was speaking a foreign language. "You okay?"

"Sure, why?"

"Just how much coffee did you have this morning? You're like a runaway train."

"I guess I shouldn't have had that extra cup." As long as he was offering me an out, I wasn't going to turn it down. "I'll be fine. Lead the way."

Jorge was wearing painter's overalls with so many layers of paint that he looked like a living canvas of modern art. He had an assistant working with him. If I understood Jorge's introduction, his name was Carlos and he was a fourth cousin on his mother's side. He hadn't bothered with painting gear, but he might be rethinking that decision now that his jeans were speckled with white paint.

Jorge took us into an empty bedroom and offered us seats on the hardwood floor. I was glad I'd opted for pants instead of a skirt. "What would you like to know?" he asked in accented English. Travis nodded at me to take the lead.

"When you think back to the night before Ava was killed, do you remember hearing any arguments or raised voices coming from her apartment?"

"*Sí*, I hear two woman—they shouting from where is Miss Duncan's apartment. I recognize her voice. I think the other voice must be the lady I see go past the apartment where I finish up painting for new tenant." I opened my purse and took out the photo I'd brought along of Lolly and her family. I pointed to Dani and asked if she could be that woman.

Jorge wiped his hands on his overalls before taking the picture from me. He squinted at it. "*Sí*—is her."

"Do you remember what time that was?" I asked.

"It was after dinner, because my wife, she says to me her usual 'work after eating is no good for digestion.'" He chuckled, then whispered, "Between you and I, nagging is less good for digestion." Travis and I laughed with him. Jorge had his delivery down pat.

I repositioned myself on the floor, thinking that hardwood was aptly named. It made me aware of every bone in my body that didn't have enough padding. "Could you tell what the women were saying?"

He shook his head. "Only just one word or two. I say to myself, Jorge, maybe you go knock on the door and see if they are okeydokey. But before I can decide, the visitor lady is coming out and I see in her face how angry she is. I have relief there isn't blood on her. I knock on Miss Duncan's door, but she isn't opening up. We talk through the door. She say she is fine, but she sound upset. What more I can do?" He shrugged. "I go back to mind my business."

We thanked him for his help and Travis gave him his card. "You know," Jorge said, "there was a man who came one, no two weeks before and he argues with Miss Duncan too."

"Liam," Travis and I said at the same time.

"Did you have a chance to see this man?" Travis asked, getting to his feet. I followed. Standing was preferable to the floor.

Jorge shook his head. "You know, Miss Duncan is being so nice to me and my wife, I am not understanding why is people angry at her?"

Travis clapped him on the back. "That's what we're trying to find out, my friend. You have my number. Give me a call if you remember anything else."

"Are you heading straight back?" Travis asked in the elevator.

"If you have time, I was hoping we could discuss what Jorge told us."

"We can grab a quick lunch. How's pizza—or what people here call pizza?"

We stepped off the elevator into the lobby. "I'm not really in a pizza mood." I stopped so I could face him. "Have you ever been to the Deli Café? Good sandwiches and great pickles," I added lightly. And a chance to find out if you're going to be upfront or secretive about your recent lunch there.

He hesitated and I could almost see the workings of his brain through his expressions. For those few seconds his head was like the see-through watch I'd had as a teen. "Sure—it's the best sandwich place in the Glen," he said matching my carefree tone. "Besides it's hard to pass up a great pickle." That moment would have been the time to admit that he'd been there yesterday with Whitney, but the moment passed in silence. He had no intentions of telling me. My heart was leaden. He spent the five-minute trip to the deli talking about Ava, Dani, and Liam. I didn't absorb a word of it. Didn't he wonder why he was having a conversation with himself, my only contribution a few monotone *uh huhs?*

It wasn't quite eleven-thirty—early for lunch. There was no line at the counter. I stared at the menu board on the wall without seeing it and ended up ordering turkey and brie on rye, because it was the first item on the menu. I thought the deli guy might say something offhand to Travis about seeing him with a different woman earlier in the week, but he was as tight-lipped as a priest in the confessional.

Travis ordered roast beef and cheddar on a Kaiser roll. We both opted for bottled water. He led the way to the table in the corner. Wasn't that the table Beverly had mentioned? People have little habits they're not even aware of—in poker they're called *tells*. Preferring corners was clearly one of Travis's. We unloaded our trays and started eating.

"Do you still want to canvas the apartments on either side of Ava's?" he asked. "It might net us some specifics about the arguments she had."

"We already know what they were fighting about. We can always circle back to it if we're stuck."

The teenage boy who bussed the tables offered to take our trays away. We handed them over. As he turned to leave, he gave Travis a chin thrust. "Like your style man." If he were of an older generation he might have added a strategic wink only Travis could see.

It was doubtful he was talking about Travis's establishment beige chinos and blue polo, his conservative hair, or table etiquette. He was clearly referring to his style of juggling women. It was the opening I needed. "What an odd thing for that kid to say."

Travis took a long drink from his water bottle. "Who knows what kids today are thinking." I couldn't decide whether to ask him outright about seeing Whitney or wait and see if he'd back himself into another corner. It really wasn't much of a choice—I don't like playing mind games, especially with someone I care for.

I put my sandwich down. "I think he was congratulating you about having lunch yesterday with Whitney and with me today."

"Possibly," he said, studying me like I was an abstract painting he was trying to interpret. At least he racked up a point in my book for not denying it. "Was I expected to clear it with you?" And instantly lost two points for attitude. I hadn't counted on such a defensive answer. It might mean he was more invested in her than I'd thought.

"No, I'm just surprised you didn't mention it."

"I didn't mention it, because it didn't mean anything."

"See, that's where we disagree. If it didn't mean anything you would have told me. You tell me if you saw an interesting bird, if you lost another sock in the drier, if someone brings in donuts and you were able to resist having one. The fact that you didn't, well…"

Travis sighed in the way men sigh when they think women are being difficult. "To be honest, I was trying to avoid *this*."

"How's that working for you?" I heard the sarcasm slither into my voice, but I didn't care.

"Look, she called and asked if we could meet for lunch to catch up on old times. She's not trying to pick up where we left off."

"Did you seriously expect her to tell you if she was? I'm sure you would have realized it eventually—about the time they started playing the wedding march."

"You're not giving me much credit."

"I'm giving you a lot of credit—for recognizing how poorly you treated her, for feeling guilty about it, and for wanting to make amends. But take it from a woman, that's what she's counting on."

"I'm a good judge of character too, Kailyn, and I'm telling you that you're wrong."

"When is your next date?" I asked in a cool measured tone.

"There isn't one. For that matter, yesterday wasn't a date either."

"All right, when will she be back in town?" I could play semantics too.

"In two weeks, specifically to check on how her design plans are being implemented."

"Did she say something like 'let's touch base then?'"

He hesitated. "No, not exactly in those words." If he didn't see it yet, he never would.

I wiped my mouth and screwed the cap on my water. "I don't seem to have much of an appetite after all," I said, standing.

Travis sprang out of his chair and put his hand on my arm as if to stop me. "I don't want to leave it like this."

"Like what?" I said softly. I'd had my back to the small dining area and when I turned I was surprised to see that half the tables were now occupied, with more patrons at the counter ordering. From what I could tell, everyone was either in conversation with their seatmates or on their phones. No one appeared to be interested in Travis and me. I was glad we weren't in New Camel.

"With you upset and angry," he whispered.

"No, don't try to make this about me. *You* have to decide how far you'll go to make things right with Whitney." I turned and threaded my way between the tables to the door.

Chapter 36

I tried not to think about my relationship with Travis, which only made me think about it more. I wrote a spell that failed to banish it from my thoughts. I asked Tilly if she knew of one that might work. According to her, no one in my family had been successful in that endeavor. Apparently matters of the heart were impervious to magick. Merlin offered up the one he'd created to help King Arthur win Guinevere's love away from Lancelot. After some questioning, he admitted that it hadn't worked and that it had turned him into a frog for the better part of a night. He said he couldn't get the taste of flies out of his mouth for months. That settled the matter. The risk-reward ratio was too great to even contemplate.

It didn't help matters that Travis and I were still partners in the investigation to clear Lolly and her daughter in the murder of Ava Duncan. There was too much at stake to shut down that facet of our relationship while he decided where his heart lay. Before the Whitney issue arose, we had planned to drive up to Hassettville to try to talk to Angie's mother in person. When I called Travis to settle the details of the trip, our conversation was awkward. Thankfully the trip up there was under an hour, so we didn't have to deal with hotel accommodations. I ached for things to go back to the way they'd been, but that wasn't possible if Travis didn't know his own mind. I was starting to understand how Bronwen and Morgana must have felt when their husbands opted for a simpler life with less complicated women.

With the weather warming, bus tours were beginning to fill my calendar. Travis's schedule was even more hectic. Since we were both free the next morning, we agreed there was no point in waiting. With any luck, I should be back in time to open for most of the afternoon. I wouldn't even have to disrupt my aunt's day with the care and feeding of my felines. As if I'd summoned her with my thoughts, she twirled into my shop through the connecting door to show off her new pale yellow spring muumuu. It was the perfect foil for her bright red hair.

"Look, it's so light and airy, it floats," she said, losing her balance and teetering first to the left and then to the right. I ran from behind the counter to try to steady her, but only succeeded in joining her in a heap on the floor. "All that whirling around made me dizzy!" she giggled. "Remind me never to do that again. Are you okay, dear?"

"I'll be fine," I said, getting to my feet and trying to help her up.

Merlin ambled into my shop with a half-eaten mini pie in his hand and cherry juice in his beard, making him look like a down-on-his-luck vampire. "What was that crash I—? Why are you on the floor, Matillda? You know how hard it is for you to get up from there."

"I like a challenge," she said wryly. "Do you think you could put down the pie for a minute and help me up?"

He set the pie carefully on the counter and had Tilly off the floor in no time. "In spite of his appearance, he's surprisingly wiry," she said in answer to my stunned expression. I helped her into the customer chair. Merlin retrieved his pie and hurried back to Tilly's shop before he could be asked to do anything else.

"How is the great search going?" I asked her.

"Nowhere. It's going nowhere. On the positive side, I am helping to support the oil companies."

"How much longer are you going to drive him around looking for a reason the ley lines may have shifted?" Although I had suggested the idea, it had to be hurting her bottom line. Psychic readings aren't the type of work you can delegate to an assistant.

"I don't know. It does seem to have stopped his sleepwalking, except for the incident the other night when I found him in the kitchen eating the seven-layer cake I made for Lolly's birthday. He claimed he was sleepwalking and sleep-eating, but I don't buy it."

* * * *

I made sure I was ready when Travis picked me up at ten o'clock. I slid into his SUV and immediately noticed that there were two coffees-to-go in the cup holders. Mine had *decaf* written in pen on the lid like it always did. He only drank what he called *hi-test*. I didn't know what to make of it—an olive branch? But there wasn't going to be any reconciliation unless he was ready to leave Whitney in his past. I'd realized back in college that dating more than one man at a time was not for me. And I expected to be the only woman in a man's life. If Travis and I were to work things out, I'd have to make that clear.

* * * *

We were both on our best behavior during the drive, the conversation polite and suffocating. I had to open my window for fresh air. The investigation seemed to be the least emotionally charged topic we could discuss. We went over everything we had on each of the suspects, hoping to catch something that had escaped us before. Lolly had the best alibi. She'd been at the Camel Day Fair at the time of Ava's death and the other merchants could vouch for her. Although she'd had a bitter argument with Ava, we were pretty sure Duggan didn't know about it or he would have interrogated her again. Her daughter, Danielle, was a different story. Ava was having an affair with Dani's husband, providing her with a great motive. Unfortunately, Dani had no equally great alibi. In fact, she had none, unless the checkout clerk at the grocery store remembered seeing her on that day at that time.

The list continued with Liam, who stood to lose his inheritance if Ava told their parents about his continued gambling. Brock, Ava's ex-boyfriend, had been stalking her since she broke up with him. Angie rounded out the list, but we hadn't been able to find a reason, let alone a motive, for the way she'd suddenly turned against Ava. To complicate matters, Angie had disappeared with her kids a month before Ava was killed.

We had no trouble locating the Neumann home. We drove by once, without stopping, to get a general impression. It sat on a block of small colonials and ranches that were probably built by the same developer long enough ago that some of them had fallen into disrepair. The Neumanns took care of their property. The grass had been mowed, all the bushes were neatly trimmed and the flower beds were freshly mulched. The vinyl siding was a slate blue, the trim and shutters a sparkling white. A late model gray sedan was parked in the driveway. There was no way to tell if another car was behind the closed garage door. Since it was a weekday, we'd just have to hope that Christopher Neumann was at work. If he was home, our chances of talking to his wife Susan were slim to none.

We parked at the curb and walked up the brick path to the front door. Travis rang the bell. There was a peephole through which we were no doubt being eyed. When the door opened, it revealed a well-groomed woman on the cusp of sixty. She regarded us warily, her eyebrows pinched over the bridge of her nose.

"Can I help you?" She sounded poised, but wary.

"Susan, I'm Kailyn Wilde. We spoke on the phone the other day." I held out my hand. She placed hers lightly in it as if she was afraid I might grab it and drag her away.

"I remember. You shouldn't have come here. If my husband were home..." her voice trailed off.

"It's important we speak to you. We're afraid Angie may be in danger." I'd tweaked the truth to appeal to Susan's maternal instincts. Even if she knew her daughter was safe at the moment, my concern might raise just enough doubt in her mind that she would want to hear more. She looked from me to Travis and back to me, clearly uncertain about what to do.

"Anything you want to discuss with me, we can discuss right here," she said finally. It wasn't ideal, but I had no problem conducting our meeting on her doorstep.

"Susan," I said, getting down to business, "do you know where your daughter is?"

"We're not asking you to tell us *where* she is," Travis interjected. "We just want to know if she's all right."

She shook her head. "We can't be sure. I haven't slept properly in weeks."

"Have you heard from her at all?"

She hesitated and when she spoke, her voice cracked and tears welled up in her eyes. "She's called a couple of times to tell us not to worry. We live in limbo—day and night—waiting for her to call again."

I opened my purse and rummaged in its depths until I found a packet of tissues. I offered her one, which she took with a *thank you.* She dabbed at her eyes and nose. "Have you filed a missing person's report with the police?"

"Oh no—she made it very clear that if we went to the police it would put her in jeopardy."

"We're not with the police," Travis assured her. "We're private investigators. You have our word that we wouldn't do anything to compromise your daughter's safety. We just want to talk to her, because she might have information that could help us."

"My husband wouldn't even want me talking to you. He believes family matters are only discussed within the family."

Instead of repeating the same request six different ways, I tried another tack. "Are your grandchildren with her?"

"Yes—I... I probably shouldn't be telling you any of this," she fretted.

I didn't have to be my aunt to predict that any moment now Susan was going to send us away. I tried one more question. "Did Angie tell you why she left her job and her life in Watkins Glen?"

"No, all she keeps saying is that the less we know the better it is for everyone." Susan checked her watch again. "You have to leave now. I have nothing more to say."

As the door swung shut between us, there was the unmistakable sound of children giggling. Susan made a heroic effort to mask the noise with a loud coughing fit and throat clearing that didn't bear the slightest resemblance to giggles.

"I'm sure you heard that too," Travis said as we walked down to the car. "It seems Susan lied about at least one thing—she definitely knows where her grandkids are. And if they're staying here, you can bet Angie will make an appearance sooner than later."

Chapter 37

We'd only driven a few blocks, when Travis hit the brakes. I looked around to see why he'd stopped in the middle of the road. No kid on a bicycle was flying out of a driveway. No one was trying to cross the street. No dog was chasing a runaway ball. "What's wrong?"

"Any chance we could hang out in Hassettville and keep an eye on the Neumann house? I think we'd have a good shot at catching Angie when she comes home from work."

It would mean keeping Abracadabra shuttered all day and asking my aunt to care for the cats if I wasn't home by their dinnertime. But as long as Travis and I were in Hassettville, it seemed foolish not to try waiting for her. It could be weeks before we both had the time to come back. And if she was amenable, there was a lot we could learn from her. When Tilly heard my request, she said she'd be delighted to open my shop for the afternoon. It would be a welcome reprieve from driving around searching for something that might not even exist.

"I figure Angie's at work," Travis said. We were seated in a booth at the diner in the small business district of Hassettville. We needed a decent lunch to carry us through our stakeout. I put down the menu, defeated by too many choices.

"It makes sense. She has two kids, and kids come with a lot of expenses. She can't expect her parents to take on that burden at this stage of their lives."

"We probably don't have to stake out the house much before five."

"Some offices close at four or four thirty," I pointed out. "I wouldn't want to miss her by half an hour after waiting all day."

The waitress came by before I'd settled on what I wanted. Travis ordered a bacon cheeseburger with fries. I wasn't in the mood for anything that heavy. At the table next to us, I saw a woman digging into a Belgian waffle with two huge scoops of ice cream—bingo. I hadn't indulged in one since last summer and now that the weather was milder it seemed like the perfect time. I caught Travis grinning at me. "Do you have something to say about my lunch?" I asked after the waitress walked away.

He shrugged. "Just that you're like a little kid when it comes to ice cream."

"Or like an old wizard," I added. Travis opened his mouth as if he was about to say something, then closed it again. We were both having trouble finding a neutral topic of conversation now that we'd talked the investigation to death. The other tables near us were having no such problem, which made our situation even more distressing. A niggling little voice in my head told me the ball was in my court. I could end our estrangement if I wanted to. But the voice was wrong. Until Travis could leave Whitney in the past, I had no play.

Out of desperation, I dredged up a question. "So—how are your folks?"

"Good—they're good," he said, grabbing onto it like it was a lifeline. "Have you heard from Morgana and Bronwen recently?"

"No, they must be busy. It seems the hereafter has quite a curriculum." And we were back to uncomfortable silence. I hadn't thought much about it before, but one of the best things about diners was the speed of their kitchens. In less than ten minutes our food arrived, rescuing us. When you eat without chatting, it's astonishing how little time it takes. Travis was down to his last few fries. I still had a quarter of my waffle, but I'd finished all the ice cream. Now what? He suggested a movie at the mini multiplex. I couldn't come up with a better plan, so off we went. There were three movies to choose from—war movie, chick flick, dumb comedy. Dumb comedy won by a landslide.

There were two other people in the theater, napping or wasting time like we were. As it happened, Travis and I had never gone to a movie together. It was weird sitting beside him in the darkened theater. If not for Whitney, he might have put his arm around me; I might have reached for his hand. The dumb comedy was dumber than we'd imagined. We didn't laugh once, but our moods may have been to blame for that. We walked outside into blinding sunlight with another hour to kill.

We were out of things to do and I, for one, wasn't interested in anymore pointless conversation. The only other option was to start the stakeout early. Travis parked at a curve in the road from which we had a decent view of the house, but anyone inside would have had difficulty seeing us. I was drained from the emotional turmoil of our relationship. Spending the entire day with him under these circumstances was exhausting. He seemed worn out too. There was no point in discussing why we were tired. Instead I proposed we take turns napping. I let him go first and I kept watch. Fifteen minutes crept by. It was my turn, and since no good deed goes unpunished, I had just drifted off to sleep when Angie came home.

She parked at the curb in front of her parent's house and sprinted across the lawn to the front door as if the boogey man was after her. For all we knew, maybe he was. "Does that look like a woman who's been held hostage for weeks?" Travis asked.

"Nope," I said. "That looks more like a woman who doesn't want anyone to find her here."

"The question is why? Did she rob a bank before leaving the Glen? Embezzle money from Eagle Enterprises? Abscond with proprietary information?" Since catching her before she ran into the house was no longer an option, we'd have to ring the bell and try to convince her to talk to us. One thing was clear—her mother was a gifted liar.

We waited another ten minutes to give Angie time to let down her guard and hopefully be more receptive to our visit. Susan answered the bell. "What are you doing here again? If you came back to call me a liar, I'm not the least bit sorry I misled you. I did it to protect my family. Chris was right. I should have slammed the door shut in your faces. Well no more questions—you are not welcome here and if you keep harassing us, I *will* call the police!"

I had one last card to play—the commonality of motherhood. "Susan, you have every right to your privacy. But can you spare one thought for a mother who's grieving, who wants to know why her daughter is dead? Angie may have information that could bring her some peace."

"I'm sorry for her—I truly am, but I have to concentrate on *my* family now." She shut the door on us for the second time that endless day. Travis and I looked at each other. Now what? We were turning to leave when the door opened halfway. Angie stood in the doorway, her mother behind her, glaring at us.

"You want to know about Ava Duncan?" Angie asked.

I stepped forward. "Yes. If you have any information, any theories about who killed her, we'd be really—" Angie grabbed my arm and pulled me into the house. Travis didn't wait for an invitation. He cleared the threshold a second before she shut the door. Susan Neumann walked off, muttering and shaking her head.

Angie led us into a small living room with furniture that was too bulky for the space. It reminded me of a store with too much inventory. A television was playing in another room. I figured that's where the children were. It was a good bet that Chris Neumann was still at work.

Travis and I sat at one end of the sectional couch; Angie chose a chair to our right. "I'll try to help you," she said, "but I have to be careful about what I say. I hope you understand."

"We'll be grateful for anything you can tell us," I assured her.

"Please forgive my mom—she's a lot more sociable than she seems. She's trying to protect me and the kids. My sudden homecoming has been hard on her and my dad. They should be nominated for sainthood. They went from a serene empty nest to a rowdy full house overnight without a single complaint."

"You're a lucky woman," I said.

"I suppose that's one way of looking at it. I sure don't feel lucky having to uproot my kids and leave behind everything I worked for in Watkins Glen."

"Why did you feel the need to do that?" Travis shot straight to the heart of the matter.

Angie took a deep breath "In order to answer that, I should give you an idea about my tenure with Monroe Enterprises. I took the job there, because the salary was higher and there were better benefits than at the other firms I'd looked into. It was a financial decision pure and simple. When you have two kids to support that's how it is. Monroe, and later Eagle, made it clear that security was a priority, because they were working on a federally funded project. I'm sure you ran into the armed guards at the gate if you tried to get in there." We both nodded.

"I'd been working there for about six months," she continued, "when Ava joined the staff and took an apartment in the building where the kids and I were living. We became instant friends. Things were going great. I should have known it couldn't last." Her mouth curved up in a rueful smile. "Isn't that the way life goes?" I murmured agreement.

"We heard the company started laying off people," Travis said when she seemed lost in thought. She shifted her focus back to us again.

"Right. The government funding for the project had been cut. Rumors circulated that we were heading for bankruptcy. We were living in limbo for a good few months. I can't tell you what an enormous relief it was when we found out the company had new funding for the project and all our jobs were safe. That's when the name changed from Monroe to Eagle Enterprises. Living through those scary days, Ava and I became very close—like sisters. At least that was how I thought of her." A deep sadness colored her tone.

"We heard your relationship hit a rough patch sometime after that," I said. "Can you tell us what happened?"

Angie closed her eyes and wagged her head as if she still couldn't believe it. "Ava and I had a horrible argument. We'd both applied for the newly vacated position as the head of accounting. It paid more and had better benefits. Given that I had seniority there, I'd hoped she would back off. But Ava was competitive, a real go-getter. Her philosophy was *may the best woman win.* I didn't want to lose her friendship, but I needed the money more than she did—she was only supporting herself. It created a wedge between us." Angie bit down on her lower lip as if debating how much more to say.

"Before we found out who got the promotion, something happened at work that made me realize I didn't want to continue working there. I told Ava about it and suggested she consider leaving too. She blew up and accused me of making up the story to get her out of the way." Angie's voice wobbled; tears glistened on her lower lashes. "That was the end of our friendship."

"What happened at work that made you decide to quit?" Travis asked.

"I can't tell you that."

"Did someone threaten you?" Seated side by side as we were, I couldn't catch his eye to tell him to drop it. I put my hand under his elbow and squeezed it as discreetly as possible. He pulled away. Maybe I was overreacting, but I didn't want this to turn into *pizza with Liam* all over again.

Angie put her hands up as if to stop the questions. "I... I told you there were things I can't go into."

"It's getting late, Travis," I said pointedly. "We should let Angie get dinner ready for her kids." I stood up so he'd know I meant business. He seemed about to protest, but Angie had risen too. He was outmaneuvered.

She walked us to the door. "I hope someday the circumstances will be different and I'll be free to tell you everything." I said I understood. Travis thanked her for seeing us, but there was an edge of irritation to his words.

"I thought we were on the same team," he said when we were driving home. We hadn't said a word to each other for the first fifteen minutes of the trip.

I held myself back from saying, *what the hell is that supposed to mean?* No good could come of ratcheting up the tension between us. "Of course we're on the same team," I said evenly. "I'm just not sure we're working with the same set of ethics."

"How many more opportunities to question her do you think we'll get? We wasted an entire day with nothing to show for it." He took one hand off the wheel and ran his fingers through his hair the way he did when he was frustrated.

"That's not true. We learned what broke up her friendship with Ava. We know she's worried about her kids' safety—worried enough to leave everything she worked for and start over again. But I don't think that's because of Ava. It's more like two different issues that are somehow linked."

"Is that women's intuition?" he asked dryly.

I didn't answer him. I knew he wasn't just arguing with me about Angie. He was lashing out because he was caught between Whitney and me. But that didn't mean I had to sit there and take it. I did some deep breathing to relax and when I reached the proper state of mind, I took a shortcut home.

Chapter 38

Travis called the next morning before I left for the shop. When I saw his name on the screen, my heart twisted. I much preferred the happy dance it used to do. "I just got off the phone with one of my contacts," he said after a quick *hi*. "According to him, Eagle Enterprises did lose the government contract—he doesn't know why. They were about to go belly-up when they got new funding. He's been trying to find out if the infusion of capital came from a private source or if Washington just had another change of heart."

"That agrees with what we've been told by everyone from the Duncans to Angie."

"Yes, but he also told me something interesting. The original contract Eagle Enterprises had with the government was to develop and produce a new class of weapons using magnets—things called coil guns and rail guns and electromagnetic pulse bombs—the stuff sounds like science fiction."

"Wow—I'd hang on to this *guy* of yours, at least until the government catches up with him. Then deny ever knowing him—deny, deny, deny."

Travis chuckled. "Yeah, he's one of my higher-class contacts." Despite the subject matter, for a moment it felt like we were having one of our old comfortable conversations, where we didn't parse every word before speaking—the kind we used to have before Whitney showed up.

As the laughter wound down, a heavy silence rushed in to fill the void. It was getting awkward again fast. One of us had to say something, so I repeated the obvious. "I wish we knew what Angie discovered about Eagle Enterprises that made her leave."

"Wait a minute—didn't she say that she told Ava about it, but Ava didn't believe her?"

"You're right." My mind shifted into overdrive. "It's possible Ava passed it on to her parents. They knew about her argument with Angie. But another trip to Williamsville isn't in the cards right now with our day jobs. I can call the Duncans and see if they're willing to talk about it over the phone."

"It's worth a shot. You're good with people—empathic. They can feel that you care." He'd never said anything like that to me and this was a heck of a time to start. It rocked me back on my proverbial heels. "Kailyn?" he said when I didn't respond.

It took me a second to reel my thoughts back in. "Right—I'll call them after the tour bus leaves. Speaking of which, I've got to run." I shoved my feet into a pair of flats. They weren't as classy-looking as stilettos, but tour bus days were hard on my feet. Was this how my aunt Tilly had started the slow slide from sexy chic into bunion-kind footwear? I shook the thought from my head and tripped over Sashkatu, who'd fallen asleep on the braided mat by the door. To avoid hurting him, I made a last second course correction that twisted my ankle and sent me crashing down next to him on the hardwood. He opened one critical eye that said, *You really must pay more attention to clocks.* "Thanks, that's a big help," I said, pulling myself up from the floor.

We arrived at the shop in time to answer a tentative knock on the front door. I unlocked it and greeted my first customers of the day, a senior couple who teetered in, arms entwined so that if one fell the other was sure to follow. They both had short white hair and the years had whittled away at their features until they appeared elfin-like. With a mischievous twinkle in her eye, the woman whispered that they'd never been inside a real magick shop before. I asked if they were looking for anything in particular. She took me aside.

"Would you have something to help Bobby's hearing? I'm ever so tired of repeating things," she said without resentment. A minute later Bobby whispered to me, "Maybe you could give Fanny something to make her voice stronger? She thinks I don't listen, but I can't listen to what I don't hear."

"I told them each that I had just what they needed. Now there's a chair at the counter and another one behind it if you'd like to sit down. This will only take me a minute." I left them to it and headed for the first aisle. I plucked two products off the shelf and took them back to the supply room. For Bobby's hearing, there was a mixture of gingko biloba, rosemary leaf, passion flower, plantain leaf and yarrow flower. For Fanny's voice, there was propolis, collected by honeybees from tree buds and sap. I opened the bottles and added a little spell of Morgana's to ensure they'd do the trick:

Let not ear or voice grow dim,
Rather may this keep them clear.
Be for her and be for him
All they need to say and hear.

I found Bobby in my desk chair and Fanny in the customer chair. She was speaking so softly that I barely heard her. There was little chance that Bobby could, but he was smiling at her and nodding. I wondered what secret, what formula had brought them to this late stage of life together, not without problems, but without acrimony. Even if I could replicate that formula and even if it wasn't considered black magick, I knew in my heart that it would never work on any other couple. It had to be as unique as the individuals themselves.

I explained the ingredients to them and printed out the spell. They would need to rewrite it in pencil before using it, and then recite it three times. If the benefits faded, they should recite it again and if that no longer worked, they could recite it up to ten times. Beyond that they would have to return to me. They spent the next twenty minutes browsing through the aisles. Bobby didn't appear all that interested, but he followed dutifully behind his wife. They left with a tote bag full of remedies to treat everything from hiccups in humans to hairballs in cats.

By the time they left, the shop had filled with customers, and when the bus drove away at three p.m. sharp, I had a lot of empty shelves to restock and my register was flush with cash. I'd recently instituted a ten percent discount to encourage customers to use cash instead of plastic and it seemed to be working.

In the quiet that followed, it occurred to me, or more specifically to my stomach, that I hadn't eaten lunch. I poked my head next door to see if Tilly had any leftovers from her teas. She always baked more than she needed, but since Merlin's arrival, it was no longer a foregone conclusion that there would be anything remaining. I found her asleep, head down on one of her tea tables. A full day of baking and readings was becoming too much for her. She should think about cutting back. But whenever I broached the subject, she pooh-poohed my concerns. I'd recently walked in on a discussion between Morgana, Bronwen and her. They'd stopped talking the moment they realized I was there, but not before I'd heard Tilly say that she worried about the time when I'd be left on my own, adrift in the world without the anchor of family.

The following day, my mother had popped in when I was giving the familiars their dinner. Her cloud was an indistinct mixture of colors and she got straight to the point. "There's no need to beat around the bush, Kailyn. You're aware of our concerns for the future. We'd hoped that you and Travis would get married and have a family. But to be frank, what matters most is that you have a child or better yet, children, to continue the Wilde magickal genome as well as to provide you with family as you grow older."

"You're having this conversation with the wrong party," I'd grumbled, realizing my mistake a second too late. "But don't you dare say anything to Travis!"

"I had no such plans. If he's not the one, then you need to move on."

"I intend to," I had assured her, although my heart still hoped that he'd come to his senses.

I left Tilly sleeping and found Merlin in the kitchen watching baseball on his iPad. I made a point of not asking when he'd found this new interest. All I wanted was a snack. He pointed out the three mini Linzer tarts he hadn't eaten. I wrapped them in a napkin and headed back to my shop. Sashkatu was snoring on his window ledge, exhausted from the nonstop parade of tourists. I downed the tarts as if I hadn't eaten in a month, and with the sugar swirling through my blood stream in the guise of energy, I was ready to call the Duncans.

Valerie answered my call and asked permission to put me on speaker so that Teddy could be a part of the conversation. I told them I needed to discuss certain matters pertaining to Ava, along with the fact that neither Travis nor I could make the trip up to see them in person in the foreseeable future. Valerie didn't want to speak about private matters on the phone. Teddy was more receptive. "Privacy is an illusion these days," he said. "Big Brother is the reality. But if my Val is more comfortable speaking to you in person, there is another possibility. What if we were to come down to the Glen?"

"Are you both up to the trip?" I asked.

"We won't know unless we try. It would do us a world of good to get out of this house for a couple of days." Val raised objections and Teddy shot them down. "How about we call you back once we work out the details," he said to me, which I took to mean he had to work on getting Valerie onboard.

Chapter 39

Grannies on the Go was a small tour group that came to New Camel at least once a year. They ranged in age from sixty all the way up to a hundred and one. Most of them didn't even need a walker to get around. Although Abracadabra wasn't their favorite shop, they always came in to say *hello* and usually left with products to address the most recent indignities their advancing ages had visited upon them. They were a lovely group of women, funny and feisty. I'd enjoyed talking to them in the past, but that day I had to stick to business if I didn't want to miss lunch with the Duncans and Travis.

The three of them were already seated when I arrived at the Grotto. Travis had chosen the restaurant, because it was quiet enough for conversation and the tables were far enough apart to allow for privacy. The Duncans stood up to hug and kiss me. If they noticed that Travis and I said polite but distant *hellos,* they wisely chose not to say anything. The moment I took my seat, the waiter appeared to see if I wanted a beverage other than water. Travis was drinking a cola and there were two iced teas with lemon parked in front of Valerie and Teddy. I was sticking with water.

He inquired if we needed a few more minutes to look at the menus, but I knew he was talking to me. I asked him to start with the others while I glanced at the lunch special—soup and salad or a personal pizza. The men ordered pizza; Val and I went for the minestrone and strawberry salad.

I asked the Duncans how they'd been doing. Valerie shook her head, lips compressed. "It doesn't get any easier," Teddy answered for both of them. Maybe I shouldn't have inquired, but it didn't seem right not to ask. I almost fell back on the old *it will take time,* but I caught myself. Instead I said, "How is Liam?" In for a penny, in for a pound.

Teddy shook his head. "Sad, distant. For a long time now we've wished he would meet someone, get married, have a family…" That seemed to be going around.

"I wonder if we could get right down to your questions," Valerie said, cutting him short. I'd never heard her interrupt her husband that way, but to be fair I hadn't spent all that much time with them. Curiosity must have gotten the better of her.

"Of course," I said, "that's why you made the trip. During one of our earlier talks, I remember you saying that Ava confided in you about the rift between her and Angie."

"Yes, they'd both applied for a new position—that's when things got dicey. Angie wanted Ava to withdraw her name from consideration. She said if Ava were a true friend, she'd realize how much more she and her kids needed the extra money. Ava replied that she was still paying off her student loans and that they should let the company make the decision based on merit. Then Angie made up some story about the company, in hopes of scaring Ava into leaving." Bingo.

"What kind of story?" Travis asked.

"According to Angie, she was having lunch in the cafeteria and needed to go to the bathroom. The cafeteria is located between the business office and the research and development wings. Instead of walking all the way back to the bathroom in her wing, she decided to use the closer one in R&D, even though she didn't have the necessary clearance to be in that area." Val looked from Travis to me as if to be sure we were following her. Teddy was busy buttering a roll. He seemed fine with letting his wife do the talking.

"She said she was walking back to the cafeteria when she heard someone coming. She opened the closest door and ducked inside."

"Wait, I must have missed something," I said.

"No, no—I'm just getting to the crux of the story. The room where Angie hid was a conference room. It was occupied by four men and a woman. Angie recognized two of the men as company bigwigs. The others she'd never seen before. She said they were speaking a foreign language and the woman was translating. They all stopped talking the moment she barged in. One of the Eagle men grabbed her by the arm and hustled her out of the room. He told her to report to his office before leaving for the day. That's when he tore into her. Said if she was ever found in that wing again, she'd regret it."

At that moment, the waiter arrived with our lunch, and we sat quietly while he served it. Angie's story was ricocheting around in my head. It must have been a chilling threat to hear from her boss. He had the power to fire her, and with the right words whispered in the right ear, render her unhireable. I wondered if the story had undergone some embellishments in the retelling by Angie to Ava, Ava to her mother and now to us. Travis caught my attention with one raised eyebrow that usually meant he had similar concerns.

I tasted a spoonful of the soup that was more like a hearty vegetable stew. "What did Angie do after that?" I asked.

"Nothing at first, but then one morning she just didn't show up for work. Her colleagues and friends couldn't reach her online or by phone. The superintendent at her apartment house confirmed she was gone. That's when Ava began to think she might have dismissed Angie's story too quickly. Angie would never have left her job if she wasn't really scared." Val paused to sip her iced tea and add a squeeze of lemon. "Ava felt awful about not believing her and about the way their friendship ended."

Travis wiped pizza sauce off his mouth. "Did she try to reach out to Angie?"

"Yeah," Teddy said, "She left messages like everyone else, but never heard back."

I was busy chewing a mouthful of salad, wishing, not for the first time, that spring mix came without stems. "Did Ava wind up with the promotion?" I asked when I could finally speak again.

Teddy pushed his empty pizza tray away. "Yes, it basically fell into her lap, but by then I don't think she could take any joy in it." Travis gave up on his pie with one slice left. Val and I gnawed our way through the better part of our salads. I wondered how many calories I burned off with my jaws.

"There is something else," Val said hesitantly. She glanced at her husband and he nodded. "Ava made it her mission to find out why the company's executives were so alarmed when they found Angie in the restricted area. As the new head of accounting, Ava had access to a lot of Eagle's financial files, and she figured if anything strange was going on, there would have to be a record of it somewhere. Everything comes down to money in the end, you know. It took her a while, but she came across a wire transfer of a large sum of money into Eagle's account from an international bank she'd never heard of. She was able to trace the transfer back through the Cayman Islands and Singapore to a branch in Moscow."

The waiter reappeared with a large tray of desserts to tempt us. He described them in detail, but we all declined. He looked personally crushed. "Coffee, cappuccino, espresso, tea?" he offered with less enthusiasm. Maybe we all felt bad about disappointing him, because the men asked for coffee and Val and I opted for tea. All I really wanted at that point was for Val to finish her story. The waiter vanished, but the busboy came right on his heels to remove the detritus of our lunch and brush the crumbs off the tablecloth. If anyone else showed up to further delay us, I might have strangled them. Judging by Travis's expression, he might have beaten me to it.

"The Russians are financing Eagle Enterprises?" he whispered hoarsely across the table once the busboy left.

"That's what Ava thought," Val replied, "but she never found any other transactions or memos like that one. She said it was for a large sum, but not large enough to buy the company outright. She thought there were probably other payments, but she couldn't find any proof. She figured that the one transaction she found was mistakenly sent to a file she could access.

"Ava even considered looking into the Dark Web for more information," Teddy added. "If Eagle Enterprises was making some kind of deal with Russia, they'd want to keep it under wraps. But she didn't get far with it, because, frankly, it scared her."

The Dark Web? I had no idea what he was talking about, but Travis didn't seem thrown by the term. I must have looked lost, because he summed it up for me. "The Dark Web is a catchall name for thousands of shady websites that you can't reach by regular browsers like Chrome or Firefox." The busboy returned with our mugs of steaming coffee and tea along with cream and sweeteners.

"It sounds illegal," I said after he left.

Val stirred a packet of sugar into her tea. "That's what I thought when Ava first mentioned it, but apparently it's not."

"Neither is using Tor or other browsers that can access those websites." Travis paused to taste his coffee. "But most of the people who use the Dark Web are involved in criminal activities. They like it because it's much harder to track anyone there. However it's not impossible. Users make mistakes all the time that lead the feds right to their doors."

"I feel like I've been living with blinders on," I said.

Val set her mug down. "I know exactly what you mean. Scares me to wonder what else I don't know."

"Listen," Travis said so softly that we all had to lean forward to hear him, "if there's even a chance that the Russians are buying Eagle Enterprises or the new weapon systems they're developing, we have to inform the FBI. If there are no objections, I'll take care of it." Teddy and Val looked relieved that it was out of their hands. And I was no longer surprised that Travis had contacts just about everywhere.

Chapter 40

Travis and I were both speechless after what the Duncans told us. We stood near my car, watching them drive away. I'd expected to hear details of the quarrel between Angie and Ava that escalated beyond reason. But the ramifications of their argument reached far beyond Watkins Glen and the state of New York. When I'd corralled my thoughts enough to speak, Travis started speaking too. We stopped, waiting for each other to speak, then began again, stepping on each other's words. It might have been funny under other circumstances—if we were not estranged and if the Russians weren't buying the newest high-tech weapons from right under the federal nose.

"Go ahead," Travis said.

"Is this FBI guy you know from around here?"

"No, he's in the city, but it doesn't matter. I'll tell him what we heard, which isn't all that much. He'll know what to do with it."

"Over a secure line I guess?" Was I seriously telling him how to go about it?

"No, I thought I'd just call from my cell phone in the most public place I can find that has free Wi Fi."

"Sorry—I'm a little rattled."

"I'm actually going to rework my schedule so I can drive down to the city and speak to him in person. If I give my news director a general idea about what I'm looking into, he'll probably grant me *carte blanche* to follow the story to its end."

"When do you think you'll go?"

"Possibly this afternoon, early tomorrow the latest. Why?"

Because I care about you and I like knowing where you are. Great—now *I* sounded like a stalker. I quickly dredged up a better answer. "Because we're partners." I opened the car door and slid beneath the wheel. Travis knocked on my closed window, so I turned on the engine and rolled it down.

"Kailyn—please don't get into trouble while I'm gone. There's nothing that can't wait until I get back. I'm serious."

I wasn't up to a round of flirtatious sarcasm. I gave him a single nod, wished him a good trip and waited for him to step back so I could leave without driving over his feet.

When I got back to the shop, I went through the connecting door to Tea and Empathy. My aunt must have taken the day off, because there weren't any tantalizing aromas of freshly baked goods lingering in the air. Odds were she was driving around under Merlin's direction, searching for the cause of our magickal woes.

I went back to Abracadabra and opened for business. Sashkatu was on his tufted ledge, but he squinted at me and started to stretch away the remnants of his sleep, before changing his mind and closing his eyes again. "You're just lucky I can't fit on that comfy ledge of yours or you'd have to fight me for it," I said. He ignored me.

Half a dozen locals filtered in during the remaining hours of the afternoon. They kept me from dwelling on Travis and Eagle Enterprises, which was good because there wasn't anything I could do about either one.

When Sashki and I arrived home, I fed him and the rest of my brood, and then called Tilly to find out how her day had gone. She didn't answer. I tried her cell, but it went straight to voice mail. All of their previous trips had seen them home by six. Of course it was possible her phone's battery had died, because she regularly forgot to charge it. Maybe they'd stopped somewhere for dinner. I waited another hour and tried her again with the same results. I checked with her friends, but no one had seen her or knew where she might be. I'd exhausted all the acceptable reasons for not being able to reach her. All I had left were worries and they were piling up fast.

There was no point in talking to the police. An adult had to be missing for forty-eight hours before they would do anything, unless said person had been diagnosed with dementia. I tried Tilly's phone every half hour and was actually startled when it rang. *Pick up Tilly, please pick up.* The words repeated in my head like a mantra, but it was her voice mail that picked up. I left a message asking her to call me ASAP. It occurred to me that since her phone was on now, I could activate the app on my cell to locate her. A map popped onto my screen with a little headshot of Tilly in a building somewhere. It appeared to be at the end of a road with only one other road nearby—Eagle Enterprises. I was on my feet and moving the second I made the connection.

I grabbed my purse, locked the door behind me and jumped into the SUV. I didn't waste time wondering what awaited me when I got there. It didn't matter. Tilly and Merlin were in trouble. The math was simple—I had to rescue them.

The roads around New Camel would have benefitted from more lighting. It occurred to me every time I had to drive at night. Maybe this time, I'd remember to bring it up at the next town meeting. There was no lighting at all at the turnoff, which was why I drove right by it. I'd gone a mile down the road before I realized my mistake. I spun a U-turn and headed back at a crawl, my headlights burrowing through the darkness like moles forging their way underground. I turned onto the side road that was little more than a hard-packed dirt path with trees crowding the edges. I bounced along, hitting every depression and hole because I couldn't see them. It took a lot longer than I remembered to reach the place where the path curved before becoming the smoothly paved macadam road. I turned my SUV around, parked it at the edge of the path and doused the headlights. All ready for a fast getaway.

I opened the door and stepped down. I'd have to go the rest of the way by foot. Charging the gate at full speed was great in action movies, but hardly practical. It would alert any guards who might be in the building or around its perimeter, plus it would destroy my SUV in the process. I had a much lower budget than Hollywood.

The only light I could see from my position was most likely coming from the little guard house. I didn't know if they kept a guard on duty there at night, but I couldn't take any chances. If I snuck through the trees to get an up-close look, there was a good chance I'd step on crackling old leaves from autumns past and give myself away. On the other hand, if I approached by the roadway, I would almost certainly be seen. I didn't even have the luxury of time to decide. If Tilly and Merlin were being held captive in Eagle Enterprises, I had to get to them as soon as I could.

I briefly considered teleporting into the building, but that would waste psychic energy I might need later. A spell would do the trick, providing I could come up with one fast enough. Rushing magick was never a good idea, but better ideas weren't exactly tripping over each other in my brain. In less than five minutes I came up with something workable if not elegant.

Let my feet in silence pass
Over leaves and twigs and grass.

No sound reach another's ears
If I do not hold them dear.

I recited the words three times and set out through the trees. So far so
good. It was a strange feeling to be walking on a forest bed of crinkling,
crunching material that made no noise. When I was parallel with the
gate, I paused to look for a guard. I spotted him sitting in the guard house
thumbing through a magazine, listening to music through earbuds. I could
only hope that the rest of the security contingent was as apathetic as he.
The odds were against it.

I worked my way down to the building where there was one armed guard
outside the main entrance. I waited to see if there were more. It didn't take
long before a second man came around the right side of the building. He
stopped to talk to his colleague. I couldn't hear what they were saying,
but it must have been funny, because they both laughed. Then the second
man continued on his rounds. Based on the footprint of the place, I figured
I had three minutes before he would come around again. But that didn't
solve the problem of getting past the guard who was there all the time, or
of getting inside the building without tripping the alarm. Like it or not, I
would have to teleport in. At least the distance was short, which seemed
to play a part in how much of my energy would be consumed

While I was coming to this decision, I must have moved my feet without
realizing it, because the rustling sound they made startled me. The spell
had worn off. I peered between the trees to see if the guard had heard it.
He was looking straight at me, but then his eyes moved on, still trying to
locate the source of the noise. My heart was beating so hard it felt like it
was in my throat. I was surprised he couldn't hear it too. But he shrugged
to himself and focused his attention on the cigarette he was trying to light.

I teleported into Krista's cubicle again. It had the advantage of walls even
if it didn't have a door. More important, it was a pathway I'd established on
my first foray into Eagle Enterprises. I was all about saving my energy for
later. The building was silent. I needed to search for sound—the sound of
voices in particular. Merlin and my aunt were not quiet people. I suspected
their captors wouldn't be quiet either.

I gave the business wing a cursory inspection before moving on to the
cafeteria. I knew from Valerie Duncan's description that it was located
between the business offices and the larger research and development wing.
The cafeteria was empty. The hallway into R&D was empty. Walking
down there, I'd be out in the open with nowhere to hide, unless the closed
doors along its length were unlocked. I remembered that Angie had used

the bathroom off this hall. There it was—halfway down on the right. The words on the door were almost the same color as the wood of the door—hard to see if you weren't looking for it. I headed toward it, the carpet swallowing the squeaking of my sneakers.

I peered out from the bathroom, looking for another place I could hide along the way if I heard someone coming. This hall ended on another hall perpendicular to it, but from my vantage point, I couldn't see far enough down in either direction to locate any doors on that hallway. I had to assume that when I left the bathroom I'd be out in the open, without refuge. I was about to leave my sanctuary when I finally heard voices. Two men were talking. They were far enough away that their words were incomprehensible mumbles, but the agitation in their voices carried to me as clearly as if they were only a few feet away. I had to assume they were part of the night security force inside the building. A door closed, blocking what little I had heard. If I was ever going to leave the bathroom, this was the time to do it.

I held the door and closed it quietly behind me before taking off for the intersecting hallway. Left or right? As if in answer to my thought, I heard Tilly's voice from somewhere on my right. I changed directions, relieved to know that she was alive and not far away. Why didn't I hear Merlin? I pushed that worry to the side; I couldn't afford to let it distract me. I moved along the hall, wishing I knew if the two men were in a room between Tilly and me or past her. *Keep talking, Tilly. Keep talking!* I urged her with my mind, even though telepathy had never worked for me. I paused at each door I came to and listened for a moment. A door somewhere behind me clicked open. I grabbed the knob of the door I was next to and turned it. Thankfully it opened and I slipped inside as I heard the two men come into the hallway. I was sighing with relief when they burst into the room. I'd never seen the taller one before, but I recognized the shorter one as the driver who'd kidnapped me. But this was no time for reminiscing. I recited the spell in my head—the one I'd used in the cabin.

I am razors; I am knives,
I am needles in your eyes.
I will burn you like hot coal;
I will freeze you like North's pole.

There was a brief skirmish, during which I managed to kick the taller one in the shin and elbow the driver in the eye. Bellowing in pain, the driver grabbed my wrists and started to pull them behind me when the spell kicked in. He tried to ride out the pain. "It ain't real! It ain't real! It ain't real!" he chanted. The words sounded like they were coming through clenched teeth.

"What's going on with you?!" his partner demanded.

"Shut up," the driver mewled. The pain was winning. I could hear it in his voice. Even so, he'd hung on longer than I expected. He finally let go, sputtering a string of profanities. "Don't just stand there, Carillo, where's your gun? What's the point of carryin' it if you don't use it on an intruder?!"

Carillo pulled the gun from his shoulder holster and pointed it at me.

"Shoot her in the leg if she tries anything, but whatever you do—don't touch her."

The driver ordered me to put my hands together behind my back. It was slow going, but he managed to tie my wrists without touching me. He pulled the coarse twine tight, until it bit into my skin—payback for sure. He picked up my purse and rummaged through it.

"Where's Boscoe?" I asked him.

"That dimwit? He was canned after your escape."

"So you blamed it all on him." What a standup guy. He was too busy tossing tissues, gas receipts, keys, and lipstick out of my purse to pay attention to me. He found my phone and pocketed it, along with three hundred dollars in cash I'd intended to take to the bank in the morning. He didn't seem interested in my credit cards. Maybe it was company policy. He tossed my bag onto the floor with the rest of its contents. "How'd you pull off that Houdini stunt anyways?"

"Magick."

"Yeah, right. If my partner here would walk out of the room for a minute or two, I'm sure I could encourage you to tell me."

"Forget it," Carillo said. "You'd probably throw me under the bus like you did the last guy. I don't understand how come you both didn't get sacked after you blew that job."

"We were only supposed to give her a scare, get her to drop her investigation."

"Yeah, I see how well that worked." He turned to me. "You come looking for the ditzy redhead and the weirdo?"

"Are they all right?" I asked. I wanted to demand an apology on behalf of my aunt, but first things first.

"If you ask me, they weren't all right when we caught them. You can wait for the boss together. It'll be a regular reunion."

The driver grabbed the gun from him and nudged me out of the door with the business end of it. We didn't go far before he told me to stop at another door. He pulled a ring of keys out of his pants pocket and opened the door one-handed. He shoved me into the room and slammed the door shut behind me, locking it from outside.

Tilly was sitting against the opposite wall. Merlin appeared to be sleeping on the floor next to her. There was a bruise on his temple that had bled down his cheek before drying.

"Kailyn!" Tilly cried, struggling to lever herself off the floor. With my hands tied, I couldn't help her. When she was on her feet, she hobbled over and hugged me tightly to her. "Am I glad to see you!" she said. "Wait, no—I'm not. I mean I'm always glad to see you, but given the circumstances, I'm not glad to see you. Are you okay?"

"I'm fine. Are you? What happened to Merlin?"

"When they threw us in here, I stumbled and hit the wall. I've never seen Merlin so enraged. He got right up in their faces, screaming at them, until the short one hit him with the butt of his gun and knocked him out. I checked his pulse and it seems okay, but I'm no doctor. Let me get you untied."

"What on earth are you and Merlin doing here?" I asked while she worked at the twine.

"Merlin felt what he called *a disturbance* every time we drove along this section of road. After all the fruitless days we spent looking for the cause of our problems, we thought we should at least check out this hunch of his before we gave up."

It all came together in my head. "Merlin told us that the ley lines were magnetic and that our ancestors built their house and shop on the lines to enhance their magick. Then Eagle Enterprises moved in and started developing magnetic weapons."

"That must have been around the same time we first noticed problems with our magick," Tilly said, finally untying the knot to set me free.

"They must be working with magnets powerful enough to have pulled the ley lines out of their normal position." It all made sense. We'd pinpointed the cause of our trouble, but that didn't help our more immediate situation. We sat down on the floor beside Merlin who was snoring away peacefully.

"Now that you're in here with us," Tilly said with a heavy sigh, "there's no one left to save us." I almost said *Travis,* but then I remembered he was probably on his way to the city. I took a few deep breaths to calm myself and once I was on a more even keel, I realized that it didn't matter if there was no else to save us, because we were perfectly capable of saving ourselves.

Chapter 41

I checked Merlin's pulse to confirm what Tilly said. It was slow, but steady, and he seemed to be breathing quietly. Any plan to save ourselves couldn't depend on his help. Even if he were to open his eyes and sit up in the next moment, we wouldn't know if his ability to ply his magick had been compromised, especially in the short term.

The best idea I could come up with was to teleport out of the building, alert authorities, then return to help Tilly and Merlin and await our rescue. If only I could teleport with them. *Forget the if onlys,* I told myself. *Wishful thinking isn't a strategy.* I explained my plan to Tilly. She didn't raise any objections, but I'm pretty sure she'd thought of the one big problem with it just like I had. The driver might fly into a psychotic rage over my second escape on his watch. He might beat her until she told him about my talent. And then beat her more for what he'd assume was a lie. I didn't know if the taller man could stop him or if he'd want to, since his neck was also on the line. I had to get back to my aunt and the wizard as quickly as possible. With any luck, the two company goons wouldn't check on their prisoners before I did.

To that end, I teleported myself directly into a stand of large evergreens at the back of the New Camel precinct's parking lot. I opened my eyes, afraid to find myself staring back at Duggan, Hobart, Paul Curtis or any number of New Camel residents who happened to be in the lot when I arrived. I was relieved to find myself alone. The downside of my landing choice was a few scrapes and bruises from nearly becoming one with the trees.

I trotted up to the precinct house to find that the door was locked. Whoever was on duty was out on a call. Residents who dialed 911 at such a time had their calls automatically shunted to police headquarters in Watkins

Glen. Maybe it was for the best. A lone police officer would have been at substantial risk facing down the security forces at Eagle Enterprises. But first things first—I needed a phone and it was the middle of the night. I couldn't just run next door to one of the nearby shops. Instead, I teleported over to my shop, praying that I'd still have enough energy to get back into Eagle Enterprises. I was never so glad to see an old-fashioned landline. I placed the call and explained the situation to the woman who answered. A minute later Detective Duggan called me back. I had to go through it a second time with him. He asked too many questions. I tried to impress upon him that time was of the essence.

"The safety of my officers is too," he responded with a contemptuous edge to his words. "This is precisely why civilians shouldn't be conducting their own investigations." I could just picture the smug expression on his face. I swallowed my rebuttal, desperate to get off the phone and back to Tilly and Merlin. When he finally let me go, I dialed Travis. My call went straight to voice mail. I left a message with the pertinent details. I'd been gone from Eagle Enterprises for thirty-five minutes. If I ever needed to be strong enough to teleport—it was now.

I focused on the room where I'd left Tilly and Merlin. A second later I landed in a heap on the floor there, completely spent. I looked around me—I was alone. Was I in the wrong room or had they been taken away? Fear for them gave me the punch of energy I needed to get off the floor and plan my next move.

"Kailyn." I thought I heard a tiny high-pitched voice call my name. I had to be hallucinating from exhaustion. "Kailyn." There it was again and it sounded oddly like my aunt's voice after a hit of helium. I looked around again, not the usual way you look for a person. I scanned the walls, the ceiling, the floor.

"We're in the corner near the door." It sounded like a micro-mini duet. I stretched out flat on my belly. Squinting into the corner I saw a couple of ants.

"Tilly? Merlin?" I felt silly addressing ants.

"Yes, yes—it's us!" Tilly squealed. I inched closer. "Merlin finally woke up and transmuted us so they'd think we escaped and they'd leave the door open."

"Can't you get through the space between the bottom of the door and the floor?"

"I think we can," Merlin said, "but Matillda is afraid of getting stuck."

"They haven't been back?" I asked.

"Not yet, but I wish they'd get on with it. I don't know how much longer I can maintain our present forms."

"I prefer bees to ants," Tilly grumbled. "It's awful to constantly worry about being squashed."

"Constantly?" Merlin said. "Kailyn is the only one who's been in here."

"I just know I wouldn't like it," Tilly replied in a huff. We waited for the inevitable return of the tall man and the driver. I remained stretched out on the floor as a barrier to keep the ants safe if they did walk in.

"Get ready," I whispered when I heard the key turning in the lock. "This is your chance to escape." A moment later the driver and the tall man walked in.

"What the—" the driver spun around looking for Tilly and Merlin as if they might be hiding in plain sight. "You," he said, turning his anger on me. "Where are they?"

"How would I know? I fell asleep. I can't believe they left me behind to deal with the two of you."

"Now I'm angry," the tall man snapped. "How'd they get out of here?"

"Maybe you left the door unlocked by accident," I said, looking straight at the driver. The tall man turned his glare on him too.

"No, no way this is on me," he sputtered. He pulled out his gun and pointed it at my head. "I want answers and I want them now!"

"Think about it—if I knew how they escaped, why would I still be hanging out here?" That brought both men up sharply. I checked on the ants' progress. They were traversing the doorway.

The tall man said, "You better start praying we find your friends or we'll be taking our frustrations out on you." They turned to leave. The ants were not quite out of danger.

I needed to give them more time. "Wait, I have an idea."

"Yeah? This better be good." The driver's tone dared me to lie.

"My cousin can't resist sweets. Seriously I've seen him eat a box of cookies and a whole banana bread in one sitting. He can sniff out baked goods from a mile away. It's like he's half hound dog. If there's a cafeteria, that's where you'll find them." I glanced at the doorway, which appeared to be ant-free. I could only hope my family was out of harm's way. The guards left. I heard the lock engage.

Being imprisoned in a small room, with no means of telling time and no way of knowing the fate of my loved ones had to qualify as its own level of Hell. Dante might argue the point, but I could hold my own against any man.

Staring at the blank walls, I wondered why it was taking Duggan so long to rescue us. Maybe he was trying to teach me a lesson. I didn't want to believe he could be that vengeful, but I'd never seen anything in the man that pointed to a generosity of spirit.

The next time the door opened, I jumped up ready to thank whoever it was—even Duggan. My heart sank like a stone when the tall one propelled Tilly and Merlin back into the room and locked the door behind them. Tilly's curls were matted down and her muumuu was ripped and wrinkled, no doubt the result of being miniaturized. "What happened?" I asked them.

"Well," she said, trying to smooth out her clothing, "although becoming ants made it possible to escape from the room, we realized too late that it would take us a month of Sundays to reach an exit on our teensy weensy ant feet. So Merlin changed us back and not five seconds later, we turned a corner and literally ran into the big ape. He was not happy to see us."

"Are we to be rescued or not?" Merlin asked crossly, as if this whole misadventure was my fault.

"I'm sure we will be," I said with all the confidence and patience I could muster. For once my words seemed to have the force of a director calling *Action!*

A man shouted, "Stand back," which was followed by two powerful kicks that sent the door flying open to slam into the wall where the doorknob left its imprint. The kicker stood in the doorway dressed in full tactical gear. A second man in his forties was standing behind him, wearing street clothes and a bullet-proof vest. The SWAT agent and Street Clothes switched places in a neat little do-si-do. "Federal agents," Street Clothes said, holding up his badge for us to see. "Ms. Kailyn Wilde?"

My hand shot up. "Here," I said, waving as if I was at risk of not being seen. Relief can make you act like a fool.

"Ms. Matillda Wilde and Mr. Merlin Wilde?" They followed my embarrassing lead. The Three Stooges couldn't have looked any sillier. Neither of the agents seemed to notice. Travis squeezed past Street Clothes and ran straight to me. He threw his arms around me and pulled me to him without a word. Then he hugged Tilly, who kissed him on the cheek, and with a what-the-hell wink at me, he hugged Merlin.

Street Clothes introduced himself. "I'm agent Reilly. I'm mighty happy to meet all of you. Is anyone in need of medical attention?" We all declined. "In that case, I will be accompanying you to a secure location for debriefing." Travis took my hand in his as we followed Reilly through the halls. "When did you get my message?" I asked, trying to figure out how he and the FBI made it here before Duggan.

"I was a couple of hours into my trip to the city. You must have called when I was talking to my FBI contact—I'll call him Ed. I got off the first exit I came to and headed back. Meanwhile Ed got in touch with the field office in Ithaca and told them we had a hostage situation. I gunned it all the way to Ithaca—Ed fixed it so I could ride along with them. I'm surprised we made it here before the cops." Once things settled down, I'd tell him about my conversation with Duggan.

I counted half a dozen federal SWAT agents on our way to the door. When we passed the cafeteria, I caught sight of Detective Duggan talking to another agent in street clothes. The detective was wearing a sour expression, clearly unhappy to be relinquishing control to the FBI in what he must think of as *his* territory. I couldn't work up any sympathy for him.

"When we get there do you think we can order pizza or something?" Tilly asked in a stage whisper.

"I'm famished too," Merlin chimed in. "None of our captors thought to offer us dinner!" As a friend of King Arthur's court, he'd apparently never been taken hostage or mistreated in any way. I suspected his view of the Middle Ages was quite different from that of the average peasant.

Reilly looked over his shoulder at the wizard and cracked a grin. "I'll see what I can do."

Outside Eagle Enterprises there were armored vehicles, unmarked sedans, police cars and a couple of ambulances parked every which way. Reilly led us to a sedan that was halfway into the tree line. I had no idea how he intended to get past all the other vehicles without playing Bumper Cars, but he did a masterful job of it. He asked Tilly to ride upfront with him, even though Merlin had called shotgun. It simply made more sense, given her age and girth. The wizard wisely chose not to complain, but he made no attempt to hide his disgruntled expression as he squeezed into the back seat with Travis and me.

I asked Reilly when Tilly and I could come back for our cars. He made a quick call to the ranking agent at Eagle Enterprises. "They'll be dropped off tomorrow—just give me the license numbers and your addresses when we reach the field office."

"I have my car here in Ithaca," Travis said. "I'll drive you all home." Everything was settled in five minutes, flat. I sat back and tried to relax. Merlin was better at it. He was slumped in his seat, snoring, before Reilly said goodbye.

The trip to Ithaca normally took forty minutes. But in the wee hours of the morning, going FBI-sanctioned speed, we arrived in half an hour. To Tilly's dismay, there were no pizzerias or anything else open at that hour in the college town. Although I'd expected as much, it was easier to let her discover it on her own than argue about it all the way there. Reilly told us there was a diner that opened at five and delivered.

The field office was equipped with a Keurig machine. Reilly invited us to help ourselves. Travis opted for coffee, Tilly and I wanted tea, and Merlin was all over the hot chocolate. He'd never seen such a machine before, so he was tickled to make all of our drinks. He looked crestfallen when the agent didn't want anything. Not to be denied, he finished his cocoa and made himself another. Reilly found an open box of powdered sugar donuts from a local grocery store. Although they weren't as fresh as they once were, they were still edible. Hunger made up for their deficiencies.

Reilly asked us to recount everything from our time in Eagle Enterprises. Tilly began, because Merlin was busy stuffing donuts in his mouth and coughing from the powdered sugar.

"Merlin and I had been riding around trying to find the cause of our magick problems, when we saw the dirt road and decided to find out where it leads."

Reilly's brows bunched together. "Magick? I'm afraid I don't follow."

Think fast, Kailyn! "That's what my aunt calls her psychic ability." It was the best I could do on the spot. ESP had come into the mainstream enough that Reilly wasn't likely to refer her for psychiatric evaluation. "You may have heard of her," I added to lend more gravitas to my words. "She's been on several talk shows over the years. She was on the track to celebrity status when she decided to stop the train. She didn't want to give up her quiet life in New Camel." Tilly sat up straighter, apparently pleased with my appraisal.

"I'm afraid I don't follow that sort of thing," he said, without any judgment in his tone. He turned his focus back to Tilly. "Why did you think Eagle Enterprises might be compromising your... your talent?"

"It involves ley lines and magnets," Merlin supplied between coughs.

This time Travis jumped in. "Thanks, Merlin, but I don't think we have time for that right now."

"We do need to move things along or we'll never get you out of here."

Tilly told him about their capture up to the point when I arrived. I finished the narrative, leaving out the parts about ants and teleporting. Since the diner would be opening in a few minutes, Travis took us out for breakfast. Despite all the donuts he'd eaten, Merlin put away pancakes, eggs, bacon and potatoes.

After Travis dropped Tilly and Merlin at their place, he drove to my house. He put the car in *park* and turned to me. "We did it. We took down Eagle Enterprises."

"I know that's a good thing, even if it was accidental, but we still don't know who killed Ava."

"We will." He ran his index finger along the side of my cheek. "More importantly, you're all right." A yawn snuck up on me. Travis laughed. "You need sleep—lots of sleep and you'll be good as ever."

"Wait, if you need a place to crash…"

"I'm good—three cups of coffee and leftover adrenaline. Besides, I have things to take care of. We'll talk later." I let myself into the house and found Sashkatu atop the couch as if he'd been too worried about me to stay in bed. I figured I had a couple of hours before the other cats would be demanding breakfast. I didn't have the strength to climb the stairs, so I curled up on the couch, and Sashki left his high ground to snuggle with me.

* * * *

Travis was at my door in the late afternoon. I was surprised he'd driven all the way back from the Glen instead of calling. "Did you get any sleep?" I asked, closing the door behind him.

"Some, but I wouldn't turn down a cup of coffee."

"How about tea—one of Tilly's special blends?"

"Sure." He followed me into the kitchen and sat at the table while I put the water up to boil.

"I thought you were going to call," I said, mystified about why he would choose to make the trip back instead.

"Certain things need to be said in person." I turned away from the stove and found him standing behind me. He took my hand. "Like an apology. I want to apologize for acting like a fool with Whitney. I guess I was flattered that she still had feelings for me. And I felt guilty about the way I'd treated her back in school. I don't know how I thought I could make it up to her. But the other night, when I didn't know if I'd find you alive or… well it put things into perspective. This morning I told Whitney I wouldn't be seeing her or speaking to her again." He took a deep breath. "I hope you can forgive me for being an idiot."

"Since you admit to being a fool and an idiot, I'd say we have some common ground to build on." Travis's mouth turned up in one of his charming, lopsided smiles. "I do have certain terms you have to agree to," I continued. "When you're with me, you're only with me. And by my rules, two strikes and you're out—forever." He folded me into his arms and whispered *agreed* in my ear as the kettle whistled.

Chapter 42

The news about Eagle Enterprise's deal with the Russians hit the media big time. The story was everywhere—the internet, TV, radio, and newspapers. Hudson Monroe, the CEO, and several of the board members were arrested and the company shut down pending a thorough investigation.

After the federal government reneged on its contract with Eagle Enterprises and pulled its funding, the board had one option—declare bankruptcy. Monroe was irate; he wanted revenge. The Russians showed up at the perfect time, flush with cash and ready to bargain. The most serious charge against Monroe and his cohorts was treason. And it carried the death penalty.

Travis called two days after Eagle Enterprises blew up, figuratively speaking. He sounded altogether too chipper. I was still down about not being any closer to finding Ava's killer. "If you're handing out jolly pills, I could use a few," I said.

"You mean you don't have a handy spell to tickle you pink?"

"I did try one on myself when I was teenager, but when it wore off I was more depressed than ever."

"What if I share some good news? Would that help?"

"It couldn't hurt."

"I just got off the phone with Ed. Agents have been scouring the Dark Web for any additional evidence on the deal between Eagle Enterprises and the Russians. They turned up something that may help us nail Ava's killer."

"Travis—didn't anyone ever teach you not to bury the lede? What did they find?

"An add soliciting wet work."

"Wet work? You mean like laundry?" Either I was being obtuse or he was talking in code.

He chuckled. "No, I mean like murder."

There appeared to be a whole lexicon I knew nothing about. Growing up in tiny New Camel, I'd been living in a cushy bubble much like Sashkatu on his tufted window ledge. "Okay—now you've got my attention."

"Most people use an alias on the Dark Web. An agent came across a user there who contacted Eagle Enterprises on multiple occasions and later used the same alias to solicit murder. Big mistake. Now Ed wouldn't confirm or deny my theory, but I believe the alias belongs to one of the Russians looking to hire a killer for someone at Eagle Enterprises who stumbled onto the deal and could have exposed it to authorities."

"The wire transfer Ava found." A chill flashed along my spine. "She might have signed her own death warrant by going to her boss with it. Angie was lucky to get out of Eagle Enterprises before they decided she also posed a threat."

"Or so it appears. But what if Angie saw the ad for murder and decided it could solve her financial problems? To cover her tracks, she left the company and went back home to live with her parents a month before she killed Ava. I'm sure her parents would swear to any alibi she came up with."

"This is going to sound naive, but I can't imagine Angie killing her friend for money."

"For a large sum of money she needs for her kids," Travis said, putting a finer point on it. "You'd be shocked to know how many seemingly normal people out there are sociopaths with no conscience at all."

"You still haven't told me what aliases the agent found."

"Sorry," Travis said, "I got ahead of myself. The person who placed the ad went by *Ursa Major,* which is why they think he's Russian. The one who answered his ad used *Orion.*"

"The Hunter." I'd expected a killer's name to be along the lines of Avenger or Grim Reaper, names that resonated with darkness and death. Even if I hopped aboard Travis's theory, I still didn't know how to figure out who applied for the job of killing Ava. "Now what? We can't ask our suspects if they ever cruised the Dark Web as Orion and expect them to tell the truth."

"No, but I have an idea."

* * * *

It was nearly show time. A lot of work had gone into planning the event. I'd reserved a meeting room in the Sherwood Hotel near Henrietta, NY, approximately halfway between Watkins Glen and Buffalo. It was important to make the venue equally accessible to all five of our suspects. At the last minute, I'd unilaterally taken Lolly off the list. Yes, she had a motive and an opportunity to kill Ava. And yes, she was probably pleased the woman was dead. But I couldn't bring myself to believe Lolly was capable of murder. If I was wrong, I didn't have much hope for the rest of humanity. Travis thought I was making a mistake, but he didn't try to change my mind.

The five suspects received the same letter informing them they were finalists in a contest held by Granite Financial to promote the opening of their first office in the state of New York. The winner would be selected by a random drawing in the meeting room of the hotel—the prize a cool half million. Travis and I had debated the amount. It had to be large enough to ensure that all the suspects attended. But it couldn't be so large that they shrugged it off as a joke or a scam. In an age when national lottery prizes approached a billion dollars, a half million felt about right for this small a group.

Travis and I arrived at the hotel that morning to make sure everything was in place for the event. The invitation called for three o'clock. At two, we secreted ourselves in the small anteroom off the meeting room. It was used to store extra tables and chairs, but there was plenty of space for the two of us and the monitors on which we'd be watching the drama unfold. It didn't take long for Travis to set up the video cameras around the meeting room. The images and sound would feed directly to our monitors. Without it we'd essentially be blind and deaf.

The door already had the requisite lock to prevent any of the suspects from wandering in and finding us. Since some of the suspects knew each other, there had to be enough other people there to prevent the killer from becoming spooked. We decided on fifty additional guests. It was imperative they be strangers to the suspects. We contacted acting troupes, veterans' groups, Moose and Elk lodgers, firefighters and EMTs from towns and cities in the Henrietta area. We told them the truth—we were conducting a sting to flush out a killer. Although the odds of anyone being hurt were tiny, in life there were no guarantees. I didn't mention that I intended to cast a spell of protection over the room and everyone in it, because that might scare some people more than reassure them. We were surprised by how many people wanted to take part. When I asked one of the actors why he volunteered for the non-paying gig, his answer saddened me.

"Safety is a figment of the imagination in our world. People are mowed down in public places on a daily basis. They're killed in their homes by drive-by shootings. Kids are shot by assault weapons in their classrooms. I'll be safer in the controlled environment you're creating than in most other places."

Travis enlisted the help of the cameraman he'd partnered with for the last five years to make the whole thing look genuine to the suspects. He added two brawny security guards, who owed him favors, to nab the killer when he or she fled. And last, but in no way least, Travis's director of news loaned us one of the studio's metal detectors in exchange for an exclusive on the killer.

Our emcee was Elise's beau, Jerry the dentist. He said *yes* before I finished asking the question. He confessed to having dreamed of a career in acting, until reality came knocking with fistfuls of unpaid bills. Dentistry had the allure of solvency albeit after his student loans were paid off.

As the clock ticked down to the hour, Travis and I toasted our enterprise with lemonade and waited for the first guests to arrive. By three o'clock, all the suspects were there along with most of the additional guests. We made the decision to start on time even if a few of our extras were late.

Jerry stepped up on the podium and waited for the crowd to quiet down. Next to him was a glass fishbowl filled with the names of everyone assembled. He started off with a few dentist jokes that elicited some laughs and maybe served to relax folks. They didn't relax me, but then I was wound tighter than an old-fashioned watch spring. From there he worked his way through a reiteration of who was holding the contest and why, not that anyone seemed interested. Cell phones were pulled out of pockets and purses. Before getting down to picking the winner, Jerry had one more story to tell and it was one Travis and I had written for him.

"I know you're all anxious to find out who will be walking out of here with a check for a half million dollars, but I have one more little story to impart." A soft grumble rippled through the audience. The extras were either doing an admirable job of acting or they too were disgruntled by the delay. Jerry held up his hand and once again waited for silence.

"This story has its origins in ancient Greece, where the poet Aratas first named the groups of stars in the night sky. Two of these constellations are particularly important today—Ursa Major and Orion." I stared at the TV, trying to focus on all five of the suspects scattered around the room, waiting for one of them to make a move toward the door. Without thinking, I reached for Travis's hand. He closed his fingers around it.

Dani looked over her shoulder as if to check how far she was from the door. Liam was busy with his phone. Brock shook his head. Angie was still as a statue. Had the killer slipped beneath our radar? Was it Lolly after all? Jerry stared straight into one of the cameras and shrugged for our benefit, clearly as baffled as we were.

I turned to Travis. "Why isn't one of them bolting?"

He ran his fingers through his hair. "Let's not jump to conclusions. At this point, the killer has to realize this is a setup, a trap. And they've also figured out that no one knows who killed Ava or there'd be no need for this elaborate ruse. They've chosen to bide their time. Running at the first mention of their alias might be the worst mistake they could make."

For that matter, the killer could walk out of there with everyone else and we wouldn't be any closer to knowing their identity. Why hadn't we foreseen this possibility? Had we been so caught up in taking care of every little detail that this huge glaring error had gone unnoticed until now? I was holding out hope that the killer wouldn't be able to take the pressure of hanging around for much longer.

"Stop stalling," Brock called out. Other voices joined his. Instead of risking an uprising, Jerry continued with the story. "Orion means the hunter. Ursa Major means greater she-bear. In this story, the bear tries to hire the hunter to kill someone for him."

Dani was shifting her weight from one foot to the other. Liam popped his phone into his shirt pocket. Brock shook his head again and checked his watch. Angie dialed her phone as she turned and headed in the direction of the door. She didn't run, but she walked with purpose as if she had somewhere to be and was running late. Was this what we'd been waiting for?

She stopped once she was past the crowd and covered her other ear as if she was having trouble hearing the person she'd called. I was so focused on her that my heart leaped into my throat when the room erupted in screaming and shouting.

Travis jumped up from his chair and grabbed my arm. "Kailyn!" I saw Angie and everyone else hit the floor. Everyone except Liam. While I'd been focused on Angie, he'd made his way to the other side of the room and was now facing the audience, his arm outstretched, a gun in his hand. What the hell? He'd passed through the metal detector—I'd seen him. Half of my brain was refusing to believe what was on the monitor. The other half was yelling at me to do something. I heard Travis talking to the 911 operator. The door of the meeting room flew open and the security guards ran in. In a split second, they assessed the situation and flattened themselves just as bullets flew past them. Travis unlocked the door of the anteroom. I pushed in front of him to block him from leaving.

"You can't go out there. If he could kill his sister, he'll kill you without a second thought."

"Maybe I can talk him down."

"You've got a great voice, but it's not magickal. I'm the one who should go." Repeating the protection spell in my head, I pulled the door open and was gone before he could stop me. Once I was in the meeting room, I realized I didn't have a plan. Aside from Liam, I was the only one standing—the perfect target. But I wasn't there to cower, I was there to save the people who'd accepted my invitation to this shindig. Telekinesis would be the simplest way to accomplish that. I'd just pull the gun out of his hand. I'd done it successfully on other occasions. My only hesitation was the distance between me and the gun. I might be too far away for it to work properly. But if I started walking toward him, he might panic and pull the trigger.

"Hello, Ms. Wilde," Liam said wryly, "why am I not surprised?! You and your boyfriend have been hounding me from the get-go. Well whatever happens here today is *your* fault. You're the one who'll be to blame."

"You're right. Your beef is with me. There isn't another person here who deserves to be involved in this. Let them go and you can have me as your hostage. I imagine you're going to need a hostage to get out of this situation."

He squinted at me as if trying to read beyond my words. "I don't trust you. What's your angle?"

"You've outwitted me. I have no angles left." It galled me to admit that I was playing catch up. I hadn't even figured out how he'd smuggled in the gun.

He gave a short bark of a laugh. "I doubt that. Here's what I think. It's in your best interest to draw things out until the police arrive to save the day. I bet you'd like it if I let the people go slowly—like one at a time—would that make you happy?"

"No, Liam, I don't want anyone to get hurt, *including* you." He chewed on my words for half a minute. This might be my only chance. I had to take it. I concentrated all my energy on the weapon and tugged hard with my mind. Liam started sliding closer to the crowd. He had a bewildered and mildly panicked look on his face. I'd hooked onto him *with* the gun. I couldn't hold onto them. The connection between us snapped. He flew backward, crashing into the wall behind him, the gun skittering across the floor. I fell on my butt. Good old inertia. The words from physics 101 flashed in my head, mocking me… *for every action there is an equal and opposite reaction.* I'd never experienced anything like it before with telekinesis, but then I'd never tried to move this much weight from this far away.

I got to my feet as fast as I could, but my legs were rubbery, threatening to give way and my head was spinning. The only thing I'd accomplished was to weaken myself. Liam was already standing. He retrieved the gun and trained it on the crowd. "I don't know what just happened, Wilde, but if you had anything to do with it, don't be foolish enough to try it again."

If I did, I'd have to be closer to him and even that might not be enough. I walked toward the front of the room, navigating around the people on the floor. "Please let them go, Liam." Even my voice sounded frail. "Let everyone go and take me hostage to make your getaway. Things will be easier for you if you don't have to worry about all these people. Sooner or later one of them is going to try to be a hero."

"For once you're right. I don't need them. Go on, all of you—get out of here." I could see that they were hesitant to stand up and become targets. They had no reason to trust him. Some of them started crawling toward the door. It was slow going. When they were temptingly close to the door, they stood up and ran. No bullets rang out, emboldening the rest of the group to follow them, including the security guards. Maybe they thought they could find another way into the room and outflank him, or maybe they decided security work wasn't worth it after all. I was enormously relieved that Liam had let them all go, free and unharmed. This mess was on me. He was right about that much.

As soon as I was close enough, Liam grabbed my forearm, fingers digging in deep enough to hit bone. They felt like they were gouging holes in my flesh. He pressed the gun against my temple and cocked it. I thought about trying the spell I'd recently used at Eagle Enterprises. There was only one problem. A spell against other people had hard limits even if it was used defensively. If it was too weak, it might just irritate Liam, make him decide to punish me. Having Merlin's ability to transmute or even glamour would have come in handy. *Why didn't I hear any sirens yet?*

I felt Liam stiffen and the gun dig deeper into my skull. *What happened?* I followed his line of sight. Travis had come out of the anteroom, hands in the air. Why didn't he stay in there until the police arrived and had things under control? *Would you have?* He probably would have asked me.

"I should have known your partner wouldn't be far away," Liam muttered. He called out to Travis, "Today's your lucky day, Anderson—I only need one hostage. You get to walk away."

"I want to make you an offer," Travis said coming slowly toward us.

"Yeah? What do you have in mind?"

"I want to tell your side of the story. No one knows what you've been through, how hard your life has been from the beginning." I could feel the tension in Liam's body start to loosen as Travis spoke, the pressure of his gun and fingers eased. Travis was reaching him on a visceral level. "Don't you want everyone to know the truth? You're not some crazy bad guy. Life has brought you to this." He was only a few yards away from Liam and me.

"Stop right there," Liam shouted, shaking off their connection. "You come one step closer and I'll blow her head clean off."

Travis stopped. "Think about it, Liam. I know the right people who can make it happen. They might even make a movie—" A bullhorn blasted the air. The police had arrived.

"Liam Duncan, this is Lieutenant Thomas Van Buren of the Rochester PD. Let your hostages go now and we can resolve this incident in a peaceful manner. We don't want anyone to die here today. You have two minutes to release the hostages and walk out unarmed, your hands in the air."

"What do you say," Travis asked. "Do we have a deal?"

Liam was chewing on his bottom lip. "Yeah, okay."

"All right, but for that to happen, you have to let Kailyn and me go."

"No."

"It's the only way you walk out of here alive," I said.

"Shut up both of you! I can't think with you jabbering at me."

Travis's phone rang, making the three of us jump. He asked Liam's permission before retrieving it from his pants pocket. He listened for a moment and then held the phone out to him. "Lieutenant Van Buren wants to talk to you." Liam kept his gun at my head, but he let go of my arm and took the phone gingerly as if he thought it might be booby-trapped. He listened to Van Buren, growled "rot in Hell," and smashed the phone onto the floor.

From beyond the open door of the room, I picked up the muted sound of rubber-soled shoes. Liam had heard it too. He pulled his gun away from my head, aimed it at the doorway and fired a warning round. I ducked under his arm, Travis grabbed my hand, and we ran to the far back corner where we'd be safer if the police stormed the room. We curled together there, his arms around me, my head against his chest, his head resting on mine.

A cop in tactical gear peered inside and immediately drew Liam's fire. But he must have seen what he was looking for—the hostages far enough away from Liam to take him down. They didn't have much time.

Liam realized he'd lost us, his tickets out of there. Keeping his eye on the doorway, he did a sideways shuffle toward us. I had one card left to play. The odds were against me being strong enough to pull it off, but I didn't want to spend eternity regretting that I didn't at least try. "Hold on to me no matter what happens," I told Travis. "No matter what!"

"Got it." He tightened his grip on me.

I pushed the negative thoughts and *what ifs* from my mind as best I could. In another few steps, Liam would be close enough to grab one of us. It was now or never time.

From here and now, to there and then,
Attract not change, nor harm allow.
Safe passage guarantee to souls
As well as lesser, mindless things.

I thought it worked. I thought we'd made it to my shop. I'd felt the unique *whoosh* associated with teleporting, but when I opened my eyes we were in the same corner. My heart sank. Travis looked bewildered. *But where was Liam?* I found him on the other side of the room, his eyes bugging out of his head. Maybe my attempt hadn't been a complete failure after all. It was possible I'd teleported us away, but I wasn't strong enough to complete the journey. Much like the problem I'd experienced with the telekinesis, we'd been snapped back here by a sort of magickal bungee cord. It was better than having our molecules adrift in the ether. All of this went through my mind in the second before the assault began and ended.

Liam couldn't tear his eyes away from us to watch the doorway. By the time he did, it was too late. The SWAT team was coming through the door. He managed to squeeze off two shots that didn't hit anyone. He took a bullet to his lower leg and went down screaming. It was over.

One of the tactical officers escorted Travis and me out of the room to a waiting ambulance where we were checked out briefly by an EMT even though we told him we weren't injured. Two other EMTs ran into the hotel with a stretcher. Across the street, a crowd had formed behind a police barricade. Reporters and photographers were being held in a separate area, slightly forward of them. They called out to us, their questions swallowed by the cloud of noise around us. We were talking to the lieutenant when Liam was brought out on the stretcher and loaded into the ambulance. I was glad they hadn't killed him. I had a lot of questions that needed answers.

Chapter 43

Liam's lawyer wouldn't allow him to talk to Travis and me until after his trial. The good news was that Watkins Glen didn't have a large backlog of cases awaiting adjudication. It was just a matter of giving the prosecution and the defense time to mount their cases. Travis coped by throwing himself back into his work. I was grateful for every tour bus that came to New Camel. On slow days, I restocked all of my products until every shelf was full, and then made extras to keep in the storeroom for when the tourist season was in full swing.

To say that I was surprised to hear from Valerie Duncan was an understatement. She called late on the morning of July Fourth. Two days had passed since the verdict came in. Liam had been found guilty of murder one, premeditated murder, among other serious charges. He was sentenced to life in prison without the possibility of parole. Val and Teddy had taken a month-by-month rental in Watkins Glen, so they could be there in the courthouse every day. I couldn't begin to imagine how gut wrenching it must have been for them.

When I answered the phone that morning, I had trouble recognizing Valerie's voice at first. She sounded diminished, hollowed out by the dreadful twist of fate that had been visited upon her family. "You treated us kindly during the investigation," she said, "so we wanted to let you know the truth about what happened minus the hype of the media coverage or the innuendos, and drama of the trial."

"Would you like me to come up to Williamsville?" It didn't seem like much to offer, since I would have jumped through hoops of fire to hear what she had to say.

"I appreciate that, but I'm not up to seeing folks. I'm barely up to making this call."

"Whatever works for you is fine with me," I said.

She took a deep wobbly breath before she began. "I'm going to assume that you know about Liam's gambling problem among other things." I murmured that I did. "Teddy and I made it clear that we would cut him out of our will unless he went for help. He never went. He refused to believe it was an addiction. Ava helped him out of a few tight spots by loaning him money to cover his debts. But the last time he went to her, he was in big trouble. He owed a large amount to some bookie with ties to the Mafia. They threatened to cut off his arm or leg to teach him a lesson. Ava couldn't help him—she didn't have that kind of money. For that matter, we wouldn't have been able to help him either.

"According to Ava, a friend of his said he could pick up serious money on the Dark Web. After he figured out how to navigate it, he found an ad for wet work, which I have since learned is a euphemism for murder." Her voice cracked and she excused herself to ask Teddy for a glass of water.

While I waited for her to get back on the phone, I thought about her and Teddy. Despite all they'd endured, they hadn't lashed out at each other or assigned blame. They'd shared the burden and come through it together. That had to count for something.

Val returned to the phone with an apology. "I spent so many weeks in that courthouse where I wasn't allowed to speak that my voice seems to be out of practice." I assured her there was no need for apologies. "Now where was I?" she asked.

"Liam found an ad...?"

"Yes, right... the person who put up the ad went by the name Ursa Major. Liam signed on for the job and was paid half of the fee, the remainder to be paid upon completing his assignment. When he was given the victim's name, he thought it was a joke. Ursa Major made it clear that it was no such thing. Liam tried to explain that Ava was his sister and that he couldn't possibly be expected to kill her. He was told he had a choice—either kill Ava or lose his own life. Now Liam would be the first to tell you that he's no hero. He'd already given the bookie the first half of his payment, so he couldn't have given the money back to Ursa Major even if that would have changed things."

I tried to imagine myself in Liam's place. Although I didn't have any siblings, I thought of my aunt Tilly. Would I be able to kill her to save my own life? My mind recoiled—no way, never, not for any reason. "Did Liam ever find out who marked Ava for death?"

"Eagle Enterprises, but who was actually calling the shots at that point is still a little murky. As you know, they'd made a deal to sell the weapons system to a Russian company aka the Kremlin. Putin has his hands in everything.

"Are you up to answering one more question?" It had bothered me from the beginning of the case.

"Go ahead," she said, but I could hear the fatigue dragging at her. I had to let her go after this.

"Why did Liam leave Ava's body in Lolly's backyard?"

"Ava had told him about her affair with Dani's husband. That meant Dani had a motive for killing her. Lolly did too—a mother protecting her young—practically archetypal. By leaving Ava's body in Lolly's backyard, Liam hoped to frame one or both of them." I thanked Valerie for her call. After we said goodbye, I found myself wondering if she and Teddy still loved their son and if they would visit him in prison. I would probably never know the answers, because I would never ask the questions.

When the doorbell rang, I realized Valerie's call had me running behind. I opened the door for Travis, who was stuck firmly in spring with his beige chinos, navy polo, and loafers. Summer was taking its time coming north this year. I'd taken the opposite tack, rebelling against the below normal temperatures in white jeans with a navy and white striped tee and sandals. My toes were cold, but I didn't want to give in and go back to closed shoes. I was in a standoff with the weather.

My cat pack had finally sanctioned my relationship with Travis. They no longer headed for their hidey holes when he arrived. Three of them came to greet him by rubbing against his legs. The other two, along with Sashki, remained on the couch and chairs, but meowed an invitation to come over and pet them.

Travis kissed me, then noticed that my hair looked like I'd just fallen out of bed. "You're not ready," he said bemused. "Did the Earth fly off its axis?"

"Funny. I had an important phone call."

"Not more important than Merlin's party!" He sounded scandalized. The party had gone from being a passing thought to a full-fledged celebration of the wizard's first year with us. Or as Tilly put it, "How did we survive the year?!"

"You be the judge. Come upstairs and I'll fill you in while I comb my hair."

"How do I know you're not just trying to get me upstairs to have your way with me?"

"You'll just have to take your chances."

By the time my hair was beaten into submission, Travis was up to date. I put him to work filling the cats' water dishes. I pulled out all the items Tilly had assigned me to bring—a chopped salad with a dozen vegetables and three kinds of lettuce, twice baked potatoes and the ice cream cake Merlin had campaigned for. My aunt baked two pies, cherry and blueberry, to be served with vanilla ice cream, because it was the Fourth.

"With an ice cream cake, we'll be awash in ice cream," she'd groaned, "but if I don't buy the vanilla, my dessert won't be red, white and blue." To equalize things, she made a chocolate layer cake. I didn't agree with her math. Too many desserts always equaled too many desserts, but I'd learned a long time ago not to argue over the small stuff.

Elise, Jerry and the boys were already at Tilly's house when we arrived. "I guess you ran into traffic on your way here," she said, hugging me.

"It was one rough block." I kissed my aunt and admired her wild new paisley muumuu that was a party all by itself. I gave Merlin a kiss on the cheek that left him flustered.

"These days people are entirely too free with their affections. It's most unsettling."

Tilly gave each of us something to carry—paper goods, drinks and things to nibble on—and led the way out to the back patio, where the sun held the promise of warmer days to come. Zach and Noah put their phones down to play volley ball. Merlin had installed the net, resorting to magick when the ground proved too compacted for him to dig. As a result, it seemed that the net was now a permanent structure. Tilly worried it would raise her taxes. None of us had an answer for her. To be safe, she made us promise not to ever mention it to anyone.

"You'll never guess who called me," I said when there was a pause in the conversation.

Tilly took a handful of potato chips from the basket she'd placed on the little glass table beside her chair. "Valerie Duncan."

I laughed. "Hey, no fair. You just plucked that out of my head." Tilly didn't admit or deny the charge, but she never could keep a straight face when she was caught doing something improper. Everyone wanted to hear what Valerie told me, so I spent the next few minutes repeating it for the second time.

Jerry drained his beer. "Did you ever find out who hired those goons to kidnap you?"

"Monroe sent them to scare me into shutting down my investigation." Elise laughed. "They had no clue who they were dealing with."

"It might not be as good for our investigations, but I'd prefer it if she kept a lower profile," Travis put in. "Too many people hear about super sleuth here and the bad guys will up their game when they go after her. All it takes is one mistake, one miscalculation…"

"There's always a party pooper at every party." I gave him a wink.

"It doesn't take a detective to figure out why Liam stabbed his sister in the back," Tilly said. "He probably couldn't have done it facing her. But here's my question: why did that bio-whatever scanner indicate Liam was in the office when he wasn't?"

"Liam's firm was using the scanners primarily to keep strangers out. So everyone had to scan to get into work, but didn't have to when leaving. Liam scanned in, then left and drove down to New Camel where he had a lunch date with Ava. He killed her, then drove back up to his office in Buffalo and left with everyone else at the end of the day."

Zach and Noah challenged Travis and Jerry to a game of volley ball.

"Didn't anyone notice that Liam was gone for most of the day?" Elise asked me.

"Apparently it wasn't unusual for the CPA's to be out in the field from time to time. Home visits were a service the firm offered their wealthier clientele. Besides, Liam wasn't exactly a social butterfly. He kept to himself, never formed any close friendships with his colleagues."

The calls and laughter from the volley ball game drew our attention. It was a fight to the finish—muscles and experience against youth and enthusiasm. Youth won to the men's dismay. By then Zach and Noah had had enough, so Elise and I were recruited. We gave it our all, but Travis and Jerry pulled it out at the end, salvaging their male pride. When it was time to fire up the grill, another male dominated sport, Tilly was happy to hand over the tools and prep the sides in the kitchen. I ran home to feed Sashkatu and company and was back well before the food was ready.

An hour later, we'd all overeaten. Merlin's normal pallor had taken on an edge of green. "I think he's finally reached his limit," Tilly said. "I never thought I'd live to see the day."

Since Jerry hadn't yet been given clearance to the Wilde family secrets, I took the wizard aside with a question that had been nagging at me. "Is there any chance we could move the ley lines back into their original position with magick?"

Merlin frowned. "On one hand, I suppose it might be possible. But on the other, it could cause a worse disruption in the entire matrix of ley lines. They're interconnected in complex ways that not even I fully comprehend." I suspected as much, but I needed to hear it from him.

At eight thirty we piled into our cars and headed to the town park to watch the fireworks. Merlin was stretched out on the couch recovering from too much of everything. Tilly claimed she was too tired to go. She would enjoy the networks' coverage of the spectacular shows in Manhattan, DC, and Boston from the comfort of her home.

* * * *

My cats were not fans of fireworks. They spent every July Fourth cowering in the basement. Sashkatu, who'd grown deafer with each passing year, was finally able to take the holiday in stride. But he grumbled when he felt the reverberations that shook the house with each rocket blast. He probably chalked it up to human nonsense. What were more highly evolved creatures like him to do?

Travis had the next day off, so he was able to spend the night. I awoke to a tingling in my shoulder. Since it was still dark out, it couldn't be the cats wanting breakfast. And it wasn't Travis who was sleeping soundly beside me. I decided it must have been a dream and turned over to go back to sleep. The tingling started again, this time accompanied by whispers. I opened one eye to find two energy clouds floating beside the bed.

"Come," Morgana said softly as she and Bronwen moved to the bedroom door. There was no point in ignoring them, they wouldn't give up and leave. I dragged myself out of bed and padded downstairs after them. "We didn't want to wake Travis," my mother said once we were all in the kitchen. I sank onto one of the chairs, wishing I were Travis.

"We're pleased to see that he is back in the fold," said Bronwen.

"Is that why you woke me?"

"Not at all," she replied. "I just wanted to start out with a pleasantry." *Uh oh.* Words like that were guaranteed to shake the last vestiges of sleep from my brain.

"It occurred to us that it won't be too long before you turn thirty," Morgana said.

"Since I still have a few years before that, couldn't this little meeting have waited at least until daylight?"

"From our cosmic perspective, that's no more than a second or two," Morgana said, taking the high road instead of calling me out for my attitude. Whatever they needed to tell me was important enough for her to turn the other cheek—assuming energy clouds had cheeks. "What if we're whisked away to the next—"

"Morgana!" my grandmother cried, cutting her short.

"What? I was just going to say the next *thing*—before we were able to warn her."

"Warn me? Warn me about what?"

Bronwen nudged my mother aside so that she was floating directly in front of me. "Somehow or other we never mentioned this to you when we were incarnate."

"I thought your grandmother was going to take care of it," Morgana said, "and she thought I was handling it."

"What is *it?* What did you forget to tell me?!" I heard the irritability in my voice and immediately regretted it.

Bronwen's cloud flickered red at the edges. "You needn't get snippy. I dare say you'll miss us when we can no longer pop in for a visit."

"Sorry." She was right. I would miss them. Most of the time anyway.

"That's better." The red faded from her cloud. "What we failed to tell you is that whatever powers you may possess must be exercised at least once before you turn thirty or you will lose them forever." I sat up straighter in the chair as if that would help me better understand what she was saying.

"But what if I have powers I'm not even aware of by then?"

"Not to worry," my mother said. "You won't miss what you've never had. As it happens, there is one ability you've mentioned, but haven't as yet tried."

"Time travel."

"Precisely. We understand that you may be afraid of trying it. Who wouldn't be? Lord knows you could encounter any number of problems, like not being able to find your way back home." *Not helping your cause, Mom.*

"But if you intend to set things right and take Merlin back where he belongs," Bronwen added, "you'll need to start addressing the matter sooner than later."

"Okay, I get it."

"One last thing," Morgana said. "I would be remiss if I didn't mention that you look peaked. You young people don't assign enough importance to the restorative powers of sleep." It was a good thing she and Bronwen said their *goodbyes* and winked away before I finished counting to ten.

I sat in the kitchen for a while longer, trying to sort out my feelings. In the end, I realized my mother and grandmother were right about time travel, but for the wrong reason. Fear *was* holding me back. Only it wasn't the fear of becoming lost in time. It was the fear of losing Merlin from our lives. He'd driven us crazy and made our lives chaotic during the past year, but he'd also managed to insinuate himself into our hearts. If our lives would be more serene without him, they would also be a lot less colorful. I would heed the warning about losing skills left untried. That didn't mean I had to take him back. But should there come a time when he wished to go home, I'd be prepared, although reluctant, to accommodate him. Should he choose to live out his life with us, history might note that the legendary wizard simply vanished one day.

Acknowledgments

Bringing a book to the public may not take a village, but it does take a team of dedicated professionals. My thanks to Michaela Hamilton and her team! A special thanks to the artists who captured Sashkatu so perfectly and created all the beautiful, eye-popping covers!

Don't miss the next delightful book in the Abracadabra mystery series...

This Magick Marmot

Coming soon from Lyrical Underground,
an imprint of Kensington Publishing Corp.

Chapter 1

Tilly stood in the doorway, surveying my bedroom. Dresses covered the bed, shoes littered the floor. I was standing in the middle of the mess in my bra and panties, no closer to a decision than I had been thirty minutes earlier. Sashkatu, who had no interest in fashion or human dilemmas, had fallen asleep on the high ground of my pillow, safe beyond the tide of clothing. The five younger cats had run for their hidey holes when the second dress hit the bed.

"I expected to see you all decked out by this time." My aunt sounded disappointed. "If you don't get moving, you'll miss the whole cocktail hour."

"You just want to hear the reunion gossip when I get home," I teased her.

She lifted her double chin in mock indignation. "I'll have you know that I merely wish to learn how everyone is doing in their fields of endeavor, who married whom, and how many little ones they have." In her defense, I couldn't think of a single time she'd relished hearing ugly gossip, with the possible exception of Beverly. But I couldn't fault her there.

She moved a few of the dresses aside and sat on the edge of my bed. "It's not like you to be this indecisive. Any one of these frocks will look smashing on you. But that isn't the real problem, is it?" She arched one eyebrow at me.

She was right of course. From the day back in January when I received the first email about my ten year high school reunion, I'd been dealing with a mixture of nostalgia, curiosity, and dread. Now that the Welcome Back Dinner was upon me, *dread* had claimed top billing. It thrummed in my veins like the background music in a thriller. I'd considered skipping the entire weekend, but that wasn't a practical solution in a town the size of New Camel. If I didn't show up for the reunion, the reunion would come and find me.

I plucked a red-and-white flowered sun dress off the bed and shimmied into it. I would look festive even if I didn't feel that way. "This reunion is going to be like reliving the terrible night of the prom."

"Ten years is a long time. I guarantee you that most of the kids won't bring it up or even think about it."

"That's almost worse. My gut still tells me Scott didn't have to die that night. The police investigation didn't go far enough."

Tilly patted the bed beside her. "Come sit here so I can zip you." I sat. She zipped.

"He and I were friends since first grade, Aunt Tilly. He was never a risk taker. His voice was always the voice of caution."

She took my hands in hers. "There's no way to pursue it after all this time. Memories grow fuzzy and unreliable. Scott is at peace. You need to find a way to let it go, dear girl. Now," she continued in a more Tilly-like tone, "that dress is simply begging for those red patent leather peep-toe sling backs. If I didn't have arthritis and bunions, I'd be strutting around in them every day." An image of her *strutting around* in a muumuu with my shiny red heels on her feet made me smile. I kissed her cheek.

"That's more like it. My work here is done." She consulted her watch and sprang to her feet so quickly that I heard her knees pop and creak. She winced, but didn't complain. "I'd best get home before Merlin runs out of patience waiting for dinner and orders a dozen pizzas." That wasn't hyperbole. We'd been down that particular road before.

* * * *

Half an hour later, I slapped on what felt like a serviceable smile and walked into the lobby of the brand new Waverly Hotel. It had opened just two weeks earlier. All the finishes were high end, so dazzling and bright they made me a little dizzy—like looking into the headlights of oncoming cars. I sank into one of the elegant armchairs and waited until I felt properly anchored to the ground again. I had no problem finding the room where the cocktail hour was being held. All I had to do was follow the noise.

The reunion invitation had specified that the Friday night dinner was strictly for alums. It was described as a time to catch up with old friends without boring spouses and significant others. Saturday night would include everyone. Travis had beamed with relief when I told him he wasn't expected to attend the Friday night *shindig*—his word.

When I walked in, the cocktail hour was already in full swing. A highly polished bar ran the length of the room, the shelving on the wall behind it filled with gleaming glassware and liquor bottles of every shape and color. Small tables were scattered around the rest of the space, but no one was seated. There was too much catching up to do.

Before I could take another step into the room, two of my close friends from kindergarten through high school spotted me and shrieked like adolescents at a boy band concert. They rushed over to me, trying not to spill their cocktails on the way. Seeing them brought back a rush of good memories that made me glad I'd come. They'd both gone to colleges out west and stayed out there. At first we'd tried to keep our relationships going by email, phone, and a few cross-country visits, but it became clear to me early on that life was pulling us in different directions, the threads that had drawn us together as kids unraveling as we spread our wings.

Genna caught me around the shoulders. "The third musketeer!" My mother had dubbed us the three musketeers when we entered elementary school. None of us had known what it meant until third grade when Genna bothered to look it up.

"One for all and all for one!" Charlotte cried, stumbling in her stilettos and plowing into me. Instead of pressing her cheek to mine, she came in hard and we smacked cheekbones. She grabbed on to Genna for balance, her drink splashing everywhere. We all would have gone down in a heap if not for the silent spell I remembered from childhood:

We stand up tall; we do not fall,
I know we have the where-with-al.

The spell stopped us on our downward trajectory, suspending us in midair for a split second before reversing our course. As soon as we approached vertical, our equilibrium kicked back in. It all happened so fast, I was probably the only one who noticed the blip. If someone *had* seen it, they were apt to blame the alcohol.

When we didn't hit the floor, my pals dissolved into giddy laughter and I joined in. Genna was breathless. "I was sure we were going down."

"It's the alcohol," I said, "it messes with your inner ear and how you perceive things." They were both inebriated enough not to question it further.

"Are you okay?" Charlotte gingerly touched the spot on my cheek. I pulled back, surprised by the pain. "We have to get this girl some anesthetic," she said threading her arm through mine and steering me toward the bar.

Genna ordered me a club soda and lime. "That's not going to make her feel better," Charlotte protested. Genna reminded her discreetly that I couldn't drink. As far as anyone knew, I abstained due to stomach issues.

I hated to lie, especially to close friends, but I was forbidden from telling anyone about our magick. There were few exceptions. "It's for our safety," my grandmother Bronwen had explained when I'd railed against the restriction as a child. Since it only took a little alcohol to loosen Charlotte's lips, I realized now that my family had been right to enforce the rule.

"I'm sorry I forgot," Charlotte murmured. "Sorry about your cheek too." Her tone was so pitiful and out of character that it bought us another round of laughter.

"Hey, I'd know that laugh anywhere." The voice came from behind us. I turned around to find Adam Hart grinning at me. His face was fuller, his hairline starting to recede. He had been my first boyfriend in high school. I recalled a movie date, a dinner date, a few dates studying, and a couple of kisses I'd had to initiate. He was that shy. No hearts were broken when it was over—perfect first boyfriend material.

Genna and Charlotte excused themselves and left us to chat. When I asked Adam how he was doing, he held up his left hand with its band of gold and pulled out a picture of his two young daughters wearing tutus and ballet slippers.

"They're adorable. Looks like you got started right out of the gate."

He tucked the photo back in his wallet with great care. "Stacy and I met at freshman orientation and we married the day after graduation. They were the longest four years of my life. How about you?" he asked, glancing down at my hands. "Hasn't anyone swept you off your feet yet?"

"There's someone working hard on it. You'll meet him tomorrow night. Will I get to meet the special woman who's made you so happy?"

"She'll be there, and I know you'll love her. She is special."

A guy whose name eluded me clapped Adam on the back. "Look at you," he said with a short bark of a laugh, "gaining weight and losing hair ahead of schedule."

Adam turned to him with a wide grin. "Says the guy who had to attend summer school so he wouldn't get left back."

"Hey man, I was all about priorities—studying women instead of chemistry and math."

I left them to their put-downs. I've never understood the way men insult and ridicule each other. If we women did that with our friends, we'd be friendless in no time. I went looking for a place to discard my glass. Between the air conditioning that was cranked up to frigid and the cold drink, my fingers were getting numb. A moment later, a busboy came by carrying a tray of discarded drinks as if I'd cast a spell to make him appear. Could I have subconsciously summoned him? I'd have to look into it. According to Morgana, any skills I left untried by the age of thirty would lie dormant for the rest of my life. I chafed at having a deadline, but it had made me more vigilant.

I spotted a knot of women across the room—the three other founding members of the Green Love Circle we'd started in our junior year. The club arranged for people in the environmental field to address the student body several times a year. It also raised money and awareness to shut down puppy mills and promote no-kill animal shelters. I was headed in their direction when Ashley Rennet stepped into my path.

My heart clenched. She and Scott had been voted most likely to wed. I hadn't seen her since his funeral. According to the grapevine, she'd gone off to college in New Hampshire as planned, but dropped out after the first semester. I felt bad about not reaching out to her back then to see how she was doing, but I'd lost Scott too, and I didn't know how to comfort either one of us.

In my mind, I had imagined Ashley losing weight, her face wan, dark circles beneath her eyes. I was relieved to see I was wrong. She looked exactly as I remembered her. However heartbroken she might have been, she'd made it back to herself. That was before I noticed Scott's class ring on its silver chain around her neck the way she'd worn it all senior year— engaged to be engaged. It was possible she'd just put it on for the reunion, but it was more likely she'd never taken it off.

She had to know it would deter men from asking her out. And if a man did approach her, when he asked about the ring, her explanation would surely have sent him running. The ring was like a silver cross worn to keep vampires away. Only in Ashley's case, she wanted to keep life from moving on.

Earlier in the day, I'd come up with a few neutral things I could say that wouldn't upset her. But when I opened my mouth, they all gushed out at once. "It's so good to see you. You look wonderful. How are you? Where do you call home these days?"

Sidestepping my embarrassing attempt at conversation, she answered the last question. "I'm still in New Hampshire. It's quiet—folks there mind their own business." She spoke softly, slowly, as if the whole cadence of her being had been transformed by the pace of her life there. "Turned out college wasn't for me. I went to baking school instead and found my niche. Now I'm part owner of a thriving bake shop." There was satisfaction in her tone. Who's to say that didn't qualify as happiness? "Are you still here in New Camel?" she asked.

I nodded. "Still working in Abracadabra." I decided not to mention that Morgana and Bronwen had died. I didn't want our conversation to be about death.

"I used to love browsing in your shop," she said wistfully. "All the great natural cures and the best makeup. Everything worked like magic. I've never found products anywhere else that measured up. Plus they cost a fortune. I have to make time to stop into Abracadabra before I head home."

"I hope you do. I'll show you all the new products." We smiled at each other. I tried to think of something else to say, but came up empty. Our smiles were wilting and the silence was growing awkward. Ashley finally rescued us both.

"So tell me, what do you do when you're not running the shop?"

I could tell her about Travis, but that might bring her down. Besides, she'd meet him on Saturday night. What else...."In my spare time, I've been hunting down killers." And just like that I shoved my foot in my mouth and halfway down my throat—what my grandmother used to call *hoof in mouth disease.* When I made a social blunder, I didn't do it by half measure.

I heard Ashley's breath catch in her throat. "Seriously? Are you good at it?"

"I've done okay, but I've only tackled a few cases." I knew what was coming next. I'd set myself up for it. Was my brain back home snoozing with Sashkatu?

"Have you looked any further into Scott's death?" Like me, she had believed there was more to his passing than the official version.

"I haven't," I admitted. "I doubt I could find anything after all this time. And Duggan, he's the chief of detectives, he would never give me access to the old files. We're not exactly on good terms. He'd like nothing better than an opportunity to lock me up and throw away the key."

"Would you try—as a favor to me?" Ashley's voice wobbled. "No, forget me. Do it for Scott and what his friendship meant to you."

I don't like being manipulated. Attempts to *handle* me that way are usually doomed to failure. But I told her I'd do what I could, because there was a chance that with more information she might finally be able to put Scott's death behind her.

The lights flickered a few times and as the room quieted, the maitre d' invited us into the adjacent room for dinner. There were no cards telling us where to sit. The reunion committee had wanted it to be more organic, letting the alums decide on the spot with whom we wished to eat. As a result, there were several chaotic minutes that resembled the Oklahoma Land Rush. There were arguments about who claimed which table first.

Since the tables only held six, many of the alums had to settle for seats wherever they could find them. There was almost a skirmish between a group of cheerleaders and a group of computer nerds for possession of one table. The maitre d' came to the rescue, setting up an additional table before things got out of hand. The reunion committee would have been wise to take note if they had any intention of presiding over another milestone event in the years ahead.

I headed straight for the table Green Love had staked out. They were holding the last seat for me. I made my way around the table saying a proper hello, since I hadn't had the opportunity earlier. I'd worked so closely with the other members that the bonds we'd formed were easily reclaimed.

I'd meant to pay attention to the food we were served, because the Waverly was winning raves from local food critics. Travis had shrugged them off. "These are the same people who think New Camel pizza is great," he'd reminded me. We made a friendly little wager over which of us would be vindicated by the food Saturday night. The Welcome Back Dinner provided me with a preview of it, but my friends' stories stole my focus.

The evening flew by too fast. We were all groaning about overeating and simultaneously wondering what we'd be served for dessert. Charlotte stopped at my table to hug my neck on her way to the bathroom. "I love you. You're like the sister I never had."

"You have two sisters," I said.

"Wow, you're right—I do! How about that?!"

I grabbed her hand before she could walk away. "Charlotte, promise me you won't drink any more tonight."

"I promise. Just coffee. *Strong* coffee." She kissed my cheek and teetered off to find the restroom. Less than a minute later, a horrific scream ripped through the air. I just knew it was Charlotte. I jumped out of my seat and ran into her as she hobbled back into the dining room. She was sobbing hysterically, her face stark white. Black mascara was streaming down her cheeks with her tears, giving her a macabre appearance. What could have happened to her in the brief time she'd been out of sight?

Her knees gave way. I grabbed her around the waist in time to ease her descent as she crumpled to the floor. "Are you okay? What happened?" By then everyone was on their feet. Someone offered her water, but she pushed it away. The nurse and two doctors in our midst knelt beside her to assess her condition.

"It's Genna," she said between sobs. "I think she's dead." A siren screamed in the distance, punctuating her words. Whoever was manning the New Camel police station was already on his way. Paramedics wouldn't be far behind. One of the benefits of living in a small town.

I left Charlotte to the ministrations of the medical alums and hurried to the restroom off the lobby. A small crowd had gathered there, trying to figure out what was going on. I pushed past them with an air of authority, my face set in a grim expression that dared anyone to question me. I used the back of my hand to open the bathroom door. I had no intention of disturbing the crime scene. I just wanted to get a look at the victim. Maybe Charlotte was wrong. She'd had far too much to drink. If the victim had the same color hair as Genna, or similar clothing, Charlotte might have jumped to conclusions.

I didn't have far to go. Genna was lying on her back on the porcelain tile near the gleaming bank of sinks. There was blood on the floor that appeared to have come from her head, most likely when she fell unconscious. Foam oozed from her mouth and down her chin. Her eyes stared back at me as if she too were wondering what on earth had happened.

About the Author

Sharon Pape launched her delightful Abracadabra mystery series with *Magick & Mayhem* and continued it in *That Olde White Magick* and *Magick Run Amok*. Sharon is also the author of the popular Portrait of Crime and Crystal Shop mystery series. She started writing stories in first grade and never looked back. She studied French and Spanish literature in college and went on to teach both languages on the secondary level.

After being diagnosed with and treated for breast cancer in 1992, Sharon became a Reach to Recovery peer support volunteer for the American Cancer Society. She went on to become the coordinator of the program on Long Island. She and her surgeon created a nonprofit organization called Lean On Me to provide peer support and information to newly diagnosed women and men.

After turning her attention back to writing, Sharon has shared her storytelling skills with thousands of fans. She lives with her husband on Long Island, New York, near her grown children. She loves reading, writing, and providing day care for her grand-dogs.

Visit her at www.sharonpape.com.

SHARON PAPE
MAGICK & MAYHEM
LYRICAL UNDERGROUND
An Abracadabra Mystery

SHARON PAPE

THAT OLDE WHITE MAGICK

An Abracadabra Mystery

SHARON PAPE

MAGICK RUN AMOK

LYRICAL UNDERGROUND

An Abracadabra Mystery

Printed in the United States
by Baker & Taylor Publisher Services